Carl Hiaasen was born and raised in Fl_____ ___ ___
author of twelve previou_ _____ ____ _____ _ Sick
Puppy, Lucky You, Stormy _____ ___ _____ ____se, Skin
Tight, Skinny Dip and, mo__ _e___tly, Hoot and Flush,
both novels for children.

He also writes a weekly column for the Miami Herald.

www.booksattransworld.co.uk

Acclaim for *Nature Girl*:

'Combines the comedic energy of Molière with
Mark Twain's lightness of phrase'
Independent

'Carl Hiaasen's latest screwball thriller . . . is sometimes
ludicrous but always engaging and frequently hilarious'
Observer

'Read, embarrass yourself in public by laughing
yourself to near apoplexy, then sign up for the
"Declare Hiaasen an International Treasure" league'
Sunday Telegraph

'Hiaasen once again makes the case that life in his
backyard really is more absurd than in ours . . .
Nature Girl deserves the laughs it will get,
from sea to shining sea'
New York Daily News

'Hiaasen isn't just Florida's sharpest satirist –
he's one of the few funny writers left in the whole
country . . . I think of him as a national treasure'
Newsweek

'Hiaasen's pacing is impeccable . . . I purred
warmly through the novels' twists and further
twists . . . An entertaining ride'
New York Times Book Review

Also by Carl Hiassen

Fiction
Skinny Dip
Basket Case
Sick Puppy
Lucky You
Stormy Weather
Strip Tease
Native Tongue
Skin Tight
Doubly Whammy
Tourist Season

For Young Readers
Flush
Hoot

NATURE GIRL

CARL HIAASEN

BLACK SWAN

TRANSWORLD PUBLISHERS
61-63 Uxbridge Road, London W5 5SA
a division of The Random House Group Ltd
www.booksattransworld.co.uk

NATURE GIRL
A BLACK SWAN BOOK: 9780552773713

First published in Great Britain
in 2006 by Bantam Press
a division of Transworld Publishers
Black Swan edition published 2007

A CIP catalogue record for this book
is available from the British Library

Addresses for Random House Group Ltd companies outside the UK
can be found at: www.randomhouse.co.uk
The Random House Group Ltd Reg. No. 954009

The Random House Group Ltd makes every effort to ensure that the
papers used in its books are made from trees that have been legally
sourced from well-managed and credibly certified forests. Our paper
procurement policy can be found at: www.randomhouse.co.uk/paper.htm

Typeset in 11/13pt Melior by
Falcon Oast Graphic Art Ltd.

Printed and bound in Great Britain by
Cox & Wyman Ltd., Reading, Berkshire.

2 4 6 8 10 9 7 5 3

For Pete Hamill,
the best in the business

Once again I am indebted to Liz Donovan for her peerless research skills, and to Bob Roe for his clever eye and sharp advice. I'm also extremely grateful to Capt. Steve Huff, who suggested Dismal Key as a location for this story and took me there to see it; and to his wife, Patty, who helped me stay true to the wild history of the Ten Thousand Islands.

NATURE GIRL

One

On the second day of January, windswept and bright, a half-blood Seminole named Sammy Tigertail dumped a dead body in the Lostmans River. The water temperature was fifty-nine degrees, too nippy for sharks or alligators.

But maybe not for crabs, thought Sammy Tigertail.

Watching the corpse sink, he pondered the foolishness of white men. This one had called himself Wilson when he arrived on the Big Cypress reservation, reeking of alcohol and demanding an airboat ride. He spoke of ringing in the New Year at the Hard Rock Hotel and Casino, which was owned by the Seminole tribe on eighty-six acres between Miami and Fort Lauderdale. Wilson told Sammy Tigertail that he'd been sorely disappointed not to find a single Indian at the casino, and that after a full night of drinking, hot babes and seven-card stud he'd driven all the way out to Big Cypress just to get himself photographed with a genuine Seminole.

'Some dumbass bet me a hundred bucks I couldn't find one,' Wilson said, slinging a flabby arm around Sammy Tigertail, 'but here you are, brother. Hey, where can I buy one of them cardboard cameras?'

Sammy Tigertail directed Wilson toward a convenience store. The man returned with a throwaway
Kodak, a bag of beef jerky and a six-pack. Mercifully,
the airboat engine was so loud that it drowned out
most of Wilson's life story. Sammy Tigertail heard
enough to learn that the man was from the greater
Milwaukee area, and that for a living he sold trolling
motors to walleye fishermen.

Ten minutes into the ride, Wilson's cheeks turned
pink from the chill and his bloodshot eyes started
leaking and his shoulders hunched with the shakes.
Sammy Tigertail stopped the airboat and offered him
hot coffee from a thermos.

'How 'b-b-bout that picture you promised?' Wilson
asked.

Sammy Tigertail patiently stood beside him as the
man extended one arm, aiming the camera back at
them. Sammy Tigertail was wearing a fleece zip-up
from Patagonia, a woolen navy watch cap from L.L.
Bean and heavy khakis from Eddie Bauer, none of
which would be considered traditional Seminole garb.
Wilson asked Sammy Tigertail if he had one of those
brightly beaded jackets and maybe a pair of deerskin
moccasins. The Indian said no.

Wilson instructed him not to smile and snapped a
couple of pictures. Afterward, Sammy Tigertail
cranked up the airboat and set out to finish the swamp
tour at the highest-possible speed. Because of the cold
weather there was practically no wildlife to be
observed, but Wilson didn't seem to mind. He'd gotten
what he came for. Squinting against the wind, he
gnawed a stick of dried beef and sipped on a warm
Heineken.

Sammy Tigertail took a shortcut through a prairie of tall saw grass, which flattened under the airboat's bow as neatly as wheat beneath a combine. Without warning, Wilson arose from his seat and dropped the beer bottle, spraying the deck. As Sammy Tigertail backed off the throttle, he saw Wilson begin to wobble and snatch at his own throat. Sammy Tigertail thought the man was gagging on a chunk of jerky, but in fact he was trying to remove from his doughy neck a small banded water snake that had sailed out of the parting reeds.

The creature was harmless, but evidently Wilson was in no condition to be surprised by a flying reptile. He dropped stone-dead of a heart attack before his Seminole guide could get the boat stopped.

The first thing that Sammy Tigertail did was lift the little snake off the lifeless tourist and release it into the marsh. Then he took Wilson's left wrist and groped for a pulse. Sammy Tigertail felt obliged to unbutton the man's shirt and pound on his marbled chest for several minutes. The Indian elected to forgo mouth-to-mouth contact, as there obviously was no point; Wilson was as cold to the touch as a bullfrog's belly.

In his pockets the Seminole found the disposable camera, $645 cash, a wallet, keys to a rented Chrysler, a cellular phone, two marijuana joints, three condoms and a business card from the Blue Dolphin Escort Service. Sammy Tigertail put back everything, including the cash. Then he took out his own cell phone and called his uncle Tommy, who advised him to remove the dead white man from the reservation as soon as possible.

In the absence of more specific instructions, Sammy Tigertail wrongly assumed that his uncle meant for him to dispose permanently of Wilson, not merely transport him to a neutral location. Sammy Tigertail feared that he would be held responsible for the tourist's death, and that the tribal authorities wouldn't be able to protect him from the zeal of Collier County prosecutors, not one of whom was a Native American.

So Sammy Tigertail ran the airboat back to the dock and carried Wilson's body to the rental car. No one was there to witness the transfer, but any casual observer – especially one downwind of Wilson's boozy stink – would have concluded that he was a large sloppy drunk who'd passed out on the swamp tour.

Having positioned the corpse upright in the backseat, Sammy Tigertail drove directly to Everglades City, in the heart of the Ten Thousand Islands. There he purchased four anchors and borrowed a crab boat and headed for a snook hole he knew on the Lostmans River.

Now a single coppery bubble marked the spot where the dead man had sunk. Sammy Tigertail stared into the turbid brown water feeling gloomy and disgusted. It had been his first day working the airboat concession, and Wilson had been his first customer.

His last, too.

After returning the crab boat, he called his uncle Tommy to say he was going away for a while. He said he wasn't spiritually equipped to deal with tourists.

'Boy, you can't hide from the white world,' his uncle told him. 'I know because I tried.'

'Do we own the Blue Dolphin Escort Service?' asked Sammy Tigertail.

'Nothing would surprise me,' said his uncle.

At about the same time, in a trailer not far from the

fishing docks, a boy named Fry looked up from his dinner plate and asked, 'What is this crap?'

It was not an unreasonable question.

'Salisbury steak,' Honey Santana said. 'It tastes better than it looks.'

'Did you get fired again?'

'No, I quit,' Honey said. 'Now hush up and eat.'

As her son well knew, she resorted to frozen dinners only when she was out of work.

'What happened this time?' he asked.

'You remember Aunt Rachel's Chihuahua? Yum-Yum Boy?'

'The one that got killed, right? Trying to hump a raccoon.'

'Yeah, well, that's what Mr. Piejack is like,' Honey said, 'only bigger.'

She took a small bite of the tough gray meat. It was gruesome but she managed a smile.

Fry shrugged. 'So, did he make a move or what?'

'You could say that.'

Mr. Piejack was the owner of the fish market, and he'd been sniffing after Honey for months. He was married and had numerous other unsavory qualities.

'You know those little wooden mallets we sell at the register?' Honey said.

Fry nodded. 'For cracking stone-crab claws.'

'Right. That's what I whacked him with.'

'Where?'

'Where do you think?'

As Fry pushed away from the table, Honey hurried to explain.

'He grabbed my breast. That's why I did it.'

Her son looked up. 'For real? You're not making this up?'

'My right breast, I swear to God.' Honey solemnly entwined her hands over the object of Mr. Piejack's lust.

'What an a-hole,' Fry said.

'Totally. After I hit him, he started rolling on the floor, moaning and whining, so I grabbed a slab of tuna out of the cooler and shoved it down his pants. You know, to keep the swelling down.'

'What kind of tuna?'

'Yellowfin,' Honey said. 'Sushi-grade.'

Fry grinned. 'He'll throw it back on the ice and sell it to some snowbird.'

'That's gross,' Honey said.

'How much you wanna bet?'

'Hey, I could fix us some soup.' She got up and scraped the Salisbury steaks into the garbage can. 'Minestrone or cream of tomato?'

'Whatever.' Fry scooted his chair back to the table. Sometimes he believed that his mother was on the verge of losing her mind, and sometimes he believed that she was the sanest person he'd ever met.

'Now what, Mom?'

'You know my friend Bonnie? She's doing these ecotours where she takes tourists kayaking out to Cormorant Key,' Honey said. 'She says it's a ton of fun and the money's pretty good, too. Anyway, driving home from Marco this afternoon I noticed a string of bright yellow kayaks crossing the bay, and I thought: What a heavenly way to spend the day, paddling in the sunshine through the mangroves!'

'Kayaks,' Fry said skeptically. 'Is this the same Bonnie with the solar-powered sewing machine?'

'You sound like your ex-father.'

'He's not my ex-father, he's *your* ex-husband. Anyway, what'd I say wrong?'

'Oh, just the look on your face.' Honey took the soup pot off the stove. 'What was I supposed to do, Fry? The man squeezed my boob. Did he deserve to be clobbered with a crab hammer in the testicles, or did he not?'

'How much does a kayak cost?'

Honey set two bowls on the table. 'I'm not sure, but we'll need at least two or three, for starters.'

'And where would you take these goobers on your "ecotour"?' Fry asked. 'I mean, since Bonnie's already locked up Cormorant Key.'

Honey laughed. 'Have you looked out our window lately? Have you noticed all those gorgeous green islands?'

The phone began to ring. Honey frowned.

'Every night,' she said, 'like clockwork.'

'Then don't answer it,' her son said.

'No, I've had it with these clowns. Enough is enough.'

More than a thousand miles away, a man named Boyd Shreave stirred a latte and listened on his wireless headset to a phone ringing somewhere distant, in the 239 area code. A photocopied script lay on the desktop in front of him, but Boyd Shreave no longer needed it. After three days he knew the pitch cold.

Shreave was employed by Relentless, Inc., a tele-marketing company that specialized in outbound sales calls to middle-income residential addresses in the United States. The firm's call center was a converted B-52 hangar in Fort Worth, Texas, where Boyd Shreave and fifty-three other solicitors toiled in individual cubicles that were padded to dampen ambient noise.

In the cubicle to the right of Boyd Shreave was a woman named Eugenie Fonda, who claimed a murky connection to the famous acting family and in any case had recently become Boyd Shreave's mistress. To the left of Boyd Shreave sat a man named Sacco, who was cavern-eyed and unfriendly and rumored to be a dot-com burnout. During work hours, Boyd Shreave rarely spoke to any of his co-workers, including Eugenie, due to the onerous calling quotas imposed by Relentless, Inc. They were on the phones from 5:00 p.m. to midnight, strafing east to west through the time zones.

It was a dreary and soulless job, though not the worst that Shreave had ever held. Still, at age thirty-five he realized that the feeble arc of his career had more or less flatlined during his six months in tele-marketing. He probably would have quit were it not for six-foot-tall Eugenie, the ash-blond crest of whose head he could gaze upon at will in the adjoining carrel.

Boyd Shreave had been in sales since the age of twenty-six: corrective footwear, farm equipment, auto-mobiles (new and used), fertilizer, herbal baldness remedies, high-definition televisions and exotic pet supplies. That he had failed to succeed, much less prosper, surprised no one who knew him. In person, Boyd Shreave was distinctly ill-suited for the craft of persuasion. Regardless of his mood there was an air of sour arrogance about him – a slant to one thin reddish eyebrow that hinted at impatience, if not outright dis-dain; a slump of the shoulders that suggested the weight of excruciating boredom; a wormish curl of the upper lip that was often perceived as a sneer of condescension or, worse, a parody of Elvis.

Almost nobody wanted to buy anything from Boyd Shreave. They just wanted him to go away.

He'd all but abandoned his ambitions in sales when, upon the occasion of his most recent firing, his future ex-boss had suggested that he consider telephone work. 'You got the pipes for it,' the man had said. 'Unfortunately, that's about *all* you got.'

It was true that strangers were often unnerved when Shreave opened his mouth, so mismatched was his voice – smooth, reassuring and affable – with his appearance. 'You're a natural,' Eugenie Fonda had told him on his first day at the call center. 'You could sell dope to the Pope.'

Shreave didn't set the world afire at Relentless, but for the first time in his life he could honestly claim to be semi-competent at his job. He was also restless and resentful. He disliked the late shift, the confined atmosphere and the mynah-bird repetition of the sales script.

The pay blew, too: minimum wage, plus four bucks for every lead he generated. Whenever Shreave got a hot one on the line – somebody who actually agreed to a callback or a mailout – he was required by company policy to punt the sucker's name to a floor supervisor. Shreave would have gladly forgone the shitty four-dollar commission for a chance to close the deal, but no such responsibility was ever dealt to rookie callers.

A woman picked up on the fifth ring.

'Hello, is this Mrs. Santana?' Boyd Shreave asked.

'It's *Ms.*'

'So sorry, Ms. Santana, this is Boyd Eisenhower calling—'

Eugenie Fonda had told Shreave not to use his real

last name with customers, and coached him on selecting a telephone alias. She said research had proven that people were more likely to trust callers with the last names of U.S. presidents, which is why she'd chosen 'Eugenie Roosevelt' for herself. Initially Shreave had selected the name 'Boyd Nixon' and in four days failed to churn a single lead. Eugenie had gently advised him to try a different president, preferably one who had not bolted from the White House with prosecutors camping on the doorstep.

'Eisenhower, like Dwight?' asked the woman on the end of the line.

'Exactly,' Shreave said.

'And your first name again?'

'B-o-y-d,' said Shreave. 'Now, Ms. Santana, the reason I'm calling this afternoon—'

'It's not the afternoon, Mr. Eisenhower, that's the problem. It's the evening, and I'm sitting down to eat with my family.'

'I'm sorry, Mrs. Santana, this won't take long. Or perhaps you'd like me to try back later.'

It was a line designed to keep the customer on the phone. Most people didn't want a callback; they wanted to get it over with.

The woman's voice began to rise. 'Do you know how many telephone solicitations I get on this number? Do you know how aggravating it is to have your dinner interrupted by strangers every night?'

Boyd Shreave, unruffled, was already fingering down the call list. 'Is Mr. Santana available?' he asked perfunctorily.

To his surprise, the woman replied, 'As a matter of fact, he is. Hold on.'

Moments later, a new voice said, 'Hullo?'

'Mr. Santana?' Shreave thought the person sounded too young, although there was always the possibility of a sinus infection.

'What're you selling, mister?' the voice demanded.

Shreave let it fly.

'Mr. Santana, I'm calling about a unique real-estate opportunity that we're presenting to specially selected candidates. For a limited time only, Suwannee Bend Properties is offering ten pristine wooded acres in north-central Florida for only $3,999 down—'

'But we already live in Florida,' the voice said squeakily.

'Yes, Mr. Santana, this valuable offering is being made exclusively to residents of the southwest coast.' Boyd Shreave glanced at his pitch sheet. 'You live in the fastest-growing part of the United States, Mr. Santana, and in recent years many of your neighbors have gotten fed up with the traffic, high taxes, crime and big-city stress. A lucky few of them have relocated to beautiful Gilchrist County, the heart of traditional old Florida – a safe, peaceful and affordable place to raise a family. Instead of being packed like rats into a gridlocked suburb, you can relax on a lush, secluded ten-acre ranchette, not far from the historic Suwannee River. May I send you some printed information, or perhaps arrange for a qualified sales associate to call back at your convenience?'

The voice said, 'A ranchette? Is that like a dinette?'

'No. It's a real-estate term, Mr. Santana.'

'But we don't live in a crowded suburb. We live in the Everglades,' the voice said. 'There's only five hundred and thirteen people in the whole town.'

By now, Shreave had figured out that he was speaking to a kid, and that his time was being wasted. He was itching to say something really snide, but he had to be cautious because Relentless randomly monitored outgoing floor calls for 'quality control.'

'Mr. Santana,' he said with exaggerated politeness, 'would you mind putting Mrs. Santana back on the line?'

'I'm right here,' the woman piped in, catching Shreave off guard. Obviously the bitch had been listening on another phone.

'Then I guess I don't need to repeat our offer,' Shreave said thinly.

'No, you do not,' Mrs. Santana said. 'We categorically have no interest in buying a "ranchette" in Gilchrist County, wherever that might be.'

'Well, you *have* heard of the Suwannee River, right?'

'I've heard the song, Mr. Eisenhower. There's no reason to be sarcastic.'

'That wasn't my intention.' Shreave's eyes drifted to the top of Eugenie's head. He wondered if the fool listening on the end of her line would have ever imagined that she had a real pearl stud in her tongue.

Mrs. Santana went on: 'The song's actually called "Old Folks at Home" and it was written by Stephen Foster, and you know what? He never floated way down upon the Suwannee, because he never set foot in "beautiful Gilchrist County" or anywhere else in Florida. The man lived in Pennsylvania, and he got the name Suwannee River off a map and took out the *u* to make the syllables fit the music. By the way, Mr. Eisenhower, what is your supervisor's name?'

'Miguel Truman,' Shreave said dully.

'And *his* supervisor's name?'

'Shantilla Lincoln.'

'Because I intend to speak with them,' Mrs. Santana

said. 'You sound like such a nice, decent fellow – does your mother know what you do for a living, Mr. Eisenhower? Harassing strangers over the phone? Trying to talk folks on a fixed income into buying things they don't need? Is this what she raised you to be, your mother? A professional pest?'

At that moment, Boyd Shreave should have calmly apologized for inconveniencing the Santanas, and then disconnected. That was the drill at Relentless: Never argue with people, never abuse them, never lose your cool. Do not under any circumstances give them a reason to complain to the feds.

Those on the receiving end of Boyd Shreave's grating sales calls had at various times called him a deadbeat, a maggot, a polyp, a vulture, a douchebag, a cocksucker, a shitbird, a pussbucket and even a rectal ulcer. Never once had Shreave replied in kind.

And most likely he would have held his composure on this particular evening had Mrs. Santana not touched a sore spot by referring to his mother, who had in fact expressed bilious objections to his move to telemarketing; who herself had pelted him with unflattering names, each preceded by the word *lazy*.

So, instead of hanging up and moving down the list to the next call, Shreave said to Mrs. Santana what he had longed to say to his mother, which was: 'Go screw yourself, you dried-up old skank.'

This was articulated not in Shreave's friendly-neighbor telephone voice but in a corrosive snarl, emitted so loudly that both Sacco and Eugenie Fonda sprang up in their cubicles and stared at Shreave over the padded partitions as if he'd wigged out.

On the other end, Mrs. Santana sounded more wounded than angry. 'What an awful thing to say, Mr.

Eisenhower,' she said quietly. 'Please connect me with Mr. Truman or Miss Lincoln right this minute.'

Boyd Shreave chuckled acidly and plucked off his headset, thinking: No wonder they're moving all the call centers to India – the poor saps there don't know enough English to insult the customers.

Eugenie passed him a note that said 'Are you fucking crazy?'

'Only for you,' Shreave scribbled back.

But as he sat there sipping his latte, he reflected upon the exchange with Mrs. Santana and conceded he had been harsh, considering that she hadn't called him anything worse than a pest.

Maybe I *am* losing it, Shreave thought. Jesus, I need a vacation.

Honey Santana stared at the phone in her hand.

'What'd he say?' Fry asked.

Honey shook her head. 'Never mind.'

'You know, there's a do-not-call list. Why don't you put our number on it? Then we won't have to deal with these turds anymore.'

'Could you please not use that word?'

Honey already paid extra for a service that rejected calls from blocked phone numbers. To get around it, many telemarketing firms used rotating 800 exchanges, which is what Honey found when she pressed the caller ID button. She jotted the number down next to the name Boyd Eisenhower.

Fry said, 'Thanks for the soup. It was good.'

'Welcome.'

'What are you doing now?'

'I'm calling the company to complain.'

'Like they care,' Fry said. 'Mom, please, not tonight.'

The line was busy. Honey put down the phone and popped a Tic Tac. 'I wouldn't mind speaking to that guy again. He called me a truly awful name.'

'So, let's hear it.'

'You're only twelve and a half, Fry.'

'Hey, you let me watch *The Sopranos*.'

'Once,' Honey said ruefully. 'I thought it was about opera, honest to God.'

'Was it b-i-t-c-h? That's what he called you, right?'

Honey said no and dialed again. Still busy.

'You shouldn't have brought up his mom,' Fry remarked.

'Why not?' Honey said. 'You think she bled and suffered to bring him into this world, nursed him at her breast, bathed him when he was soiled, held him when he was sick – all so he could grow up and nag people in the middle of their suppers!' Honey shook a finger at her son. 'You ever take a lame-ass job like that, I'm writing you out of my will.'

Fry glanced around the double-wide as if taking inventory. 'There goes the trust fund,' he said.

Honey ignored him and dialed again. Another busy signal.

'Maybe his mom's a pest, too. Ever thought of that?' Fry said. 'Maybe he was raised by pests and he just can't help the way he is.'

Honey slammed the phone on the kitchen table. 'For your information, he called me a shriveled-up old skank.'

'Ha!' Fry said.

'That's funny to you?'

'Sort of.' Fry had never mentioned that his friends considered her the hottest mom in town. He said,

'Come on – you're not old, and definitely not skank material.'

Honey Santana got up and started banging dishes around the sink. Fry wondered when she was going to wind down – sometimes it took hours.

'What is it with men?' she said. 'First Mr. Piejack wants to jump my bones and now this person I don't even know tells me to go screw myself. My day starts with dumb animal lust and ends with rabid hostility – and you wonder why I don't date.'

Fry said, 'Hey, did Aunt Rachel ever get another dog?'

'Don't you dare change the subject.' Again, Honey snatched up the phone and started punching the buttons.

'Mom, you're wasting your time. You'll never get through to that creep.'

She winked at him. 'I'm not calling the 800 number. I'm calling my brother to have him *trace* the 800 number.'

'Oh wonderful,' said Fry.

'And don't roll your eyes at me, young man, because – oh, hello. Could you ring Richard Santana please?' Honey covered the mouthpiece. 'I will most definitely find this person,' she whispered emphatically to her son, 'one way or another.'

Fry asked, 'And then what, Mom?'

She smiled. 'And then I'll sell him something he can't afford. That's what.'

28

Two

After nightfall Sammy Tigertail ditched the rented Chrysler in a canal along the Tamiami Trail. Then he hitchhiked to Naples and met his half brother Lee in the parking lot of an outlet mall.

'Come home. You'll be safer on the reservation,' Lee said.

'No, this way is better for everyone. You bring the gear and the rifle?'

'Yep.'

'What about the guitar?'

Sammy Tigertail had only once set foot inside the tribe's Hard Rock operation. The whole scene was gruesome, except for the rock-and-roll artifacts on display. Sammy Tigertail had zeroed in on a blond Gibson Super 400 that had once belonged to Mark Knopfler of Dire Straits, his late father's favorite band.

'It's in the truck,' Lee said, 'and you owe me big-time, brother. They didn't want to give it up.'

'Yeah, I bet.'

'But I got the big boss to make a call.'

'No shit?' Sammy Tigertail hadn't known that Lee held any sway with the tribal chairman. 'Let's go,' he said.

His brother drove him to the Turner River, where together they dragged a small canoe from the bed of the pickup; not a native cypress dugout but a shiny blue aluminum model, manufactured at some factory in northern Michigan.

After they loaded in the gear, Lee said, 'You see the Man coming, first thing to go overboard is the gun.'

'All depends,' said Sammy Tigertail.

They stood in a thickening darkness, silent but for the oscillating hum of insects.

Lee asked, 'You didn't kill that white man on purpose, did you?'

Sammy Tigertail took a heavy breath. 'No, it wasn't me.'

He told the story of the banded water snake, and Lee agreed that it was clearly a spirit at work. 'What do you want me to do with your checks?' he asked.

Every month the tribe sent three thousand dollars to each Seminole, remittance from the gambling profits.

'Give it to Cindy.'

'Sammy, don't be a fool—'

'Hey, it's *my* goddamn money.'

'Okay,' Lee said. Cindy was Sammy Tigertail's ex-girlfriend, and she had issues.

Lee put a hand on his brother's shoulder and said good-bye. Sammy Tigertail got into the canoe and pushed it away from the bank.

'Hey, boy, since when do you play guitar?' Lee called out.

'I don't.' Sammy Tigertail dipped the paddle and turned the bow downriver. 'But I got all the time in the world to learn.'

'Sammy, wait. What do I tell Ma?'

'Tell her I'll be back someday to play her a song.'

* * *

Eugenie Fonda had been briefly famous as a mistress in another relationship. In the summer of 1999 she had dallied with a man named Van Bonneville, a self-employed tree trimmer in Fernandina Beach. Soon after the affair had begun, a hurricane pushing thirteen feet of tidal surge struck the coast and smashed Van Bonneville's house into toothpicks. He survived, but his wife was lost and presumed drowned.

Hurricanes being to tree cutters what Amway conventions are to hookers, Van Bonneville was an exceptionally busy fellow in the days following the tragedy. While neighbors were impressed by his stoicism, his in-laws were disturbed by what they considered an inadequate display of grief by the young widower.

Certain grisly suspicions were floated before the local police, but no one paid much attention until Mrs. Bonneville's body was found in her Pontiac at the bottom of the St. Johns River. It was her husband's contention that Mrs. Bonneville's Bonneville had been swept away by the onrushing flood as she wheeled out of the driveway in a frantic quest for Marlboros. Doubt fell upon this story as soon as police divers revealed that Mrs. Bonneville had been snugly strapped into the driver's seat. Well known among her friends was the fact that on principle Mrs. Bonneville never buckled her seat belt, even though it was required by state law; an ardent libertarian, she opposed government meddling in all matters of personal choice.

Another clue was her knockoff Seiko titanium, which, unlike the genuine item, was not even slightly water-resistant. The face of the wristwatch was frozen on a time and date that preceded by a full nine hours the hurricane's landfall, suggesting that the Pontiac had gone into the river well in advance of the fierce weather, and that Mrs. Bonneville's corpse had been strapped inside to keep her from surfacing prematurely.

In the end, her husband's fate was sealed by the Duval County medical examiner, who retrieved from a blunt indentation on Mrs. Bonneville's scalp several sticky ligneous flakes that were later identified as bark particles from a sawed-off mahogany branch. The branch segment measured three feet long and seven inches in circumference on the day it was confiscated from the bed of Van Bonneville's obsidian-flecked Ford F-150 pickup.

The 'Hurricane Homicide' trial was broadcast live on Court TV and later featured during prime time on *Dateline*. Prosecutors depicted Van Bonneville as a philandering shitweasel who had conspired to do away with his loving wife and blame it on the storm. The motives were laid out as greed (a $75,000 life-insurance policy) and lust, Van Bonneville having acquired a new girlfriend who then went by the name of Jean Leigh Hill. Tall and smoky-eyed, her long languorous walk to the witness stand was the un-disputed highlight of the trial.

Eugenie testified that she'd taken up with Van Bonneville believing he was a widower, having fallen for his claim that his wife had perished in a freak tanning booth mishap. It wasn't until three days after the hurricane that Eugenie had spotted a newspaper story about the missing Mrs. Bonneville. The enlightening article included several quotes from her 'tearful and apprehensive husband.' Immediately Eugenie located the one and only love letter that Van Bonneville had scrawled to her, and marched to the police station.

Scandalous headlines were followed by the obligatory book deal. Soon a ghostwriter arrived from New York to help Ms. Hill organize her recollections of the romance, although there wasn't much to recollect. Eugenie had known Van Bonneville all of eleven days before the crime. They'd gone on one lousy date, to play putt-putt golf, and afterward they'd had putt-putt sex in the cab of his pickup. That it was enough to leave Van Bonneville smitten and dreamy-eyed had been mildly depressing to Eugenie.

Initially she'd been drawn to his rugged looks, particularly his knuckles, which were intriguingly striped with scars. Eugenie had occasionally been a sucker for marred, rough men, but on that first and only night with Van Bonneville she would discover that his wounds were the results of frequent tree-trimming miscues, and that he was as clumsy at foreplay as he was with a pruning saw.

Fortunately for her publisher, Eugenie had a fertile imagination. The manuscript that she and the ghost-writer produced was thin but sufficiently tawdry in content to become an instant best-seller. For seven weeks *Storm Ghoul* ran neck and neck on the *New York Times* non-fiction list with a collection of Ann Coulter's most venomous Al Gore columns. So torrid was Eugenie's account of Van Bonneville's sexual talents that he got swamped with marriage proposals from complete strangers. From Death Row he sent Eugenie a thank-you note and a Polaroid photograph of his hands.

Her share of the book advance was half a million dollars, a cheering sum. Eugenie's new boyfriend, a stockbroker who'd seen her on *Oprah* and contacted her Web site, advised her to invest the windfall in a red-hot Texas outfit called Enron, the shares of which he was pleased to acquire for her at a discount fee. Within twenty-four months Eugenie was dead broke, alone again and working the phone bank at Relentless. By that time a barrage of anti-bimbo invectives had caused her to shut down the Web site and adopt the name of Fonda, a demented aunt having declared herself a third cousin to Peter and Jane.

Eugenie was still not entirely sure why she'd seduced Boyd Shreave, a charmless and dyspeptic presence in the adjacent cubicle. Perhaps it was because he had shown so little interest that she felt the tug of a sexual challenge. Or perhaps she'd sensed something in his glazed indifference that hinted at a secret wild side, a raw and reckless private life.

Yet, so far, Boyd Shreave had failed to deliver a single surprise. He was a man without mystery and, except for an odd stippling on his pubic region, also without scars. On the upside, he was decent-looking enough and fairly dependable in the sack. He kept assuring her that he was angling for a divorce, a blatant lie with which Eugenie gamely played along. Boyd's wife had inherited a small chain of pizza joints, the profits from which provided the Shreaves with a comfortable existence in spite of Boyd's serial failures as a salesman. It would have been idiotic for him to run out on his wife, much less snuff her in the manner of Van Bonneville, a fact in which Eugenie Fonda took comfort. She had no desire to reprise her role as the paramour of a murderer.

To Eugenie, Boyd Shreave was not a love interest so much as a timely distraction. Their relationship was the natural backwash of being stuck together in the most boring, brain-numbing job on the planet.

On the night Shreave had so loudly berated the customer on the phone, he arrived at Eugenie's apartment carrying a six-pack of Corona, to which he clung even as he hugged her. 'I got canned,' he announced.

'Oh no.' Eugenie, who in her heels stood four inches taller than Boyd, kissed his forehead. 'Don't tell me they were taping you!'

Shreave nodded bitterly. 'Miguel and Shantilla called me in and played back the whole goddamn call. Then they sent some Mexican ape from Security to clean out my desk and hustle me out of the building.'

'What happened to probation?' Eugenie asked. 'I thought they aren't supposed to fire you the first time you lose it.'

'They will if they catch you tellin' somebody to go screw themselves.'

'Jesus, Boyd, *screw* isn't so bad. You hear it on TV all the time. If it was *fuck*, I could understand you gettin' axed, but not *screw*.'

Shreave uncapped a beer and settled in on the couch. 'Apparently *skank* is a no-no, too.'

Eugenie seated herself beside him. 'I'm so sorry,' she said.

'Oh well. It sure felt good to say it at the time.'

'Have you told Lily?'

'Not yet,' Shreave muttered. Lily was his wife. 'She'll be pissed, but what else is new. It was a shit job, anyway,' he said. 'No offense.'

Eugenie was wondering how best to inform Boyd that she wasn't devoted to the idea of continuing their affair now that he was no longer employed at Relentless and they couldn't pass horny notes to each other. It exhausted her to think about carrying on with him by telephone.

'The only good thing about that goddamn place,' he was saying, 'was meeting you.'

Swell, thought Eugenie. 'Boyd, that's so sweet.'

Shreave began unbuttoning her blouse. 'You wanna take a shower?' he asked. 'I'll be the Handsome Drifter and you can be the Hula-Hula Queen.'

'Sure, baby.' She didn't have the heart to give him the bad news. Maybe tomorrow, she thought.

Honey Santana's brother was busy on a story, but he promised to try to help. While waiting, Honey robotically kept dialing the 800 number. She was well aware that telemarketing companies deliberately rigged their outgoing phone banks to thwart incoming calls, yet she continued to punch the buttons. She felt more powerless than usual against this latest compulsion.

'It's driving me up the wall, this guy was so awful,' she said to her brother when he finally got through. 'And, the thing is, he had such a nice voice.'

'Yeah, so did Ted Bundy,' said Richard Santana. 'Sis, what are you going to do with the name if I give it to you? Be honest.'

Richard Santana was a reporter in upstate New York. Among the many Internet databases available to his newspaper was a nifty reverse telephone directory. It had taken about six seconds to trace the 800 line for his sister.

'All I want to do is file a complaint,' she lied.

'With whom? The FTC?'

'Right, the FTC. So, you got the name?'

Richard Santana was aware that Honey sometimes reacted to ordinary situations in extreme ways. Having been burned before, he was now wary of all her inquiries. This time, however, he felt confident that the information he was providing could result in nothing worse than an angry letter, since the offending company was in Texas and his sister was far away in Florida.

'I'll E-mail you what I've got,' he told her.

'You're a champ, Richard.'

Honey Santana didn't inform her brother that she could no longer retrieve her E-mails without her son's permission. Fry had locked her off the computer the day after she'd fired off ninety-seven messages to the White House complaining about the president's support for oil drilling in the Arctic National Wildlife Refuge in Alaska. The E-mails had been sent within a four-hour span, and their increasingly hostile tone had attracted the notice of the U.S. Secret Service. Two young agents had driven over from Miami to interview Honey at the trailer park, and they'd departed believing, quite mistakenly, that she was too flighty to present a credible threat to anyone.

She hurried into Fry's bedroom, flipped on the light and began to shake him gently. 'You asleep, sweetie?'

'Not anymore.'

'I need to get on the computer. Richard's E-mailing the goods.'

'Mom, look at the clock.'

'It's only eleven-fifteen – what's the matter with you? When I was your age, I used to stay up until midnight writing love letters to Peter Frampton.' Honey felt Fry's forehead. 'Maybe you're coming down with a bug.'

'Yeah, it's called the Psycho Mom flu.'

Fry untangled himself from the sheets and stumbled over to his desk. He shielded the computer keyboard from his mother's view as he tapped in the password. The screen illuminated with a beep, and Honey sat down intently. Fry aimed himself back toward the bed, but she snagged him by one ear and said, 'Not so fast, buster.'

'Lemme go, Mom.'

'Just a minute. Lookie here.' Honey tapped the mouse to scroll down her brother's message. 'It's RTR Limited, Fort Worth. That's the name of this outfit.'

'So?'

'I need you to Google it for me.'

'Google yourself,' Fry said.

'No, kiddo, you got the touch.' Honey rose and motioned him into the chair. 'I'm too wired to type, honest to God.'

Fry sat down and searched for RTR Limited, which came up as Relentless Telemarketing Resources, Relentless Wireless Outreach and Relentless, Inc. He surfed through the entries until he found a self-promotional Web site that listed an office-park address and a direct toll number.

'Bookmark that sucker!' Honey cried triumphantly.

'Okay, but that's it.' Fry signed off and darkened the screen. 'We're done, Mom.'

'Come out and watch Letterman with me. Please?'

Fry said he was beat, and dived into bed. When Honey sat beside him, he rolled over and faced the wall.

'Talk to me,' she whispered.

' 'Bout what?'

'School? Sports? Anything you want.'

Fry grunted wearily.

'Hey,' Honey said. 'Did you see on the news about the wolves out West? They're trying to take 'em off the endangered list so that we can wipe 'em out all over again. Does that make any sense?'

Her son didn't answer. Honey turned out the light.

'Thanks,' Fry said.

'I didn't forget my medicine, if that's what you're thinking.' Which was true in a way – she'd thrown the pills in the trash weeks earlier. 'Certain things still set me off, no matter what,' she said. 'But I'm getting better, you've gotta admit.'

'Yeah, you're definitely gettin' better.'

'Fry?'

'I'm serious,' he said.

'Other things I just can't let slide. You understand? Starting with matters of basic civility.' Honey closed her eyes and listened to her son's breathing. Tomorrow she would go find another job, and then after she came home she'd get on the phone and track down Mr. Boyd Eisenhower.

'He had such a nice voice, didn't you think?'

'Who?' Fry asked.

'That man who tried to sell us a place on the Suwannee River,' Honey said. 'I thought he had an exceptionally agreeable voice.'

'I thought he sounded like a total dick.'

'What are you saying, kiddo? That I've lost my marbles?'

'No, Mom, I'm saying good night.'

* * *

The private investigator's name was Dealey, and his office was downtown near Sundance Square. Lily Shreave was fifteen minutes early, but Dealey's assistant waved her in.

Dealey, who was on the phone, signaled that he'd be finished in a minute. Pinned under his left elbow was a large brown envelope on which 'Subject Shreave' had been printed with a black Sharpie.

After the private investigator hung up, he asked Lily Shreave if she wanted coffee or a soda. She said, 'No, I want to see the pictures.'

'It's not necessary, you know. Take my word, we got him cold.'

'Is she in them?' Lily Shreave pointed at the envelope.

'The pictures? Yes, ma'am.'

'She pretty?'

Dealey eased back in his chair.

'You're right, it shouldn't matter,' Lily Shreave said. 'What's her name?'

'The one she's using now is Eugenie Fonda. She works at Relentless with your husband,' Dealey said, 'and she has an interesting back-story. You remember the "Hurricane Homicide" case a few years ago? The guy who whacked his wife and tried to make it look like she drowned in a storm?'

'Down in Florida,' Lily Shreave said. 'Sure, I remember.'

'She was the husband's girlfriend,' Dealey said, 'the one who wrote that book.'

'Really? I read the first chapter in *Cosmo*.' Lily Shreave was puzzled. The woman had made the tree cutter out to be a stallion in the bedroom. So why on earth would she want Boyd?

'Let me see those pictures,' she said.

Dealey shrugged and handed her the envelope. 'It's the typical routine. Drinks after work, then back to her place. Or sometimes a late lunch before they punch in. Did I mention she was single?'

Lily Shreave held up the first photo. 'Where was this one taken?' she asked.

'At a T.G.I. Friday's off the 820. He ordered ribs and she got a salad.'

'And this one?'

'The doorway of Miss Fonda's apartment,' Dealey said.

'She's a real amazon, huh?'

'Six feet even, according to her driver's license.'

'Age?'

'Thirty-three.'

'Same as me,' Lily Shreave remarked. 'Weight?'

'I don't recall.'

'Are those flowers in his hand?' Lily Shreave studied the grainy color print.

'Yes, ma'am,' Dealey said. 'Daisies and baby's breath.'

'God, he's so lame.' Lily Shreave couldn't remember the last time her husband had brought her a bouquet. They had been married five years and hadn't slept together in five months.

'This is the first time he's cheated on me,' she volunteered.

Dealey nodded. 'You got your proof. My advice is take him to the cleaners.'

Lily Shreave laughed caustically. 'What cleaners? The man can't hardly pay for his own laundry. I want a speedy divorce, that's all, and no trouble from him.'

'Then just show him the pictures,' Dealey said. 'And save number six for last.'

Boyd Shreave's wife thumbed through the stack until she found it. 'Good grief,' she said, and felt her face redden.

'Deli over on Summit. Broad daylight,' said Dealey, who'd taken the photograph from a parked car. The camera was a digital Nikon with motor drive and a 400-mm telephoto.

'Is she actually blowing him?' Lily Shreave asked.

'That would be my expert opinion.'

'And what in the hell is *he* eating?'

'Turkey and salami on a French roll with pickles, shredded onions, no lettuce,' Dealey said.

'You can remember all that, but not her weight?' Lily Shreave smiled and fitted the stack of pictures back into the envelope. 'I know what you're up to, Mr. Dealey. You're trying to spare my feelings. When I get stressed, I tend to put on a few pounds, sure, and lately I've been stressed. But don't worry, I'll get down to a size six again once I dump this jerk. So tell me – how much does she weigh?'

'A buck forty,' Dealey said.

'Oh, get real.'

'Exactly. People always lie on their driver's license.'

'I mean, she's six feet tall, so come on.'

'Like you said, Mrs. Shreave, it doesn't really matter. Adultery is adultery.'

Boyd Shreave's wife took out her checkbook. 'Let me ask you something else about Miss Fonda. Do you think she put him up to it? I'm talking about the tree trimmer who murdered his wife. Is it possible this slut had something to do with it?'

Dealey said, 'The cops tell me no. I already called down to Florida because I was wondering the same thing. They said she passed the polygraph with flying colors.'

Lily Shreave was somewhat relieved. Still, she made up her mind to move swiftly with the divorce, in case her husband got any nutball ideas.

'Copies of the pictures are locked in my safe box. They're yours if you want 'em,' Dealey said. He'd already made a dozen prints of the sub shop blow job, which he considered to be a classic.

'I'm sorry things turned out this way,' he added.

'No, you're not,' Lily Shreave said, 'and, frankly, neither am I.'

She wrote out a check for fifteen hundred dollars. The private investigator put it in the top drawer and said, 'It was a pleasure meeting you, Mrs. Shreave.'

'Whoa, you're not done yet.'

Dealey was surprised. 'You want me to keep tailing your husband? What for?'

'The oral stuff is okay, but I'd prefer to see documentation of actual intercourse.'

'They usually don't give out receipts, Mrs. Shreave.'

She said, 'You know what I mean. Pictures or video will do.'

Dealey tapped two fingers on the desk. 'I don't get it. You've got more than enough to bury him already.'

'The deeper the better,' said Lily Shreave, snapping shut her purse.

Three

Fry's father was the only man that Honey Santana had ever married, and they astonished themselves by staying together seventeen years. The sea change took place after Fry was born. He spent two weeks in the hospital, fighting to breathe, and it was during that wrenching time that Honey began hearing musical static in her head; battling uncontrollable spells of apprehension and dread; overreacting, sometimes radically, to the bad behavior of total strangers.

From the day she brought Fry home, Honey was gripped with a fear of losing him to a random act of nature, an incurable illness, or the criminal recklessness of some genetically deficient numskull. The fright sometimes manifested itself in unacceptable ways. Once, when Honey had seen a car speeding down her street, she'd dashed out and hurled a forty-gallon garbage can in its path. Brandishing the demolished receptacle, she'd then accosted the stunned driver. 'This could've been my kid you flattened!' she'd screamed. 'You could've killed my little boy!' Another time, when Fry was in the fourth grade, she'd watched a motorcycle blow through the school zone and nearly strike one of his classmates. Honey had hopped into her husband's truck and trailed the biker to a tourist bar on Chokoloskee. When the man emerged two hours later, his motorcycle was missing. The next day, a purple plume of smoke led park rangers to a high-end Kawasaki crotch rocket, burned to scrap on a gravel road near the Shark River Slough.

Honey understood that every dickhead she encountered was not necessarily a menace to her son, yet still she struggled with a rabid intolerance of callousness and folly, both of which abounded in South Florida. It exasperated Fry and his father, who couldn't understand how she'd turned out that way.

Honey had tried many doctors and many prescriptions, with imperceptible results. Eventually she came to believe that her condition was one that couldn't be treated medically; she was doomed to demand more decency and consideration from her fellow humans than they demanded of themselves. What her husband wrote off as loony obsessiveness, Honey Santana defended as spells of intense and controlled focus. While denying she was mentally unsteady, she never claimed to be normal, either. She was alert to the uncommon impulses that took hold of her like a bewitchment.

'Yes, ma'am, I'm trying to reach a Mr. Boyd Eisenhower.' Honey held the receiver in her left hand. In her right was a ballpoint pen, poised over a paper napkin.

'What was the last name?'

'Eisenhower,' Honey said, 'spelled just like the president.'

'I'm sorry, there's no employee here with that name.'

45

'This is RTR, correct? In Fort Worth, Texas?'

'That's right. I show an Elizabeth Eisenberg in Accounting, but no Boyd Eisenhower.'

'He's in the telephone solicitations department,' Honey said.

'That would be our call center at Relentless, but there's still no Eisenhower listed. Sorry.'

Honey hung up. The guy who'd tried to sell her a ranchette on the Suwannee River had apparently given a fake name, or at least a fake surname. It occurred to Honey that Boyd wasn't something that a man would make up for himself.

So she waited ten minutes and tried again. As she'd hoped, a different switchboard operator answered. Honey identified herself as an investigator with the Texas Department of Motor Vehicles. There'd been a bad rollover in Denton, she said, involving a man who claimed to work for RTR.

'Unfortunately, his driver's license melted in the fire,' Honey said. 'We're just trying to confirm an ID.'

'What name do you have?' the operator asked.

'Well, that's the problem. Right now the poor guy can't remember anything except his first name – Boyd,' Honey said. 'He was doin' about eighty on the interstate when he swerved to miss a rabbit and flipped his car like seven times. Gonged his melon pretty bad, but he finally came out of the coma.'

'Did you say "Boyd"?'

'That's correct.' Honey spelled it for the operator. 'Is it possible to do an employee search by first name only? If not, we can send an officer over to look through your payroll records.'

'Hold on, I'm scanning the directory,' the operator said.

'I sure appreciate this.' Honey laid on a touch of what she imagined to be a mild Laura Bush accent. 'I tell ya, the guy must have a real soft spot for bunnies—'

'I found only one Boyd,' the operator said. 'Last name is Shreave. S-h-r-e-a-v-e.'

Honey Santana scribbled it on the napkin.

'But the thing is, he doesn't seem to work here anymore,' the operator added. 'Says here on my screen that he left the company as of today.'

'What a weird coincidence. Did he resign, or get fired?'

'I'm sorry, but I don't have any additional information. You say he's gonna be all right?'

'The doctors are hopeful.' Honey tried to sound encouraging.

'Well, I'll say a little prayer for him.'

'That's probably not a bad idea.'

Honey hung up and did a dance through the trailer.

Boyd Shreave saw no reason to inform his wife that he'd been canned. His plan was to persuade Eugenie Fonda to quit the call center and find a day job. That way they could hook up after work and cavort at the apartment until midnight, Lily assuming that he was still pounding the phones at Relentless. He figured it would take weeks for her to notice that he was no longer depositing a paycheck, so paltry was his contribution to the family finances.

At breakfast Lily surprised him by asking, 'So, what's on the schedule today?'

Boyd Shreave had no schedule, as his wife well knew; no hobbies, interests or intellectual appetites. To ingratiate himself with certain bosses and large-account customers, he had over the years taken up (and soon abandoned) tennis, rollerblading, skeet shooting, dry-fly tying, backgammon, contract bridge and even bonsai cultivation. In truth, nothing filled his spare hours more pleasingly than daytime television, which never failed to make him feel superior. In particular he was enthralled by the many talk shows that featured dysfunctional cretins debating the paternity of unplanned offspring. To Shreave, their raucous misery was more than idle entertainment; it reaffirmed his own higher place in the natural order. Comfortably stationed with a snack tray in front of the plasma screen, he drew hope from the cavalcade of cursing, frothing idiots – these were the prey, and one day Boyd Shreave would find his niche among the predators. He was sure of it.

'I haven't got much planned,' he told his wife. 'Just hang out and watch TV, I guess.'

'You want to meet for lunch?'

Shreave was rattled by the offer. 'Um, I'm supposed to get the oil changed in the car. I just remembered.'

'What time?'

'Noon sharp,' he said.

Lily smiled a smile that Boyd Shreave hadn't seen in a long time. She said, 'Excellent. That leaves us the whole morning.'

'For what?' Shreave croaked.

'Guess.' Lily reached under the table and squeezed him. 'You know how long it's been?'

Shreave plucked her hand from his crotch and edged out of reach.

Gravely his wife said, 'One hundred and fifty-six days.'

'Really?' Shreave was confused. In all that time Lily

48

hadn't once complained about his lack of attention, so he'd assumed that the disinterest was mutual.

'That's more than five months,' she added.

'Wow,' Shreave said.

'Too long, Boyd. Way too long.'

'Yeah.' Already the back of his neck was moist and clammy.

'What's the matter, honey?' Lily leaned forward, letting her robe fall open. Shreave couldn't help but observe that her breasts seemed larger than Eugenie Fonda's. He wondered if he'd somehow forgotten what they looked like, or if his wife had secretly been to a plastic surgeon.

She touched his arm softly, then lobbed a question that lay there like a ticking grenade: 'Boyd, is there something you want to talk to me about?'

Oh Christ, does she know? he wondered anxiously. *Or is she fishing?*

Working from slickly worded scripts had dulled Shreave's talent for the improvisational lie. He knew he needed something better than an oil change to handle Lily's current line of interrogation.

'It's not you, it's me,' he began.

Slowly she pulled her robe closed and crossed her arms.

'It's a flashback from the accident in Arlington,' he said, aware that he was raising a touchy subject.

'Three years ago?' Lily raised her eyebrows, but Shreave soldiered on.

'I'm what they call "clinically depressed." The doctor says it's affected my . . . you know . . .'

'Libido.'

'Yeah,' he said. 'Anyhow, I got some of those pills, but they haven't helped at all.'

CARL HIAASEN

'What brand? The kind Bob Dole uses?' Lily was very active in the local Republican leadership committee, and a longtime admirer of the former senator from Kansas.

Shreave said, 'The exact same stuff, but it doesn't work on me. I still haven't got the slightest interest in . . . you know . . .'

'Fucking?'

'Right. Off the agenda completely.' He shrugged in resignation.

His wife said, 'Well, what do you suppose you're so depressed about?'

'Hell if I know. But the doctor says that's pretty common.'

Lily nodded sympathetically. 'And who's your doctor?'

'Kennedy,' Shreave said, following Eugenie Fonda's presidential advice on made-up names. 'Some hotshot shrink over in Irving. Don't worry, he's on the company HMO.'

Lily got up to refill his coffee cup, which Shreave interpreted positively. 'Is something wrong at work?' she asked.

'Are you kidding? They love me. I'm up for a promotion.'

'That's great news.' Lily bit her lip. 'This is my fault, too, Boyd. I've been so tied up with the restaurants that I didn't notice what was happening between us.'

In fact she'd been very busy – quietly closing a deal to sell her six pizza joints to the Papa John's corporation for a boggling sum of cash and common stock, none of which she intended to share with Boyd Shreave in the upcoming divorce. Lily felt sure that her husband's unfaithfulness would make him an

unlikely candidate for alimony in the eyes of most
Texas judges, especially the Republican ones. In the
meantime, Lily was finding it strangely enjoyable –
almost exciting – to toy with him.

She said, 'Hey, I've got an idea. Let's get dressed.'

Shreave frowned. 'Where are we going?'

'It's a surprise.'

'But Judge Joe Brown is on in fifteen minutes.'

'Great. Now I'm married to Rain Man.' Lily steered
Boyd out of the kitchen, saying, 'When's the last time
Judge Joe gave you a hard-on?'

Later, in the car, Shreave sat solemn and petrified.
He feared that Lily was taking him on a shopping
adventure to the adult-video store a few blocks from
their house – the same place he'd been renting DVDs
for his clandestine visits to Eugenie Fonda's apartment. Shreave had no faith that the video-store clerk
would be merciful enough to pretend not to recognize
him, or to not mention the $37.50 in late fees he'd
piled up.

But Lily went speeding past the porn parlor, and
Shreave sagged in relief. She wheeled into a busy strip
mall and led him into a bagel shop, which he vaguely
recalled from a long-ago date, before they were
married.

'We came here the morning after our first night
together,' Lily reminded him.

'Oh, I remember,' Shreave said.

'The night, or the bagels?'

'Both.' Shreave forced a laugh. He was sweating like
a hog with typhoid.

Lily clearly was planning something dramatic, and
Shreave waited in a state of pale dread. He couldn't
possibly resume sexual relations with his wife and

still carry on with Eugenie; it would be way too much work. While some men were able and even eager to juggle the needs of many women, Shreave withered at the thought. Whether on the job or in the sack, he'd never been burdened with an abundance of ambition.

'We'll have two raisin cinnamons,' Lily told the waiter, 'with cream cheese.'

'And ice water for me,' Shreave added urgently.

For some reason his wife had not removed her sunglasses. She appeared to be smiling to herself as she pulled her frosted hair back into a ponytail. From her handbag she took the car keys, which she let fall with a jingle to the linoleum floor.

'Oops,' she said, and disappeared beneath the tabletop.

Shreave gripped the arms of his chair as if plummeting on a crippled jetliner.

'What are you doing!' he whispered bleakly.

The question was answered by the sound of a zipper, his own. 'Sshhh,' came the muffled counsel from his wife. 'Just relax, sweetheart.'

Never before had Boyd Shreave felt a need to fake impotence, and he was not up (or rather, down) to the task. As Lily rapidly got the better of him, he floundered in a state between panic and marvel – not once in thirty-five years had he been publicly fellated, and now it had happened twice in as many weeks, with different women! Most men would have found the coincidence thrilling, but Shreave worried about the heavy implications. He understood that yielding to his wife would officially reinitiate his marital obligations, and compromise his secret life.

He ignored the gapes of other diners and pretended to study the menu listings printed on the paper place mat, all the while endeavoring to compress his knees together. However, Lily would not be dislodged.

Just as surrender seemed imminent, the raisin cinnamon bagels arrived. Shreave seized the moment to stage a mishap, overturning a tumbler of cold water on his lap. Lily came out sputtering from beneath the table, Shreave loudly chastising the innocent waiter for his clumsiness.

The restaurant manager picked up their tab for breakfast, but the couple rode home in a slack and deflated silence.

The circumstances of Sammy Tigertail's conception had not been concealed from him. His father drove a Budweiser truck three times a week between Naples and Fort Lauderdale, and was a regular customer at the Miccosukee service plaza where Sammy Tigertail's mother worked in the gift shop. Because she had serious doubts about trying to raise a half-white son on the reservation, Sammy Tigertail's mother reluctantly agreed to let his father keep the boy.

So, for his first fourteen and a half years, Sammy Tigertail was Chad McQueen. He lived in a middle-class subdivision in Broward County with his father and, beginning at age four, a stepmother who aggressively attempted to acculturate him. Growing up, the boy showed no interest in soccer leagues or video games or skate-boarding. His passion was roaming the outdoors, and learning the rock music that his father played on the car radio. By the time he was in first grade, the kid was singing along to Creedence and the Stones and the Allman Brothers. Everybody said he was going to turn out fine, despite his Indian genes.

Then one day his father died suddenly. After the funeral, the boy's stepmother drove him back to the Everglades and dropped him at the truck stop. He had sensed it coming, and he was privately looking forward to the move. Every other Sunday his father had taken him to visit his real mother at the Big Cypress, and the boy liked it out there.

'I should've never let go of you,' his mom said when he arrived with his suitcase and fishing rod. 'This is where you ought to be.'

'I believe so,' the boy said.

'Remember the time you caught that cottonmouth with your bare hands? You were only seven.'

'I didn't know it was poisonous,' the boy reminded her. It had been an embarrassing episode. 'I thought it was a water snake,' he added.

'But you weren't afraid!' his mother said supportively. 'That's when I knew you belonged here, and not in that other world. First thing we do now is fix your name – starting today you're a Tigertail, same as me.'

'Chad Tigertail,' the boy said proudly.

His mother winced and shook her head. The boy agreed: Chad was definitely too white for the reservation.

'What about Sammy?' he suggested.

'Perfect. That was your great-grandfather's name.'

'Was he a fighter?'

'No, a trapper. But your great-great-great-grandfather was a chief.'

'Tiger Tail?' the boy cried excitedly. '*The* Tiger Tail?'

It was true. Sammy was descended from one of the last great Seminole warriors, Thlocklo Tustenuggee, a cunning leader whose fate Sammy chose to regard as a mystery. Most accounts said the U.S. Army had shipped the chief off to New Orleans, where he'd died of tuberculosis in a stinking military dungeon. But at least one teller of the Tiger Tail legend claimed he'd committed suicide by swallowing ground glass on the ship to Louisiana. Another said he'd escaped to Mexico and ultimately made his way back to Florida, where he'd lived to be a very old man.

Sammy felt honored to be half of a true Tigertail and, except for his Irish blue eyes, he looked full-blooded. To make up for the time lost during his white childhood, he spent hours listening to the stories of the elders. He envied them for having grown up in a time when the tribe lived in relative isolation, buffered by swamp from the other world.

Now things were different. Now there were casinos and hotels and truck stops, and the stampede of outsiders meant big money for the Seminole corporations. A few of the tribal bosses even flew around Florida in private jets and helicopters, which impressed some people but not Sammy Tigertail. He remained on the reservation and worked hard, although his frequent bad luck caused others to whisper that he was cursed by the paleness in his past. It was a thought that also had occurred to Sammy Tigertail, and shadowed him now like a buzzard as he paddled alone across Chokoloskee Bay.

He wondered about the man named Wilson, held fast with trap ropes and anchors on the bottom of Lostmans River. The sun was high and the water was warming, so it was possible that bull sharks would cruise in from the Gulf. Wilson wouldn't feel a thing.

A half dozen fishing boats flew past the young Seminole as he made his way through Rabbit Key Pass.

Some of the anglers waved but Sammy Tigertail looked away. It had been nearly two days since he'd slept, and his senses were dull. Shortly after noon he beached the canoe on a small boot-shaped island. He unloaded his gear, taking special care with the guitar and the rifle, which was wrapped in a towel. He found a crown of dry land and made camp. It occurred to him that he hadn't brought much food, but he wasn't worried – his brother had sent along two spinning rods and a useful assortment of hooks and lures. Sammy Tigertail was not as resourceful in the wild as some of his full-blooded kin, but he did know how to catch fish.

With noisy seabirds wheeling overhead, he lay down beneath a tree and fell into a hard sleep. The spirit of Wilson arrived, strung with slimy ropes and dragging all four anchors. The sharks hadn't yet found him, although the blue crabs and snappers had picked clean his eye sockets. He was still half-drunk.

'I was expecting you sooner,' said the Indian.

'*How come you didn't take my money before you dumped me in the river?*'

'Because I am no thief.'

'*Or at least the doobs. That was a waste, my friend,*' Wilson said.

Sammy Tigertail allowed that he was sorry Wilson had died on the airboat excursion.

'*It was that fuckin' snake, wasn't it?*' Wilson asked.

'Naw, it was your heart.'

'*Well, I'll be damned.*'

'What do you want from me?'

The dead tourist held up the disposable camera. The cardboard was sodden and peeling apart.

'*How about another picture?*' said Wilson. '*For my*

guys back at the bar on Kinnickinnic Avenue – something they could frame and hang in the pool room.'

Kinnickinnic sounded like an Indian word, though Sammy Tigertail didn't know which tribe had been run out of Milwaukee.

'Aw, come on,' Wilson said. *'They got an autographed photo of Vince Lombardi and a game jersey signed by Brett Favre. But a picture of me, dead and with my eyeballs chewed out – that'd be tits!'*

Sammy Tigertail said, 'Sorry. No more photos.' He was extremely tired, and he wanted the dream to be over. He hoped that a shark would devour the disposable camera while chewing on Wilson. Sammy Tigertail wanted no one to see the humiliating, though undeveloped, images of him posing with the obnoxious white tourist.

'It's freezing in that damn river,' Wilson complained.

'I had to move your body off the reservation. There weren't many options.'

'I didn't know the water got so cold in Florida.'

'Just wait till summer. It's like soup,' Sammy Tigertail said.

Wilson scowled and spit out a clot of brown muck. *'You sayin' this is it for me? I gotta spend the rest of eternity out in this goddamned swamp? Dripping wet and smellin' like fish shit? Not to mention these fuckin' anchors.'*

Sammy Tigertail said, 'I can't blame you for being angry.'

'I shoulda croaked in the casino. I shoulda had my heart attack in the bar when that hooker was bouncin' on my lap. That's how I should be spendin' the hereafter,' the spirit of Wilson fumed, *'not out here all alone in the middle of nowheres.'*

'Deal with it,' the Indian said.

'*Fuck you. This was the worst vacation I ever had.*'

The dead tourist stomped the camera to pieces and shambled away, the anchors screaking across the floor.

Sammy Tigertail awoke in a state of prickly agitation. It was dusk, with a chilly northwest wind blowing in off the Gulf. He put together one of the spinning rods, tied on a plastic minnow plug and hurried to the beach in hopes of fooling a redfish or a snook.

But while the young Indian had been arguing with the white man's spirit, a big tide had rolled in. It was not good for beach fishing, and even worse for an untethered canoe.

In the fading light, Sammy Tigertail paced the shore, scanning anxiously in all directions. There was no sign of the bright blue craft. The wind and the fast-rising water had carried it away and possibly overturned it.

Again he felt cursed. He trudged back to camp and built a fire. Then he took out the Gibson guitar and placed it across his lap. Running his hands along the instrument's magnificent curves, he found himself soothed by the dancing flames reflected in the cool polished wood.

Since he didn't know any chords, Sammy Tigertail began strumming with a wild and random vigor. He had no amplifier, yet he imagined that he was filling the night universe with music. It was good therapy for a stranded man.

Four

The crab boat that Sammy Tigertail had borrowed to transport Wilson's body belonged to a man named Perry Skinner, Honey Santana's ex-husband and the father of her only son. Skinner hadn't asked Sammy Tigertail why he needed the boat, because Skinner didn't care to know. He was vice mayor of Everglades City and therefore inoculated from official scrutiny in most matters criminal and otherwise.

'How's school?' he asked Fry.

'Electrifying.'

'And your mom?'

'That's sorta why I'm here.'

'I figured,' Perry Skinner said. 'Pass the catsup.'

They were the only ones eating burgers at the Rod and Gun Club.

'She still call me your "ex-father"?'

'Sometimes,' Fry said, 'and sometimes it's just "your worthless dope-smuggling old man."'

'That's cold.' Skinner drew a smiley face in mustard on his burger. 'Such bitterness ain't real attractive,' he said.

'I don't know that she means it.'

Like practically every red-blooded male of his

59

generation in Everglades City, Skinner and his brother had gotten popped running loads of weed. 'What happened was a long time ago, Fry. I went away and did my time,' he said. 'Thirty-one months at Eglin, I made a point of improving myself. Where you think I learned to talk Spanish?'

'I know, Dad.'

'Your mom coulda divorced me while I was gone, but she didn't.'

Fry emptied two packets of sugar into his iced tea. He'd already heard everything his mother and father had to say about each other. It was interesting to him that neither had remarried.

Skinner tore into his hamburger and asked, 'How much does she need this time?'

'A thousand bucks,' his son said.

'For what, may I ask?'

'Two kayaks.'

'How nice,' Skinner said.

'Plus paddles and life jackets.' Fry hesitated before telling his father the rest. 'See, she quit her job at the fish market.'

'Yeah, I know. Only she got sacked is the way I heard it.'

'Now she wants to do ecotours through the back-country – nature trips for bird-watchers and stuff,' Fry said.

His father took another big bite and grunted.

'She might be good at it.' The boy spoke loyally but without conviction.

'What the hell happened at the fish market? Did she say?'

'What did you hear?'

Skinner put down his burger and sanded his chin

with a paper napkin. 'I heard she flipped out and attacked Louis Piejack with a claw hammer.'

'After he grabbed her boob,' Fry said. 'And it wasn't a hammer. It was a crab mallet.'

His father blinked slowly. 'Louis grabbed her?'

'Yes, sir, that's what Mom told me. And I believe her.'

Skinner nodded as if he believed it, too. 'Then he's damn lucky she didn't crack his skull instead of his nuts.'

Fry could tell that his father was angry.

'Did he hurt her? Tell the truth.'

'No, sir, I don't believe so.'

Skinner got up from the table and went out to his truck. He came back with a folded wad of hundreds, which he pressed into Fry's left hand.

'Dad, there's something else,' the boy said.

'How come I'm not surprised?'

'Mom needs two plane tickets. She wondered if maybe you could cash in some of your miles.'

Skinner was instantly suspicious. 'She takin' you somewheres on a trip?'

'Not that I know of.'

'You'd clue me in if she was, right?'

'For sure,' said Fry. 'She didn't say what the tickets are for, but she told me to tell you don't worry, it's no big deal.'

Skinner waved the waitress over and paid the bill. 'Plane tickets are too a big deal,' he said.

'Mom said you could cash out your miles and it wouldn't cost you anything—'

'Son, you don't understand. Come on, let's go.'

When they were outside, in the parking lot, Skinner lowered his voice and said, 'I'm not worried about how much the tickets cost or don't cost. I'm worried about what she's up to.'

Fry thought: If only I knew.

But to his father he said, 'So, what do I tell her?'

'Tell her to come talk with me.'

'Aw, Dad.'

'What – you think that's *my* idea of a good time?' Skinner snorted. 'Tell her to swing by and see me if she wants the damn tickets. Tell her it won't take but a minute.'

He got in the truck and lowered the window. 'What kind of grades are you makin' these days?'

'Not bad. *B*'s and *A*'s,' Fry said. 'Hey, thanks for lunch.'

'Anytime. Always great to see you, buddy.' Perry Skinner put on his sunglasses and fitted a plug of Red Man into his cheek. 'I'm countin' on you to let me know if your mom starts actin' up again. You'll call, promise?'

The boy got on his bike.

'Don't worry. She's all right,' he said, and pedaled away before his father could get a good look at his eyes.

Honey Santana didn't despise her ex-husband as much as she claimed. She felt compelled to bad-mouth Perry Skinner because it was he who had filed for divorce, beating her to the punch. By that time they'd already agreed that staying married would be lunacy, their feelings for each other having been flayed raw by one emotional upheaval after another. Honey's attorney had been fumbling around, trying to draft a basic divorce petition, when she'd received the court papers from Perry. Her pride had been scalded, because among the women she knew, it was always the wife who divorced the husband and never the other way around.

After the split, Skinner had been shockingly prompt with the alimony and child support. He'd also been cooperative on the numerous occasions that Honey Santana needed extra cash, mainly because these requests were passed along by Fry, whose affections Skinner prized. Honey felt lousy about sending her son on these begging missions, but she couldn't bring herself to do it. Being alone with Perry still flustered her, four years after the divorce. It wasn't his attitude that was intimidating but rather the way he'd look at her – like he still cared yet didn't want her to know, which was, for Honey, difficult to handle.

Sometimes she envied her divorced friends, who seemed liberated by toxic and spiteful relationships with their exes. Of course most of those husbands had been caught screwing around, which wasn't the case with Skinner. Honey Santana had simply worn him out with her bewildering projects and antic crusades. He was feeling whipsawed and she was feeling caged, and there had seemed to be no practical solution except splitting up.

Still, Honey couldn't forgive Perry for filing first, which made it appear as if the whole damn thing was her fault when it wasn't. He could have been a more patient and empathetic partner. He could have been a better listener, and not so quick to believe the doctors . . .

'I'm sorry, but at the customer's request this number is not published.'

Oh please, Honey thought. He's a nobody, for God's sake.

She tried again, spelling the name more slowly, but she got the same recording. It was unbelievable: Boyd Shreave, anonymous low-life salesman, kept an unlisted home number.

Honey went outside and picked up a section of lead drainpipe and whacked it half a dozen times against the siding of the trailer.

Feeling somewhat better, she went back inside and sat down at Fry's computer, which he'd forgotten to disable, and Googled the name Shreave. Although only one match turned up, her spirits sailed.

It was a story from the *Fort Worth Star-Telegram*, appearing under the headline JURY BOOTS SALESMAN'S LAWSUIT.

A Tarrant County jury has awarded only $1 to a local salesman who claimed he was permanently injured while demonstrating corrective footwear to a prospective customer.

Boyd S. Shreave had sought more than $2 million in damages from his former employer, Lone Star Glide-Boots, following the mishap in August 2002.

According to the lawsuit, Shreave was making a sales visit to an elderly Arlington woman when he inserted a graphite orthotic device in one of his own shoes. While parading back and forth to show off 'the comfort and unobtrusiveness' of the item, Shreave allegedly stumbled over the woman's oxygen tank and ended up painfully straddling a potted cactus.

He claimed that the accident resulted in 'irreparable cervical trauma' to his neck, and that the cactus needles 'grossly disfigured' his groin area, causing 'inestimable mental anguish, humiliation and loss of marital intimacy.'

Attorneys for Lone Star Glide-Boots argued that the incident was entirely Shreave's fault because he'd mistakenly put a left-footed corrective wedge into his right shoe. They also charged that he had 'flagrantly' violated company policy by attempting to sell such devices to a person who had long ago lost the use of both legs to diabetes.

The customer, 91-year-old Shirley Lykes, testified that Shreave was 'a slick talker, but clumsy as a blind mule.'

The six-member jury deliberated less than an hour. The foreman later explained that the panel decided to give $1 to Shreave 'so he could go out and buy some tweezers' – an apparent reference to the lingering cactus thorns that the salesman had complained about.

Shreave, who now works for another company, declined comment.

Honey Santana printed out the article. Gleefully she waved it at Fry as soon as he walked in the door after visiting Perry Skinner.

'Check this out!' she said.

'Don't you even want to hear his answer?' Fry asked.

'Your ex-father? I already know his answer.'

Fry handed her the cash. 'He wants to talk about the plane tickets.'

'Fine, I'll call him tomorrow.'

'No, Mom, in person.'

Honey frowned. 'What crawled up *his* butt and died?'

Fry sat down at the table and skimmed the newspaper article. After finishing, he glanced up and said, 'I thought his name was Eisenhower.'

'Nope. He lied,' Honey said, 'per the usual.'

'Sure it's the same guy?'

'Sweetie, how could it *not* be?' She took the printout and taped it to the refrigerator. 'Listen, I've got another small favor to ask. I need you to go on the computer and do your magic.'

Fry said, 'No chance. I'm done for the day.'

'Please? It won't take long.'

The boy headed down the hallway, Honey trailing behind. 'He's got an unlisted number, can you believe that?'

'Easily,' Fry said.

'But thank God for that stupid lawsuit,' his mother went on, 'because it means there's a court file somewhere in Texas with Mr. Boyd Shreave's address and home phone number in it. If you can find it on-line, then I can . . .'

Fry fell into bed and shut his eyes. 'You can what? Call up this a-hole and give him a piece of your mind?'

'Yeah. Exactly,' Honey Santana said.

'And that's all you're gonna do? Promise?'

'Well, I might have a little fun with him. Nothing he doesn't deserve.'

Fry sighed. 'I knew it.'

'Jesus, I'm not gonna do anything dangerous or against the law.'

Fry opened his eyes and gave her a hard stare. 'Mom, I'm not going to Texas with you.'

'What on earth are you talking about?'

'Oh, come on. Even if you con Dad into givin' you the plane tickets, I'm not going.'

Honey laughed lightly. 'Well, I'm not flying to Texas, either. Fry, that's the nuttiest thing I ever heard – you honestly think I'd jump on a jetliner to go chasing after this slug? Just 'cause he called me a dried-up old whatever.'

'Then who are the tickets for?' her son demanded.

Honey got up and cranked open a window. 'I'm starving. You want a snack?'

Fry groaned and yanked the sheet across his face. 'I told Dad you were doing okay. Please don't make a liar out of me.'

'Hush,' said his mother. 'How about some popcorn?'

To distance himself from an overhead air-conditioning vent, the haunted-looking Sacco had moved into the cubicle left empty by Boyd Shreave. When Eugenie Fonda passed him a playful note, Sacco swatted it away as if it were a scorpion. His skittishness hinted at a bruised and volatile soul, which naturally piqued Eugenie's curiosity. Even the man's telephone voice sounded spent and frayed, although he still managed to churn plenty of leads. After Eugenie slipped him a second note, casual and innocuous, Sacco scrawled a one-word response — 'GAY!' — and sailed it back to her desk. By the end of the shift she found herself missing Boyd, dull lump that he was.

When she got home at half past midnight, he was waiting at her front door.

With more flowers.

'Oh Lord,' said Eugenie Fonda.

'Okay if I come in?'

'You look terrible, sugar.'

'Bad day,' said Shreave, following her inside.

They began to make love on the sofa, Eugenie bouncing with her customary determination upon his lap. Within moments she found herself detached, literally, Boyd having waned to limpness.

'Sorry,' he mumbled.

Eugenie climbed off and pulled on her panties. 'Tell me what's wrong,' she said.

'It's Lily. She's acting really weird.'

'You think she knows?'

'How could she? We've been so careful,' Shreave said.

'Right. Like that day in the sub shop.' Eugenie clicked her teeth.

She went to get a vase for the flowers, Shreave calling after her, 'I'm telling you, Genie, she doesn't know about us. There's no way.'

What a voice, she thought. Sometimes when Boyd was talking, she'd close her eyes and imagine for a moment that he looked like Tim McGraw. That's how good he sounded.

By the time she returned to the living room, he'd removed his shoes and socks and was sucking loudly on a lime Jolly Rancher candy that he'd taken from a silver bowl on the end table.

Eugenie Fonda put down the vase and got two beers from the refrigerator. 'So,' she said, stationing herself beside him on the sofa, 'what'd your wife do that was so weird?'

Shreave spit the sticky chunk of candy into an ashtray and attacked the beer. Eugenie waited.

'Just a strange vibe,' he said finally. 'Things she said. The way she was looking at me.'

Eugenie nodded. 'She wanted to have sex, right?'

'How'd you know?' Shreave was amazed.

'Boyd, we need to talk.'

'I didn't bone her, Genie, I swear to God!'

Eugenie smiled. 'Sugar, she's your wife. An occasional orgasm is part of the deal.'

Shreave reddened and lunged for his beer once again, dark crescents blooming under his arms.

'Boyd, I can't do this anymore,' Eugenie told him. 'And please don't say you're going to ask Lily for a divorce, because you aren't. And even if you did—'

'I haven't told her I got fired. That means we can be together every night!'

'How, Boyd? What about my job?'

He set down the beer bottle and damply clasped her right hand. 'Suppose you quit Relentless and started working days somewhere else. It'll be great – I could have dinner ready when you get home and stay here till midnight, Monday through Friday. Lily won't suspect a thing. She'll think I'm at the call center.'

Eugenie Fonda withdrew her hand and dried it on his shirttail.

'Boyd, listen up,' she said. 'I really don't want to be your full-time fuck buddy. Call me a dreamer, but I still think I could wind up with a normal guy in a normal relationship, once I stop sleeping with married men.'

Shreave sat back, ashen.

'Now don't you dare start to bawl,' Eugenie said.

Shreave's head drooped. 'I can't believe this. First I lose my job, and now you want to break up with me. Maybe tomorrow I'll find out I've got cancer.'

Eugenie led him toward the door, saying how sorry she was and what a blast they'd had together and how it was time for both of them to figure out what they truly wanted from life.

'But I *know* what I want,' Shreave said. 'You.'

'Good-bye, sweetie.' She bent down to kiss him, but then he didn't leave.

'Boyd, I said good-bye.'

He remained rooted and defiant in her doorway. 'I'm not going anywhere till you tell me the real reason you're dumpin' me.'

Seriously, Eugenie Fonda said to herself, do I need this?

'It's the least you can do,' Shreave said.

In addition to the best damn hummers you ever had in your life, Eugenie thought.

'Genie, I want the truth.'

'Fine,' she said. With some guys, cold and cruel was the way to go.

'Boyd, you're boring. You're gonna put me into a coma, you're so fucking boring. I'm sorry, but you asked for it.'

He looked up at her with a twisting and skeptical smile. 'Boring? Nice try. What's his name?'

Eugenie Fonda took hold of Boyd's shoulders. 'There is no *him*. Now, adios, cowboy,' she said.

He shook free. 'No, wait – how'm I boring?' His strong, silky voice had shrunk to a tubercular rasp.

'No, sugar, the question is: How are you *not* boring?' Eugenie Fonda felt a disquieting nibble of guilt, so she hastily unloaded both barrels. 'When's the last time you did anything interesting? Anything at all?'

'With you?'

'*With* me. *To* me. Anything that wasn't totally predictable,' she rolled on.

'But—'

'But nuthin. I don't care to spend the rest of my days servicing a couch potato. When's the last time you were even out in the sunshine, for God's sake? Michael Jackson's got a better tan.'

'But I told you about my accident!' Shreave interjected.

Eugenie waved him off. 'Don't even start. You fell on a cactus, big fucking deal. Everything still works fine.' Then, letting her gaze drift below his belt, she added: 'More or less.'

That did the trick. Wordlessly Shreave plunged down the steps and reeled toward the parking lot.

As his car screeched away, Eugenie Fonda experienced a tug of remorse. If only he'd surprised me just once, she thought.

Flowers just don't cut it.

Five

From 1835 to 1842, the United States government for the second time directed its military might against a small band of Indians settled in the wilderness of Florida. During those years the Seminoles were pursued by almost every regiment of the regular army, and more than fifty thousand volunteers and militiamen. By the time it was over, the Second Seminole War had cost the United States an estimated thirty million dollars, a mountainous sum in that era, and more than three thousand lives.

The toll was all the more astounding because, at the peak of its strength, the Seminole tribe had no more than a thousand warriors.

Absurdly outnumbered, braves would lure the white infantry deep into the boggy swamps and pine barrens, then attack in lightning flurries. The strategy proved highly effective at first, but in the end the Indians were overrun. Their home camps were razed, hundreds of families were wiped out and nearly four thousand tribal members were deported to Indian Country, the bleak plains of Oklahoma. Nevertheless, the small numbers of Seminoles who remained in

Florida refused to surrender, and to this day their descendants have never signed a peace treaty with Washington, D.C.

In late 1880, the Smithsonian Institution's Bureau of Ethnology dispatched the Rev. Clay MacCauley to Florida 'to inquire into the condition and to ascertain the number of Indians commonly known as Seminole.' MacCauley spent the winter of 1881 traveling to tribal settlements at Catfish Lake, Cow Creek, Fisheating Creek, the Miami River and Big Cypress. His account, published six years later, was praised for its rich descriptions and perceptive commentary.

Sammy Tigertail's father bought him a copy for four dollars at a used-book sale at the big public library in downtown Fort Lauderdale. The volume became one of the boy's most treasured belongings, and it was not exaggerating to say that it changed his life.

'They are now strong, fearless, haughty and independent,' MacCauley wrote in summary of the Indians he met, then added:

> The moving lines of the white population are closing in upon the land of the Seminole. There is no farther retreat to which they can go. It is their impulse to resist the intruders, but some of them at last are becoming wise enough to know that they cannot contend successfully with the white man. It is possible that even their few warriors may make an effort to stay the oncoming hosts, but ultimately they will either perish in the futile attempt or they will have to submit to a civilization which, until now, they have been able to repel and whose injurious accompaniments may degrade and destroy them.

From the moment he first read those words, Sammy Tigertail had dreamed of shedding his plain life as a Chad and disappearing into the Big Cypress, hideout of Sam Jones and Billy Bowlegs and other heroes of the second war. Above all, the great-great-great-grandson of Chief Tiger Tail would not allow himself to be degraded and destroyed by the white man, a process he feared had already commenced during his suburban childhood. He planned grandly to recast himself as one of those indomitable braves who resisted the intruders, or died trying.

But then he was only a teenager, stoked with idealism and newfound native pride.

Now, re-reading MacCauley by firelight, Sammy Tigertail struggled to envision the noble and fiercely insulated culture so admiringly documented in those pages. He wondered what the journalist-preacher would say about the twenty-first-century clans that eagerly beckoned outsiders to tribal gambling halls, tourist traps and drive-through cigarette kiosks. For not the first time the young man contemplated the crushing likelihood that the warrior he aspired to become had no place to go.

As much as Sammy Tigertail cherished the Mark Knopfler guitar, embracing it made him think of the casino from whose garish walls it had been lifted. The great Osceola would not have allowed his people to put their name on such a monstrous palace of white greed; more likely he would have set a torch to it.

But Osceola was long gone, dragged in chains out of his beloved Florida and left to die on a dirt prison floor at Fort Moultrie, South Carolina. As for Dire Straits, the band had split up while Sammy Tigertail was still in grade school.

Morosely he closed the MacCauley book and reached for the Gibson. He didn't feel torn between two cultures so much as forsaken by both. Soon, he knew, the spirit of the dead tourist would appear again. Sammy Tigertail was certain that what had happened to Wilson on the airboat was no ordinary heart attack; it had been arranged by the Maker of Breath, to touch off the events that now found the Seminole marooned on a mild winter night in the Ten Thousand Islands.

Obviously the high spirits were testing him.

Sammy Tigertail let his left hand wander up and down the frets of the guitar while he chopped at the strings with his right. For a pick he used a broken seashell, half of a pearly pink bivalve. The music he made was in its dissonance both melancholy and defiant, the bass notes pounding a martial beat. He played until his fingertips stung, and then he stretched out on the ground near the fire.

Before long he drifted off, lulled by the soft crackle of the embers and a breeze moving through the leaves. After a time his sleep was interrupted by singing, which he assumed was the ghost of Wilson returning to pester him. Who else would be warbling 'Ninety-nine Bottles of Beer' in the sacred dead of night?

Yet Wilson didn't show himself, and the unseen chorus began to swell. Soon Sammy Tigertail could make out several voices, some unmistakably female.

He sat up, realizing it wasn't a dream – the wind had switched direction, bringing not only white man's music but harsh bursts of laughter and acrid whiffs of lighter fluid. Hurriedly the Seminole arose and kicked sand over his campfire. Then he loaded his rifle and headed upwind into the darkness. He was not an experienced tracker, nor was he particularly light-footed in the bush, but his heart was true and his aim was improving.

Lily Shreave hadn't expected to see her husband when she walked in the front door.

'What're you doing here? It's six-thirty – you're late for work,' she said.

'I called in sick,' Boyd Shreave told her. 'You were right. We need to talk.'

'Well, well.' Lily motioned him to the couch. 'I'm gonna have myself a cocktail. You want one?'

Her husband said definitely not, and sat down. He felt steadier than the last time they'd spoken, having now devised a more compelling explanation for his monkish behavior. In a fog of vanity, Shreave believed that Lily's simmering hunger for him was genuine. He would have been poleaxed to learn that she'd just returned from meeting a private investigator who was compiling evidence for a divorce.

When Lily returned to the room she was sipping a martini. She had also stripped down to thong panties as red as a pepper.

'So.' She put down her drink and straddled him. 'Let's talk.'

But Shreave couldn't. He sat mute and immobilized as Lily planted both fists in his sternum and began churning piston-like against his crotch. That her gyrations reminded him of Eugenie Fonda wouldn't have been so bewildering had he known that only an hour earlier his wife had been studying his mistress's upright style of lovemaking on a videotape recorded by the private eye, shooting through a window of

Eugenie's apartment. Later, while viewing the tape, Lily had commented with clinical neutrality upon Boyd's weak performance.

He wasn't doing much better on his own couch. His wife's uncanny mimicry left him numb with confusion.

'Lily, please don't,' he bleated.

'Oh, just sit back and enjoy.'

'I saw another doctor today!' Shreave practically shouted. 'The news is bad!'

Lily ground to a halt. 'You went to a new shrink? Why?'

Shreave nodded somberly. 'After what happened at the bagel shop, I was desperate. His name's Dr. Coolidge.'

'Yeah?'

'He says it's much worse than depression.'

'Go on.' Lily seemed in no hurry to dismount.

'I wrote it on a piece of paper. It's in my pants,' he said.

'Right or left pocket?'

'Right one, I think.'

As his wife went delving for the note, Sheave squirmed. He had mixed feelings about the stubbornness of his erection – as reassuring as it was after the humiliating episode with Eugenie, it definitely sent the wrong message to Lily.

'Is this even in English?' She frowned at the lined scrap of paper she'd found.

'It says "aphenphosmphobia,"' Shreave said. He'd practiced pronouncing it all afternoon – the weird stuff you could find on the Internet was amazing.

'So, what *is* it exactly?' Lily didn't sound nearly as concerned as her husband would have hoped.

He said, 'Aphenphosmphobia is the fear of being touched.'

'By your wife?'

'No, Lily, by anybody.'

'Touched where?' she asked. 'Just on your pecker?'

'*Anywhere*,' Shreave said impatiently. 'Fingers, toes, lips, ears – all skin-on-skin contact triggers what they call a "phobic reaction." Could be anxiety, the sweats, even a panic attack. Dr. Coolidge says it's a very rare condition.'

'Yeah, I'll bet he's only seen a handful of cases – get it? *Handful* of cases.'

'Oh, that's hysterical.' Shreave was appalled at her heartlessness. What if he'd been telling the truth?

He said, 'You think this is funny?'

'What I think, Boyd, is that you're still hard.' Slowly she pressed down on him. 'That means one of two things: Either you've been miraculously cured, or you're totally full of shit. Here, let's take off your pants and try a little experiment—'

Shreave bucked loose and bolted for the den, locking the door behind him. 'Look it up yourself!' he called out. 'A-p-h-e-n-p-h-o-s-m-p-h-o-b-i-a.'

Lily knocked lightly. 'Open up,' she said.

'Not 'til you apologize.'

'Boyd, I'm sorry. I had no idea.' Lily was smiling on the other side of the door.

Shreave said, 'And could you please go put some clothes on? This is torture.'

I'll bet, thought his wife. 'You chill out. I'll be right back.'

Alone in the den, Shreave began to pace. Being rejected by Eugenie Fonda had imbued him with something that resembled determination, a trait heretofore lacking from his flaccid personality. A quitter by nature, Shreave now felt positively propelled. He was resolved not to let his girlfriend slip away, and not to be diverted by his wife in her fiery thong underwear.

The phone rang on the desk. Shreave didn't feel like answering; however, he'd been harboring an inane fantasy that his boss at Relentless would call to offer him a second chance. Of course he would demand his old cubicle next to Eugenie.

He picked up the handset. 'Yes?'

'Hello, is this the Shreave residence?'

It was a woman. She sounded remotely familiar but then so did everybody these days. Shreave had calculated that during his call shifts at Relentless he'd conversed with at least seven thousand strangers, and had heard just about every kind of accent, dialect, pitch, timbre, drawl, twang and speech impediment on the planet.

He glanced at the caller ID, which read BLOCKED.

'I'm Mr. Shreave,' he said curtly.

'Oh, good. My name is Pia Frampton and I'm calling with a very special offer—'

'Save your breath, lady.' Shreave chuckled mordantly. In happier times he'd been working at the call center during the dinner hour, so he hadn't had to deal with telemarketers phoning his own damn house.

'Please don't hang up, Mr. Shreave. If I could just have a minute of your time—'

'You're new at this, aren't you, Pia?'

'No, sir—'

'Come on, tell the truth.'

'Okay, yeah. It's my first week on the job.'

'Thought so,' Shreave said. 'Free piece of advice: Don't ever tell the sucker not to hang up, because all you're doing is putting the idea front and center in his head. Just keep talkin', okay? Stick to the script. And don't beg for a minute of his time because then you sound desperate, and nobody trusts a desperate salesman.'

'Wow,' the woman said.

'It's what I do for a living, Pia.'

'Seriously? You work at a call bank, too?'

'One of the biggest.' Shreave told her she had a nice voice, almost too nice for the phone.

'What do you mean?' she asked.

'Lacks authority. It's too, I dunno, creamy-sounding.'

'Creamy?'

'See, the guys on the other end might want to date you, but that doesn't mean they're gonna buy whatever it is you're selling,' Shreave explained. 'Sexy doesn't work when you're hawking Krugerrands or discount equity loans. You ever thought about hiring on with one of those adult chat lines? I hear the pay's pretty good.'

There was silence on the line. Shreave wondered if he'd offended her.

'I was just thinking,' the woman said finally. 'Talking to you is just what I needed – all my friends said I wasn't cut out for this job, and I guess they're right. Thanks for being so straight with me.'

'Now hold on, don't give up so easy.' The new Boyd Shreave, dispensing motivational advice. 'Tell me what you're pitching.'

'Real estate.'

'In Florida?'

'Where else,' she said. 'West of Naples, on the edge

80

of a swamp. Royal Gulf Hammocks is the name of the company.'

'Raw lots?' Shreave asked.

'Oh yeah. Underwater at least half the year,' she said. 'That's why they save the sales push for winter, when it's dry.'

'Beautiful. What's the deal – a free weekend, I bet. And all they've gotta do is sit through a sales seminar.'

'And sign a purchase option,' she said, 'which you can cancel within thirty days, or so they promise.'

Shreave thought the pitch sounded stale. 'It's been done to death,' he told her.

'No, they also give 'em an ecotour,' the woman said. 'That's the newest angle.'

'A what?'

'A breathtaking ecotour through the Ten Thousand Islands,' she recited, 'in kayaks.'

'Well, it's different.'

The woman said, 'I've heard it's real pretty down there. You and Mrs. Shreave ought to go. Heck, you don't have to buy a darn thing – like I need to tell *you*.'

'You get a commission on the sign-up?'

'Right, but it's not much.'

'Never is,' Boyd Shreave said. She'd gotten him thinking.

'Travel included?' he asked.

'Yessir. Two round-trip plane tickets.'

'What about the accommodations?'

'A four-star eco-lodge,' the woman said. 'If you can stand the sales push, it's a pretty sweet deal.'

'Yeah, not bad,' Shreave agreed. He and Eugenie had never taken a trip together. They'd never even gone to a motel.

'Only thing is, the offer expires in two weeks,' the woman added. 'That's what it says here on the read sheet.'

Shreave heard the doorknob rattle, then Lily saying: 'Let me in, Boyd. I promise not to touch you *anywhere.*'

Shreave covered the handset and told his wife he'd be out in a minute.

'Let me ask you something,' he said in a low tone to the telemarketer. 'Are there really ten thousand islands, or did they just make that up to con the tourists?'

Honey Santana had ferreted out Boyd Shreave's home number all by herself. Fry had refused to help, and then her brother had made up some fishy excuse, claiming he couldn't track down Shreave's lawsuit because the courthouse computers were down.

So, after talking Fry into letting her on-line, Honey had found a person-locator service that was offering a one-day trial – supposedly free, although she had to give a credit card number. Once the Web site was accessed, she typed in 'Shreave' and got twenty-seven hits, including several repeats. There were three Boyds, four B.S.'s and two Lilys with the same telephone number and South Willow Street address in Fort Worth.

Honey timed her call for 6:45 p.m. in East Texas. She was hoping Boyd and his wife were in the midst of dinner.

I'm Mr. Shreave.

Honey knew it was him. That voice, dripping confidence and cordiality, was unforgettable.

She was caught off guard when he interrupted her pitch, but she rolled with it, letting him play the wise old pro. His description of her telephone style as 'creamy' was amusing, since she'd deliberately softened her tone to sound different from their only previous conversation.

The moment he asked about travel expenses, Honey knew he was hooked. It was a total high; she was almost ashamed by how excited she felt. Now all she had to do was talk her ex-husband out of the plane tickets.

In the car Honey reached to turn down the radio, only to find that it was off. The music she heard was coming from inside her skull, one of the usual symptoms. Today it was two oldies – a wretched disco number, and the peppy 'Marrakesh Express' by Crosby, Stills & Nash. The static, over which Honey had no control, was worse than on the Cuban stations from Miami.

Her mouth was dry by the time she pulled into Perry Skinner's driveway. The house sat on the Barron River, up the bend from the Rod and Gun Club. It wasn't a huge place but she liked its old, comfortable look. The floors and beams were made of real Dade County pine, which these days was practically impossible to find. Perry Skinner had purchased the house shortly after the divorce, Honey suspecting that the down payment was left over from his smuggling days. Three doors down lived a famous fishing guide who'd taught Fry how to cast for tarpon.

Skinner was alone on the front porch, having a drink.

'Where's the boy?' he asked when Honey got out of the car.

'Track practice. He'll be home around nine,' she said, letting Perry know she couldn't stay and chitchat – she had a tight schedule.

He nodded toward a wicker rocking chair.

Honey sat down but made a point of not rocking. This was a business appointment, after all.

'Fry said you had some problems with the plane tickets.'

Skinner said, 'Not problems, just questions.'

'All I need is two coach seats on American. I remembered you had tons of frequent-flier miles from visiting Paul out West.'

Paul was Perry's older brother and former partner in the marijuana trade. Thanks to his arrogant Tampa attorney, Paul got heavier time, and for spite the feds stuck him in a prison camp way out in Oregon.

Skinner said, 'I can *buy* you the damn tickets, Honey. That's not the issue.'

'Then what is?'

'Are you taking Fry somewhere? I've got a right to know – it says so in the settlement.'

Honey puffed her cheeks and blew out the air. 'Honest to God, the kid's like a mini-you. He asked me the same ridiculous thing.'

'So the answer is no.'

'A big fat capital N-O! What – did you think I was moving away?' she asked. 'I wouldn't do that to Fry. He loves it here.'

Skinner said, 'I heard you quit the fish market.'

She shrugged. 'There's other things I want to do with my life. And don't give me that sideways look of yours.'

Lord, he's still a handsome guy, she thought. Nobody could ever say I didn't have a good eye.

'Did Louis Piejack really grab one of your boobs?' Skinner asked matter-of-factly.

Honey Santana felt herself blush. 'Word sure gets around. Yeah, but don't worry – I fixed his sorry wagon.'

Skinner leaned close and whispered, 'Hold still.'

Honey almost broke into a tremble, thinking he was going to kiss her, yet all he did was very gently brush a mosquito from her neck. She wasn't sure if she was relieved or disappointed.

Skinner said, 'So who are the plane tickets for?'

'A couple of friends of mine from Texas,' she said. 'I'll pay you back as soon as I get another job. I already put in for cashier at the Super Wal-Mart in Naples.'

He smiled. 'You don't have to pay me back. And, no offense, Honey, but Wal-Mart ain't ready for the likes of you.'

'Hey, I've been doing real good,' she said defensively. 'Didn't Fry tell you how great I was doing?'

'Still on the medicine?'

'Twice a day.'

'Because otherwise I'd offer you a drink,' he said.

'No mixing booze with the happy pills. Doctor's orders.' It was the easiest part of the charade; Honey had never cared much for alcohol. 'So, we're cool with the tickets?'

'I'll need the names of your two friends.'

'Here, I wrote everything down.' She took a paper from her purse and handed it to him. 'I appreciate it,' she said. 'This is important.'

Skinner turned toward the river, where a snook was blasting minnows under the dock lights.

'It sucks that you're not tellin' me everything,' he said.

'When are you gonna stop worrying?'

'Maybe when you get a grip on the world.'

'Boy, that's a shitty thing to say.' But Honey could barely hear her own words above the melodies clashing in her brainpan.

Six

Three days later, Eugenie Fonda sat cross-legged on the bathroom floor, listening to Sacco's theory that Bill Gates was not only the Antichrist but the illegitimate spawn of Jesse Helms and Grace Slick.

Evidently it had been Sacco's misfortune to sign on with a software company that vaingloriously decided to compete with some arcane pop-up blocking service provided by Microsoft. The technical details were beyond Eugenie's grasp, or interest, but she had no difficulty understanding the reason for Sacco's consumptive bitterness. At one point the young man had been worth approximately two million dollars on paper, a figure reduced to bus change by his firm's brief skirmish with Sir William Gates.

Sacco's sorrowful tale was related from the depths of Eugenie's claw-footed tub, where he'd retreated morosely after a late lunch at which he'd refused wine, beer and several choices of hard liquor. Eugenie was perturbed to see he had no intention of relaxing, not even for a fifteen-minute hump on the sofa. Sacco was obsessed, and nothing was more tedious than a man with an obsession.

'It's getting late,' Eugenie hinted.

'They talk about free enterprise but in America it's a myth. They talk about a level playing field, ha! It's tilted sideways,' Sacco declared, 'so that every last penny rolls into Bill Gates's pocket. That four-eyed fucker's wired himself a monopoly over the whole damn universe!'

He arose, dripping and agitated. 'Where's your PC? I'll prove it to you, Genie.'

'I don't have a PC,' she said.

Sacco looked mortified. 'You aren't serious?'

'Listen, sport, you want to do it or not? Because I need to get ready for work.'

She'd had her hopes up, having persuaded Sacco first to admit that he was a heterosexual, and then to visit her apartment. It was the inaugural step of her commitment to refocus on unmarried men.

Yet, appraising the bony, mirthless figure in her bathroom, Eugenie Fonda thought: Am I hard up or what?

Sacco said, 'You don't give a damn what they did to me, do you?'

Eugenie tossed him a towel. 'Hey. Sometimes life is a shit-flavored Popsicle.'

'Don't you at least want to hear about the lawsuit, and how they paid off the judge with a free laptop and lifetime DSL?'

'Not really.'

Sacco mulled over this information, then stepped purposefully out of the tub. 'Well, I suppose we could try having sex,' he said.

Try? thought Eugenie.

'Lord, I wouldn't want you to damage yourself,' she said. So much for the quiet, brooding types.

'No, Genie, it'll be great,' Sacco said.

She doubted that. 'Why don't you go wait for me on the couch.'

'How about the bed?'

'It's broken. Don't ask.' Eugenie nudged him out the door, removed the pearl stud from her tongue and dashed cold water on her face. She peeled down to her underwear, but that was as far as she could go.

When she came out, Sacco was obediently stationed on the sofa. He had folded the towel triangularly across his lap, a quaint act of modesty that Eugenie might have found charming under other circumstances.

'I cannot believe you haven't got a PC,' he remarked. 'Don't you feel totally lost and out of touch?'

'You have no idea.'

Sacco flinched when she jerked the towel away.

'How tall are you, anyway?' he asked.

'Six feet even, but don't be intimidated,' she said, hoping just the opposite.

Sacco said, 'You wanna hear something weird? I'm the exact same height as Gates.'

'Cool. Are your cocks the same size, too?'

Sacco looked down at himself in a clinical way, pondering the possibility. Eugenie Fonda was alarmed to think that she'd once regarded this man as intriguing. He was simply fucked-up, and not in a particularly interesting way.

'It's getting late,' she repeated, hoping he'd pick up on her lack of enthusiasm.

'Then let's get busy. I'm ready,' Sacco said.

'You are?'

He patted the tops of his spidery-haired legs, inviting her to hop aboard.

'I don't want to hurt you,' Eugenie said.

'You can't hurt me. I'm beyond pain.'

Just my luck, Eugenie thought. She placed herself on Sacco's lap, facing away. He made a growling sound and said they should pretend they were riding a Harley.

'More like a Lark scooter,' she muttered.

'What'd you say?'

Miraculously the doorbell rang. Eugenie briskly unsaddled and snatched up the towel, covering herself as she hurried to the foyer. Through the peephole she saw him.

'Boyd?'

'Please, Genie.'

She opened the door and whispered, 'What's all this?'

He had shown up in flip-flops, baggy surfer shorts and a loose citrus-colored shirt with palm trees all over it.

'Can I come in?' he asked.

'Absolutely not.' She stepped outside into a cold drizzle, shutting the door behind her.

'You just get out of the shower?'

'No, Boyd, I'm dancing in the Dallas ballet. What are you doing here?'

Nervously he ran his tongue across his teeth. 'I've been thinking about what you said the other night. About me being so . . .'

'Dull?' Eugenie Fonda said.

'Predictable. And you're completely right.'

'It's forty-eight degrees out here, Boyd, and I'm wearing a towel. Could you get to the goddamn point?'

'Here's the point: I'll change.'

'Sure you will.'

'Give me a chance,' Shreave said. 'Just look at me!'

Eugenie was certain she heard breathing on the other side of the door – her hot date, eavesdropping. She couldn't decide which sight was more comical, Sacco ranting in the nude or Boyd Shreave dressed up like one of the Beach Boys and freezing his ass off.

'Genie, close your eyes and hold out your hand.'

'Oh for Christ's sake.'

'Please,' Shreave said.

Eugenie did what he asked, thinking: If he gives me a ring, I'll throttle him.

'There. You can look now,' he said.

In her palm was a ticket envelope bearing the red-and-blue logo of American Airlines.

'Where to?' she asked warily.

'Florida. You and me are going kayaking through the Ten Thousand Islands,' Shreave announced in his platinum voice, 'where the weather today is seventy-four degrees Fahrenheit under clear and sunny skies.'

Eugenie Fonda felt her heart begin to hammer. She shivered and blinked the chilly raindrops from her eyelashes. Inside the apartment, Sacco was lurking like some randy underfed ape, and Eugenie felt appalled that she'd come so close to seducing him. Boyd Shreave was a lump and also married, but at least he wasn't a paranoid geek.

And Florida was Florida, especially in the dead of winter.

'When do we leave?' she asked.

Shreave beamed in triumph. 'Day after tomorrow,' he said, and kissed her so hard that it curled some if not all of her toes.

* * *

Fry waited until they were almost at the Naples city limits before telling his mother. Otherwise she would have whipped a U-turn and hauled back to Everglades City and made a scene.

'Somebody hurt Mr. Piejack real bad,' Fry said.

'Hurt him how?' Honey Santana pivoted in the driver's seat.

'Eyes on the road, Mom.'

'Tell me what happened.'

'They jammed one of his hands into a stone-crab trap,' Fry said, 'while it was full of stone crabs.'

Honey grimaced. 'Ouch. Mediums or larges?'

'Jumbos,' the boy said.

'Uh-oh.'

'Three of his fingers got pinched off and the other two got broken. It happened yesterday afternoon.'

Honey nodded. 'I thought I heard an ambulance coming across the causeway.'

Fry said, 'Here's where it gets nasty. The paramedics opened the trap and busted off all the crab claws, with his fingers still caught in the pincers. They put 'em on ice in a cooler, but supposedly they forgot to mark which of the fingers went where—'

'Oh stop!'

'I'm serious. They finally got Mr. Piejack into surgery, but then the nurses started arguing with the doctors about who'd get to keep the claws for dinner,' Fry said, 'and then the lights went out in the middle of the operation – anyhow, it was a major cluster. Somehow Mr. Piejack ends up with his pinkie sewn to his thumb stump, and his thumb stitched to the nub of his index finger, I don't remember exactly . . .'

Honey whistled softly. 'I guess he'll be selling his piano.'

'Mom, what are you doing? Why're you stopping here?'

'I'm not stopping. I'm waiting for the traffic to pass so I can turn the car around,' she explained. 'I need to speak with your ex-father.'

Fry deftly snatched the keys from the ignition.

'Give me those,' his mother said.

'No, ma'am.'

'Do you want to kill us both? We're parked in the middle of Route 41, or didn't you notice?'

She has a point, Fry thought. It was a good way to get flattened by an eighteen-wheeler.

'Dad's in Miami,' he said, 'so there's no point racing home.'

'Did they catch whoever did this? Have they arrested anybody?'

'No, but Mr. Piejack told the cops it was three Spanish-speaking guys he'd never seen before. So don't automatically assume Dad was involved,' Fry said, though he himself assumed the same thing.

His mother laughed. 'Who else could it be? A normal person would've had Louis beat up or shot. It's just like Perry to get carried away and hire a gang of sadistic gangsters. Stone crabs, I mean, how sick is that!'

Cars and trucks and campers were stacking up, honking behind them.

'The keys, please.' Honey held out a hand.

'What – you think he was trying to impress you or something?' the boy asked. 'Maybe he was just pissed off.'

Honey sighed and adjusted the rearview mirror in order to better appraise the chaos mounting behind them. Fry sullenly tossed her the car keys.

'Attaboy. Now let's go buy some kayaks,' she said.

'Whatever.'

Fry didn't know what his mother was planning, but he feared that she was slipping into one of her manic spirals. She'd made no credible effort to land another job, even though the manager at Wal-Mart had left two phone messages asking her to come in for an interview.

Meanwhile she was spending hours at the kitchen table poring over marine charts of the Ten Thousand Islands. The more she gibbered about starting an ecotour business, the more Fry regretted not telling his father how concerned he was. Honey Santana had no innate sense of direction, frequently getting lost in broad daylight in an automobile, on a grid bristling with street signs. Out on the water, the possibilities for calamity were infinite.

Still, Fry tried to remain optimistic. After all, several days had passed since his mother had mentioned the foulmouthed telemarketer. That could only mean she'd already confronted (and probably crucified) the a-hole, either by telephone or snail mail.

Which was good, Fry thought. She'd gotten all that venom out of her system without harming a soul, including herself.

On the other hand, she continued to skate around all questions pertaining to the two airline tickets. Fry was exasperated, and more than a little suspicious.

'So, who are these friends that you're flying in?' he asked when they were stopped at a traffic light.

'I told you about seventeen times – it's been like forever since I've seen 'em.'

'You guys go to high school together or something?'

'Junior high.' Honey kept her eyes fixed on the

highway. 'But we've stayed in touch. They send a fruitcake every Christmas.'

Fry pointed out that he'd never seen a fruitcake in their home.

'That's because I throw the damn things out immediately. Stuff'll rot your teeth like battery acid,' his mother said.

She was obviously winging it, so Fry dropped the subject. He also decided not to inquire why she'd stopped shaving her right leg – he couldn't imagine any response that would put his mind at ease.

They stopped at an upscale outfitter's shop, where some over-tanned Yuppie wearing razor-pressed khakis informed them that a thousand dollars wasn't nearly enough for two new tandem ocean kayaks. Prowling in the rear of the shop, Honey Santana discovered a pair of used fifteen-footers, one red and one yellow. In no time she talked Khaki Jack into selling her both, plus paddles and travel racks, for nine hundred even.

'That guy couldn't have been more than twenty-five, twenty-six years old,' Honey remarked on the trip home. 'I can't believe he asked for my phone number.'

'I can't believe you *gave* it to him,' Fry grumbled.

'Actually, I didn't.'

'Then whose number was that?'

'Oh, I just made one up.'

Again Honey wasn't being truthful. It was Perry Skinner's number she handed out to men who wanted to call her but whom she had no intention of dating. One conversation with her ex-husband usually cooled their interest, Honey had found, while simultaneously serving to remind Perry that not all guys thought she was a basket case.

'Hey, I need a favor,' she said to her son. 'Would you mind crashing at your ex-father's place for a few days?'

'Can you please stop calling him that?'

'Thing is, I invited my friends to stay at the trailer, which means I'll have to sleep in your room,' Honey said.

Fry hitched his eyebrows.

'Honest to God, I won't peek in the closet.'

'Damn straight.'

'Or under your mattress.'

'How do you know what's under the mattress?' Fry demanded.

'Because that's where all teenage boys hide their porn, isn't it?' Honey said. 'It's only for three or four days, I promise. And I won't touch the computer, either.'

'Why can't they get a motel?'

'Because they're on a budget, young man. Not everybody's rolling in dough like the president's millionaire pals in the oil racket. Or Mr. Perry Skinner, the dope smuggler.'

'Knock it off, Mom. And watch where you're going, 'kay?'

'I'm doing fine!' she snapped.

'In England you'd be doing fine. In this country we use the other side of the road.'

His mother's driving skills eroded dramatically whenever she got frazzled.

'I don't mind going to Dad's,' Fry told her in a calming tone. 'I'll ask him as soon as he gets back from Miami.'

'Thank you.' Honey exhaled with relief. 'I owe you a big one.'

She seemed to relax, and almost immediately the car

found its way back to the proper lane. Later she began humming a tune that resembled in no way the song on the radio.

Another ominous sign, her son knew.

He said, 'So when will they be here? Your friends.'

'Day after tomorrow,' his mother replied.

'You never even told me their names.'

Honey Santana drummed her fingernails on the steering wheel. 'Oh, we'll all get together for dinner one night. I promise.'

He counted three young men and three young women. Their beer cans glinted in the firelight. Thanks to a thundering boom box (with which one of them was now doing a tango), they hadn't heard Sammy Tigertail's somewhat unstealthy approach. He crouched in a line of palmettos and watched the kids frisking around a wind-whipped fire that they'd built on a dry spit of beach. Nearby were three gum ball–colored canoes that had been dragged ashore and emptied. Numerous articles of clothing, including bras and bathing suits, had been laid out to dry on the upturned hulls.

Sammy Tigertail guessed that the intruders were about his age, probably college students on holiday break. Most likely they were harmless, yet he wanted them to go away. He wished not to be seen by any other humans. The battery in his cell phone had died, so for all he knew, a police manhunt was under way for the missing Wilson and the Indian airboat driver with whom he'd last been seen.

It was Sonny Tigertail's third night of spying on the strangers, and finally he'd settled on a plan.

Frightening them off would be easy; a couple of rifle shots over their pale heads would do the job. But first he needed to steal a canoe, a small crime requiring grit and patience.

He stretched out behind a dune to nap, waiting for the campers to pass out. He envisioned himself as his great-great-great-grandfather, stalking General Jesup or that swine Zachary Taylor. The grandiose fantasy was jarringly interrupted by Wilson, the dead tourist. An underwater scavenger had nibbled off one of his earlobes, and a colony of purple barnacles had taken up residence on a bare patch of his scalp.

'*Man, I need a favor*,' Wilson's spirit said.

'Like what?'

'*I want you to move me.*'

'That's not funny,' said Sammy Tigertail.

'*Get my body out of that river, please? Come on, bro, it's so goddamn cold at night. Move me someplace dry.*'

'No, sir. I can't.'

'*Someplace where there's no sharks.*' Dripping algae, Wilson turned to reveal a jagged excavation in one of his thighs; a pallid wound the size of a salad bowl. He said, '*Jesus, I hate those sharks.*'

Sammy Tigertail assured him that he wouldn't like the turkey buzzards any better. 'And that's what'll get you on dry land. Buzzards and fire ants.'

'*But at least I won't be freezing. At least I can rot to dust in the warm sunshine.*' The spirit of Wilson playfully clanked his anchors. '*Come on, whatta ya say?*'

The Indian felt a sting of remorse, which was ludicrous. The white man was deceased and experiencing no discomfort; his spirit just happened to be a royal pain in the ass.

Sammy Tigertail said, 'I don't have time for you. I've gotta deal with these kids.'

'*Move me out of the damn river. It's the least you can do,*' the dream spirit implored. '*Aren't doomed men s'posed to get one last wish?*'

'Only in the movies,' said the Seminole.

Wilson snorted. '*We'll talk later, you and me.*'

The dead tourist disappeared. Sammy Tigertail opened his eyes and got up. He peeked over the crest of the dune, toward the raucous campsite of the college kids.

One chamber-of-commerce myth about the Everglades is that the insects disappear all winter. Mild nights can be hellish, and Sammy Tigertail found himself enshrouded by famished mosquitoes and sand flies. Having foolishly forgotten to baste himself with repellent, all he could do was remain at his post and accept the punishing stings.

To maintain a clear view of the beach, he slashed one arm back and forth, like a windshield wiper, through the buzzing horde. With grim envy he observed that the radiating heat from the campfire seemed to shield the college students from the marauding swarms; either that, or they were too bombed to notice the bites. Sammy Tigertail wondered how long until his eyelids and nostrils swelled shut. He also wondered what Micanopy or Jumper or Sam Jones would have done in the same wretched predicament. One time he'd asked his uncle if there was a secret Seminole potion to ward off bugs, and his uncle had advised him to drive to the CVS in Naples and buy the biggest can of Cutter spray he could find.

As the campfire began to ebb, so did the carousing. The boom box racket faded away, and one by one the college kids teetered in exhaustion. Moments after the last of them had fallen, Sammy Tigertail liberated himself from the palmettos. Rifle in hand, he headed for the beach where the canoes were lined up. He selected the tangerine-colored one and quietly flipped it over, scattering boxer shorts and bikini bottoms.

'Take me with you,' said a voice from the shadows.

Sammy Tigertail whirled and raised his rifle.

'Don't shoot,' the voice said.

'Come closer,' the Indian whispered hoarsely.

It was one of the student campers. She had tangled chestnut hair and wide-set green eyes and sand stuck to her chin and nose, from dozing facedown on the beach. She wore a fanny pack on her waist, and a rumpled sleeping bag was bunched like a blanket around her shoulders. She reminded Sammy Tigertail of Cindy, his ex-girlfriend, except that Cindy had a better complexion. The college girl's cheeks were mapped with angry crimson welts.

'Take me along,' she said.

Sammy Tigertail lowered the gun. 'Go away before you get hurt.'

'The guy I'm with, he's such a loser.' She motioned with her head toward the campfire. 'He brought along these rubbers with SpongeBob and Mr. Krabs on the tip. Cartoon condoms, and he can't figure out why I won't fuck him. What's your name? I'm Gillian.'

'Sit and be quiet,' Sammy Tigertail said. He remembered that he was being tested by mystical forces.

'You an Indian?' she asked.

He was pleased that she'd noticed, but he tried not to let on. He glanced back at the camp to make sure that none of the other kids were stirring.

'Why can't I come with you?'

'I said be quiet.' Sammy Tigertail grabbed the bow of the canoe and began sliding it toward the water.

'These aren't zits,' Gillian said, pointing to her cheeks. 'They're mosquito bites. I'm allergic.'

'Please shut up.'

'Look, I'm a Seminole, too!' With a playful smile she shed the sleeping bag to show off a baggy gray sweatshirt. FSU was emblazoned in tall burgundy letters on the front.

It was too much for Sammy Tigertail. He let go of the canoe and walked up to the girl and touched a hand on her neck to make sure she wasn't a spirit. Her skin felt warm and she smelled like stale beer and marijuana.

'School's a drag,' she said.

'Not my problem.'

'I'm majoring in elementary ed. What was *I* thinking?'

Sammy Tigertail said, 'Do you ever stop talking?'

He nudged the canoe into the water and waded in behind it, aiming the bow into the light chop. Carefully he set his rifle between the seats and prepared to climb in.

Gillian asked, 'And where do you think you're goin'?'

'To find a new island.'

'Yeah? Then you might need this.' She held up the paddle.

Sammy Tigertail grimaced.

'I had a sorority sister, the one who talked me into my major,' Gillian said, 'her senior year she did spring break at Panama City. And one night she gets supertrashed, right? So when this crew from *Girls Gone Wild* shows up at the tiki bar, she jumps up on a chair and flashes her titties. And she was so hot they put it in the video – *Girls Gone Wild* number six. You ever see that one?'

Dazedly, Sammy Tigertail shook his head.

'After graduation she ends up teaching sixth grade down in Delray, right? First week on the job, some smartass kid brings in the video and switches it out for one on the Battle of Gettysburg. And this little shit's only eleven years old! What's with *that*?' Gillian was indignant. 'Anyway, there was my sorority sister up on the screen, shakin' her hooters for her whole class to see. Can you believe she got fired? And the kid who switched out the tape, all he gets is detention!'

'Give me the paddle,' said Sammy Tigertail.

'I want to be your hostage.'

'I don't need a hostage. I need peace.' He sloshed toward the beach, hauling the canoe behind him.

Gillian backed up. 'What if I start screamin' and wake everyone else? You got enough bullets for all of us, Tonto?'

Sammy Tigertail thought: This one is not like Cindy. This one is worse.

'Get in the canoe,' he said.

Seven

Disappointment was the fuel that cranked the aging pistons of Della Shreave Renfroe Landry – disappointment in the father who'd cashed out his Shell Oil pension early and invested every dollar in the DeLorean Motor Company; disappointment in the mother who'd refused to hock her heirloom earrings and send Della to a prep school favored by the tall rangy sons of petroleum tycoons; disappointment in the three successive husbands who'd died without leaving Della wealthy and carefree; disappointment in the one daughter who'd run off to follow a rock band called Phish, then married a public defender who was a known Democrat and quite possibly a Jew; disappointment in the other daughter, who'd taken a nursing degree and, instead of bagging the first available neurosurgeon, hooked up with the World Health Organization and moved to Calcutta.

And disappointment – corrosive and bottomless disappointment – in her only son, who after thirty-five years had failed to distinguish himself either professionally or socially, displaying to Della's hardened eye not a speck of ambition.

'Don't tell me you got fired again,' she said as he sat down across the table.

'As a matter of fact, I'm getting promoted,' Boyd Shreave said, and then to the waiter: 'I'll have the jerked chicken sandwich with extra mayo.'

Della glared. 'Are you trying to make me vomit? Extra mayo?'

'Why would you think I got fired?'

' 'Cause that's the only time you ever have lunch with me, when you've got stinking rotten news and you don't want me to make a fuss. You know damn well I won't raise my voice in a restaurant.'

Boyd Shreave shrugged. 'Last time you called me a lazy sack of muleshit.'

'Yes, but quietly.' Della stirred her jumbo Diet Coke with a straw. 'So what are you getting promoted to – deputy chief telephone harasser?'

'Floor supervisor,' Boyd Shreave lied pleasantly. Not even his mother's taunting could spoil his sunny mood. He was flying away with Eugenie Fonda!

'That come with a raise, or is it all glory?' Della grumped.

'Two hundred extra a week, plus commission bumps.' Boyd Shreave was pleased to see that his mother was disarmed by his fictional success.

'Guess what else,' he said. 'I had the most sales leads of all callers last month, so Relentless is sending me on a free vacation to Florida.'

Della studied him doubtfully. 'Where in Florida?'

'It's called the Ten Thousand Islands.'

'Never heard of 'em. How many did you say?'

'Thousands. It's just like the Bahamas,' Boyd Shreave said. That's what the lady telemarketer had told him, and that's what he believed.

Wistfully Della said, 'Your father and I honey-mooned in Nassau. I liked it so much I made both your stepdads take me there, too.'

With horror Boyd Shreave realized that his mother was angling to accompany him. 'I wish I could bring you along,' he said tightly, 'but they only gave me one ticket.'

'And you couldn't spring for another? Now that you got this big fat raise?'

Shreave felt the sweat collecting under his collar. 'Mom, it's a company junket. I can't even take Lily.'

Della Shreave Renfroe Landry grunted and reached for the soup crackers. 'Boyd, are you screwing some-body from work?'

He gripped the edge of the tabletop. '*What?*'

His mother gnawed at the cellophane wrapper on the crackers. 'Oh, come on,' she said. 'Who gives away a free vacation where you can't bring your wife or even your mom? For all I know, you could be running off with some dumb tramp from the call center.'

Boyd Shreave was shocked to hear himself say: 'She's not a tramp. She's one of the Fondas.'

Della spit half a saltine into her lap.

'A cousin of Jane's,' Shreave added.

His impulsive burst of candor made it official: Like a lizard, he'd shed his old skin. He felt like dancing on the table.

'This is *not* funny,' his mother wheezed. She couldn't picture her chronically unmotivated son as a philanderer.

'If you tell Lily,' Shreave said, 'I'll never forgive you.'

The waiter brought their sandwiches. Della tidied herself and said, 'Well, does this girl at least *look* like Jane?'

'More like Bridget. Only taller.'

'You got a picture?'

He shook his head. 'I meant what I said – if you rat me out, you'll be sorry. Everybody's got ugly little secrets.'

Della didn't need her son to spell it out. She had cheated on her last husband, Frank Landry, with one of the hospice workers who'd been caring for him in the final days. If the incident were made known, it would surely incite Landry's grown and highly litigious offspring. There were still a few bucks kicking around probate that Della had no wish to forfeit.

She said, 'Of course I won't say a word. But seriously, Boyd, where are you headed with this thing?'

'To happiness, Mom. Where else?'

He bit into the jerked chicken and smiled, pearls of mayonnaise glistening on his chin.

While Fry scrubbed the kayaks, Honey Santana sat down to write a letter to the *Marco Island Sun Times* about what had happened to Louis Piejack. One of Honey's past therapists had told her to do this whenever she got worked up. The therapist had said writing was a healthy and socially acceptable way of expressing one's anger.

So far, Honey had gotten forty-three letters published in thirteen different newspapers, including the *Naples Daily News*, the *Sarasota Herald-Tribune* and the *St. Petersburg Times*. Once she'd almost had a letter about the Alaska oil drilling printed in *USA Today*, but the editors had objected to a sentence suggesting that the president had been dropped on his head as a child.

Honey kept scrapbooks of all her newspaper letters, including the 107 that had been rejected. Sometimes she felt better after writing one; sometimes she felt the same.

To the Editor:

Regarding today's front-page article about the violent assault on Mr. Louis Piejack, I certainly agree that the perpetrators of this act ought to be pursued and brought to justice.

However, as a former employee of Mr. Piejack, I feel obliged to point out that his own conduct has occasionally bordered on the criminal, particularly the way he treats women. I myself was the victim of both verbal and physical abuse from this man, though I derive no pleasure from his current troubles.

Perhaps during his long and excruciating recuperation, Mr. Piejack will take a hard inward look at himself and resolve to change. As for the unfortunate mix-up during the reattachment surgery on his fingers, Mr. Piejack should be grateful to have all five, in any order, considering the places he has put them.

Most sincerely,

Honey Santana
Everglades City

She slipped the letter into an envelope and affixed three first-class stamps, even though it was traveling only thirty miles up the road.

Fry came indoors and flopped down in front of the television. 'Did you ask your ex-father if you can stay there?' Honey asked.

A sour glance was the boy's only response.

She said, 'Sorry. I meant your "dad." '

'Not yet, but I will,' Fry said.

'Be sure to tell him it's just for a few days.'

'Mom, chill, okay? It won't be a problem.'

When the local news came on, Honey sat down beside her son to watch. The lead story was about a red tide that had killed thousands of fish, the majority of which had inconsiderately washed up to rot on the public beach in Fort Myers. The tourists were apoplectic, while the Chamber of Commerce had been scrambled to Defcon Three crisis mode. A video clip showed acres of bloated fish carcasses on the sand, pallid beachcombers fleeing with towels pressed to their noses.

'Look, it's the seafood festival from hell!' Fry said.

His mother frowned. 'That's not funny, young man. We're poisoning the whole blessed planet, in case you hadn't noticed.'

Fry didn't want to get her fired up, so he said nothing.

The last story on the TV news was about a missing Wisconsin salesman named Jeter Wilson. After a night of partying at the Hard Rock Casino, he'd announced that he was driving alone to the Seminole reservation in the Big Cypress Swamp. Wilson's family back in Milwaukee hadn't heard from him in days, and it was feared that he'd dozed off and run his rental car into the canal somewhere along Alligator Alley. A search was under way, and in the meantime the Hard Rock had provided a photograph of the missing man, taken at the hotel bar. In the picture, Jeter Wilson's ample lap was occupied by a full-lipped woman wearing a blue-sequined halter, whom the TV reporter identified as a 'local part-time masseuse.'

Fry said, 'What kind of a touron would go straight from the casino to an Indian reservation?'

'He's a salesman,' Honey Santana said. 'He probably wanted to sell them something – like we haven't done enough harm to those poor Seminoles.'

'Poor? They're rakin' it in big-time off the gambling.'

Honey thumped her son on the head and ordered him to go Google the name Osceola and write a four-hundred-word essay about what he learned. Then she changed into some cutoff jeans and went outside to wait for the mosquitoes.

She was conducting an experiment based on information supplied by the night cashier at the Circle K, an amiable older gentleman who'd grown up in Goodland. When Honey had told him of her upcoming ecotour, the man had advised her to pack plenty of bug repellent in case the wind died and the temperature got warm, which could happen even in the heart of winter. He'd also counseled her to stop shaving her legs, explaining that hair follicles served as a natural obstacle to the hungry insects.

Honey had never heard this theory. Being somewhat vain about her legs, which often drew whistles when she jogged along the causeway, she was reluctant to relax her grooming habits. Moreover, it was possible that the guy at the Circle K was conning her, and that he was just some crusty old degenerate who had a thing for hairy women.

Still, Honey couldn't summarily discount his advice. She'd listened to enough lore about the ferocity of Everglades mosquitoes to desire every possible advantage when kayaking through the Ten Thousand Islands with Boyd Shreave.

So as a scientific test she'd decided to let the hair on

her right leg grow, and to observe the buggy response. She sat barefoot on the steps of the double-wide and wiggled her toes enticingly. On a yellow legal pad she noted that it was dusk and dead calm, and that the air temperature was a mild seventy-one degrees. The middle bars of a Tom Petty song, 'Breakdown,' kept cycling through her head, although she didn't write that in the bug journal.

The first mosquito showed up at 6:06 p.m. and alighted on Honey's left knee, where she swatted it dead. Soon a second one arrived, and then a full airborne battalion. By the time Fry emerged with his essay from the trailer, Honey's tan legs were covered with black-and-red smudges.

His face pinched with worry, Fry peered at his mother in the light from the open doorway. Eagerly she told him about the experiment, declaring: 'See, there's no damn statistical difference! Eleven bites on the shaved one and eleven bites on the unshaved one – I'm keeping a chart.'

Her son nodded uncomfortably.

'But maybe I should wait,' Honey said, running two fingers along her right shin. 'It's just a stubble now. Maybe it's gotta grow in thick and curly before it works.'

Fry handed her his paper about the warrior Osceola. Then he went back inside and came out with a towel that he'd soaked with warm water from the kitchen tap. While Honey read through the essay, he wiped the dead mosquitoes from her legs.

He said, 'Mom, let's go in. We need to talk.'

'This is pretty good,' Honey said, tapping a fingernail on the pages he'd written, 'except you got Jesup's name wrong. There's only one *s*.'

'I'll fix it later. How about some dinner?'

'You didn't put in the part about them stealing Osceola's head after he died. About that army doctor keeping it at home in a jar, and taking it out to frighten his kids.'

'Are you making this up? Because it's incredibly twisted,' Fry said.

'I did *not* make it up!' Honey Santana slapped the essay pages into his hand. He could see she was telling the truth.

'Mom, you're getting all torqued up again. Maybe you should go back to the doctor.'

She smiled and stretched like a cat. 'Oh, I'm perfectly fine,' she said. 'You up for pizza? I've got a coupon somewhere.'

Dealey was tired of the Shreave case. He'd done his job, nailing the knucklehead in the act, and now he was ready for fresh meat.

'Trust me. Your husband won't give you any trouble over the divorce,' he assured Lily Shreave. 'After seeing what you've got on him, he'll sign anything.'

She said, 'I want more, Mr. Dealey.'

'But why? I got you dinner tabs and floral receipts and eight-by-tens and video.' Dealey could not suppress his exasperation. 'You said the photos of the blow job weren't enough. You wanted "documentation of intercourse," so I got that, too – on tape, for Christ's sake! What else do you need, Mrs. Shreave?'

'Penetration,' she replied.

Dealey waited for her to chuckle and tell him she was only kidding. When it became apparent that she was serious, he shut the door to his office so as not to offend his assistant, who had recently found religion.

'That video you took was good,' Lily Shreave said, 'but I want something a hundred percent irrefutable.'

'Excuse me? I got you a naked woman grinding your husband on the sofa of her living room, and you say that's not proof of adultery?' Dealey had his share of wacko clients, but Lily Shreave was breaking new ground.

He said, 'I'd kill to be in court when Bouncing Boyd tries to explain that little scene. "Honest, Your Honor, she's not my girl-friend. She's a pelvic chiropractor."'

'Yes, but in the video all you really see of him is the back of his head,' Lily remarked.

'The lady nearly knocks him unconscious with her tits, Mrs. Shreave! In my business, it doesn't get any better than that. Seventeen years, I've never seen a tape of that quality,' he asserted with no small measure of pride.

Lily Shreave had replayed the video over and over during her last visit to Dealey's office. He remembered her sitting unusually close to the screen – not angry or tearful, but hunched forward and studious. At the time, Dealey had thought it was a little creepy.

He said, 'This is a slam dunk, Mrs. Shreave. Ask any divorce lawyer in Texas.'

Lily was unswayed. 'I'd prefer to see penetration,' she said flatly. 'That would be the smoking gun.'

'No, that would be a fucking miracle,' said Dealey, 'literally.'

'I suppose I could find another private investigator.'

'And I'd understand completely.' He passed his invoice across the desk. 'That includes gas and expenses.'

As Boyd Shreave's wife wrote out the check, she said, 'You never told me if this slut was really a Fonda.'

'Not even close. No family connection,' Dealey said. 'It's in my report.'

'Right. One of these days I'll have to read it.' Lily took a tube of mint lip balm from her purse and applied it conservatively.

Dealey glanced at his wristwatch. 'Mrs. Shreave, I've got another appointment across town.'

She closed the purse and said, 'Ten thousand dollars if you get me proof of penetration.'

'That's just crazy.'

'Cash,' she said.

Dealey sat down slowly. The woman obviously was getting off, watching her old man do it with somebody else. One time Dealey had been hired by a husband who got his kicks the same way, except he didn't have ten grand lying around.

'Well?' said Lily Shreave.

Dealey pondered the unappetizing dullness of his next case – a fireman who'd claimed he injured his shoulder while hosing a burning Airstream was now playing thirty-six holes of golf daily while on disability leave. The city's claims adjuster had expressed an interest in either stills or videotape.

Lily said, 'Think of it, Mr. Dealey. You pull this off, you'll be a legend in your business.'

'But logistically, it would be . . . it would be . . .'

'A triumph?'

'A bear,' the investigator said. 'Just so you know, I don't do break-ins and I don't do disguises. That means I'd have to figure out some other way to sneak a camera into her apartment.'

'Not necessarily,' Lily said. 'This morning my husband informed me that his company is sending him to Florida to be treated for a rare condition called aphenphosmphobia.'

Dealey winced. 'Holy crap. Is it fatal?'

'If only,' said Boyd Shreave's wife. 'It's a fear of being touched. And as we both know from your excellent surveillance, my husband has no fear whatsoever of being touched. Or sucked, fucked and fondled, for that matter.'

'So he's faking.'

'Here's what else: Boyd was fired several days ago from the call center. He was out banging Ms. Fonda when his boss called to ask where to mail his final paycheck – minus the cost of some missing office supplies.'

Dealey said, 'Mr. Shreave has no idea that you're onto him?'

'No, it's pathetic. I'll give him as much rope as he needs to hang himself,' Lily said. 'The only thing he's not lying about is going to Florida. A friend of mine works at a travel agency – she went in the computer and found Boyd's reservation on a flight to Tampa. Guess who's got the seat beside him.'

'Where will the happy lovebirds be staying?'

'I haven't a clue. But for ten grand I'll bet you can find out.' Lily got up and headed for the door.

'Hold on,' Dealey said. 'You expect me to do what exactly – hide in the closet of their motel room? This thing you're asking for, Mrs. Shreave, would take some special planning. Not to mention luck.'

Lily told him to go rent some porn, if he needed tips on the camera work.

'But those are actors. They couldn't care less if some

stranger with a camcorder is crouched between their legs,' Dealey said.

'You'll think of something.' Lily walked out of the office.

Dealey, who couldn't recall accepting her offer, followed two steps behind. 'It's ten thousand plus expenses, right?'

'If you get me penetration, yes. Absolutely.'

'And what if I don't?'

'Then all you get is a free trip to Florida,' said Boyd Shreave's wife, 'which isn't such a bad deal, is it?'

Eight

Sammy Tigertail was doing fine until the girl named Gillian started messing with his guitar. That's when he stripped a palmetto frond and wove the leaves into a twine rope and tied her wrists to her ankles. Oddly, she did not resist.

'You don't dress like an Indian,' she remarked as he cinched the knots. 'Those are pretty nice threads.'

'Haven't you heard? We're all richer than Trump now.' He resumed packing his belongings into the stolen canoe.

'I had a boyfriend who played in a rock group. He had a Gibson, too,' Gillian said, 'only not as cool as yours. His band was called the Cankers. Mostly they did covers of Bizkit and Weezer. Know what else? He got his thingamajig pierced.'

'I'm warning you,' said the Seminole.

'His scrotum. They all did – it was the bass player's idea.'

Sammy Tigertail crouched directly in front of her. 'If you go on with this story,' he said, 'I'll leave you here for the buzzards.'

Gillian squirmed. 'You don't scare me,' she said, but

116

dropped the subject of her ex-boyfriend's pierced privates.

'So where are you taking me?'

Sammy Tigertail didn't answer because he didn't know. He gagged her mouth with a balled-up pair of athletic socks and carried her to the canoe, which was wedged in some mangroves. Then he picked up the rifle and jogged back across the island.

In the moon glow he saw that Gillian's friends were sleeping where they'd dropped, not far from the wisping campfire. Sammy Tigertail raised the gun and fired a shot over the beach. Quickly he stepped back into the tree line. As soon as he heard voices, he fired twice more.

Now the college kids were all on their feet, yelling and scrambling for their belongings. A male voice called Gillian's name, and soon others chimed in. The Seminole squeezed off another round and the kids fell silent as they clambered into the remaining canoes.

Sammy Tigertail waited until they were out of sight and he could no longer hear their frantic paddling. He walked to the water's edge and stood there, listening to the waves and trying to decide what to do next. Gillian had screwed up the whole plan. Her friends would go back to Chokoloskee and tell everyone that a sniper had chased them off the island, and that Gillian was missing. Airplanes and helicopters would be sent to search for the tangerine-colored canoe, which – Sammy Tigertail realized glumly – would stand out like a burning flare on the tea-brown creeks.

He hurried back to where he'd left the girl. Somehow she had gotten out of the canoe but he found her nearby, grunting and thrashing among the mangroves. He lugged her to a small clearing, where he cut off the palmetto ropes and uncorked the socks from her mouth and cleaned the scratches on her shins and arms.

'Stop crying,' he said.

'You killed my friends! I heard the shots.'

'Your friends are fine. All I did was scare 'em away.'

'What about me?' Gillian wiped her eyes with a sleeve of the sweatshirt. 'They just left me here to rot?'

'I spooked 'em off with the gunfire.'

'What about Ethan? That guy I was with? I bet he just ran and never looked back.'

Sammy Tigertail said, 'You remind me of my last girlfriend.'

Gillian sniffled and smiled. 'Yeah?'

'It's not a compliment. Take off that goddamn sweatshirt.'

'No way. I'm cold.'

He opened his duffel and dug out a gray fleece pullover, which he tossed to her. Grudgingly she removed the FSU sweatshirt.

'Give it here,' Sammy Tigertail said.

'I don't see why you're so pissy. It's just a name,' she said, zipping up the fleece, 'like the Atlanta Braves.'

He unsheathed a Buck knife and shredded the sweatshirt. Gillian sat stunned.

'It's *not* just a name,' said Sammy Tigertail. 'Do you have any clue what your people did to my tribe?'

Gillian said, 'Chill, okay?' She didn't take her eyes off the knife. 'It wasn't my people. My people were up in Ohio.'

'Yeah, screwing the Shawnee and the Chippewa.' Sammy Tigertail was depressed to think that this bubblehead would soon be a schoolteacher. It affirmed his view that white people were devolving with each generation.

He sheathed the knife and told her to take a seat in the canoe. 'We're outta here,' he said.

'Can't we wait until the sun comes up? What if we flip over in the water?' Gillian was slapping haplessly at a mosquito. 'Ethan said there's sharks all over the place. He's majoring in marine biology. My girlfriend's engaged to his roommate. Well, practically.'

'I'm gonna count to three.'

She frowned. 'You want me to shut up, I'll shut up.'

Sammy Tigertail knew it was foolish to bring her along. If she remained on the island, the marine patrol or the Coast Guard would find her within hours after her friends reported her missing. She'd be hungry and sunburned, but unharmed . . .

Unless the other kids got hung up on the way back to the mainland. In that case, it might be several days before Gillian was located. By then the insects would have made a wreck of her and she'd be dangerously dehydrated, not that Sammy Tigertail should have cared.

Yet he did care – not much, but enough to unsettle him. He felt corrupted by the sentiment, which he blamed on his polluted half-white blood.

Into the night he paddled as fast as he could, the canoe gliding in a wash of moonlight. It occurred to the Indian that since he had no idea where he was going, it was technically impossible to get lost. At daybreak he'd stop at the nearest island, conceal the canoe and construct a lean-to that would be invisible from the air.

From the bow came Gillian's voice: 'What should I call you? I mean, since you won't even tell me your name.'

'Thlocklo Tustenuggee,' he said.

119

It was his great-great-great-grandfather's Seminole name.

'Thlocka *what*?' said Gillian.

Sammy Tigertail pronounced it again, although not as mellifluously as the first time. Since returning to the reservation, he had struggled to master the traditional Muskogee dialect.

'Never mind,' Gillian mumbled.

'Tiger Tail,' he said between strokes. 'That's my other name.'

'Cool. I like 'em both.'

The tip of the paddle struck something hard under the surface, jolting the canoe. Gillian yipped and said, 'Easy, dude!'

Sammy Tigertail cursed under his breath as the hull screaked across a submerged oyster bar.

A few minutes later the girl said, 'I did two semesters of crew.'

'What?'

'Rowing. We can take turns with the paddle,' she offered. 'I'm serious. It'll give me somethin' to keep my mind off the damn bugs.'

'Why'd you ask to come with me?'

'I dunno, Thlocko. Why did you let me?' Gillian laughed. 'I'm semi-drunk and totally stoned. What's your excuse?'

'I'm weak,' Sammy said flatly. He dug harder against the tide.

'So, am I your first-ever hostage?' she asked.

He thought of Wilson, the tourist. 'The first *live* one,' he said.

'You're funny.'

'Yeah,' he said. 'Me one funny Injun.'

* * *

Honey Santana grew up in Miami, where her parents owned a jewelry store on Coral Way. She had three older sisters, each of whom married urologists and moved across the causeway to Miami Beach. Honey was different. Even as a child she'd felt suffocated and disoriented in the city. Crowds made her dizzy and traffic gave her migraines.

She inherited her father's impatience and her mother's lousy sense of direction, a combination that made her teen driving years exceptionally eventful. On the night of her senior prom, Honey's date got blasted on Cuervo and passed out on top of her in the spacious backseat of his father's Continental Mark IV. The task of navigating homeward fell to Honey, who missed the turn off Eighth Street and continued due west on the Tamiami Trail, all the way to the opposite coast of Florida. Honey's date, who would grow up to be a heartthrob on a popular Latin soap opera, awoke to the surreal vision of Honey skipping barefoot in her ice-blue prom gown along the Naples beach.

On the return drive across the Everglades, the young man pulled over numerous times to throw up. The last of these pit stops occurred near a kidney-shaped pond in which a large alligator was wolfing down a purple gallinule. Honey got out of the car to watch, aghast but fascinated. After a while she went back to the Lincoln and found her date snoring in a splash of his own vomit. She took a long thoughtful walk around the pond, counting three more alligators and five old beer cans, which she gathered up.

From the road came the sound of squealing brakes. Honey turned and saw a westbound pickup skid to a halt, tires smoking. The man who stepped out wore a dark flannel shirt and pale dungarees and white rubber boots that came up to his knees. He walked over to Honey and asked if she was all right. Then he took the rusty beer cans from her arms and lobbed them one by one into the bed of his truck.

Immediately Honey Santana forgot about the tuxedoed nitwit passed out in the Continental.

The man in the rubber boots had broad shoulders, his hair was sun-bleached and his face was baked caramel brown. Honey thought he was uncommonly good-looking. He told her he was a commercial fisherman from Everglades City, and a volunteer firefighter. He said he was heading home from Dania, where he'd purchased two new propellers for his crab boat. He said his name was Perry Skinner.

'Perry, do you have a pen I can borrow?' Honey asked.

In the console of the truck he found a black marker that he used for numbering boxes of crab claws.

'That'll do fine,' Honey said.

She walked over to the Lincoln and picked up the limp right arm of her date. She removed the silver cuff link and rolled up the sleeve. With the black marker she wrote out the word LOSER in fat block letters stretching from the young man's wrist to his elbow.

Perry Skinner, who was standing behind Honey, said, 'I can't take you home. I've gotta work tomorrow.'

'I don't want to go home,' she told him. 'Anywhere except home would be lovely.'

'Look, I'm married,' he said.

'Liar.'

He grinned. 'How'd you know?'

Honey hooked a finger in the waistband of his dungarees. 'See, you missed a loop with your belt. My mom would never let my dad out of the house if he did that. No wife would – or girlfriend. I got ten bucks says you live alone.'

Skinner raised his hands in surrender. Honey let go of his pants.

'What's your name?' he asked.

Honey told him. She was thinking about his outstanding smile.

'How old are you, Perry?'

'Twenty-nine.'

'Well, I'm only eighteen and a half,' Honey said, 'but if I stay in Miami 'til my next birthday, I'll go totally fucking insane. Honest to God.'

Perry Skinner said he'd seen it happen before. He opened the passenger door of the truck and she climbed in.

'You didn't even ask about my ridiculous dress,' she said.

'And you didn't ask about my rubber boots.'

Three weeks later they got married.

Honey Santana was surprised to see Fry's skateboard on the sidewalk when she parked in front of her ex-husband's house. The screen door was half-open so she knocked lightly and let herself in. The two of them were in the kitchen, pretending to talk about something other than her. Honey wasn't fooled.

'Don't you have homework?' she asked her son.

'Just algebra. Quadratic equations – totally easy.'

'Get a move on.'

Fry looked to his father for a reprieve. Perry Skinner tossed him an apple and said, 'See you at the track meet tomorrow.' Fry slung his book bag over one shoulder, shuffled out the door and skated away.

Honey said, 'Let me guess – he thinks I need to start back with the shrink.'

'Be grateful you've got a kid that gives a shit,' Skinner said. 'Want something to drink?'

'I'm fine, Perry.'

'How about an orange?'

'No, I mean I'm *fine*. As in, not loony,' Honey said. 'Fry worries too much, same as you.'

Skinner went out on the porch and sat down in his rocking chair. Honey followed but remained standing.

'He said you found some decent kayaks,' Skinner said.

'I didn't really come to talk about that.'

'Or say thanks, either, I guess.'

Honey was stung. 'Knock it off,' she told him.

'I'm dying to hear more about these ecotours. Where exactly do you plan to go?'

'Back in the islands.' She waved her hand toward the river. 'I've got the trip all charted out. Give me some credit, okay?'

Skinner took out a joint and lighted it up.

'Oh, *that's* polite,' Honey said.

Skinner ignored the bite in her tone. 'You got your medicine, I got mine. By the way, Fry can stay with me for as long as he wants.'

'What?'

'He said you needed his room for those friends who're coming into town.'

'Oh. Right,' Honey said. 'Thanks.'

'See, that wasn't so painful.'

She let it slide. She was watching an osprey fly upriver with a fish wriggling in its talons. Her skull had filled up with two songs playing simultaneously. It sounded like 'Bell Bottom Blues,' which she loved, and 'Karma Chameleon,' which made her bowels cramp. Honey wilted under a churning wave of vertigo.

'You okay?' Skinner got up and guided her into the rocker.

She waited until the boom box in her brainpan went quiet. Then she said, 'You heard what happened to Louis Piejack.'

'Sure did.'

'You hire those thugs to maul him?'

Skinner smiled. 'And why would I do that, Honey? To avenge your honor?'

'Did you or didn't you?'

'Go get your purse. I want to check your prescription bottles.'

'That's real funny.'

Skinner took a heavy drag off the joint. 'Louis owed money to lots of people, including one old dude in Hialeah who I know for a fact has a wicked sense of humor and no appetite for excuses.'

'So you're saying it wasn't you? You didn't pay those guys to feed Louis's fingers to the crabs?' Honey said.

Skinner blew smoke up at the cedar beams. 'You act disappointed.' He pinched the joint and dropped it into a breast pocket. 'Makes you feel better, I probably would've done something worse if I'd been there when he touched you.'

'Yeah, such as?'

'Gutting him from his asshole to his nose with the dirtiest blade I could find.'

Honey heard herself gulp. 'You're just saying that 'cause that's what you think I want to hear. Don't patronize me, Perry.'

'Unbelievable,' he said quietly.

She studied his expression for a trace of something more than the usual exasperation. He walked to the door of the porch and held it open.

Honey rose from the rocker. 'Promise me one thing,' she said. 'Promise you won't have anyone over while Fry's here – that girl who sells propane to the RV parks, and whoever else you're sleeping with these days. Not with Fry in the house, okay?'

'I'll try to restrain myself.'

'Oh, and the dentist wants him to floss twice a day.'

'For God's sake, Honey.'

'He's a teenager. Somebody's got to be the drill sergeant.'

'Is he allowed to whack off once in a while?' Skinner asked.

Honey jabbed him in the ribs on her way out. 'Only after he's done his algebra,' she said.

Packing for Florida, Eugenie Fonda endeavored to convince herself that she truly wasn't a desperate woman. Chronically restless maybe, but not hard up.

She expected that the trip would cause Boyd Shreave to get so carried away that he would stamp a romantic interpretation upon every casual sigh and gesture. This was common with inexperienced philanderers. Eugenie was determined not to repeat the big mistake she'd made with Van Bonneville, which was to underestimate the besotting power of routine sex. Certain men could misread the most perfunctory hand job as a pledge of lifetime devotion. Although Boyd Shreave wasn't the type to rush out and murder his wife, he was probably capable of other lust-crazed misbehavior.

Eugenie was certain that she could control him. To that end, she packed four bikinis, in escalating degrees of skimpiness. She applied the same unsubtle strategy to her selection of travel panties and bras. Boyd was not a complex machine.

While struggling to shut her suitcase, Eugenie Fonda caught a sideways glimpse of herself in the bedroom mirror. She shook off her robe and stood there for a minute of blunt self-appraisal. At the end she concluded that she looked pretty darn good – nice legs, premium tits and not a crease on her face; nothing that a light foundation couldn't hide anyway.

Undoubtedly she was the best thing that had ever happened to Boyd. He, unfortunately, was destined to be at most a very short paragraph in her future autobiography.

Eugenie slumped on the edge of the bed. *What am I doing?* she wondered. *Why am I hopping on a plane with this slacker?*

Of course he'd promised he would change. They all said that, and they never changed one little bit. Yet Eugenie always tried to persuade herself that the men she dated weren't really dim, just deceptively shy; that deep in their souls glowed something precious and rare, which they were waiting for just the perfect moment to share.

She straightened up and told herself to get a grip. It wasn't like she was whoring on the streets; she was vacationing with a guy who wasn't physically repulsive and whose companionship was not entirely unbearable. Life is a ride, so what the hell.

From a hand-carved jewelry box she took the pearl

stud that had been given to her by a man she'd met on a Denver talk show during her book tour. He was a famous self-help guru – blissfully married, of course – who by coincidence was also staying at the Brown Palace. At half past midnight he'd shown up at her suite toting a two-hundred-dollar bottle of cabernet, a girl-on-girl porn tape and an elephant's dosage of Levitra, every last milligram of which he would ultimately require for a six-minute erection.

Eugenie stuck out her tongue at the mirror and deftly inserted the glossy pearl.

She understood that she must be heedful, and she must be firm. The trip to the Ten Thousand Islands meant something very different to her than it did to Boyd Shreave.

He wanted to make a whole new man of himself.

She just wanted to get out of Texas for a spell.

Nine

Fry was fast enough to run relays but he preferred the mile because it gave him time to think. When things were all right at home, Fry typically won by ten or eleven seconds. When he was worrying about his mother, he usually came in dead last.

One time he didn't even finish the race. He was in second place with a quarter mile remaining when he heard sirens, at which point he veered off the track and sprinted nine blocks home to see if his mom was being arrested. That morning she had threatened to hunt down and emasculate the plumber who'd sold her a defective toilet fixture that had flooded the trailer. Knowing she didn't believe in idle threats, Fry assumed from the sound of the police cars that she had carried out the revenge mutilation. Fortunately, it turned out to be a routine fender bender in the traffic circle. The errant plumber was alive and unlacerated, mopping the double-wide under Honey Santana's glowering supervision.

The day before the mystery couple was due to arrive, Fry returned from track practice and found his mother painting extravagantly on the outside wall panels of the trailer.

'What's with the parrot?' he asked.

Honey said, 'It's a scarlet macaw, and don't tell me there's no macaws in the Everglades because I know that, okay? The store didn't have any pink paint so I couldn't do a flamingo.'

Fry said, 'Why not a spoonbill?'

'Same difference.'

'No, they've got more red in the feathers.'

'Thank you, Mr. Audubon,' Honey said, 'but I wanted something more – what's the word? – iconic. Spoonbills are okay, but let's face it, they look like ducks on stilts. Now, when you see a big regal macaw' – Honey was beaming at her florid masterpiece – 'you think of a tropical rain forest.'

She dunked her brush in the paint can and went back to work. Fry failed to curb himself from saying, 'Mom, we don't have rain forests here, either.'

'Get busy on your homework, wiseass.'

'Can I ask why you're painting the place?'

'So it won't look like a mobile home,' Honey said. 'Nothing fancy, a basic jungle motif – palms, vines, banana plants. I bought, like, four different shades of green.'

Fry sat down on his backpack and contemplated the obvious futility of opening an eco-lodge in a trailer park. Based on what he saw, he didn't have high hopes for his mother's nature mural. She had bestowed upon her psychedelic macaw the lush eyelashes of a dairy cow and the dainty tongue of a fruit bat.

He said, 'Next you'll be doing monkeys.'

'Matter of fact, I am.' She spun around to face him. 'Look, kiddo, this ain't the frigging Smithsonian. This is a sales job, okay? Once we get the tourists into the kayaks and out in those islands' – she was pointing fervently with the paintbrush – 'they'll be so blown away by how gorgeous it is, the mural won't matter. Instead of macaws and gibbons they get bald eagles and raccoons. Instead of a rain forest they get mangroves. So what.'

Fry said, 'You're right, Mom.'

'And you know what? If they *don't* get it, then screw 'em. They should go back to the big city and commune with the pigeons and rats, 'cause that's all the wildlife they deserve.'

Fry regretted questioning the realism of her artwork. Once Honey Santana launched a project, extreme delicacy was required in commentary. To criticize even mildly was to risk agitating her or, worse, sparking a more fanciful initiative.

'You have any more questions?' she asked sharply.

'Yeah, one.' Fry stood up. 'Got an extra paintbrush?'

Boyd Shreave hurried to pack before his wife came home. He didn't want her to see his Florida wardrobe, seven hundred dollars' worth of Tommy Bahama boat shorts and flowered shirts that he'd charged to her MasterCard. They all fit neatly inside a new Orvis travel bag that he'd spotted at a high-end fishing shop downtown.

He was finished by the time Lily walked in the front door. With evident skepticism she eyed the Orvis bag. 'What's the name of this place you're going?'

Falling back on Eugenie's advice, he dredged up another dead president. 'The Garfield Clinic,' he said.

'Garfield, like that lazy cat in the comics?'

'No, it's the name of the doctor who discovered my disease.'

'No offense, Boyd, but *leprosy* is a disease. The fear of being groped is a mental condition.'

'Disorder,' he said stiffly.

'What's it called again?'

Shreave paused long enough to nail the pronunciation. 'Aphenphosmphobia – you can look it up. Dr. Millard Garfield was the one who first documented it.'

His wife said, 'Is that right.'

'He died a few years ago.' Boyd Shreave hoped she would wait until tomorrow morning, after he was gone, to get on the Internet and check his story. 'So they named the clinic after him,' he added.

'Quite an honor,' Lily said dryly.

Shreave didn't waver. 'I'm feeling worse every day. I sure hope they can help.'

'And Relentless is picking up the tab?'

'They said they've got an investment in me. They said I have a big future with the company.' It felt like he was working the phones, the lies were rolling so comfortably off his tongue.

'So what exactly is the therapy for this kind of thing?' Lily asked. 'You sit in a rubber room with a bunch of other nuts and practice fondling each other?'

'That's *so* funny.'

'I'm serious, Boyd. I want to know if you're ever going to get better.'

'Why do you think I'm making the trip?' he said. 'Garfield is like the Mayo Clinic for aphenphosmphobics.'

'If you say so.' His wife headed for the kitchen. 'I'm having a drink. Want one?'

Boyd Shreave stood at the window and watched the neighbor's tiny Jack Russell take a mastiff-sized dump on his lawn.

Lily returned with two strawberry daiquiris and thrusted one at him. 'Might as well get into the tropical spirit.'

Shreave raised the glass and said, 'To Dr. Garfield.'

'Ha! To hell with that quack,' Lily said. 'I bet I can cure you quicker.'

Her mischievous tone caused Shreave to hack out a nervous chuckle. He had not forgotten the aborted bagel-shop blow job, or the attempted red-thong seduction on the couch.

'Sit down,' she said, motioning toward a wingback chair. 'Sit and enjoy.'

'Lily, this isn't a game.'

'Oh relax. I promise not to lay a hand on you.'

'You better not.'

'I swear on Daddy's grave.'

What grave? Shreave thought. The man was cremated and scattered over a golf course designed by Fuzzy Zoeller.

'Boyd, *sit*,' said his wife.

He surrendered his daiquiri and sat.

'Excellent. Now shut your eyes,' she instructed.

'What for?'

Lily put down the two glasses and said, 'You want the cure, or not?'

Shreave squeezed his eyelids closed, half-expecting her to latch onto his crotch. He decided to stage a fainting episode if that happened – complete with convulsions and flecks of spittle.

'Clear your mind of every distraction, every random thought,' his wife said, 'except for one. I want you to focus all your concentration and energy on this simple image until it fills your whole consciousness, until

133

you can't possibly think about anything else even when you try.'

'Okay, Lily.' Shreave assumed that she was cribbing from Deepak Chopra or some other flake.

She said, 'Boyd, I want you to focus on the fact that I'm not wearing any panties.'

That's original, he thought.

'Think about the tight jeans I'm wearing. Think about what you could see if you really tried,' Lily said, 'but don't you dare peek.'

That's what Boyd Shreave was tempted to do. Despite his determination to remain unaroused, he found himself imagining in all its velvet detail the very thing that his wife wanted him to imagine. How she loved tight pants! 'Smuggling the yo-yo,' she called it.

'What's the point of this?' he asked somewhat shrilly.

'Hush.'

He heard a zipping noise and then the unmistakable sliding of fabric on skin as she pulled off the jeans.

'Come on, Lily, don't.'

'Just take a deep breath. Let yourself go.'

'You don't understand. This is an irrational fear that's out of my control.' He was quoting from the unofficial aphenphosmphobia Web site. 'Are you trying to humiliate me, or what?'

'Boyd, open your eyes,' his wife said, 'and look down.'

He did.

'Now, tell me you don't want to be touched,' she said. 'Tell me that's not a happy, sociable cock.'

It was hard to argue the point. As Boyd Shreave assessed the telltale tent pole in his pants, he began to reconsider his staunchly monogamous commitment to Eugenie Fonda. The sole reason he'd been deflecting Lily's advances was to avoid the rigors and inconvenience of maintaining two sexual relationships simultaneously. However, Shreave's domestic agenda recently had changed, as had his outlook. Tomorrow he was jetting off to start a thrilling new chapter of an otherwise drab and forgettable life; what possible harm could come from a quick good-bye fuck with his wife?

'Boyd?' said Lily.

He looked up and saw her stretch like a sleepy lioness on the Persian carpet. He noted approvingly that she'd been truthful about her lack of underwear. Her blouse and heels lay in a pile with the blue jeans.

He said, 'Okay. You win.'

'What do you mean?'

Shreave rose and briskly began to unbuckle his belt. Lily studied him curiously.

'Go to town,' he said, dropping his pants.

She sat up and drew her knees together, blocking her husband's view of the shadowy treasure.

By now he was nearly levitating with lust. 'It's okay, honest,' he said. 'Grab all you want.'

Lily's brow furrowed unpromisingly. 'That's not how this therapy goes. The first stage is look but don't touch.'

'Excuse me?'

'Like you said, Boyd, this is a very serious disorder. I'd never forgive myself if you had a coronary or something while I was sucking you off.'

'I'm willing to take that chance,' Shreave declared with a desperate stoicism. 'I feel good, Lily – in fact, I feel terrific. It's what they call a breakthrough!'

'No, let's wait to see what the experts at Garfield say. We shouldn't try anything too wild until we're sure it's safe.'

'But I'm fine,' he squeaked, watching sadly as his wife wiggled into her clothes.

'We definitely made progress tonight,' she added brightly. 'I can't wait till you get back from Florida – we'll do it all night long, if the shrinks say it's okay. We'll touch our brains out.'

'Yeah. All night long,' he said.

Lily blew a kiss and vanished down the hallway.

Boyd Shreave tugged up his pants, sat down and, during detumescence, polished off the slushy dregs of his daiquiri. He was not one who appreciated irony, so at that moment all he experienced was a loutish sense of deprivation.

Because he had no intention of coming back from Florida. He would never again see his wife naked on the carpet.

Dismal Key is a crab-shaped island located on the Gulf side of Santina Bay, between Goodland and Everglades City. Local records list the first owner as a Key West barkeep named Stillman, who planted lime groves on Dismal and shipped the fruit to market on a schooner called the *Oriental*. Stillman died in either 1882 or 1883, and thereafter the mangrove island was purchased by a hardy South Carolinian named Newell, who took residence with his wife and their four children. They stayed until 1895, no small feat of endurance.

After the turn of the century, Dismal Key became a way station for itinerant fishermen and a home for a series of self-styled loners, the last of whom was a whimsical soul named Al Seely. A surveyor and machinist, Seely was diagnosed with a terminal illness in 1969 and informed that he'd be dead in six months. With a dog named Digger, he took a small boat to Dismal Key and occupied an abandoned two-room house with its own cistern. There he began writing an autobiography that would eventually fill 270 typed double-spaced pages. For a hermit, Seely was uncommonly gregarious, providing a guest book for visitors to sign. Still very much alive in 1980, he welcomed a group of local high schoolers who were working on a research project. To them he confessed that he'd moved to the Ten Thousand Islands with the notion of killing wild game for food but had found he didn't have the heart for it. He lived off a small veteran's pension and the occasional sale of one of his paintings.

'People often ask how Dismal Key got its lugubrious name. I wish I knew,' Seely wrote in his journal, discovered years after he vacated the island. 'But since I haven't as yet turned up even a clue, I suggest that they visit me during July or August when the heat, the mosquitoes, and the sand flies are at their rip-roaring best and they will at least discover why it's not called Paradise Key.'

On the January morning when Sammy Tigertail beached his stolen canoe on Dismal Key, the temperature was sixty-nine degrees, the wind was northerly at thirteen knots and insects were not a factor. Gillian was, however.

'I'm starving,' she announced.

Sammy Tigertail tossed her a granola bar and hurriedly began unpacking.

'Is this supposed to be breakfast?' she asked.

'And lunch,' he said. 'For dinner I'll catch some fish.' He worked fast, expecting at any moment to hear the ranger helicopter that patrolled Everglades National Park. That he was two miles outside the park boundary would have been pleasing news to Sammy Tigertail, who knew neither the name of the island nor the route that had led him there.

Gillian gobbled down the granola bar and complained of a killer hangover. 'You got any Tylenols?'

'Sleep it off,' the Seminole advised unsympathetically.

He hauled the canoe into the mangroves and carefully covered it with loose debris from what appeared to be a rotted dock. Using the paddle as a machete, he began hacking his way uphill through a thicket of formidable cactus plants. Gillian followed, toting the guitar case. Jagged shells crunched under their feet.

Beneath a vast and ancient royal poinciana was a half-sunken concrete structure that Sammy Tigertail recognized as a cistern. It had a blistered tin roof that seemed intact, promising not only shade but concealment. The Indian was relieved that he wouldn't need to construct a lean-to, a wilderness task he had never before attempted.

Farther along they came to a rubble of sun-bleached boards, cinder block, trusses and window frames – the remains of Al Seely's homestead. In a nearby ravine lay hundreds of empty Busch cans older than Gillian, who picked one up and studied it as if it were an archaeological treasure.

Sammy Tigertail walked back to the shoreline to retrieve the rest of the gear. He returned to see Gillian slashing at a cactus with the end of the paddle.

'I heard they use 'em for food in the desert. I heard they taste pretty good,' she said.

'This ain't the Sahara, girl.'

'Fine. You're the Indian,' she said. 'Tell me what's safe to eat around here.'

Sammy Tigertail didn't have a clue. Since returning to the reservation from the white man's world, he'd been unable to shake a fondness for cheeseburgers, rib eyes and pasta. Because of modern commerce coming to the Big Cypress, there had been no need to familiarize himself with the food-gathering skills of his ancestors, who'd farmed sweet potatoes and made bread flour from coontie. Sammy Tigertail wouldn't have recognized a coontie root if he tripped over it.

'Later I'll go catch some fish,' he said again.

'I hate fish,' Gillian stated. 'One time when I was only four, my dad brought home a salmon he caught on Lake Erie and we all got really, really sick. Our cat, Mr. Tom-Tom, he took two bites and dropped dead on the kitchen floor. Me and my sister threw up for about five days straight, and swear to God the puke was, like, radioactive. I mean, it practically *glowed*.'

Sammy Tigertail said, 'You're so full of crap.'

'No way! It really happened,' Gillian said, 'and ever since then I can't eat fish.'

'You will now. You're on the South Beach hostage diet.'

The cistern was littered with leaves and animal scat. It looked like a solid place to hide, because there was no sign that it had held water in many years. Sammy Tigertail squeezed through an opening under the roof, chased off a wood mouse and announced: 'We picked the right island.'

Unfazed by the scrambling rodent, Gillian said, 'Are

139

we up on a hill? I didn't think they had hills around here.'

'It's made of oyster shells. The whole thing.' Sammy Tigertail stripped off his shirt.

'Made by who?' she asked.

'Native Americans – but not my people. Hand me the rifle, please.' He tied his shirt around the barrel and methodically went through the cistern taking down spiderwebs.

Long before the Seminoles arrived, southwest Florida had been dominated by the Calusa tribe, which fought off the Spaniards but not the sicknesses they brought. The most striking remnants of the sophisticated Calusa civilization were their monumental oyster middens, engineered to protect the settlements from flooding and also to trap fish on high tides. Sammy Tigertail felt proud, and inspired, to be camping on an authentic Calusa shell mound. He hoped to be visited in his sleep by the spirits of their long-dead warriors – perhaps even the one whose well-aimed arrow had been fatal to the invader Ponce de León.

'They must've been the horniest Indians anywhere,' Gillian mused, 'if all they ate was oysters.'

Sammy Tigertail stared at her. 'What kind of grades do you get in college?'

'I made the dean's list twice.'

'God help us.'

'Screw you, Tonto.'

Once they finished cleaning the cistern, they loaded in the gear. Gillian lay down on top of her sandy sleeping bag and said she was going to crash.

'What's that music?' Sammy Tigertail asked. 'You got an iPod or something?'

It sounded like the opening bars of 'Dixie.'

Gillian rolled over and said, 'Shit. My cell.' She took it out of her fanny pack and checked the caller ID. 'Oh great, it's Ethan.'

The Indian snatched the phone. 'What're you going to tell him?'

'That he's an asshole. Seven hours later he calls to see if I'm alive!'

'Say one word about me, I'll—'

'What – kill me? Rape me? Stake me to an anthill?'

The phone stopped ringing.

'Hey, where you goin'?' she asked.

'To make a call,' Sammy Tigertail said.

'Watch my battery. I didn't bring a charger.'

He laughed. 'I didn't bring any electricity.'

He went outside and dialed his mother's house at the reservation. Her machine answered, so he left a message saying that he was camping in the Fakahatchee, collecting tree snails.

Next he phoned his uncle Tommy, who answered on the tenth ring.

'Who's Gillian St. Croix?' he said, reading from his caller ID, 'and why are you calling from her number?'

'Long story. Is anybody hunting for me?'

'No, but they've been out to the reservation asking about a man from Milwaukee.'

Sammy Tigertail's heart quickened as he thought of Wilson at the bottom of Lostmans River. 'Do they know about the airboat ride?'

'My guess is no. But that drunken shithead ran the SunPass lane on Alligator Alley, so they got a photo of his car heading west. They figure he probably drove into the canal on his way to Big Cypress.'

'I like that theory.'

'We're doing what we can.'

'What kind of questions are they asking?'

'Don't sweat it,' Uncle Tommy said.

Sammy Tigertail was worried. What if the dead tourist had big-shot kin back in Wisconsin? The search might drag on for months.

'Where the hell *are* you?' asked his uncle.

'Some island near Everglades City. I don't even know the name.'

'No problem. I'll get the air force up and we'll find you.'

Tommy Tigertail had been the financial architect of the tribe's early bingo enterprises, which had made him a power player in the Seminole hierarchy. He was not a fan of white men, but he liked their toys. A Falcon jet and several luxury turboprops were available to him on an hour's notice.

'You can stay at the town house on Grand Bahama until the heat's off,' he told his nephew.

'Thanks, but I'm okay out here,' Sammy Tigertail said. 'I'm learning the guitar.'

'Your brother told me. Is she with you – this Gillian girl?'

'Temporarily.'

'Don't lose your senses, boy. White pussy is bad medicine.'

Sammy Tigertail chuckled. 'Speaking of which, you seen Cindy?'

'Yeah. She says she's finally off the crystal and dating a real-estate man from Boca Grande. I told her she'll be getting your remittance, and she said you're a prince.'

'Hang on a second.' Sammy Tigertail flattened himself against the cistern wall and scanned the sky.

'She said she's going to take the first check and buy herself some new boobs,' his uncle continued. 'She wanted me to be sure and tell you thanks.'

Sammy Tigertail heard the thing clearly now, coming in fast from the south. 'Uncle Tommy, I gotta go,' he said, and vaulted through the narrow opening.

He landed hard on the bare cement floor, and lay there listening as a small plane passed very low over the island. A shadow moved to block the sunlight, and there was Gillian standing over him – pointing the rifle at his chest. Sammy Tigertail noticed that she'd removed his shirt from the point of the barrel, indicating a possible seriousness of purpose.

'Are you arresting me?' he asked.

Gillian sighed in exasperation. 'Gimme the damn phone.'

Ten

Eugenie Fonda didn't complain about flying coach, although she let it slip to Boyd Shreave that her book publisher had always sent her first-class.

'Book publisher?' he said.

'Didn't I mention?' Eugenie thinking: Damn those Valiums.

'That you wrote a book? No, I definitely would've remembered,' said Shreave. 'What was it, like a cookbook?'

'Not exactly, sugar.'

The plane was sitting on the runway at DFW, eleventh in line for takeoff. Eugenie would have killed for a pre-flight vodka tonic, but there was no prayer. Not in fucking coach.

'It was a few years back,' she said. 'I was involved with a man who turned out to be a seriously bad guy. Later they asked me to do a book – wasn't *my* idea.'

'What was it called? Maybe I read it,' he said.

Eugenie Fonda would not have been shocked to learn that Boyd Shreave hadn't cracked a book since twelfth grade.

She said, '*Storm Ghoul.* How's that for a title? Sounds like a Halloween movie.'

'You make some bread off it?'

'I did okay. It was on the best-seller list for a while.'

'Oh, really.' Shreave sagged into a pout. 'I thought you and me weren't going to have any secrets.'

'I don't recall such an agreement, Boyd.'

'You wrote a best-seller! That's huge, Genie. Why didn't you tell me?'

'Because it was a long time ago and the money's all gone.'

'Fine. Anything else I should know?'

'Yeah, there is,' she said. 'I don't date nine-year-olds, or guys who act like them. So sit up straight, paste a smile on your face and show everyone on the plane that you're proud to be flying with a hot-looking lady like me.'

They didn't speak again until they were somewhere over Louisiana, where Boyd Shreave screwed up the nerve to ask about the other man.

'Well, he turned out to be a killer,' Eugenie said, emptying the last droplet from the vodka miniature into her cup. 'Bonneville was his name. The story was all over the media.'

'And you were married to this lunatic?'

'No, I was his girlfriend. He drowned his wife and blamed it on a hurricane.'

'Holy Christ. I *do* remember that one,' Shreave murmured. 'It was on Court TV, right?'

Eugenie said, 'Let's talk about a happier subject – like famine, or polio.' She signaled a flight attendant for another drink.

They were passing over Panama City when Boyd leaned closer and whispered, 'So, besides being totally beautiful and sexy, you're also a famous writer. That's pretty flippin' cool.'

Out the window Eugenie could see the gleaming crescent shoreline of the Florida Panhandle. For one fine moment she was able to imagine that she was traveling alone.

She said, 'I'm not a famous writer, Boyd, I'm a famous mistress. Big difference.'

He placed a hand on one of her legs. 'But think about it, Genie. A man *killed* for you. How many girls can say that?'

'Somehow it didn't seem all that flattering at the time.' She was irritated that he'd gotten aroused by the thought of her consorting with a homicidal nutball.

'It wasn't exactly the high point of my life,' she added, thinking: But what if it was?

Boyd smooched her neck and simultaneously sent his fingers reconnoitering beneath her skirt. Eugenie Fonda clamped her knees so emphatically that he yipped and jerked away, drawing an amused glance from a young cowboy across the aisle.

'You behave,' Eugenie said to Boyd, who decamped into another slouch.

As she drained what she vowed would be her final cocktail of the flight, she observed through the clear bottom of the plastic cup that the young cowboy was smiling at her. She did not smile back, although her outlook vastly improved.

Five miles below, the green Gulf of Mexico licked at the coast-line. Somewhere toward the east, nuzzled by the Suwannee River, was Gilchrist County, which in scraggly ten-acre parcels Eugenie Fonda and Boyd Shreave had hawked over the phone to all those innocent saps. From high up in the clouds it didn't seem like such a bad deal.

Eugenie closed her eyes and sucked on the last ice cube, which clacked lightly against the pearl in her tongue.

Dealey was seated in first class, an expense he would fondly tack on to Lily Shreave's invoice after the job was done. His camera gear was stowed in waterproof Halliburtons; his targets were sixteen rows back, in steerage.

He could have booked a different flight to Tampa but there was no point, since the lovebirds had no idea who he was or what he was doing. To them he would have looked like just another weary middle-aged suit, skimming the sports section of the *Star-Telegram* while the other passengers filed to their seats.

Penetration.

Lily Shreave was one twisted bird but she was right about one thing: If Dealey got what she wanted, he'd be a legend on the PI circuit.

Dutifully he had devoted an afternoon to surfing the voyeur-cam porn sites, but he'd found nothing instructive. There was a tedious emphasis on up-skirt shots and toilet surveillance, neither of which required a particularly advanced level of cinematography. As for the couples videos, the sex scenes were plainly staged, the participants fully aware they were being taped. There was no other explanation for why, in the throes of lust, they unfailingly paused to reposition themselves at auspicious camera angles. It was practically comical.

Unfortunately, no one would be directing Boyd Shreave and Eugenie Fonda in bed, or lighting their crotches for sweaty close-ups. Even if Dealey devised a way to conceal the taping equipment, he might end up with nothing more explicit than two grainy lumps heaving and moaning beneath the sheets.

If I live a hundred fucking years, he thought wistfully, I'll never top that delicatessen blow job.

It was golden. A classic.

Dealey had blurred out the faces on the photograph and E-mailed it to an on-line trade magazine, which had posted it the next day. Kudos (and reprint requests) continued to pour in from all over the country. A few other PIs had sent surveillance pictures of husbands being fellated by girlfriends – but none in broad daylight at a bustling lunch joint.

Some wives would've paid a ten-grand bonus just for the deli shot, Dealey thought, but my client happens to be a total kink. She wants penetration.

For a closer look at his targets, Dealey waited until the rest room in first class was occupied. Then he stood up and made his way to the back of the plane. Eugenie Fonda and Boyd Shreave were sitting in one of the emergency-exit rows. She was staring out the window; he was thumbing through the in-flight magazine.

They don't even look like a couple, Dealey noted with concern. They look like two total strangers.

Poised before the toilet in one of the aft rest rooms, the investigator pondered the dispiriting possibility that Boyd Shreave's illicit romance was already cooling. If true, the sex in Florida would be infrequent, brief and subdued.

Which would make even more improbable Dealey's quest for the coital grail.

Oh well, he thought, there are worse places to waste a few days in the wintertime. Hell, I could be flying to Little Rock instead of Tampa.

At that moment the plane hit turbulence, rocking the private investigator sideways and disrupting his otherwise-flawless trajectory.

'Goddammit,' Dealey muttered, snatching a handful of paper towels to mop the piss from his right pants leg. The stain, he observed bitterly, was the shape of Arkansas.

Stalking back to his seat, Dealey didn't bother to look at Lily Shreave's husband and Eugenie Fonda.

Who were now holding hands.

The island was quiet after the small plane passed.

Gillian shoved the rifle back to Sammy Tigertail and said, 'Scared you, didn't I, Thlocko?'

'Please go,' he said. 'Take the damn canoe, I don't care.' He wasn't sure who was the actual hostage – the girl or him.

She punched a number on her cell phone.

'Ethan? Hey, it's me. Alive and seriously pissed.'

Sammy Tigertail started to climb out of the cistern but Gillian motioned him to stay.

'Why'd you wait so long to call?' she said to Ethan. 'Know what? You're full of crap. I've got Verizon, too, and it's workin' loud and clear.'

To Sammy Tigertail, she said, 'He says he couldn't get a signal. How lame is that?'

The Indian sat down heavily and tuned out Gillian's telephone chatter. His head was beginning to ache. He rubbed his palms across the concrete floor and for a moment imagined it was Louisiana mud, like in the government prison cell where his great-great-great-grandfather might or might not have perished.

Although pained by his tribe's blood-soaked history,

149

Sammy Tigertail had never believed that all white people were evil; his own father had been an honest, good-hearted guy. During his childhood in the suburbs, Sammy Tigertail had made friends with lots of white kids, and observed several acts of decency and kindness by white grown-ups. It was also true that he'd encountered plenty of assholes, though to what degree their obnoxiousness could be blamed on race was debatable. Sammy suspected that some of them would have attained asshole status in any culture, on any continent.

His uncle Tommy had occasionally mentioned an unusual white man named Wiley, who'd written articles for a Miami newspaper. Sammy Tigertail's uncle said that Wiley had wanted to save Florida as desperately as any Seminole, and that he'd gone mad trying. Sammy Tigertail had gotten the impression that his uncle Tommy and the crazed white writer were friends of a sort. When he'd asked what had happened to Wiley, his uncle said that the great Maker of Breath had given his spirit to an old bald eagle.

Sammy Tigertail remembered that story whenever he saw a wild eagle, which wasn't often. He had yet to meet a white person like Wiley, and doubted he ever would. Gillian's flitty spirit was more akin to that of a sparrow.

'Oh, just some guy I met,' she was saying to her boyfriend, giving him the needle. 'You really want to know? Well, let's see. He's like six-one and real tan and he's got these drop-dead blue eyes.'

Tan? 'God Almighty,' the Indian said.

'And I don't even know his real name,' she went on, winking at Sammy Tigertail, 'which makes things kinda interesting.'

The Seminole whispered for her to hang up. When he made a slashing motion across his throat, she smiled and shook her head.

'Ethan wants to know if you're the same maniac who shot at them on the island. What should I tell him?'

'Tell him to lay off the weed. Nobody shot at anybody.'

Gillian said into the phone: 'My new friend's sorta shy.'

Sammy Tigertail thought he could actually feel his cranium cracking like an egg. He lay down, clutching the gun to his chest. He heard Gillian tell her boyfriend: 'I don't *know* when I'm comin' back. Tallahassee is such a drag, y'know?'

The Indian closed his eyes yet there was no hope of sleep. When Gillian turned off the phone, she said, 'You look awful.'

'Thanks for not giving me up.'

Gillian laughed. 'How can I tell him your name when I can't hardly pronounce it?'

'If they knew I was a Seminole, they'd come after me for sure.' Sammy Tigertail rose to his feet. He hoped the dizziness was from hunger and not white man's brain fever.

'Ethan promised to have them call off the search, but I can tell he's sulking. He refuses to believe I'd rather be with someone else,' Gillian said. 'You boys and your egos.'

'Speaking of names, yours is really St. Croix?'

'Ever been there? The beaches are awesome – you should take your girlfriend, or whoever.'

'No, I won't be leaving the Everglades,' the Indian said. 'Never again.'

They went outside, where Gillian counted four

kinds of butterflies. Sammy Tigertail could identify a zebra and a swallowtail, but not the others; Gillian was still impressed. She climbed halfway up the old poinciana and perched on the end of a trunk-like branch, high among the bright green leaves. 'Hey, Thlocko,' she called out. 'Why don't I want to go home?'

Sammy Tigertail was secretly pleased that Gillian remembered his Seminole name, even though she'd left out the second *l*. Others had trouble with Thlocklo, too. At the Miami public library he'd once found a copy of a muster roll of '99 Florida Indians and Negroes' delivered to the U.S. Army barracks in New Orleans on January 7, 1843. Among those on the list was 'the party of Indians with the chief Tiger Tail or Thlocko Tustenugee,' transported for involuntary relocation west of the Mississippi. The man was Sammy Tigertail's great-great-great-grandfather.

When Gillian climbed down from the tree, she said, 'I seriously need a bath.'

'Good luck with the plumbing.'

'You said you wanted me to go away. Did you mean it? Because I can tell you're not too thrilled.'

Against his better judgment, Sammy Tigertail found himself intrigued by the way she looked at that instant, how the breeze was nudging her hair and the sunlight was coloring her cheeks.

He said, 'Ethan's freaked out enough. You'd better go.'

'To hell with Ethan.'

'You don't get it. Anything could happen out here.'

'Exactly!' Gillian exclaimed. 'That's what I'm talkin' about.'

Sammy Tigertail couldn't stop himself from smiling.

She said, 'How about this – what if I told you I can play the guitar?'

'I wouldn't believe you.'

'Don't move, Cochise.' Gillian ran out, and came back carrying the Gibson. 'You got a pick?'

'I sure don't,' Sammy Tigertail said, curious.

'That's okay. Check out these fingernails.'

She played. He listened.

That evening, another telemarketer called and tried to sell Honey Santana a term-life policy for $17.50 a month. Instead of scolding the man, she was appallingly patient and polite. 'God bless you, brother,' she said before hanging up.

Aghast, Fry dropped his fork in the lasagna. 'I'm definitely tellin' Dad.'

'You'll do no such thing. I'm absolutely fine,' Honey said.

'You're not fine, Mom, you're going bipolar. Maybe even *tri*polar.'

'Just because I'm nice to a stranger on the phone? I thought that's what you guys wanted.'

'Yeah, but *that*,' Fry said, clearing his plate from the table, 'was creepy.'

Honey elected not to mention the aberrant pang of sympathy that had inspired her to visit Louis Piejack at his home that afternoon. Misled by a pleasant greeting and a seemingly benign offer of lemonade, Honey had taken a seat in her former employer's living room only to hear him announce that (a) his wife was away in Gainesville, receiving chemotherapy, and (b) his testicles had fully recovered from the pummeling Honey had delivered at the fish market. Piejack had gone on to say that the brutal stone-crab amputation and subsequent surgical reshuffling of his fingers, while problematic for his piano ambitions, promised an innovative new repertoire of foreplay. That was when Honey Santana had dashed for the door, Piejack bear-pawing at her with his bandaged left hand. Honey didn't want Fry to find out because he'd tell his father, who might do something so extreme to Louis Piejack that Skinner would end up in jail.

The boy went to pack while Honey stepped outside to test her latest mosquito remedy – citronella mixed with virgin olive oil, which she slathered on both legs. After several minutes she decided that the night was too breezy for a bug census, so instead she began rehearsing the lecture she intended to lay upon Boyd Shreave, the man who'd called her a dried-up old skank. She planned to wait until the second day of the eco-adventure, when they were so deep in the wilderness that Shreave wouldn't dare make a run for it. He'd have no choice but to sit and listen while Honey Santana straightened him out.

The theme of her rebuke would be the erosion of manners in modern society, the decay of civility. Honey was prepared to accept responsibility for her own sharp words during the sales call. Perhaps she'd begin by apologizing for mentioning Shreave's mother.

'That was wrong of me, Boyd, and I'm sorry. But I was upset, and now I want to tell you why—'

'Mom?' Fry's voice, from behind the screen door. 'Who're you talking to?'

'Nobody. Come out here and sit.'

She scooted over to make a place for him on the top step of the trailer. His backpack was slung over one shoulder and he was eating an apple.

'When's your old man showing up?' she asked.

'Ten minutes. Who were you talking to?'

'Myself. Lots of perfectly sane people do that, Fry.'

Honey leaned against him. His hair was damp, and it smelled like her shampoo. She felt like hugging his neck and crying.

'They had a plane up today,' he said, 'looking for some college girl who supposedly got snatched from one of the islands. Then her boyfriend calls up and says she's okay. She'd dumped him and took off with a poacher.'

Honey sniffled a laugh. 'Sounds like true love.'

Fry turned to gaze up at the nature mural his mother had painted on the trailer, which was partially illuminated by a street lamp. 'Your parrot turned out cool. The monkeys are killer, too,' he said.

'Thanks, but the neighbors aren't real impressed. Hey, whatever happened with that girl you used to like at school? Naomi.'

'Moved to Rhode Island. And her name was Cassie,' Fry said. 'So, what've you got planned for your friends?'

'I dunno, just hang out. I heard there's a crafts show in Naples.'

'High-octane excitement,' said Fry.

'Or maybe we'll break in those kayaks, if the weather's decent.'

'How come your eyes are all red?'

'Cat dander.' She pointed to Mrs. Saroyan's spavined gray tabby, which was squatting on the chain-link fence and spraying their mailbox.

Fry reached into his backpack and took out something that looked like a BlackBerry, only smaller. 'Here, take this. It's a GPS receiver, in case you get lost on the water.'

Honey grinned. 'Lemme guess where you got it – my guilt-ridden former spouse?'

'He had an extra one lying around. It was my idea.' He showed her how to use it, and she seemed to pay attention.

'Everybody's so damn worried about me. I suppose I should be touched,' she said.

A pair of headlights appeared at the end of the street.

'That would be him.' Fry stood up.

Honey told her son to have a good time. 'But don't forget to do your homework. I'll call tomorrow to set up a dinner, so you can meet my friends.'

Of course there would be no such gathering, but Honey had to keep up the act in case Fry was buying it.

'And, for God's sake,' she added, 'wash your jock after track practice.'

'You'd better not be crying. I mean it.'

'I told you, it's allergies.'

When Perry Skinner braked to a stop in front of the yard, Honey thought she saw him give a small wave. Fry pecked her on the cheek and said, 'Love you, Mom.'

'Love you, too. Now stop worryin' so much, would you?' She smiled and teasingly shoved him toward his father's truck.

'Don't run off with any poachers,' he said.

'Hey, I could do worse,' Honey called after him.

Eleven

The landing in Tampa was bumpy. At the airport, Eugenie Fonda charged into the first open bar on the concourse. 'Margaritaville' was playing over the sound system, so she ordered one.

Boyd Shreave had a beer. He raised the glass and said, 'To freedom.'

'I guess,' said Eugenie.

'Come on. This is the start of a brand-new lifetime.'

'What'd you rent us?'

'A mid-sized Saturn.'

Eugenie whistled. 'Whoa, baby.'

'What's wrong with a Saturn?'

She smiled. 'Very sensible, Boyd. You gonna put it on Lily's gold card?'

Shreave looked away, feigning fascination with a basketball game on the TV mounted above the Budweiser display.

'Then why not go nuts? Get an Escalade,' Eugenie was saying. 'You're not some schmuck on an expense account, Boyd. You're on safari.'

'Fine. I'll rent the biggest road hog they got.'

'Unless you're feeling guilty,' Eugenie said, 'about mooching off your wife.'

'Yeah, that's me. Crippled with guilt.' Shreave slapped three fives on the bar. 'You done?'

They stood in line at the Avis counter for forty-five minutes and departed with an ordinary Ford Explorer, the last Escalade having been rented to a middle-aged man toting two Halliburton travel cases.

Traffic out of the city was murder. Eugenie Fonda shut her eyes and leaned against the window. Boyd Shreave wondered how to draw her into the frisky spirit of a Florida adventure. Despite their rollicking sex life, Eugenie had always maintained emotional distance, and on the long drive Shreave found himself overtaken by an urge to possess her in every way. As she dozed – twitching whenever he swerved or tapped the brakes – Shreave was galvanized by a preposterous desire for her to be charmed and bedazzled and ravenously alert in his presence. Inwardly he began to speculate about what qualities might have attracted her to Van Bonneville, the killer-to-be, five years earlier. As self-deluded as he was about his own allure, Shreave understood that he had little in common with the homicidal tree whacker who'd been so chillingly profiled on Court TV. The man had shown himself as daring and decisive, traits that had never been ascribed to Shreave.

North of Fort Myers he exited the interstate, located a shopping mall and informed Eugenie that he was going to find a rest room. She acknowledged with a drowsy grunt, reclined her seat and drifted back into an ebbing haze of Valium and alcohol. Shreave beelined for a Barnes & Noble, where a bemused clerk led him to the last unshredded paperback copy of *Storm*

Ghoul, which he purchased along with a road map of southwest Florida.

The sun was setting when he and Eugenie finally rolled into Everglades City, which was not a city in the Texan sense of the word. It was, in fact, barely a town.

Eugenie lowered her window to let the cool air rouse her. 'Where's the beach?' she asked Shreave.

'I'm not sure.'

'Where's *anything*?'

'Just wait,' he said.

When he stopped at a Circle K and asked directions to the Dancing Flamingo Eco-Lodge, the clerk peered at him as if he was a registered sex offender. He had better luck at the Rod and Gun Club, where a bartender examined the street address provided by the telemarketer and said it was within walking distance. He drew a map on a cocktail napkin and handed it to Shreave.

'Let's eat first. I'm wasting away,' Eugenie said, and headed toward the restaurant.

Admiring the sway of her hips, the bartender told Shreave he was one lucky bastard. 'But I'd stick close if I were you,' he added. 'Guys around here, they don't see many women like that.'

'There aren't many of 'em to see, no matter where you live,' Shreave said authoritatively.

Dinner was excellent – hearts of palm, conch fritters, stone crabs and Key lime pie. Their table overlooked the Barron River, where jumping fish flashed like squirts of mercury under the dock lights. Eugenie ate heartily, and Shreave discerned an improvement in her mood. After dessert she even kicked off one shoe and tickled his crotch with her bare toes.

'We're gonna have some major fun tonight,' she said.

159

Nearly delirious with anticipation, Shreave decided to drive the few blocks to the eco-lodge so that he wouldn't have to schlep their bags. Following the bartender's map, he turned on to an unpaved street called Curlew Boulevard.

Eugenie stiffened in her seat. 'Boyd?'

'Yeah, I know.'

'This is a fucking trailer park.'

'I can see that,' he said grimly.

The address was 543 Curlew, and the residence was definitely a double-wide. Some wacko had painted psychedelic parrots and monkeys all over the front.

Eugenie Fonda said, 'Tell me it's a joke.'

Shreave felt prickly and light-headed.

'Boyd, are you processing all this?'

'I don't know what's going on. I swear to God,' he said.

Then the door of the trailer swung open.

Before his ill-fated employment at the airboat concession, Sammy Tigertail had briefly tried wrestling alligators. Nobody had understood why. It wasn't a popular job, most Seminole gator wrestlers having retired as soon as the gambling remissions started to flow.

Through newspaper advertisements the tribe had recruited a collection of rough young white guys to perform the alligator shows, a breach of cultural authenticity that didn't seem to bother the tourists. Sammy Tigertail took his training from a former Harley-Davidson mechanic who, by virtue of three missing toes, went by the nickname of 'Nubs.' He had lost the digits in a hatchet fight, but naturally he told audiences that a bull gator had gobbled them. For Sammy Tigertail's orientation, Nubs demonstrated a few rudimentary pinning maneuvers and counseled him not to eat cat-fish on performance days, because 'them goddamn devil lizards can smell it on your breath.'

Sammy Tigertail's first match went so well that he jokingly asked who'd dosed the alligator – an eight-footer displaying the ferocity of a beanbag chair. Sammy Tigertail was loose and cocky for the next performance, which featured an even more docile specimen, or so the young Seminole had been told.

Statistically, professional gator wrestling is only slightly more dangerous than hanging wallpaper. The low casualty rate is due less to the agility of the handlers than to the habituated tolerance of the reptiles. Having learned that the reward is a ripe dead chicken, the alligators patiently allow themselves to be dragged around a sand pit and subjected to a sequence of silly indignities. Obviously the success of these stunts relies on a certain critical level of lethargy in the animals. A freshly captured alligator is not the ideal wrestling opponent; unschooled and irritable, even a scrawny one is capable of inflicting grave and potentially crippling injuries.

For the second (and, ultimately, final) show of Sammy Tigertail's career, the redneck wrestlers thought it would be humorous to sneak a ringer into the gator pit. The chosen candidate was seven feet long and weighed roughly 110 pounds. More crucially, it had no show-business experience, having been snared from a golf-course lagoon the previous evening. Unaware, Sammy Tigertail let out an improvised war cry and leapt with gusto upon the beast, which erupted in writhing, hissing fury. The crowd thought it was fantastic.

Clawed, thrashed and tail-whipped, Sammy Tigertail somehow steered clear of the saurian's teeth. As they flopped around in the dirt, the Indian managed to lock both arms around the flailing head of his foe, at which point they rolled together into the concrete pond. The depth was barely four feet, but Sammy Tigertail knew that alligators had drowned persons in shallower water. He was also aware that the primitive creature in his grip was capable of holding its breath for hours. That fact, plus the realization that the pond itself was probably septic with gator shit, impelled Sammy Tigertail to break his clinch and kick frantically for the surface.

As he sloshed alone out of the bile-colored water, the audience rose and applauded. The Seminole took a shy bow while the announcer explained over the PA system that the defeated leviathan would remain submerged until it stopped sulking. Forty-five minutes later the alligator indeed rose to the surface and floated belly-up, a pose that suggested a far more serious condition than wounded pride. The rattlesnake-milking demonstration was immediately halted and Sammy Tigertail was summoned back to the wrestling pit. There, to a withering chorus of boos and the tickety-tick of digital cameras, he glumly hauled the scaly corpse from the pond.

A necropsy revealed that Sammy Tigertail had accidentally snapped the alligator's neck during their underwater tussle, a mishap that would cost the tribe hefty fines from state and federal authorities. Among the voluminous regulations governing the captivity and display of *Alligator mississippiensis*, none is viewed more seriously than the prohibition against harming the species. No wrestler in the history of the Seminole reservation had ever snuffed an alligator during a paid performance, and Sammy Tigertail's plea for leniency fell on deaf ears. He was banished for life from the gator pit, the incident serving to reinforce the tribal view that he was cursed by his mixed blood.

Sammy Tigertail chose not to share the dead alligator story with Gillian when he declined her request for a wrestling lesson.

She said, 'Aw, come on. I taught you how to play the guitar.'

In fact, she'd shown him the chords to one song, 'Tequila Sunrise.' It had been a favorite of his late father.

Sammy Tigertail was grateful, up to a point. 'You think all Seminoles wrestle gators? That's insulting,' he said. 'It's like saying all black men can dunk a basketball.'

The topic had arisen because they'd spotted either an alligator or a crocodile swimming across the pass near the island.

'Don't tell me you never tried,' Gillian said.

'There's a trick to it,' Sammy Tigertail replied quietly.

'Show me.'

'I said no.'

'Pretend I'm the gator.' Gillian stretched flat on her belly, arms pressed against her sides, on the floor of the cistern. 'Now, you sneak up and jump on me.'

'Some other time.'

'Don't be such a pussy. Come on.'

She was wearing pastel flip-flops, mesh panties and a white bikini top, which had become her official island ensemble. Sammy Tigertail found it extremely distracting. He wasn't sure whether Gillian was trying to torment him, or whether she was merely oblivious to his feelings.

'I'm really beat,' the Indian said. All morning he'd been chopping paths through the gnarled cactus plants, which at least had proven to be juicy and pleasantly edible.

'Please?' Gillian said. 'Just pretend.'

The Seminole aligned himself on top of her, bracing his elbows to lever some of his weight off her backside. She was warmer than an alligator and, in the absence of a corrugated hide, much softer.

Gillian laughed under the strain and said, 'Now what?'

He slipped one hand under her chin and firmly placed his other hand on the crown of her head, effectively clamping her mouth closed.

'The trick,' he explained, 'is to pin 'em without pissing 'em off.'

Gillian grunted and began to wriggle. Sammy Tigertail abruptly rolled off. He hoped she wouldn't comment about him getting hard, but of course she did.

'It's about time. I was beginning to worry about you,' she remarked as she sat up.

'This isn't a game. It's a serious deal.' Sammy Tigertail thought: Uncle Tommy's right. These girls are bad medicine.

'I totally can't believe you haven't tried to bone me yet,' Gillian said. 'It took Ethan, like, three and a half minutes the first time we went out. Not to do it, but to try – that's how long from when we got in the car 'til he jammed my hand down his jeans.'

Sammy Tigertail said, 'I'm not as smooth as Ethan.'

'I wouldn't even jerk him off, okay?'

'Listen.' He stood up and tugged Gillian off the floor. 'Hear that?'

It was another low-flying plane.

'Go outside and start waving,' he told her.

'Kiss my butt,' she said.

'What're you trying to prove?' The Indian seized her by the shoulders. 'There's not a drop of freshwater on this island – no soap, no ice, no electricity. You're gonna be livin' on bird eggs and fish, which you said makes you barf. So go on home, okay? Go back to Tallahassee and lose Ethan and start over.'

She pulled away and angrily blurted something that the Indian couldn't hear because of the plane buzzing low. When it was gone, she said, 'I thought this was a free country.'

'Why the hell are you here?' the Seminole asked.

'You go first.'

'A guy died on my airboat and I needed somewhere to go. Somewhere with no white people.'

'Is that how come you won't screw me?' Gillian said. 'That's just as prejudiced as me asking you about alligator wrestlin'. Know what? It's even worse.'

Sammy Tigertail heard himself say, 'My girlfriend's white.'

Gillian crossed her arms in mock surprise. 'No way!'

'I mean my ex-girlfriend.'

'Name, please.'

'Cindy. She's a crank freak.'

'Ha, you and I *do* have something in common. We both pick losers,' Gillian said. 'Look here, chief. Someday when I'm a gray-haired old lady I can tell my grandkids that I was kidnapped by a real live Indian and held hostage on a mangrove island in the Everglades. And that I taught him how to play the guitar, and he taught me all about gators, and we ate funky cactus berries and counted butterflies and slept in a broken cistern. That's a pretty great story.'

Sammy Tigertail could not disagree.

'And it'd be even better,' Gillian said, 'if there was a steamy romance to tell 'em about. But I guess I could use my imagination – you wouldn't mind, right? What they call "creative license"?'

'Go wild,' said Sammy Tigertail.

Lily Shreave was having a massage when the phone rang. The masseur's name was Mikko and he claimed to have trained for eleven years in Bali. Lily had found the fanciful lie endearing, given his Sooners tattoos and Oklahoma accent. She pressed a fifty-dollar bill into one of his large oily palms, motioned him out of the room and reached for her cell.

'It's not happening,' Dealey said on the other end.

'You're giving up already? But you just got there.'

'They're inside a damn trailer, Mrs. Shreave. I have no shot.'

Lily got down from the massage table. 'You mean like a Winnebago?'

'Not a motor home,' said Dealey, 'a *mobile* home. I'll never be able to get the angle I need.'

Lily wrapped herself in a towel. 'Is she with him? I don't understand.'

'Let me paint you the picture. I'm sitting in an SUV at a trailer court in some glorified fish camp in the armpit of the Everglades. I can't even get out of my vehicle because there's not one but *two* pit-fucking-bull dogs waiting to gnaw my nuts off. Meanwhile your bonehead husband and his fake-Fonda lady friend just carried their bags into a mobile home that looks like it was built when Roosevelt was president and decorated by one of Tarzan's apes.'

Dealey sounded very discouraged. Lily said, 'This doesn't make sense. Boyd always stays at Marriotts.'

'Mrs. Shreave, there are no Marriotts here. They're lucky to have running water.'

Lily asked the private investigator if it was possible to peek inside the trailer.

'Negative. Curtains on all the windows,' he reported, 'and, like I said, the dogs won't let me out of the truck anyway. I'm parked a hundred yards down the road.'

'So what's the plan?' Lily said.

'The plan is for me to drive back to civilization and get an air-conditioned hotel room with a king-sized bed, order up a sirloin steak and watch the fights on HBO. Then, tomorrow, I wake up and catch the first flight back to Dallas. That's the plan, Mrs. Shreave.'

She sensed that Dealey wasn't keen on the great outdoors. 'You can't bail on me now. Give it one more day.'

'Sorry. This is above and beyond.'

'How bad can it be? It's Florida, for God's sake.'

Dealey snorted. 'Right, maybe I'm at Disney World and I just don't know it. Maybe it's a fun ride – Trailer Trash of the Caribbean.'

Lily couldn't imagine why her husband had dragged his mistress to such a place, but she was intrigued. Perhaps it was some grungy swingers' club he'd dredged up on the Internet.

'You *cannot* leave yet,' she told Dealey.

'Yeah? Watch me.'

'Suppose I bump the fee to twenty-five.' The moment Lily said it, she knew she'd gone over the edge. This wasn't about humiliating a wayward husband; this was about getting off.

'What?' Dealey said.

'Twenty-five grand.'

'You're a sick woman – no offense.'

'I'll take that as a yes.' Lily could hear the pit bulls barking in the background. 'Boyd and his bimbo have gotta come out of that trailer eventually,' she said to Dealey. 'I bet they'll do it on the beach at sunrise. Throw down a blanket and go at it like animals – that sounds like her, doesn't it?'

'I'm not sure there *is* a beach, Mrs. Shreave.'

'Don't be ridiculous. Florida is one big beach.'

Dealey said, 'Twenty-four hours. Then I'm outta here.'

'Fair enough. But trust me on the sunrise thing.'

'I'll be sure to set my alarm,' the investigator said. 'You're not bullshitting about the twenty-five large?'

Lily Shreave smiled on the other end. 'The pizza business is good, Mr. Dealey.'

Boyd Shreave wasn't nearly as slick as Honey Santana had anticipated.

'Would you and Mrs. Shreave care for some fresh-squeezed orange juice?' she asked.

The woman accompanying Boyd Shreave started to say something but he cut her off. 'Orange juice would be fine,' he said, 'wouldn't it, Genie?'

Honey knew from her Googling expedition that Shreave's wife was named Lily. Days earlier, when he'd faxed her the information for the airline reservations, Shreave had listed his wife as Eugenie Fonda, parenthetically explaining that she preferred to use her maiden name. The slithering lie did not surprise Honey. That Shreave would bring a girlfriend only ratified her initial harsh appraisal of his character.

'So, this is the "lodge"?' He scanned the interior of the double-wide. 'We were expecting something different,' he said.

'Temporary quarters until the new facility is finished,' Honey fibbed sunnily. 'We're building it way up in the treetops, just like they do in Costa Rica.'

Shreave was skeptical. 'People give away a free trip to paradise, they don't usually put you up at a trailer court. Am I right, or what?'

'Well, I think you'll be pleased.' Honey was stung that neither Shreave nor his companion had commented upon her tropical mural on the outer wall.

'So, when do we hear the big pitch?' he asked.

'Excuse me?'

'For the swamp land you're supposed to sell us. Royal Gulf Hammocks, remember?' Shreave chuckled sardonically. 'This is some four-star operation you're running.'

'Yes – the Hammocks. Of course,' Honey Santana said. 'We'll talk about all that later.' She'd almost forgotten that she was supposed to be working a land-sales scam.

The woman named Genie spoke up. 'Isn't there a beach around here someplace? Or at least a damn tiki bar?'

'Where we're going is better than the beach – tomorrow morning we leave for the islands.' Honey smiled. 'Excuse me, would you?'

The trailer being trailer-sized, Honey could hear the couple arguing in low tones while she was in the kitchen. She was relieved that Shreave hadn't pegged her as the voice of Pia Frampton, the fictitious telemarketer who'd offered him the trip. Her Laura Bush drawl seemed to have done the trick.

Although Honey owned an electric juicer, she chose to squeeze the fruit by hand. The exercise was therapeutic, keeping at bay temporarily the two tunes – 'Smoke on the Water' and 'Rainy Days and Mondays' – that had been colliding unbearably inside her head following the unwise visit to Louis Piejack. Earlier in the evening, before the Texans had arrived, Honey had thought she'd spotted Louis in a dark-colored pickup cruising her street. She wasn't a hundred percent sure; half the guys in town owned trucks like that.

The woman named Genie materialized in the kitchen, offering to help with the tray. Honey said it wasn't necessary.

'But thank you just the same, Mrs. Shreave.'

'I'm *not* Mrs. Shreave,' Genie whispered somewhat urgently.

Honey whispered back: 'I know.'

'Really? What gave me away?'

'That pearl in your tongue, for starters.'

The woman nodded ruefully. 'My name's Eugenie Fonda. I think I've made a terrible mistake.'

'Oh, don't worry,' Honey said. 'I won't try to sell you any real estate.'

'No, you don't understand—'

Shreave called out Genie's name, and Honey touched a finger to her lips. The two women returned to the living room, where Shreave had been nosily examining the contents of Honey's bookcase, which she'd neglected to purge of personal memorabilia.

'Who's the track star?' He pointed to a shelf of trophies.

'My son.'

'Yeah? He must be pretty fast.'

Honey wanted to change the subject. 'Have some OJ, Mr. Shreave.'

'Yeah, it's really good,' Eugenie Fonda said. She was clutching the glass as if it were the rip cord on a parachute. 'Got any vodka to go with it?'

Shreave said, 'I ran some seriously swift relays myself, back in the day.'

At first Honey thought he must be joking, but she was set straight by Eugenie's scornful expression.

'Until I blew out my knees,' Shreave continued.

Soon the rising babel in Honey's skull made it impossible to follow what he was saying. She considered the possibility that she, too, had made a large mistake. Boyd Shreave didn't seem like a person who could be easily chastened, moved or transformed. He presented no convictions, or true sense of himself. He'd made the Everglades trip only to prove to his girlfriend that he wasn't a wimp.

Honey prepared herself for three challenging days. She said, 'You folks *do* know how to kayak, right?'

Twelve

Gillian's real last name was Tremaine but in college she'd changed it to St. Croix to piss off her parents. It was the same reason she was majoring in elementary education; her parents had wanted her to take a degree in finance and join them at the discount brokerage house in Clearwater. That's what Gillian's older sister had done, and her unhappiness was currently manifesting itself as sloppy promiscuity.

Although Gillian was theoretically committed to the idea of teaching school, it wasn't a true calling; it was a job she thought she could stand until she experienced a cosmic awakening, or met the right poet-musician. She'd settled on the name of St. Croix after visiting the island with her then boyfriend, the self-perforated rock guitarist. The vacation itself was not especially magical but Gillian understood that she wasn't easy to amuse. Boredom had always afflicted her like a wasting disease. Every skirt she picked out seemed drab the moment she got it home. Every CD she bought sounded old and trite the second time she listened to it. Every book she opened with high hopes turned into a slog through the mud by page one hundred. It was the same with relationships.

'I'm twenty years old and I've got nothing interesting in my life except you,' she informed Sammy Tigertail.

'That's scary,' he said.

'Don't worry. It won't last.'

Wolves that they were, Len and Ginger Tremaine had followed southward the herd of retiring, fully pensioned midwesterners. Gillian was a teenager when the family moved from Ohio to Florida. On the first day of school her tenth-grade French teacher, Mr. Hodgman, told Gillian that she was too pretty for her own good, which inspired her to reach beneath her blouse and remove her bra in front of the class. She would become so well known for such high-spirited antics that her fellow students christened her 'Psycho Babe,' not without affection. She graduated with good grades but also with enough disciplinary footnotes to kill her chances with Wharton and three other private colleges short-listed by her parents. They were aghast when she surprised them with an acceptance letter from Florida State, a notorious party school located in a notorious party town, Tallahassee, which also happened to be the state capital.

Soon after arriving in Florida, the Tremaines had read a scandalous story in the *St. Petersburg Times* about a powerful state legislator who'd put his favorite Hooters waitress on the state payroll. They feared that a similar tawdry fate awaited their youngest daughter, but they didn't know Gillian very well. She wasn't impressed by power, position or money; she was impressed by rebels.

'My cell phone finally died,' she told the Indian. 'Ethan never called back.'

'Big surprise.'

'Which is fine with me.'

'How long you gonna stay up in the tree?' Sammy Tigertail asked.

'You know why I started dating him? One night he and some other guys drove down to the Keys and freed some dolphins from a marine park. Ethan said they put on scuba tanks and used wire cutters to make a hole in the fence around the lagoon,' Gillian said. 'It made the front page of the Miami paper. He showed me the clippings. He was like a total outlaw.'

The Seminole was frying some fish that he'd caught. He told Gillian he was going to eat it all himself if she didn't climb down soon from the poinciana tree.

She said, 'Later he told me what happened. The dolphins swam out through the hole in the fence and then the very next morning they all came back, just in time for breakfast. And they never left again! They just hung around the lagoon, doin' all those corny Flipper tricks and beggin' for fish. Meantime the owners patched the fence and, like, that was the end of the big jailbreak. Of course Ethan didn't clue me in until after I'd slept with him.'

Sammy Tigertail peered up at her. 'You on dope?'

Gillian closed her eyes. 'I wish I could spend the night up here. It's so damn perfect.'

Sammy Tigertail said, 'Come on down. You gotta eat.'

Gillian rose, balancing in bare feet on the long branch. 'I'm really not so messed up. I'm just waiting for something phenomenally stupendous to happen to me.'

'On this island?'

'I don't see why not.' She hopped down and joined him by the campfire and even ate some snook, which was sweeter than any fish she'd ever tasted.

The Indian told her she was being too hard on Ethan. 'At least the guy tried. It's not his fault the dolphins didn't want to be free.'

'But he should've told me that part in the beginning,' Gillian said, 'so I wouldn't go around for weeks feeling great about somethin' that didn't really turn out that way.'

'Maybe he wanted you to be happy.'

'Sure, so I'd ball him.' She paused to pick a fish bone out of her front teeth. 'Tell me about Cindy.'

'Nothing to tell. She's a disaster.'

'All because she's white?'

Sammy Tigertail said, 'It was my mistake. I wasn't strong.'

'So, what exactly are you lookin' for out here?'

'I already told you. Peace.' He carefully poured the warm grease from the fry pan into a rusty beer can. 'Not world peace. Just peace for me – I need to shut out all the craziness.'

'Bullshit. You're hiding.'

'That's right,' said the Seminole.

'The man who died on your boat – was it your fault?' Gillian asked.

'I didn't kill him. He knows it, too. Told me in a dream.'

Gillian said, 'It's weird, but I don't hardly dream at all.'

'You will if you stay here too long.'

'Is that, like, an Indian thing?'

She dropped the sensitive subject of the dead guy. Sammy Tigertail went to pick some cactus berries, which they ate for dessert. He said, 'For fifteen hundred years this place was home of the Calusas. Spirits never go away.'

The oyster people, Gillian thought. She had never believed in afterlives but she was open to persuasion.

She said, 'Doesn't it ever rain here in the winter? Because I'm dyin' for a drink of water.'

'We'll go get some tonight, if the clouds give us a moon.'

'But where?' Gillian asked.

Sammy Tigertail said he didn't know. 'But if we can't find our own, then we'll steal it.'

Gillian thought of the loaded rifle and got worried. He didn't seem like the type who'd shoot somebody for water, but what did she know about such men? Sometimes the Indian acted hard-core, sometimes just the opposite.

'No big deal. I'm really not that thirsty,' she told him.

'Well, I am,' he said.

The first time I laid eyes on Van Bonneville, he was cutting down a grapefruit tree in front of the Elks Lodge on Freeman Street. He wore a faded indigo bandanna and a silver Saint Christopher medal that the police would find after the big hurricane, in his dead wife's sunken car.

As Van worked, sweat trickled down the cords of his neck and glistened on his bare chest. His arms were like ship cables and his shoulders looked as broad as a meat freezer. But it was his dark, weathered hands that intrigued me – they were covered with long, pale, delicate-looking scars. Van must have noticed me staring, because he smiled.

I'd been out walking my neighbor's toy poodle, Tito, who was fourteen years old and suffered from bladder problems. He was valiantly trying to relieve himself on the Elks' shrubbery (Van later told me it was a ficus hedge), and there I was, dragging him like a wagon along the sidewalk. The poor dog was yapping and hopping and struggling to keep one leg in the air, but I didn't even notice. I couldn't take my eyes off that gorgeous stranger with the chain saw.

Suddenly the tree toppled, and Van backed away in the nick of time. A flying grapefruit struck him on the temple, yet he just shrugged and put down the saw.

The first thing he said to me was: 'Canker.'

'What?'

'Citrus canker,' he explained. 'That's why this old tree had to die.'

That night I touched those magnificent hands for the first time, and they touched me.

Boyd Shreave closed the book and turned to gaze with a rush of desire at the author, who'd fallen into a deep snooze beside him. He wanted to awaken Eugenie Fonda and make crazed, howling, back-bending love to her. He wanted to shake the double-wide off its blocks. That's what Van Bonneville would have done, or so Shreave believed after reading (and re-reading) Eugenie's breathless opening passage. He couldn't remember the last time he'd picked up a book without pictures, but none of the handful he'd actually read had affected him as powerfully as this one. He was half-hoping that Genie would open her eyes and see the copy of *Storm Ghoul* on the bed. He didn't care how she reacted, as long as she did. Ever since they'd arrived at the cheesy eco-lodge, she'd been an icicle.

And now she began to snore, a moist warbling enhanced by the stud in her tongue. As Boyd Shreave reached for her, he despondently took notice of his own unmagnificent hands, which featured no masculine wounds or even a dime-sized callus. They were hands that had spent a lifetime in the safe fuzzy harbor of pockets. Shreave had only one genuine scar – the faint purple dotting of his pubic area, caused by that long-ago crash against the potted cactus – but so far Eugenie's interest had seemed more clinical than erotic.

As he endeavored to tug her into his arms, she scowled through her sleep and pushed him away. A muscular woman, Shreave thought longingly. Having invested so much hope in their illicit Everglades jaunt, he could hardly bear the idea that Eugenie might be tiring of him already. She was his future; his freedom. For Shreave, returning to Fort Worth – specifically, to his wife – seemed out of the question. Lily wasn't an idiot. She'd soon figure out that he'd lost his job at Relentless and that there was no prestigious clinic for aphenphosmphobics in South Florida, leaving Boyd's trip exposed as the sneaky tryst it was. Lily would pauperize him in the ensuing divorce, while his mother would stomp on the remaining crumbs of his self-esteem. More tragically, being both broke and unemployed would reduce to nil his chances of finding another lover as tall, beautiful and exciting as Eugenie Fonda.

After dropping *Storm Ghoul* into his Orvis bag, Shreave got up to marvel at the hokey decor of the bedroom. Honey, their goofball tour guide, had redone it like the interior of a safari tent – billows of muslin bedsheets tacked to the ceiling, and a Coleman lantern glowing on a faux-cane nightstand. Incredibly, there was no television or even a CD player.

The Dancing Flamingo Lodge, Shreave mused acidly. Try the Fleabag Flamingo. It was plain to him that the Royal Gulf Hammocks promotion was doomed; only a certified retard would buy real estate from such a lame and bumbling outfit.

He took his NASCAR toothbrush and travel tube of Colgate into the bathroom and went to work on his smile. When he came out, Eugenie was upright in bed, shedding her clothes.

'I had a god-awful nightmare,' she said. 'I'm at the call center and I've got Bill frigging Gates on the line, all hot to buy a time-share at Port Aransas. But then that damn Sacco crawls under my desk and starts licking my knees – Boyd, what does that big number three on your toothbrush mean?'

Shreave said, 'You're kidding me, right?'

Eugenie kicked off her panties. 'Okay. Never mind.'

'Come on. Number three was Dale Earnhardt's number!'

'And he is . . . ?'

'Genie, that's not even funny,' Shreave said.

'Whatever. I gotta take off my makeup.'

Hope renewed, Shreave slapped some cologne on his neck and dimmed the lantern. Kneeling on the floor, he hastily fished through the Orvis bag for his box of condoms. A black object under the bed caught his eye – it looked like a gun.

Shreave was waving it around when Eugenie Fonda walked out of the bathroom. She stopped in her tracks. He was ready.

'What's *that* for?' she asked.

'Just in case. They've got panthers down here, you know.'

'How'd you get it on the plane?'

Shreave said, 'I didn't. I bought it when we stopped at that mall.'

When Eugenie asked to hold it, he said, 'No. It's loaded.'

Sounding, he was sure, as calm and knowledgeable about firearms as Van Bonneville would have been.

She smiled. 'I didn't know you were a gun guy, Boyd.'

'It pays to be prepared.'

'What is it – a .38?'

'Good guess,' he said, having not a clue.

Had Boyd Shreave been a gun guy, he would have known that what he'd found beneath Honey Santana's bed was actually a Taser, a handheld shocking device used by police to subdue drunks and meth freaks. Instead of bullets it fired fifty thousand volts.

Shreave coolly stashed it in his bag, under a stack of Tommy Bahama shorts.

'And that little thing'll work on a big hungry panther?' Eugenie asked.

'Oh yeah.'

She climbed into bed and tugged the covers up to her breasts. 'You tired, Boyd?'

'Not really.'

'Excellent. Get your ass over here.'

Dealey drove to a Winn-Dixie in Naples and bought two pounds of ground chuck, into which he inserted his last four Ambiens. The pit bulls were still loose when he returned to the trailer park, but they keeled soon after wolfing the bloody meat.

The investigator parked one street over from the mobile home in which Boyd Shreave and his girl-friend were staying. At half past midnight, he emerged from the Escalade and began walking. He carried a small video camera equipped with an infrared attachment. He had rented it from a competitor back in Fort Worth.

Approaching the trailer, Dealey saw a faint glow through the droopy curtains on one of the windows. Quickly he stepped off the road and into the shadows. Using a penlight, he found some loose cinder blocks near the wall. He stacked them beneath the window and climbed up to have a look.

Only vague shapes and forms were discernible; the curtains turned out to be an elaborate spread of bed linens that offered no opening through which Dealey could peer. He couldn't hear a damn thing on the inside, either, thanks to the rumble of a corroded air conditioner that protruded crookedly from the wall.

'She's mine,' whispered a raw voice, causing Dealey to lose his balance and pitch sideways into a mound of potting soil. Somehow he managed to keep the video camera aloft, sparing it from damage. At first he was too startled to speak.

'Don't you move,' the man whispered. He appeared to be wearing a white glove, and he was most definitely pointing a sawed-off shotgun at Dealey's heaving gut. Unshaven and wispy-haired, the man reeked of booze, sweat and fish.

After Dealey caught his breath, he said, 'It's not what you think, mister.'

'Well, she's mine. Like I tole you.'

'Who's yours?'

'Honey. So you just put your johnson back in your pants and forget about her. Honey Santana is all mine.'

Dealey sat up slowly. 'I don't know who you're talkin' about, friend, and that's the truth.' He introduced himself, and began to explain what he was doing. 'I was hired by a rich lady in Texas to follow her husband.'

The man sniffed. 'Is he here to do Honey, too?'

'No, sir, he brought his own girlfriend.'

'Well, I don't care to believe a goddamn word outta your mouth. I think you're a sexually degenerated individual. What they call a stalker,' the man said, 'but tough shit. I was here first.'

Dealey kept an eye on the barrel of the shotgun, which was bobbing in conjunction with the stranger's agitations. It was now apparent that it wasn't a glove he was wearing; his left hand was completely bandaged except for the fingertips, one of which was poised on the trigger of the sawed-off.

'Can I ask your name?' Dealey said.

'Louis Peter Piejack.'

'What happened to your hand?'

The man was having difficulty hearing him over the air conditioner, so Dealey repeated the question.

'Crabs,' the man named Louis replied.

Dealey realized that he must have looked disgusted because the man angrily blurted: 'Not *those* kinda crabs, you asswipe. Real crabs, okay? Jumbo stoneys.'

'Oh.' Dealey thought: I should've gotten out of this damn town while I had the chance.

'It was all 'cause of my feelin's for Honey,' the man went on. 'Her ex hired some vicious Cuban bastards to scare me off, but I don't give up easy. He's gonna be sorry he fucked with me. Let's see that lil' camera.'

Dealey noticed that the bedroom window had gone dark. He lowered his voice. 'The camera's not mine, Louis.'

'You steal it or somethin'?'

'No, I borrowed it for this job.'

Piejack instructed the private investigator to stand up and start moving. Dealey didn't argue. He was waiting for an opportunity to jump the drunken twit and grab the shotgun. When they got to Piejack's pickup truck, Piejack took the video camera and ordered Dealey to get behind the wheel.

Half an hour later they were parked on a long dirt road in pitch-blackness. Dealey was demonstrating the night-vision lens, with the expectation of distracting Piejack from the shotgun that he now cradled loosely in his right arm.

Piejack blinked at the viewfinder and expressed awe. 'It's like what our boys got in Iraq' – he pronounced it *eye-rack* – 'for shootin' ragheads in the dark!'

Dealey said, 'Cool, huh?'

Piejack chortled. 'Lookie there at Momma Possum!'

Fifty yards ahead, an opossum shuffled across the road, followed by a dozen little ones, their eyes glowing like rubies in the infrared lighting.

Piejack rocked in the truck, giddy at the sight. Dealey made what he thought was a slick move for the shotgun, but Piejack swung it sideways and cracked him solidly above the right eye. With a moan, Dealey blacked out against the steering wheel.

What awoke him was warmness running down his cheeks, and the sharp gun barrel jammed against his ribs. With a shirtsleeve he dabbed the blood from his face.

'What zackly did that Texas lady hire you to take movies of?' Piejack asked.

'What do you think.'

'You serious? That's some high-class job you got, mister.'

Dealey shrugged. He had a wretched headache and was in no mood for a morality lecture.

'And I thought sellin' shrimp was a smelly business,' Piejack said.

'Can I go now?' Dealey asked. 'Take the damn camera, if you want it.'

The man grinned. 'Tell you what – I wouldn't mind havin' some private home movies of Miss Honey Santana.'

'It's all yours, Louis.'

'But see, here's the problem.' He raised his bandaged mitt. 'I can't work all them teensy video buttons with my hand wrapped up such as it is – the focus and zoom and whatnot. Shit, I can barely find the trigger on *this* damn thing.'

He turned the shotgun away from Dealey and casually blew out the window on the driver's side. Dealey screamed and clamped his hands over his ears.

Piejack himself seemed stunned by the force of the blast. He cracked the passenger door to switch on the dome light, then sourly contemplated the broken glass.

Dealey, who like many private investigators had developed a skill for lipreading, saw Piejack say, 'Shit, I thought the fuckin' window was down.'

'Let me go!' Dealey pleaded. 'Take the video camera, my credit cards, whatever the hell you want. Just let me walk.'

'Not till you get me some sexy movies of Honey. Then you're free to go,' Dealey observed the man saying. 'But till then, Mr. Dealey, you work for *me*.'

'Please don't do this.'

'Welcome aboard,' said Louis Piejack.

Thirteen

At dawn Fry got up to run. The weather was ideal, clear and cool. He went all the way to the caution light at the Tamiami Trail, where a family of tourists had piled out of an RV to snap pictures of a dead python on the road. Heading back toward town, Fry turned in to the trailer court where his mom lived. He passed two unchained pit bulls asleep near an empty black Escalade, and he thought it might be a good omen; usually the dogs were awake, waiting to chase him.

When Fry reached his mother's street, he sat down under a neighbor's mango tree. From there he could see the painted trailer, and in the front yard three figures that had to be his mom and the couple who'd come to visit her. They were strapping the kayaks – or trying to – on top of her car.

Fry considered going to help, but he decided to stay where he was. Once his mother saw him, she'd rush over and hug him and then start bragging to the visitors about his track trophies or whatever. Fry wasn't up for that scene so early in the morning.

It worried him to think of his mom leading an expedition into the Ten Thousand Islands. Any fool could mark a marine chart at the kitchen table, but once you were out there it was a jungled maze; even experienced boaters could get lost. Fry knew his mother hadn't been kayaking for years, since before the divorce, although she claimed to have been practicing while he was at school. He hoped she wasn't feeling too ambitious. A leisurely day trip around Chokoloskee Bay would be perfect – from there a blind goose could find its way back to the mainland.

As he watched the visitors get in the car, Fry was nagged by the suspicion that they weren't really old friends of his mother. She'd been too sketchy about the connection. He didn't know why she would lie about who they were, but he felt almost certain that she was up to more mischief.

After she drove away, Fry stepped from the shade of the mango tree and resumed his run, heading in the opposite direction. He made it as far as the corner when he was almost clipped by a pine-green pickup with two men in the cab. Fry darted off the road, but not before he caught a good look at the passenger.

It was Mr. Piejack.

Fry couldn't imagine a single good reason for that perverted turd to be cruising his mother's street. He watched the brake lights flicker as the truck slowed briefly in front of the painted trailer, then sped off.

On an impulse Fry ran after the pickup. He kept running long after it was out of sight.

Honey Santana had awakened to faraway harmonies. She'd filled the coffeemaker and gone to rouse the obnoxious telemarketer and his girlfriend.

Twenty minutes later they'd all sat down for breakfast. Boyd Shreave said, with his cocky half-sneer, 'Hope we didn't keep you up last night. The walls in this tin can are pretty thin.'

How very classy, Honey thought. With an innocent expression, she replied, 'I did hear some banging, but it only lasted about two minutes.'

Shreave reddened, while Eugenie Fonda stifled a chuckle.

'Would either of you like an English muffin?' Honey asked.

Shreave didn't say much after that. He inhaled a plate of scrambled eggs and went to the living room to reconnect with the television world. While Genie washed the dishes, Honey snuck outside and double-checked the gear: two pup tents, three sleeping bags, one waterproof box of matches, a first-aid kit, a fry pan, plastic forks and spoons, a short-handled ax, a dozen granola bars, six dehydrated Thai-style meals, two gallons of distilled water, a half-dozen packs of dried apples and figs, powdered Gatorade, insect repellent (a bottle of Cutter, spiced with garlic and cloves) and a jumbo Ziploc bag of Cheerios. All of it had to be fitted into two duffel bags, one for each kayak. The process of loading so much gear was further complicated by the fact that Boyd Shreave and his girlfriend didn't know they'd be camping overnight, and Honey wanted to keep it a secret.

As soon as she re-entered the trailer, she was drawn aside by Eugenie, who whispered, 'There's no beach around here, is there? Be honest.'

Honey said, 'It's still beautiful. Trust me, you've never seen anything like it.'

Shreave's girlfriend looked downcast. She turned

and said, 'Boyd, can I talk to you for a second? Hey, Boyd!'

He was gleefully enthralled by an infomercial that he'd come upon while surfing the channels. A fossilized TV actor named Erik Estrada was hawking lakefront real estate in a newly discovered 'paradise' known as Arkansas.

'Know what this proves? That absolutely *anything* is possible!' Shreave crowed. 'This is the greatest damn country in the history of the world. I mean, Erik Estrada? Good God, Genie, come look at this!'

She walked over and switched off the television and led Shreave down the hall. Even after the bedroom door closed, Honey could hear her saying: 'I don't want to stay here. I want to go to Sarasota and check into the Ritz-Carlton. I want a massage, Boyd. I want a sandy beach where I can wear my new thong. I want to go back to the room and order French wine and watch dirty movies on Pay-per-View.'

Honey Santana hurried outside and started stuffing the gear into the duffel bags. Her whole plan would be doomed if Shreave caved in, which seemed highly probable. Were he able to resist the vision of Eugenie Fonda power-tanning in a bikini, he'd surely be won over by the promise of a candlelit pornfest.

Honey feared she might crumble to pieces if Shreave bailed out now. Working late into the night, she'd fine-tuned her campfire lecture. A man such as he – a man who phoned people at the dinner hour and then insulted them coarsely when they objected – needed a lesson in manners and propriety. A few days in the wild would strip away all that smugness. A tour through the islands would expand his mind, open his eyes and deflate that superior attitude. Boyd Shreave would come back humbled and enriched. Of this Honey had convinced herself, and it was crushing to think that her mission would fizzle on the launchpad if his girlfriend bugged out.

Then Boyd and Eugenie emerged from the trailer – he sporting a new Indiana Jones–style hat; she sullenly smearing sunblock in her cleavage. Honey was practically giddy with relief. Wordlessly the couple helped her hoist the kayaks onto the car and, after a struggle, cinch them down. Shreave displayed a striking ineptitude for tying knots, but Honey didn't mind redoing the straps. She was astonished that Shreave had rejected the decadent Ritz-Carlton scenario in favor of blisters and bug bites, and she wondered if she had misjudged him. Time would tell.

'That's an awful lot of stuff for a day trip,' he remarked as they crammed the duffels into the back-seat.

'Always be prepared,' Honey said lightly.

To her boyfriend, Eugenie muttered: 'Now she sounds like you.'

They launched the kayaks next to the Rod and Gun Club. Eugenie graciously accepted Honey's offer of a life vest but Shreave said he didn't need one, citing several record-breaking performances on his high school swim team. Eugenie didn't even pretend to believe the stories and Honey had trouble keeping a straight face, especially when Shreave lost his footing and sledded on his ass down the boat ramp. The fearful look in his eyes was not that of a man who was one with the water.

With almost no arguing, he and his girlfriend chose the yellow kayak. Honey held it steady while they stork-stepped aboard. After a few dicey moments they finally got settled – Boyd in the stern, Eugenie in the bow – and Honey eased them into the current. Quickly she climbed into the other kayak and followed.

The tide was falling hard, which was promising. A downstream paddle on a deep, wide river should have been effortless, even for amateurs. Yet right away the yellow kayak began zigzagging erratically. Before Honey could catch up, it plowed into a tangle of mangroves along the far shore. Shreave was cussing so loudly that he flushed a white heron and a flock of gray pelicans. Honey arrived on scene and saw Eugenie wildly swinging her paddle at spiderwebs, Shreave using his new hat to shield his face from the hail of broken twigs and leaves.

Honey was embarrassed by their racket, which had sullied an otherwise-lovely morning. She tied the bow of the Texans' kayak to the stern of hers, and with some effort towed them out of the clinging trees. It was only a hundred-odd yards farther to the mouth of the river, beyond which lay Chokoloskee Bay, as slick as a mirror.

When they reached open water, Honey unhitched the other kayak and watched as it again started to vector wildly under Shreave's rudder. She recalled from her trips with Perry Skinner that the weaker paddler should always take the bow, and therein lay the problem: Shreave's girlfriend was clearly the stronger of the two. Knowing that he wasn't nimble enough to switch places without capsizing the craft, Honey instead suggested that Eugenie Fonda lighten her stroke.

Shreave piped: 'Yeah, I tried to show her the right way to do it but she won't listen.'

'That's because you're a spaz,' Eugenie pointed out. She was still picking dewy filaments of spiderwebs from her hair. 'My ninety-year-old grandma can paddle better than you, Boyd.'

Honey Santana began hearing distant echoes, so she covered her ears and shut her eyes. Soon there was the dreaded music – it sounded like Celia Cruz, whom her parents adored, and possibly Nine Inch Nails in the background. Honey took deep breaths, as she'd been advised to do by many therapists. If only these two would stop fighting, she thought. They're ruining everything.

Boyd Shreave shouted: 'What are you doing over there?'

At first Honey didn't realize he was addressing her.

'Are you sick, or what? Don't tell me you're sick,' he said.

She looked up, smiled lightheartedly and waved for the Texans to follow. Where, she wasn't sure. The charts were stowed in one of the duffel bags, and she didn't feel like stopping to dig them out. That she could do later, when they took a break for lunch.

With clean brisk strokes she headed across the widest part of the bay, in a direction that she correctly estimated to be north-northwest. Not far ahead was a well-marked pass, she recalled, that would lead them toward the Gulf of Mexico.

Which will be as calm as a birdbath this morning, Honey thought.

In the other kayak, Eugenie Fonda could be heard saying, 'Boyd, would you please find out where the hell this woman is taking us.'

Followed in short order by Shreave hollering: 'Hey,

Nature Girl, where we goin'? I gotta stop and unload some a that coffee.'

Honey picked up the pace. As she paddled harder, the songs in her head began to fade. 'Stay close, and watch out for oyster bars,' she called over her shoulder. 'We'll be there soon.'

Fry showered quickly and threw on some semi-fresh clothes, then grabbed his book bag and skateboarded to the crab docks. Perry Skinner was on one of his boats, taking the diesel apart. Fry climbed aboard and told him what he'd seen earlier at the trailer park.

'I'll check it out,' his father said, seemingly unconcerned. 'You get along to school now, so you won't be late.'

'But what if Mr. Piejack is after Mom?'

'Don't worry about that asshole.'

As soon as his son had gone, Skinner hopped down from the boat and drove home, where he removed a loaded .45-caliber semi-automatic from a floor safe in the laundry room. Even in Florida it's against the law for convicted felons to have a gun, but as vice mayor of the town (and one who'd successfully petitioned to have his civil rights restored), Skinner had granted himself an ad hoc exemption. None of the police officers would dare arrest him, and he was on poker-playing terms with the local sheriff's deputies. Only the federal park rangers posed a potential problem, but they mostly kept to themselves.

Skinner got on his motorcycle and went searching for Louis Piejack. Nobody was hard to find in Everglades City, which was geographically as complicated as a postage stamp. Piejack's green pickup was parked next to the boat ramp by the Rod and Gun Club. From a distance Skinner was unable to identify the two men sitting in the front seat, though he assumed one of them was Louis. There was no sign of Honey Santana or her guests. Skinner parked the motorcyle near the restaurant and strolled down to the seawall, where Piejack would be sure to notice him. The gun was tucked in the back of Skinner's pants and concealed by the tail of his work shirt.

Looking downriver he caught sight of two kayaks, one red and one yellow, heading more or less toward Chokoloskee Bay. The woman in the red kayak looked from a distance like Honey, which meant it probably was. Nobody else in the whole county looked like Honey. In the second kayak was a man in a wide-brimmed hat and a woman in a papaya-colored halter. Their teamwork with the paddles was not exactly fluid.

Skinner heard rubber peeling and glanced over his shoulder – Louis Piejack's truck, speeding away. Skinner sat down and hung his legs over the seawall and watched the kayaks slowly shrink to bright specks crossing the water. He assured himself that he was doing this not because he still cared for his ex-wife, who was certifiably tilted, but because she was the mother of his one and only son and therefore worthy of concern.

After taking the handgun home, he returned to the crab docks, where one of his young mechanics, Randy, was doing battle with the broken diesel. Skinner told him to move aside. At lunchtime a woman whom Skinner was dating stopped by with cold beer and Cuban sandwiches. Her name was Debbie but she preferred to be called Sienna. Skinner had once asked her why she'd named herself after a Crayola, and she'd gotten her feelings hurt. She was only twenty-six years old and drove a propane truck back and forth from Port Charlotte. Her brother was a tight end for the Jacksonville Jaguars, which at least gave her and Skinner something to talk about during football season. The rest of the year it was pretty slow going.

'I'm so psyched about tonight,' Sienna said. 'Aren't you?'

Skinner studied the bubbles in his beer. He was trying hard to recall what was on the agenda.

'Green Day, remember?' she said. 'God, Perry, don't tell me.'

'Sure, I remember. They're playin' in Fort Myers.'

'You said you liked 'em.'

'I meant it, too.' To Skinner's knowledge, he'd never heard any of the band's songs; he was country to the bone.

Sienna said, 'We don't have to go if you don't want. I could sell the stupid tickets on eBay in about thirty seconds.'

'Please don't pout. I already said we're going.'

'Twice I went with you to see Willie Nelson. *Twice*.'

'Yes, you did.' Skinner wasn't in the mood for a rock concert, but he figured the distraction would do him good.

'Hank Jr., too,' Sienna went on, 'or did you forget that one?'

'No, I didn't forget.' Skinner wanted lunch to be done. He wanted Sienna to go away before he was obliged to heave her overboard.

'Excuse me for a second,' he said, and stepped into the wheelhouse.

Randy was thumbing through a *MotoCross*

magazine, his rubber boots propped on the console. Skinner silently finished his beer and watched an old johnboat coming from upriver. In the bow was a paunchy, uncomfortable-looking man with a shiner over one eye. He was wearing a wrinkled gray business suit, unusual attire for a fishing trip, and on his lap he protectively embraced two metallic travel cases.

In the back of the johnboat sat Louis Piejack, his undamaged hand holding the tiller stick of the engine. He never glanced once at the crab docks as he puttered past, so he was unaware that he was being watched. Otherwise, he might have made an effort to conceal the sawed-off shotgun, which lay in plain view on the deck of the boat, between his feet.

'Goddammit,' Perry Skinner muttered.

Randy glanced up from his magazine. 'What's up, boss?'

There was no time to call the guys in Hialeah. Skinner would have to handle it himself, which was fine.

'What're you doin' tonight, Randy?'

'Not a fuckin' thing, boss.'

'You wanna go see Green Day with Sienna? It's on me,' Skinner said.

'Far fuckin' out!'

Dealey wasn't a tough guy. He'd never been a cop or Feeb, unlike many other private investigators. Eighteen years Dealey had worked for an insurance company, knocking down phony disability claims, before going out on his own.

And usually it wasn't dangerous work, spying on unfaithful spouses. Dealey had only been injured once, by a flying vibrator. It had happened while he was surreptitiously photographing an acrobatic young couple in Candleridge. The woman, having spotted Dealey, had snatched the nine-inch missile from a nightstand and spiraled it with uncanny accuracy through the open ground-floor window of her apartment. Struck in the throat, the investigator had run for five blocks before collapsing in a cherry hedge. For three weeks afterward he'd been unable to speak or to take solid foods. The vibrator had tumbled into his camera bag, and Dealey kept the flesh-colored appliance in his desk as a sobering reminder of the perils of his trade. The batteries he'd tossed in the trash.

In all his many years of surveilling cheaters, layabouts and fraud artists, nobody had ever pointed a gun at Dealey, much less fired a round past his head. Louis Piejack was both vengeful and nuts, an unpromising combination.

'I'm not a great swimmer,' he'd warned Piejack as they got in the johnboat.

'Tough shit.'

Dealey's hearing had returned to normal, so there was nothing fuzzy about Piejack's response.

'Why don't we wait for Honey to come back?' the investigator suggested. 'What kind of sexy pictures you expect me to get when she's paddling a kayak?'

'Shut your fat yap,' said Piejack.

Dealey had positioned the bulky Halliburtons on his lap to shield his vital organs from another gunshot, accidental or intended. As the small flat-bottomed craft headed downriver, he settled upon a strategy of falsely befriending Louis Piejack so that the man would let down his guard.

'What exactly happened with those stone crabs?' Dealey inquired in a plausible tone of sympathy. He couldn't stop staring at the man's fingertips, which protruded from the gauze like nubs of dirty chalk. Something wasn't right.

'It was these goddamn Cubans hired by Honey's shitwad ex-husband. They shoved my hand into a loaded trap and the fuckin' crabs went to town,' Piejack said. 'I know it was him that set me up, 'cause, first off, he speaks Cuban real good. Second off, he's jealous of my hots for Honey.'

Dealey said, 'Makes sense.'

'Then, when they got me to surgery, some doctor fucked up and sewed my fingers back all wrong. Look here.'

Louis Piejack held up what appeared to be a pinkie where a thumb ought to have been. Dealey was unnerved by the sight, although he wasn't sure if he believed any of the man's story, from the crabs to the surgeon. Piejack seemed entirely capable of self-mutilation.

He said, 'I got me a sharp lawyer, don't you worry. Come back in a year and I'll own that fuckin' hospital.'

'Can't you find another doctor to stitch your fingers back where they belong?'

'I s'pose,' Piejack said, 'but I'm gonna wait a spell and see how this new setup works.'

'What do you mean?'

'I mean, Honey might like me better this way.' Piejack attempted without success to wiggle the misplaced pinkie. 'You follow?'

Dealey nodded agreeably, thinking: What a loon.

It was tempting to blame Lily Shreave for his predicament, but Dealey knew it was his own fault.

Lily was merely rich and kinky; he easily could have said no to the Florida trip. Greed, pure and simple, had drawn him into this mess.

'I'll say this: Them doctors put me on some superior dope for the pain,' Piejack remarked as they chugged past a row of commercial fishing boats.

'Yeah, like what?'

'Vikes,' he said. 'But I et up the whole damn bottle the first day! Lucky I know this pharmacist up in East Naples – he traded me a hundred pills for five pounds of swordfish.'

Beautiful, thought Dealey. The man's not only deranged, he's overmedicated. Add the loaded shotgun and it's party time.

'If you're not feelin' good, I can steer for a while,' Dealey offered.

'Yeah, right.' Piejack coughed once and spat over the side.

Dealey turned in his seat so that he could see where the madman was taking him. Soon the brown river emptied into a broad calm bay fringed with dense trees. There wasn't a hotel or a high-rise to be seen, which Dealey found surprising. Piejack gunned the throttle and the johnboat picked up speed. Dealey hugged his camera cases and shivered at the rush of cool air.

'Now where the hell are they?' Piejack wondered, his voice rising above the whine of the motor.

Dealey saw birds diving and silver fish jumping, but no kayaks on the water.

'Maybe they turned back already,' he said hopefully.

Louis Piejack laughed. 'Naw, they're out here somewheres. I'll find 'em, too. That's a damn fact.'

Fourteen

The plan was to steal water but no food from other campers. Water was essential for life, Sammy Tigertail said. Pringles were not.

'How would you feel about beer?' Gillian asked.

'That'll do.'

They searched for hours but spotted no other fires, and encountered nobody else on the water. When the moon disappeared behind a gray-blue ridge of clouds, Sammy Tigertail began navigating back toward the island. He feared getting lost in the web of unmarked creeks, although he didn't let on to Gillian.

From the bow of the canoe she asked, 'Do you know a rain dance?'

'First I need a virgin.'

'I'm serious,' Gillian said.

Sammy Tigertail wasn't sure if the Seminoles had a dance for making rain. He knew firsthand about the Green Corn Dance, a purification and feasting ritual dating back to the tribe's Creek origins. The celebration took place every spring and required participants to swallow boiled black concoctions that induced copious vomiting. Sammy Tigertail attended with his mother and his uncle Tommy, who customarily brought a flask of Johnnie Walker to wash away the taste of the black drinks.

Gillian said, 'Speaking of virgins, you wanna hear how I lost it? I'll tell you, if you tell me.'

'Not interested.'

'It was on a riding mower.'

'Stop.'

'On the sixteenth hole of the south course at the Firestone Country Club,' she said.

'I get the picture.'

'Which happens to be the jewel of Akron, Ohio. What about you?'

'I don't remember,' said Sammy Tigertail. He spotted their island around the bend and increased the pace of his paddling, heedless of his thirst or the blister rising on his left palm.

Gillian went on: 'It was my best friend's big brother. Is that a fucking cliché or what? And you do too remember.'

'We're almost there,' said the Seminole.

'So – what was her name?'

'Sally Otter.'

'Excellent!'

After stowing the canoe, they ate some cactus berries and moved their sleeping bags from the cistern to open ground, where they could see the stars. They lay down side by side, shoulders touching.

'Hey, Thlocko,' Gillian whispered.

'I'm tired.'

'You go to college?'

'Never finished high school.'

One week after his son was born, Sammy Tigertail's father had gone to the bank and opened the 'Chad

McQueen College Fund,' into which he faithfully deposited one hundred dollars every month. When Chad/Sammy had turned twelve, his stepmother had persuaded his father to close the account and invest the accumulated balance – $16,759.12 – in 307 Beanie Baby dolls, which she grandly predicted would quintuple in value by the time the boy finished high school. Each tagged with an insipidly perky nickname, the rarest and most valuable of the small stuffed animals was reputed to be Leroy the Lemming, of which Sammy's stepmother owned four. The collection was locked inside a steamer trunk that occupied many cubic feet of the boy's bedroom. Upon the sudden death of Sammy's father, his stepmother immediately hawked her entire Beanie Babies stash for $3,400, which she put down on a new Lexus coupe.

The Indian elected not to share that memory with Gillian. His half-white past was a private matter.

'So what's your problem with college?' she asked.

'Be quiet,' Sammy Tigertail said.

'Hey, what about the Fighting Irish?'

'The who?'

'Remember you gave me a ration of shit about my Seminoles jersey? What about Notre Dame, huh? How come all the Irishmen aren't all pissed off about the name of *that* team?'

Sammy Tigertail reached out and clapped his hand over Gillian's mouth. 'Shut the hell up. I'm begging you.'

She pushed his arm away and rolled over. 'Is that how you talked to Sally Beaver?'

'Otter was her name.'

'Whatever,' said Gillian.

The Indian closed his eyes, longing for a peaceful sleep. A thousand years ago, Calusa warriors had lain under the same winter sky. When he was in the eighth grade (and still Chad McQueen), Sammy Tigertail had written a school paper about the Calusa, who had pre-dated by twelve centuries the arrival in Florida of the beleaguered Seminoles. The Calusa's highly structured society revolved around fishing, and they were accomplished makers of palm-fiber nets, spears, throat gorges and hooks. They traveled widely in dug-out canoes, dominating by trade and force all other Indian tribes throughout the peninsula. Sammy Tigertail remembered seeing photographs of intricate tribal masks, shell jewelry and delicate wooden bird carvings excavated from a Calusa midden on Marco Island. The body paint favored by Calusa braves had been mixed with the oil of shark livers, to repel mosquitoes. (Sammy Tigertail once asked his uncle why the Seminoles didn't try the same formula, and his uncle said he would rather swat a bug than kill a shark.)

But the most remarkable thing that Sammy Tigertail remembered from his middle-school project about the noble Calusa was how suddenly they were wiped out – erased from the landscape barely two hundred years after their first fateful contact with Spanish soldiers, who carried diseases more deadly than their muskets.

The Calusa brave who plugged Ponce de León with an arrow had the right idea, Sammy Tigertail thought. He knew those white fuckers were bad news.

In the end, ravaged bands of Calusa were hunted down by mercenary Creeks and other newly armed Indians, who sold them to slavers. Sammy Tigertail recalled that a few hundred Calusa were thought to have escaped with their cacique to Havana in the mid-1700s, and he wondered what had become of them. He'd always thought it sad that the Calusa had disappeared from Florida's southernmost wilderness before the Seminoles – driven by another rapacious bunch of white men – had settled there. Because the two tribes had never crossed paths, there was no chance that even a droplet of Calusa blood flowed in Sammy Tigertail's veins. In dark moments he actually worried that he might be descended from one of the slave-hunting Creeks who'd preyed upon the Calusa, for ironically it was displaced Creek clans and other *cimmarones* who would later become the Seminole Nation.

Sammy Tigertail took several deep breaths and pressed his arms against his sides. He was hoping to feel the power and wisdom of a hundred warriors rising up from the ancient bones and shells beneath him . . .

Yet when he opened his eyes, he felt no different from the way he'd felt before – like a man who didn't fit in anybody's world, red or white.

Emptily he blinked at the milky heavens. The sun had risen and the morning haze was burning off. He lay shirtless on top of the sleeping bag, clutching the Gibson guitar to his breast. Somewhere down by the shore, Gillian was saying, 'Right side, Boyd, *right* side. Watch out for those snags, Genie.'

Which made no sense, until the Indian realized that it wasn't Gillian's voice he was hearing from the water. Gillian was in the limbs of the poinciana, signaling for him to get up.

Sammy Tigertail sprang to his feet and unwrapped the rifle. Gillian dropped lightly out of the tree. She touched his arm and said, 'You think they've got water, Thlocko?'

'Time to behave,' he advised, 'otherwise I'm gonna leave you out here alone to die.'

'I can be quiet. I swear I can.' She gave a crisp salute and mimed a zippering motion along her lips.

Eugenie Fonda recognized Boyd Shreave's self-transformation from ambivalent dullard to condescending asshole as a last-ditch attempt to raise his game. It wasn't the first time one of her lovers had tried to reinvent himself, but for sheer detestability Boyd had outdone all the rest. He'd pay dearly for it, of course. Instead of lounging on a beach with chilled rum runners in hand – Eugenie's ideal of a proper Florida vacation – they were paddling through a funky-smelling, bug-infested swamp. Worse, she was doing all the hard work; as a kayaking partner, Boyd was useless, his strokes splashy and mistimed. He snottily spurned instruction from their tour guide, who – Eugenie had noticed in the light of day – was quite attractive. Most of Eugenie's past loser boyfriends would have been hitting on Honey Santana by now, but not Boyd. He'd decided to advertise his virility by behaving like a conceited dipshit.

'I gotta take another leak,' he announced to the world. Eugenie Fonda disregarded him. Honey spun her kayak and said, 'Everything okay back there?'

'No, it's not. I've gotta piss again,' Shreave said.

'We'll stop for lunch up ahead.' Honey pointed to an island a half-mile away.

'Better hurry,' Boyd growled to Eugenie, 'or you'll be up to your ankles in something nasty.'

He resumed his spastic paddling, which immediately put the kayak off course. To neutralize him, Eugenie shed her life vest and matter-of-factly unstrung her halter.

'What're you doin'?' she heard Boyd ask.

'My New Year's resolution: no more tan lines.'

'But what if another boat comes by?'

'Who cares, Boyd? They're just tits.'

From then on he was so preoccupied that he scarcely paddled at all, which had been Eugenie's objective. Unhindered by his inept flailing, she guided the kayak effortlessly with the tide. As they closed in on the mangrove island, Honey called out, 'Right side, Boyd, *right* side. Watch out for those snags, Genie.'

No sooner had the bow creased the bank than Shreave stepped into the shallows, clambered ashore and vanished. Honey Santana and Eugenie Fonda dragged the kayaks up on dry land.

'Can I ask you something?' Honey said.

'Yeah, but there's no good answer. I was bored, I guess,' Eugenie said. 'I mean *really* bored.'

'He sure doesn't seem like your type.'

'I've never met my type. That's a problem,' Eugenie said. 'How about you?'

Honey nodded. 'Once I did. We stayed together a long time.'

'I'd settle for that. You have no idea.'

Shreave reappeared. His hat was crooked and he was struggling to remove a twig from the zipper of his pants. He said, 'Ladies, you won't believe what yours truly found up the hill.'

'An ounce of charm?' Eugenie said.

'A campfire!'

'Way out here?' Honey looked concerned.

'It's still warm,' Shreave reported, 'and it smells like greasy fish.'

Honey said they should move to another island immediately.

'What're you scared of? They're gone now.' Shreave swept his arms dismissively. 'Besides, I'm starving.'

'Well, that settles it. His Majesty wants supper.' Eugenie opened her backpack and removed a light cotton pullover, which she put on despite Boyd's adolescent protests. She had no intention of marching topless through spiderwebs.

Fry woke up giggling. He didn't know where he was, and he didn't much care. He heard his father's voice say, 'Nice job, champ.'

'Whah?'

'You T-boned a garbage truck.'

Fry tried to remember.

'On your skateboard,' his dad said.

'Shit,' Fry mumbled. Normally he tried not to cuss in front of his parents, but at the moment he had no self-control. The sun was blinding and his neck throbbed when he turned away.

His father said, 'The truck was parked, by the way. Six tons of solid steel and you couldn't see it.'

'I'm sorry, Dad.' Fry laughed again and scrambled to recover. 'I know it's not funny. Really, I know it's not.'

'You're wasted,' his father said. 'Don't get too used to it.'

'Ohhhhhh.' Fry closed his eyes, floating. He comprehended that he was in his father's pickup, and it was speeding along the Tamiami Trail.

'They gave you some heavy-duty pain pills,' Perry Skinner said.

'For what?'

'Three busted ribs. Concussion with a hairline skull fracture. Plus you've got a knot on your head as big as a strawberry.'

Fry tried to touch it but all he could feel was smooth plastic.

'What's the deal?' he asked.

'The hospital wanted to hold you for observation but we had to get a move on, so I stopped at the mall and bought a football helmet.'

'Bucs or Dolphins?'

'Dolphins,' his father said. 'In case you get dizzy and fall, I didn't want you to spill your brains all over the place.'

Fry's memory was returning in muddy waves. 'Where was I going when it happened? To school, right?'

'Yep.'

'Dad, are you driving superfast, or is it the medicine?'

'Both.'

Fry recalled looking up and seeing the garbage truck broken down directly in his path, unavoidable. He wondered what he'd been thinking about at the time, what had distracted him so completely.

'Where we goin'?' he asked.

'For a boat ride,' Perry Skinner replied.

'Why?' Fry didn't feel like getting on a boat. He felt like going home and shutting the blinds and crawling under the sheets.

'Because I can't leave you alone is what the doctors told me. In case you have a damn seizure or somethin',' his father said sharply. 'There's nobody else to watch over you 'cept me.'

'What about Mom?'

Skinner didn't answer. Fry now remembered seeing Louis Piejack cruise past the trailer that morning. He also remembered rushing to tell his dad at the crab docks.

'What about Mom?' he asked again. This time he opened his eyes. 'Dad?'

'That's where we're goin', to find your mother.'

'But where is she?'

'I don't know for sure.'

'Is Mr. Piejack after her?' Fry asked.

'It's possible.'

Fry slumped to one side, the football helmet clunking against the truck window.

Perry Skinner said, 'I should've let 'em keep you in the hospital. What the hell was I thinking?'

'I would've just snuck out and hitched a ride.'

'Yeah, that sounds about right.'

Neither of them spoke again until they reached the flashing yellow light that marked the turn toward Everglades City.

Fry's father said, 'Your skateboard made out better than you. One of the wheels got snapped off, but that's it.'

'Dad, you gonna bring your gun?'

'What?'

'When we go look for Mom. Are you takin' the gun?'

'I am.' Perry Skinner cleared his throat.

'Good call,' Fry said.

Louis Piejack gazed through the binoculars and said,

'Jackpot!' Then he said it another six or seven times.

'What is it?' Dealey asked miserably from the bow.

'Get your camera ready. I see titties.'

Dealey squinted ahead. The bay was a rippled puddle of glare, and the two kayaks were at least five hundred yards away.

'No good,' he said to Louis Piejack. 'It's too far, plus they're backlit.'

'They ain't Honey's, but those are some major-league boobs. Rig up that damn camera.'

Dealey snapped open one of the Halliburtons and removed a Nikon body, which he attached to a small tripod. From the other case he took a 600-millimeter telephoto lens. Assembly was achieved with shaking fingers, for Dealey was afraid of dropping the expensive equipment overboard.

Louis Piejack laid off on the throttle, crowing, 'Jackpot! Jackpot! They stopped at the island!' His good right hand held the field glasses to his eyes while his swathed left paw steered the johnboat.

'It's still backlit, don't you understand? There's no shot from here,' Dealey complained.

'That's Dismal Key. I know another way in.'

Dealey said, 'Go slow, okay? Camera gets splashed and we're out of business.'

And I'm out two grand, he thought.

'But I want movies,' Piejack said, 'not pitchers.'

Dealey packed the Nikon away. He said they needed to get much closer to record usable videotape.

'Noooooo problem.' Piejack was fuzzy from the Vicodin tablets he'd eaten for lunch. It wasn't easy maintaining a high-level addiction to prescription painkillers with one's dominant hand swaddled so cumbersomely. Piejack had assigned Dealey – under threat of execution – to open the bottle and count out five tablets, which with lizardly flicks of his scabbed tongue he'd slurped from his captive's palm. Dealey, mortified, had said nothing.

Piejack circled to the far side of the island and poked the johnboat along an overgrown mangrove creek. The talon-like branches clawed at Dealey's skin and tore holes in his suit jacket, but Piejack seemed unconcerned. He ran the boat hard aground, snatched up his shotgun and jumped out. Dealey followed, lugging the camera gear.

'Don't get no ideas,' Piejack warned.

'You think I'm crazy?'

In fact, Dealey had thought of nothing but escape since they'd motored out of Everglades City. Now, trailing Piejack into the heart of the island, Dealey waited for the loopy kidnapper to falter. With providence, Piejack soon would pass out from the excess of narcotics, presenting Dealey with a couple of options. Running like hell would be high on the list, but where would he go? Even if he got the johnboat running, Dealey wasn't confident that he could find his way to the mainland.

A more practical idea was to snatch the shotgun while Louis Piejack slept, and then force the nimrod to ferry him back to town. Even with a plan in mind, Dealey remained anxious, for nothing on the streets of Fort Worth had prepared him for such a situation – being trapped in the Everglades with a maimed and trigger-happy fishmonger.

'Shut up,' Piejack barked.

'I didn't say a word.'

'Then who the hell did?' Piejack halted, raising a begauzed hand. Dealey heard nothing except his own rapid breathing; the camera cases were heavy.

'Over there.' Piejack pointed to a fifteen-foot hill sprinkled with scrub and cactus plants. 'You first.'

'Gimme a break.'

'How 'bout a load of bird shot up your butthole instead?'

The slope consisted almost entirely of broken oysters and seashells. Dealey's shoes crunched noisily as he advanced, Piejack goosing him crudely with the barrel of the sawed-off. As they approached the top, Dealey heard voices on the other side. Piejack directed him toward a clump of sticky vines, where they took cover.

The three kayakers were in a clearing under a big tree, about fifty yards away. Boyd Shreave and Eugenie Fonda were sitting on a duffel bag, eating from plastic containers and sharing a gallon jug of water. The woman from the trailer park, Louis Piejack's beloved Honey, stood spritzing her arms with bug juice.

'My God, ain't she a treasure.' Piejack sighed. 'Take out your camera, Hawkeye.'

'She's got her clothes on. They all do.' Dealey felt sure that in his earlier sighting, Piejack had hallucinated the naked breasts.

'Just make me a goddamn movie,' Piejack whispered menacingly.

Dealey rigged up the camera and began to tape, Piejack hovering at his left shoulder. Through the viewfinder it appeared that Boyd Shreave was talking constantly, and that neither of the women was paying the slightest attention.

Dealey felt Piejack's hot breath on his ear. Then, in a singsong voice: 'Where's my lil' Honey Pie runnin' off to?'

'How should I know?'

'Stay on her! Stay on her!'

Dealey said, 'Easy, Louis.' He kept the camera trained on Honey as she made her way into a brushy stand of small trees.

'I bet she's gonna pee,' Piejack said excitedly.

He's probably right, thought Dealey, discreetly pressing the pause button.

'Are you still shootin'? Keep shootin'!' Piejack was panting like a broken-down dog. 'Can you see her? I can't see her no more.'

The crackpot was unaware that the tape had been stopped, so Dealey easily could have faked it. He could have kept quiet and pretended to record Honey squatting in the bushes, Piejack hopping beside him in elation.

Yet even Dealey, whose life's work was invading and exploiting the most private moments of others, had moral boundaries. A sex tape was evidence; a pissing tape was trash.

The investigator pivoted with artistic deliberation, touched the record button and boldly advanced with the lens aimed squarely at his captor.

Louis Piejack began backing up. '*Now* what the hell you doin'?'

'Makin' a movie,' Dealey replied, 'about the sickest piece of shit I ever met.'

At the crest of the oyster mound, Piejack's expression changed from ragged confusion to rage. He dug his heels into the loose shells and leveled the sawed-off at Dealey's gut.

'Don't come no closer. You're done,' he said.

'I'm not so sure about that.' Dealey adjusted the exposure and continued taping.

Piejack peered at the red dot blinking beneath the lens. 'Turn that damn thing off.'

'Don't you want to be famous?'

'What for?'

'Stinking up the planet,' said Dealey.

'That's it. Get ready to die, you sonofabitch.'

'Then good luck, Louis. You're gonna need it.'

Piejack scowled. 'What the fuck's that s'posed to mean?'

'Good luck opening your precious medicine bottle without me to help,' Dealey said.

Piejack pensively nibbled his upper lip. 'It's those goddamn kiddy-proof caps. They're murder with one hand.'

'Oh, you'll figure out a way.' Dealey noticed a brown iodine-stained nub on the trigger of the shotgun. It was a thumb, sprouting from the gauze where a forefinger ought to have been. Dealey briefly zoomed in on it.

'Make up your mind, Louis.'

Piejack grunted. 'You think I won't shoot? Ha!'

Dealey heard a dull crack and the kidnapper disappeared from the viewfinder. In his place stood a muscular young man holding a rifle. Dealey lowered the camera and saw Piejack, facedown and lifeless in a cactus patch.

'I owe you, bud,' the investigator said to the stranger, who retrieved Piejack's shotgun and tucked it under one arm.

Then he walked up to Dealey and ungently pinched his nose.

'You're not real,' the man said accusingly.

'I am too,' Dealey quacked, struggling to pull free.

'Look at your damn suit.'

'I can explain!'

The man with the rifle said, 'Don't lie to me. You're a death spirit.'

Perfect, Dealey thought. Another Florida wacko.

The man let go of Dealey's nose and said, 'Take off your shoes and socks.'

Dealey stowed the video camera and did what he was told. The man balled up the sweaty socks and crammed them into Dealey's cheeks.

'You got any water?' he demanded.

Dealey shook his head apologetically.

'Hell,' the young man said. He motioned with the rifle. 'Stand up and follow me.'

When Dealey pointed to his Halliburtons, the man shrugged. Dealey hoisted the two cases and trudged heavily after the stranger. The broken oyster shells gouged the soles of the investigator's feet, and before long he heard himself whimpering.

This is the worst job I ever took, he thought. *By far.*

Fifteen

She thought she'd heard voices, but what else was new? Rarely was there a silence in her world; no peace, no quiet. Nat King Cole crooned a duet with Marilyn Manson, a sniper tripped a fire alarm at the nursing home, a parakeet landed in a margarita blender . . .

Just another day inside the head of Honey Santana.

'Some vacation,' said Boyd Shreave, the man who'd phoned during dinner and given his name as Eisenhower and tried to sucker her into buying a tract of overpriced real estate.

The man who'd called her a skank.

'Not what we had in mind,' he added. 'Right, Genie?'

'It isn't much like the Bahamas,' his mistress allowed.

Honey said, 'What were you two hoping for? Besides a beach and a tiki bar, I mean. This is raw, untouched wilderness, the very last of it. That's what people come to see on an ecotour.'

Boyd Shreave chuckled coldly. 'Just give us the damn sales pitch and take us back to town.'

'There is no sales pitch,' Honey said.

'Yeah, right.'

Eugenie Fonda stretched her arms. 'What's the name of this island, anyhow?'

'I don't know,' Honey said, 'but it'll do.'

Shreave frowned. 'For what?' He stalked up to her and flicked the half-eaten granola bar out of her hand. 'Do for what?'

'That was rude,' Honey said. She collected the pieces off the ground and placed them in a garbage tote. 'Beyond rude, as a matter of fact.'

Eugenie Fonda told Shreave to quit acting like a jerk.

'No sales pitch, she says?' He kicked at the ashes of the previous campers' fire. 'What the hell's going on?'

Honey Santana decided it was pointless to wait any longer. She was ready; he was more than ready.

She stood up and said, 'There's no pitch because there's no such development as Royal Gulf Hammocks, Mr. *Eisenhower.*'

Shreave's brow inverted in a simian portrait of vexation. He swayed slightly, working his lower jaw.

Having connected the dots, Eugenie Fonda said, 'Shit, Boyd. Shit, shit, *shit.*'

'Do I know you?' he asked Honey. The words came out as a rattle. 'Don't tell me you're the same one who called my house.'

'You called me first, Boyd. Peddling some worthless scrub in Gilchrist County, remember? I gave you a short history lesson on Stephen Foster, how he never laid eyes on the Suwannee River. Why don't you have a seat?'

Shreave spun around. Stammered. Shook his arms. Finally, Eugenie snagged him by the belt and pulled him down beside her.

'Do the voice,' he said to Honey. 'If you're really her, do the phone voice.'

She was well prepared. 'Good evening, Mr. Shreave. My name is Pia Frampton and I'm calling with a very special offer—'

Shreave's chin dropped. 'Aw, Jesus.'

'You said it was too "creamy-sounding," remember? You gave me lots of helpful pointers.'

Eugenie Fonda said, 'Incredible.'

Honey recognized the inflection of fatigue; of low expectations, unmet. *What am I doing with this loser?* Honey had more than once asked herself the same question, before she swore off dating.

'Boy, she got you good,' Eugenie said to Shreave.

'Bullshit. It was a free trip to Florida!'

'Nothing's free, Boyd. Don't tell me you forgot.'

'Yeah, but she sent plane tickets!'

'You got suckered. Get over it.' Eugenie looked over at Honey and said, 'Wild guess. There's a couple of redneck goons waiting to jump out of the bushes and rob us.'

Honey Santana had to laugh.

'Then what's this all about? Wait, I know – a ransom deal!' Eugenie guessed. 'Maybe you found out Boyd's wife has some bucks.'

Shreave said, 'Genie, shut your piehole.'

Honey popped a Tic Tac. Her attention was drawn to the debris of a cottage – peeling lumber, charred beams, broken window frames – that somebody had once called home. A squat bunker-like structure of bare cinder blocks had been erected on one slope of the shell mound, perhaps as a cistern.

Honey noticed a flurry of gulls and pelicans overhead, and she wondered what had flushed them out.

They're probably just going fishing, she thought. It was a fine day.

'Why'd you do this?' Shreave asked in a scraping voice. 'The airline tickets and all, Christ, you must be nuts.'

Eugenie Fonda said, 'She's not nuts. Are you, Honey?'

Honey was opening a packet of dried figs. The campsite was dominated by an ancient royal poinciana, and she considered climbing it to get a better fix on their whereabouts. She felt like she was a long way from her son.

A shot rang out, followed by another.

Eugenie jumped. Shreave went wide-eyed and exclaimed, 'It *is* a trap!'

'Sshhh. It's just poachers,' Honey said, thinking: They must be the ones who built the fire.

Shreave became antic, the gunfire having unstapled his nerves. He launched himself at Honey's knees and tackled her, pinning a clammy forearm to her throat.

'Get us out of here!' he rasped.

With some difficulty, Eugenie Fonda dragged him off. As Honey picked chipped oyster shells out of her hair, she recalled the time that Perry Skinner had made love to her on the beach at Cape Sable, both of them caked with sand and wet grit. It was in the middle of a wild spring rainstorm, and they were alone except for a bob-cat watching from a stand of palmettos. Honey wanted to believe that she'd become pregnant with Fry that afternoon.

'Who shot off that gun?' Shreave demanded.

'I've got no idea. That's the truth,' Honey said.

For several minutes they stayed quiet and listened.

There was no more gunfire, and Shreave calmed down.

When Honey began to unpack the pup tents, Eugenie said, 'Uh-oh.'

Shreave snickered. 'No way we are spending the night out here. I'll call for help.'

'How?' Eugenie asked. They'd left their cell phones in the rented Explorer because they were afraid of losing them overboard on the kayaks. She said, 'We're campers, Boyd.'

'Like hell we are.'

It took half an hour to set up the tents. After Honey finished, she turned to the Texans and said, 'I have one son, the boy you saw in the pictures back at the lodge. I've tried to teach him to be a decent, positive person – these days they get so cynical, you know, it breaks your heart. We watch the news together every night because it's important for young people to be aware of what's happening, but sometimes, I swear, I want to heave a brick through the television. Don't you ever feel that way?'

Eugenie said, 'Not Boyd. He loves his TV.'

'Except the news,' he cut in. 'I don't ever watch the damn news, not even Fox. By the way, we're leaving now.'

Eugenie said, 'Let her finish, Boyd. Obviously she's gone to a lot of trouble.'

Honey thanked her, and continued: 'I always tell my son, 'The world is crawling with creeps and greedheads. Don't you dare grow up to be one of them.' And what I mean is: Be a responsible and caring person. Is that so hard? To be generous, not greedy. Compassionate, not indifferent. My God, is there a worse sin than indifference?'

Shreave hoisted a water jug and glugged noisily. He

wiped his lips on his sleeve and grumbled, 'Would you get to the point, if you've got one.'

'I do. I do have a point.' Honey paused to sort out the tunes in her head. One was 'Yellow Submarine,' which she'd often sung to Fry when he was a baby. Even Perry Skinner, who preferred Merle or Waylon, knew all the words.

She said, 'I tend to get overexcited, I admit. Obsessed about certain things, though in a non-clinical way. 'Hyperfocused,' my son calls it. The dinner hour is important to me. It's the only time we really get to talk anymore.'

'You and your boy?' Eugenie said.

'Right. That part of the day is *ours*, you understand? Fry's growing up so fast – he's got track practice and homework and his skateboarding. Plus he sees his ex-father a couple of times a week, which is strictly his choice. Anyhow . . . where was I?'

'Dinner,' Eugenie prompted gently.

'Yes. Practically every night the phone rings in the middle of dinner and it's some stranger, hundreds of miles away, trying to sell me something I don't need, don't want and can't afford. The name of your company is Relentless, right? Like they're proud of how they never let up from pestering people.' Honey felt her arms flapping. She heard her voice rise. 'You call up my house, Mr. Boyd Shreave, and do not even have the honor, or spine, to give your true name!'

Shreave snorted. 'Strictly SOP.'

'Standard operating procedure,' Eugenie explained. 'We don't ever use our real last names. None of us do.'

Honey Santana was crestfallen. 'You work there, too?'

'Next time just hang up the phone. End of story,'

Eugenie said. 'They won't call back. The list of numbers we got, it's a mile long.'

'This is awful.' Honey pressed her knuckles to her temples. 'I'm talking about basic old-fashioned civility and respect. The man told me to go screw myself. He called me a dried-up skank.'

Shreave stiffened. 'After you insulted my mother.'

'I did no such thing!' Honey discarded the apology she'd rehearsed. Shreave didn't deserve it. 'All I did was ask a simple, very reasonable question: Did your mom raise you to be a professional pest? Did she bleed and suffer through your birth, Boyd, so that you could grow up to be a nag and a sneak? My guess would be no. My guess is that your folks had higher hopes for you. And what about Lily?'

Shreave wobbled, exposed once more.

'The *real* Mrs. Shreave,' Honey went on. 'Tell me she's happy that this is how your career has peaked. Tell me she's proud and content to be married to a telephone solicitor.'

Eugenie Fonda broke in. 'Okay, sweetie, we're all on board. Boyd's real sorry he called and bothered you. He'll never do it again. Now can you please get us outta here?'

'No, I don't believe he cares one bit.' Honey scrutinized Shreave for a shadow of remorse. 'He definitely does not get the point.'

Shreave confirmed this by saying, 'I get it, all right: You're as crazy as a shithouse rat.'

Eugenie glowered at him. 'Very smooth.'

'She fucking kidnapped us!'

Honey said, 'I thought you'd enjoy it out here. Be honest – did you ever see any place so amazing?'

Shreave hooted. 'Only every week on *Survivor*.'

'His favorite show,' Eugenie said, whacking a spider on her ankle. 'That and *Maury Povich.*'

Honey was lost. She felt like a sap.

'You can go now,' she said, digging into the stash of Cheerios.

Boyd hopped up and plumped his Indiana Jones hat. Eugenie Fonda said, 'Don't be ridiculous. We'll get lost in five minutes without her.' She turned to Honey. 'Come on. You've had your fun.'

'Keep heading east and you'll be fine.'

'We won't be fine. We definitely will *not* be fine.'

'Then stay with me.'

Shreave growled, 'Fuck that. Let's go.'

Honey watched them hustle down the path toward the creek. She rested her head on one of the duffels and hoped, against all odds, that they'd find their own way back to Everglades City. She truly didn't wish to see them again. Her speech had bombed, and now the whole plan seemed depressingly misguided. She hated to give up, but it appeared that Boyd Shreave was a hopeless cause.

The sky had changed color, and Honey felt a cooling shift in the wind. She didn't mind spending the night alone; poachers typically operated in secret, and the ones with the gun were probably long gone. She'd make a fire and, before sunset, go for a skinny-dip in the creek. In the morning she would return to the mainland and then wait for Fry after school. She planned on finding her way back using Perry Skinner's GPS, into which she had programmed several waypoints while leading the Texans through the islands.

Far away she heard an airplane, and soon the drone of its engine turned into a light chorus of humming.

The tune, though pleasant, was unfamiliar. She tried to hum along but couldn't nail the key. There was a rustle nearby and Boyd Shreave reappeared, silky strands of spiderwebs trailing from both earlobes. He stomped into the clearing and said, 'Okay. Get your ass in gear.'

Honey sat up. Genie emerged from the trees and said, 'You win. The joke's on us.'

'What joke? You said you were going back.'

Shreave said, 'Oh, and I guess we're supposed to swim.'

Honey got a knot in her gut. 'The kayaks are gone?'

'Surprise, surprise,' Eugenie said thinly.

Boyd Shreave whipped out a stubby pistol and leveled it at Honey's heart. 'Don't just sit there all innocent. Tell your pals to bring back our goddamn boats.'

Honey said she didn't have any pals on the island. 'I don't know who stole the kayaks. Honest to God.'

Eugenie Fonda skeptically eyed the gun in Shreave's hand. 'I don't know, Boyd. In the daylight it sure looks like a toy.'

He laid it flat in his palm for examination. 'It's not a toy,' he said, with no abundance of confidence.

'Whatever. Put the damn thing away,' Eugenie told him. 'She's tellin' the truth.'

'Great. Now you're takin' sides against me.'

'I know where he got it – from under my bed,' Honey Santana said. 'And he's right, it's not a toy.'

Shreave smirked at Eugenie. 'Told you. Ha!'

Defiantly he shoved the weapon back into his pants, which lit up with a dull crackle. Shreave yowled and pitched backward as if he'd been clipped by a freight train. For what seemed like half a minute he flopped and shuddered on the ground, clutching his groin with curled, bone-white fingers.

Eugenie Fonda watched the spectacle without comment. Honey explained, 'Actually it's not a gun, either. It's an electric Taser.'

With a sigh Eugenie said, 'What a fucking pinhead.'

'I wouldn't touch him just yet.'

'Oh, don't worry.'

With the stolen kayaks in tow, Sammy Tigertail relocated to the southeastern leg of the island. He built a new campfire while Gillian amused herself with Dealey.

When she pulled the crumpled socks from his mouth, he asked, 'Who are you?'

'Thlocko's hostage.'

'I guess that makes two of us.'

'No, you're just temporary. Like a POW,' she said. 'He also goes by "Tiger Tail." That's a Seminole chief.'

'Don't I get a chance to explain?'

'Doubtful. He's hard-core.' Gillian opened one of the Halliburtons and began tinkering with the Nikon.

Dealey said, 'Don't do that.' When he reached for the camera, she swatted his hand.

Sammy Tigertail looked up from the fire and threatened to throw both of them in Pumpkin Bay, which he had misidentified as the nearest open body of water. It was, in fact, Santina Bay, an error of no immediate consequence.

'Ten thousand islands and these assholes had to pick this one,' the Seminole said.

Retreat had fouled his mood. The place was being infested by white people and white spirits. Two rifle

shots had failed to scare off the kayakers, forcing
Sammy Tigertail to abandon the shell-mound campsite
upon which he had hoped to commune with the
ancient Calusas. Now the three tourists were settling
in, and Sammy Tigertail was stuck with both the
college girl and the spirit of the dead white
businessman.

'I'm not a goddamn ghost!' Dealey protested, displaying his bloody feet as evidence of mortality.

Gillian snapped a few close-ups and set the Nikon
down. The Indian handed his guitar to her and told
her to play something soft. She slowly worked into
'Mexico,' by James Taylor, which Sammy Tigertail
recognized and approved. It would have sounded
better on an acoustic but he couldn't complain. For the
first time he noticed that Gillian had a lovely voice,
and he feared it would add to her powers over him.
Still, he didn't tell her to stop singing.

When the number was over, Dealey stated that he
was thirsty. Gillian told him to join the club. 'We've
been living for days on cactus berries and fried fish. I'd
blow Dick Cheney for a Corona,' she said.

'What do you want with me?' Dealey asked the
Seminole, who took the Gibson from Gillian and began
twanging the B string over and over.

Gillian leaned close to Dealey and whispered,
'Thlocko won't talk to you because he thinks you're a
spirit. He says he's done hassling with dead white
guys.'

'Then tell him to let me go.'

'Go where?' Gillian smiled. 'Please. You are so *not*
getting out of here. Hey, who was that jerkoff with the
Band-Aids on his hand?'

Dealey said he didn't know the man. 'Some freak

named Louis who's stalking a woman from the trailer park. He clubbed me with that shotgun and made me go with him.'

'That's rich,' said Gillian, 'getting kidnapped twice in the same day. It might be a world record.'

'I'm not makin' this up. That's the guy who gave me the black eye!'

Gillian told Dealey that she believed him. Sammy Tigertail instructed her to stop speaking to the death spirit.

'But I think he might be real,' Gillian said, giving Dealey a secret wink.

'That could be bad for him,' said the Seminole, who'd already considered the possibility. Unlike the spirit of Wilson, Dealey hadn't faded away when Sammy Tigertail opened his eyes. More suspiciously, he'd made himself visible and audible to Gillian, who was plainly not an Indian.

Sammy Tigertail fingered a D chord and began to strum feverishly. He wished he had an amplifier. Gillian pulled out Dealey's digital Nikon and took some shots of the Seminole playing, which she showed to him in the viewfinder. She said, 'Damn, boy, you could be quite the rock star.'

The Seminole liked the way he looked holding the Gibson, though he tried not to appear too pleased. 'I don't want to be a rock star,' he said.

'Sure you don't,' said Gillian. 'All the free poon and dope you can stand, who'd want to live like that?'

'I need quiet. I can't think.' Sammy Tigertail carefully wiped down the guitar and put it away. Then he unrolled his sleeping bag and ordered Dealey to crawl inside.

'Zip him up. I mean all the way,' Sammy Tigertail told Gillian.

'Even his head?'

'Especially his head.'

Dealey turned pink. 'Don't! I'm claustrophobic!'

'Where are those damn socks?' Sammy Tigertail asked.

'No – not that! I'll keep quiet, I swear.'

Gillian said, 'Come on, Thlocko, can't you see he's scared shitless?'

'Then you squeeze in there with him. For company,' Sammy Tigertail said. 'There's room for two.'

'Gross.'

'He can't try anything. He's dead.'

'Nuh-uh,' she said.

Dealey turned on one side to make space. Gillian slid into the sleeping bag behind him, positioning her elbows for distance enforcement. The Seminole zippered the top, sealing them in warm musty darkness. He said, 'I told you, I need to think.'

After a few moments he heard their breathing level off. He sat down not far from the lumpy bulk. It was a mean thing to do, putting Gillian together with a possible death spirit, but maybe she'd finally come to her senses and abandon the notion of staying on the island. No normal young woman would tolerate the sack treatment, but then Gillian was miles from normal.

A part of Sammy Tigertail didn't want to drive her away; the weak and lonely part. But what did he need her for? Surely not to teach him the Gibson. He could learn on his own, like so many of the great ones. His father had told him that Jimi Hendrix had taken one guitar lesson in his whole life, and that the Beatles couldn't even read music.

'Hey.' Dealey's hushed voice, inside the bundle.

'Hey what?' said Gillian.

Sammy Tigertail edged closer to listen.

'There's a motorboat,' Dealey was saying.

'I don't hear anything.'

'No, there's a boat on the island. That's how we got here.'

'You and Band-Aid Man?' Gillian said.

'Yeah, his boat,' Dealey whispered. 'I think I could find it.'

'And your point is?'

A short silence followed. The larger of the two lumps shifted in the sleeping bag. Sammy Tigertail massaged the muscles of his neck, waiting.

'The point is,' Dealey said impatiently, 'with the boat we can get away from *him*!'

'And why in the world would I want to do that?' Gillian whispered back, with an earnestness that made the eavesdropping Seminole smile in spite of himself.

Sixteen

The vice mayor of Everglades City borrowed from his neighbor a skiff rigged with a 35-horsepower outboard and an eighteen-foot graphite pole for pushing across the shallows. Perry Skinner brought a cooler of water and food, a spotlight, two bedrolls and the .45 semi-automatic. Fry, who was still hammered from the pain medicine, dozed in the bow for an hour while his father poked around Chokoloskee Bay. There was no sign of Honey and her guests, or of Louis Piejack's johnboat.

Fry awoke as the sun was setting.

'What now?' he asked his father.

'We keep lookin'.'

'Can I take off this helmet? I feel okay.'

'You lie.' Perry Skinner knew that Honey would blame him if anything happened to the boy. She would, in fact, go berserk.

Fry felt his ribs and grimaced. 'It's gettin' dark,' he said.

'Better for us.'

'But they'll hear us coming a mile away.'

'Give me some credit, son.'

Perry Skinner hadn't forgotten the art of night

running, which was essential to prospering as a pot smuggler in the islands. He had never been busted on the water because the feds couldn't find him, much less catch him. They'd arrested him on dry land at daybreak, along with half the male population of Everglades City. Five DEA guys had come crashing through the screen door, Honey half-naked and hurling a fondue pot at the lead agent, who'd been too entertained to book her.

During his outlaw career Skinner had been exceptionally cautious and discreet. His only mistake was trusting a man he'd known since kindergarten. To save his own hide, the friend had ratted out both Perry and Perry's brother, betrayal being the boilerplate denouement of most drug-running enterprises. Skinner only fleetingly had contemplated revenge against the person who'd turned him in. It was, after all, his first cousin.

The shit had gone down before Fry was born, and he wouldn't have been born at all if Honey Santana hadn't been waiting for Skinner when he got out of prison; waiting in a lemon-colored sun-dress and white sandals. It was a total surprise, especially the smile. She'd mailed 147 letters to Skinner while he was locked up; few were conciliatory and none were forgiving. Yet there she'd been, all dressed up and glowing in the Pensacola sunshine when he'd stepped through the gates at Eglin. The first words from her mouth were: 'If you ever run another load of weed, I'm gonna cut off your pecker and grind it into snapper chum.'

Perry Skinner had resumed a life of honest crabbing, and things at home had been good, for a while.

'You gave the GPS to your mom?' he asked Fry.

'Yep.'

'And showed her how to use it?'

'I tried,' Fry said.

'What are the odds?'

'Fifty-fifty. She still can't figure out the cruise control on her car.'

Nothing ever changes, Skinner thought. 'How are you feelin'? And tell the truth.'

'Shitty.'

'That's more like it.' Skinner was still worried about bringing Fry. He was not a fan of hospitals, and leaving the boy with strangers in the emergency room had seemed unthinkable at the time.

'You gonna shoot him, Dad?'

'Piejack? If it comes to that, yeah.'

'But what if we're too late? What if he already did something bad to Mom?'

'Then he dies for sure,' Skinner said.

Fry nodded. It was the answer he'd expected.

Louis Piejack hadn't heard anyone sneak up behind him. The blow had caught him at the base of the skull and he was out cold before he hit the cactus patch.

At dusk he regained consciousness, roused by an onslaught of medieval pain. He thrashed free of the clinging limbs, lost his balance and skidded backward into a ravine full of Busch beer cans. His landing sounded like a Krome Avenue head-on.

In the twilight, the prone and panting Piejack surveyed upon his fishy clothing and sunburned flesh a bristle of fine needles. Incessant stinging enabled him to map mentally a pattern of perforation extending from his forehead to his shins. Miraculously spared from puncture were the tender digits protruding from the grubby gauze on his left hand. Unfortunately, because of the surgical bungling, his forefinger and thumb were now situated so far apart and at such inopportune angles as to render impossible the simplest of tweezing motions. Consequently Piejack had to rely on his weaker and less facile right hand to pluck at the tiny cactus spines, the number of which he calculated to exceed one hundred.

A less inspired degenerate might have been laid low by such a handicap, but Piejack quickly collected himself. He didn't much care who'd clobbered him, or why. He wasn't overly concerned about losing his shotgun, or forgetting where he'd beached the johnboat. Nor did he feel especially motivated to hunt down his former captive, the fatass suit with the video camera, before the law came looking.

Louis Piejack had only one thing on his mind: Honey Santana.

He was fixated in the twitchy, pathological style of true-blue stalkers, and as he lay throbbing among the rusted beer cans he found himself deliciously reliving the single lightning-quick grope that had catapulted him toward this adventure; a deftly aimed hand, snaking out to cup Honey's magnificent right breast as she'd unsuspectingly leaned over the display cooler to set on chipped ice a tray of fresh wahoo steaks. That she'd been wearing a bra had in no way diminished Piejack's thrill; if anything, the intimate crinkle of fingertip upon fabric had only heightened his arousal.

Honey's retaliatory malleting had caught him off guard, yet he'd experienced only the slightest ebb of lust as his nuts swelled to the size of Brazilian limes.

Soon thereafter Piejack had been abducted by the Miami thugs and subjected to the sadistic stone-crab torture.

In fact, his whole existence had been a scroll of searing agony since he'd fondled Honey Santana, yet he desired her more avidly than ever. He'd come to believe that she secretly felt the same way, a pathetic delusion fueled by Honey's surprise visit to his house. It was true that she'd hastily fled, but Piejack had chosen to interpret her apparent revulsion to his overtures as a tease.

Possessing Honey would be a triumph – and also a dagger in the soul of her ex-husband, the man who Piejack believed was responsible for the mutilation of his hand. He could hardly wait to be seen, arm in arm with his new mate, strolling the waterfront of Everglades City.

Piejack had no particular plan for capturing Honey; lust alone was his co-pilot. Even after the cacti encounter his focus remained singular and unbreakable, for his pain was so intense as to erase such primal distractions as thirst, hunger and exhaustion.

Under a rising moon he emerged from the pile of cans and on pricked knees began to ascend the shell mound from which he'd earlier fallen. After reaching the top he wilted feverishly, hurt pulsing in every pore. Feminine voices rose from the campsite below, and Piejack rallied with the hope that one of them belonged to Honey. He thought about the other woman in the group – the big blonde who'd gone topless in the kayak – and he fantasized for himself a star role in a writhing, glistening threesome. He recalled that the male camper was of lumpy build and not much good with a paddle, and from him Piejack foresaw minimal resistance. The man would either flee on impulse or be hurled into the creek.

Like a rheumatic old crocodile, Piejack began his long crawl, guided by the soft voices and a reddish smudge of flame at the edge of his vision.

> *Dear Geenie,*
> *Last night in my truck was magikal and prefect. I never had such amayzing you-no-what!*
> *Truly I believe we're destinationed to be together for eternalty, and I will do everthing in my par to make it happen!!! I am a man of my werd, as soon you'll find out.*
>
> > *Yours fourever,*
> > *V. Bonneville*

What a fucking Neanderthal, thought Boyd Shreave. The woman's obviously got a thing for primitive hunks.

'What are you doing down there with the flashlight?' Eugenie Fonda inquired. 'Or maybe I don't want to know.'

'Just reading,' Shreave replied crossly.

'Right. Under a blanket in the woods.'

'I'm not up for socializing. Sorry.'

She said, 'I'm not askin' you to square-dance, Boyd, I just want to know how you're feeling.'

'How do you think I feel? I Tasered myself in the schlong.'

'Did it get burned?'

'Don't pretend like you care.'

'Let me see.'

'No thanks,' Shreave said, too emphatically. Quickly he added, 'Not right now,' on the chance that Eugenie might later choose to demonstrate her concern in a more generous way.

'Why don't you come out and join us by the fire?' she asked.

'In a minute.'

Even more punishing than the fifty thousand volts was the withering embarrassment. Once the convulsions had ceased, Shreave had staggered to his feet, removed the now-broken stun gun from his pocket and mutely gimped away. He'd been sulking shamelessly ever since, certain that the two women had nothing more interesting than him to talk about.

Eugenie said, 'So, what're you reading down there?'

'A book.' He was strongly tempted to show her the front jacket of *Storm Ghoul*, just to get a rise.

'Must be a good one,' she said.

'Not really. It's pretty dull.'

Reading the tree trimmer's love letter depressed Boyd Shreave, although not because of the kindergarten spelling or even the leering allusion to Eugenie's seismic sexual energy. Shreave was bummed because the note was a black-and-white reminder that Van Bonneville was all about action. The guy had made good on his written vow, however crudely expressed. He'd actually gone out and killed his wife, in order to spend the rest of his life with the woman of his dreams.

Sure, he was a moron, but he wasn't a bullshitter. He was a man of his 'werd.'

Which was more than Shreave could say for himself.

He dimmed the flashlight and threw off the woolen blanket and followed Eugenie Fonda back to the campsite, where he surreptitiously re-stashed her memoir in the Orvis bag. The space case named Honey was heating a kettle over the fire.

'Green tea?' she offered.

Shreave sneered. 'I don't think so.'

'There was a raccoon over in the beer cans,' Eugenie reported, pointing up the hill. 'A big sucker, too, it sounded like.'

'Maybe that's who stole our kayaks,' Shreave said caustically.

'Honey also thought she heard a guitar.'

'A guitar, huh?' Shreave tossed a broken oyster shell into the flames. 'Sure it wasn't a harp? Maybe we're all dead and this is Heaven. That'd be my luck.'

Honey handed a steaming cup to Eugenie. 'Boyd's right, it probably wasn't anything. It was just in my head,' she said quietly.

Eugenie asked about panthers. Honey told her there were wild ones on the mainland. 'But only a few. They're almost extinct.'

'What a tragedy *that* would be,' Shreave muttered.

'They don't eat people, if that's what you're afraid of.'

Shreave laughed thinly. 'The only thing I'm afraid of is getting bored out of my skull. I don't suppose you two came up with a game plan.'

Eugenie said, 'We sure did. Our plan is to ignore all your dumb-ass comments.'

Honey raised a hand. 'Shhhh. Hear that?'

'Don't pay attention to her,' Shreave told Eugenie. 'She's a complete nut job, in case you didn't notice.'

Honey remarked upon how different Boyd had sounded when he'd phoned to sell her a cheap piece of Gilchrist County. 'You've got a wonderful voice when you're lying,' she said. 'The rest of the time you're just a whiny old douchebag.'

Eugenie laughed so hard that green tea jetted

through her front teeth. Shreave was furious but low on options. Honey emptied the kettle over the fire and said it was time to hit the sack.

'Big day tomorrow,' she added. 'We're gonna search the whole island 'til we find those kayaks.'

'What if they're not here?' Genie asked.

'Then I guess we start swimming. Either way, you'll need a good night's rest.'

Once it became clear that Eugenie had no intention of ministering to his wounded member, Shreave dragged his bedding out of the pup tent and relocated closer to the fire. He'd been camping only once, twenty years earlier, during a brief hitch with the Boy Scouts. His mother had signed him up as part of an ongoing (and ultimately futile) campaign to imbue her only male child with character. Almost immediately young Boyd had alienated the other Scouts with his nettlesome commentary and disdain for physical labor. By the time the troop made its first overnight expedition, Shreave had been accurately pegged as the resident slacker. Soon after midnight a prankster had opened his sleeping bag and set loose a juvenile armadillo, which innocently began to explore Shreave's armpits for grubs. The unhappy camper had reacted by clubbing the bewildered creature to death with his boom box, a second-degree misdemeanor resulting in the troop's ejection from the Lady Bird Johnson State Floral Gardens and Nature Preserve, and of course in Shreave's lifetime banishment from the Scouts.

Now, lying in the moonlight, Shreave tensely attuned himelf to the many sounds of the night. He felt foolishly exposed and defenseless against feral predators. What did that goofball Honey know about panthers? The hairs on his arms prickled when he heard an animal with heft – surely no raccoon – scraping slowly through the trees. Shreave groped around for a rock or a sturdy stick, but all he came up with was a handful of oyster shards.

'I smell fish.' It was Honey's voice.

'From the campers before us,' said Shreave. Secretly he was glad to know that someone else was awake.

'Not cooked fish. *Raw* fish,' she said. 'I swear I know that smell.'

Trying to be casual, Shreave said, 'I hear that critter you guys were talkin' about.'

'Sounds substantial, doesn't it?'

'For sure.'

'So go check it out,' Honey suggested. 'Don't forget your flashlight.'

Shreave rolled over, thinking: She's quite the comedienne.

'Nighty-night, Boyd.'

'Go to hell.'

After a while the noise in the trees stopped, and one of the women began to snore softly. Shreave had to piss like a fountain, but he was reluctant to venture out among the nocturnal fauna. Besides, the painful Taser mishap temporarily had taken the pleasure out of urination.

With no success he slapped at some gnats that had developed a fondness for his hair. Minute by wretched minute, the mystique of Florida was bleeding away. Bitterly Shreave reappraised his grandiose dream of launching a new life with Eugenie Fonda. If the trip continued on its present downward trajectory, the dimension of this particular failure would dwarf all the others in Shreave's lackluster past. As usual he deflected both blame and responsibility; cruel chance had imbedded him here – stranded on a scraggly island with a psychotic divorcée, an increasingly unresponsive girlfriend and a half-barbecued cock.

Lulled by the hiss of the dying campfire, Shreave was surprised when his thoughts turned to Lily back in Fort Worth. His longing was characteristically base and unsentimental; the memory stirring him was that of his heiress wife clad in those red thong panties, dry-humping his lap on the living room sofa. Shreave regretted not having taken advantage of that extraordinary interlude, for Lily – who by now must have figured out that he'd flown the coop – was lost to him forever.

He would have been shocked to know that he wasn't the only man on Dismal Key thinking about her.

The Indian had slipped away, leaving the young woman named Gillian to supervise Dealey. The investigator knew he was in trouble when she said, 'I think I'd make a good TV weather personality. They don't call 'em weathermen anymore – they're "weather personalities." Forget the hurricanes and tornadoes, but I'd love to do the winter ski reports. You ever been to Aspen?'

Dealey shook his head.

'Me neither. Park City?'

'I really need to sleep,' Dealey said.

'Let's make a demo tape.'

At first Dealey refused, but then the girl jabbed his gut with the sawed-off shotgun, a weapon with which she was clearly, and harrowingly, unfamiliar. So he took out the video camera and taped her holding the gun while she pretended to do a television weather report. When he replayed it for her to see, she said, 'Jesus, my hair's a wreck. Did you bring some conditioner?'

'Oh sure. And rose-petal bath crystals.'

Gillian said, 'Maybe I'll switch my major to communications. I can't see myself in a classroom full of third graders.'

'It's a stretch,' Dealey agreed.

'Or maybe I won't go back to college at all. I'll just stay here on the island with you and Thlocko.'

'Look, I need a favor. I want to call home and let my wife know I'm okay.'

Gillian looked more amused than sympathetic. 'You got a cell phone, Lester?' She'd decided he looked like a Lester and to address him that way.

'Two minutes is all I need. She's probably worried to death,' Dealey said.

'Where's your wedding ring?'

Dealey hesitated a half second too long while making up an answer. Gillian wagged a finger. 'You think just 'cause I'm young I can't tell when a guy's lying his balls off? I'm an expert, Lester, so you'd better watch out. I'm like a human polygraph!'

'Can I make the call or not?'

'To who?' Gillian was sighting the sawed-off through her toes.

Dealey said, 'I need to speak with the lady who hired me. I'm a private investigator.'

'For real? How cool is that!'

'At the moment, not cool at all.'

'By the way, I know how to use this,' Gillian said, hoisting the shotgun. 'Thlocko told me it was okay to blast away if you try anything funny. He told me to aim for the legs, in case you're really alive and not a spirit.'

'Mighty white of him,' Dealey said.

'So tell me your story, Lester, and stick to the truth.'

'Sure,' said Dealey, and he did.

Gillian thought it was fantastic. 'She's paying you twenty-five grand to tape her old man boning some bimbo! That's awesome, L-man.'

Dealey said, 'I won't see a dime, because I'll never get the triple-X shot that my client wants. She's a total kink.'

'And these are the kayak people we're talkin' about, right? The same ones camping near Beer Can Gulch.'

'The Yuppie couple from Texas, yeah. The trailer-park woman, she's not involved.'

Gillian was so delighted to learn some juicy details about the mysterious intruders that she gave Dealey permission to call his client.

'But first, my turn.' She motioned for the cell phone.

Dealey removed it from an inside pocket of his suit jacket and handed it to her. Gillian punched the number and waited.

'My mother,' she said to Dealey.

'Save me some battery.'

Gillian nodded and whispered, 'It's her machine, thank God.'

Dealey could hear the beep on the other end.

'Hey, Mom, just me,' said Gillian brightly. 'My cell's not workin' and I didn't want you guys to worry. Everything's awesome except I'm takin' some extra vacation. I broke up with Ethan, which you predicted of course, but now I met this new guy – he's real *real* different, and I bet you'll like him. Give my love to Dad, and I'll try again in a few days.'

She tossed the phone to Dealey and said, 'Whew! That's a load off. You want some privacy?'

'If you don't mind.'

'I'll be in the ladies' room.' She pointed toward a thicket at the edge of the clearing.

Dealey waited until she was out of sight. By moonlight he fished through his wallet for the scrap of paper upon which Lily Shreave had written her mobile number. She answered on the first ring.

'I hope this is good news, Mr. Dealey.'

'Yes and no,' he said.

'Uh-oh. Here we go.'

'The good part is, I got what you asked for.' He knew Boyd Shreave's wife would believe it.

'Penetration? You got penetration?'

'Yes, ma'am.'

'On the beach, right? And she was on top, wasn't she?'

'Big-time,' said Dealey. He had no intention of ripping Lily Shreave off, but a lie was still a lie. He might have felt worse about it, if she weren't such a perv.

'So what's the bad news?' she asked.

'I'm trapped. I can't get outta this fuckin' place.'

'And where exactly would you be?'

'I got no earthly idea, Mrs. Shreave. There's ten thousand goddamn islands out here, and I'm stuck on one of 'em.'

'With my twenty-five-thousand-dollar sex tape.'

'Correct,' Dealey said.

'May I ask how you got there?'

'At gunpoint.'

'Holy Christ,' said Lily Shreave. 'It wasn't Boyd, was it?'

'Get serious.'

'Please don't tell me you were kidnapped.'

'Twice,' Dealey said.

'But somehow you escaped.'

'Negative. Not by a long shot.'

'So who's got you now?' Lily Shreave demanded.

'Not important.' Dealey saw no benefit to admitting that he was the prisoner of a guitar-toting Seminole Indian and a college sorority girl.

'Here's what I need you to do,' he said to Mrs. Shreave, and he told her.

'I like it,' she said. 'You're a smart fella, Mr. Dealey. I'll call first thing in the morning.'

He held no illusion that she cared whether he lived or died. Getting her mitts on the video was all that mattered to her.

Dealey heard a rustling and Gillian stepped from the thicket. He said into the phone, 'I've gotta go.'

'Wait! One more question.'

'What?'

'The tape – how'd it turn out? Can you see ... *everything*?'

'The works,' Dealey said.

'Wow.'

'More like double wow.'

'I can't wait,' said Boyd Shreave's wife.

'Oh, you'll be surprised,' Dealey told her, and hung up.

Seventeen

Cecil McQueen died in a chokehold at a nightclub called Le Lube, where he and six friends had gone for a bachelor party. The branch supervisor of the trucking firm was being married the next day to his ex-wife's divorce accountant, and his buddies couldn't decide if it was a masterstroke or an act of self-destruction.

At the strip joint the men drank festively but set no records. Normally a shy person, Cecil McQueen surprised his companions when he bounded into the mud-wrestling pit to take on a dancer known as Big Satin, who outweighed him by fifty-three pounds and was unaware (as was Cecil) of his obstructed cardiac arteries. Afterward Big Satin felt terrible. So did Cecil's co-workers and supervisor, although the wedding went on as scheduled.

The police ruled the death as accidental, but nonetheless it dominated the TV news, which is how the victim's only son – then addressed as Chad – learned that his father had not perished while rescuing a vanload of orphans from a flooded drainage canal. That was the yarn his stepmother had cooked up.

Years later Sammy Tigertail often thought about his dad, a cheery and harmless soul who believed that the three essential ingredients of contentment were classic rock, Krispy Kreme doughnuts and a hot tub. It was the music that had cheered young Chad, even after he'd moved out to the Big Cypress and shed his name and turned forever away from white people (except for one). His affinity for rock was what had led to the foolish, soul-bruising lapse with Cindy, whom he'd met at a Stones concert in Lauderdale. Within ten seconds Sammy Tigertail had known she was poison, yet he'd willingly opened his veins.

And learned nothing from the ordeal, because the same thing seemed to be happening with Gillian.

'I'm gettin' a complex,' she told him. 'Why aren't you trying to do me?'

'You asked to be the hostage.'

'So?'

'Hostages don't get laid.'

'Who made up that stupid rule? Besides, I can tell you've been thinkin' about it.'

'Bull,' Sammy Tigertail said.

She rose on her tiptoes and tried to peck him on the chin. He dodged sideways and said, 'You don't understand.'

'About being nervous? I do so.'

He grabbed the rifle from the crook of a tree, and nodded toward Dealey. 'Keep an eye on Mr. Camera Man,' he told Gillian. 'I won't be long.'

'What if he tries somethin'? Like, jumps me and rips off my clothes?'

'Then shoot him. The shotgun's over there,' the Indian said.

'Okeydoke.'

'But aim low, in case he turns out to be real. I don't need to hassle with another dead body.'

'When you say low—'

'The legs.'

'Gotcha,' said Gillian.

On a rash impulse Sammy Tigertail leaned forward and kissed the top of her head, then he quickly moved into the night. The sky held enough moon that he was able to make headway without using a flashlight, though his sense of direction was as unreliable as ever. Fortunately, the island was small enough that it was difficult to stay lost. The Seminole eventually located the old oyster mound and took a position overlooking the campsite and the cistern. Embers from the fire glowed faintly, and Sammy Tigertail could make out the steepled shapes of two tents, and one bundled form on the ground.

He crept down the midden and, except for tripping once and dropping the rifle, his approach was practically furtive. Hearing snores, he assumed that all the kayakers were asleep. Quickly he padded into the clearing and snatched up a large duffel bag.

That's when a head poked out from one of the tents. Sammy Tigertail saw the movement and whirled, waving the rifle. His heart hammered.

'Easy, big guy,' the woman whispered.

'We need water!'

'Like we don't?'

'But I got the gun!' said Sammy Tigertail. 'Now, shut up.'

'Did you steal our kayaks?' The woman had a mild southern accent and light hair, but the angles of her face were obscured by a shadow. 'Hold on,' she said, squirming from the sleeping bag.

'What are you doin'?'

'Comin' with you.'

'No fucking way. Not again,' the Seminole said angrily.

The woman stood up and stepped into her shoes, some sort of rubberized Yuppie sneakers. She was a tall one.

'You've got the boats, and now the last of our water – I'll be damned if I'm stayin' out here to die,' she said.

A breeze stirred the mangroves and riffled the leaves of the big poinciana. The woman folded her arms against the chill and said, 'Well?'

Sammy Tigertail knew that if he left her behind, she would awaken the others, and they'd contact the authorities to report that a thieving redskin was loose on the island.

She said, 'I'll do whatever you want. And I mean *whatever*.'

The Seminole raised his eyes to the leering moon. The spirits seemed to be punishing him. He suspected it had something to do with Wilson, the dead tourist.

'You'll do anything?' he asked the woman.

She nodded.

'Then carry this bag.'

'Yes, bwana.'

'And be quiet,' said the Indian, 'or I'll cut off your tongue.'

The woman stuck it out for him to see, the pearl stud burnished by the moonlight. Sammy Tigertail frowned.

'Oh well. Some guys dig it,' she said.

'My girlfriend had one attached somewhere else. It didn't feel so good.'

The Indian turned and darted into the trees. He

heard the woman trailing behind him, breathing fast under the weight of the duffel. He expected her to start chattering like a crow, but she didn't. It was a nice surprise.

Thirty years in the seafood business combined with grossly irregular bathing habits had cloaked upon Louis Piejack a distinct and inconquerable funk. Were it cologne, the essence would have included the skin of Spanish mackerel, the roe of black mullet, the guts of gag grouper, the wrung-out brains of spiny lobster and the milky seepage of raw oysters. The musk emanated most pungently from Piejack's neck and arms, which had acquired a greenish yellow sheen under a daily basting of gill slime and fish shit. Nothing milder than industrial lye could have cleansed the man.

He stunk like a bucket of bait.

Honey Santana eventually would have pinpointed the smell – and the danger – were it not for an untimely pollen allergy that kept her clogged and sniffling. No sooner had she dozed off than Louis Piejack hoisted himself, with a hellish groan, into the old cistern. Woozy with pain, the spine-covered stalker was spying through a gap in the cinder blocks when Eugenie Fonda departed stealthily with a dark-skinned young gunman. Piejack felt no curiosity about the peculiar event; Honey was his only concern.

The person who would have been least surprised by the fishmonger's felonious pursuit was his wife, who two decades earlier had been the object of a more subtle courtship. At the time, Louis Piejack had been smoother and more attentive to hygiene, and in the meager male talent pool of rural Collier County he'd sparkled like a gem. After the wedding he'd gone downhill fast, and when his wife had threatened to leave he torched her mother's minivan and warned that it was only the beginning. Even when her family moved away to the Redlands, Becky Piejack remained with Louis out of sheer cold dread.

So awful was the marriage that she hadn't been entirely dismayed to learn she had cancer – anything to get out of the house. There were no chemotherapy facilities in Everglades City, so Becky looked forward to the twice-monthly trips to Gainesville as furloughs from her deviant and disgusting spouse. When after three years the oncologists pronounced her disease-free, Becky withheld the news from Louis and continued to travel every other week. On those long drives she often brought a young orchid collector named Armando and a box of Berlitz language tapes, with which she schooled herself in French and Portuguese. Becky Piejack was gearing up for the day when she'd gather the courage to leave her husband, which she assumed would require fleeing the continental United States. Either Paris or Rio sounded good.

In truth, it had been a long while since Louis Piejack had thought of his wife in a criminally possessive way. Except when inconvenienced by her illness, he seldom thought of her at all. Now, shivering on the concrete slab of the cistern, Piejack went about planning a new life of passion with Honey Santana. Once they returned to the mainland, he would immediately evict Becky and her hospital bed, along with the wicker furniture that he so detested. He might allow Honey to repaint the living area but not the bedroom, which would remain black with red crown molding. For a moving-in gift he'd buy his sex angel a set of new cookware, including a kettledrum fryer for wild boar and turkey. Then he'd put her back to work at the fish market, peeling shrimp or running the cash register, so that he could keep an eye on her. As for Honey's teenaged son, the smartass punk could go live with his old man.

At some point in his ruminations Louis Piejack experienced a new and unfamiliar pain – a hot welter of stings on the palm of his left hand, a location he could not access without gnawing through the surgical dressing. In the darkness Piejack hadn't seen the platoons of fire ants march the length of his aching arm and disappear through one of the ragged finger holes into the moist cocoon of dirty gauze and sticky tape. He didn't cry out, or even whimper. Stoically he ground his molars while the little red demons tore divots in his flesh.

He consoled himself with dream visions of his breathtaking goddess, who in real life lay snoring like a stevedore less than fifty feet away. To Louis Piejack, scorching physical agony seemed a small price to pay for the midlife companionship of a woman such as Honey Santana. He was morbidly amused to realize that the extremity now being devoured by insects was the same one that had touched her illicitly that tumultuous day at the market.

Go ahead and eat me, he mocked the ants. *See if I give a fuck.*

Perry Skinner followed Sandfly Pass to the Gulf and slowly headed up the coast, scouting the outermost islands for signs of campers. The wind had stiffened, pushing a troublesome chop that slapped the hull of the skiff and made silent running impossible. Another problem was debris in the water; the previous summer's hurricanes had uprooted scores of old mangroves and strewn their knobby skeletons throughout the shallow banks and creeks. To avoid an accident, Skinner was forced to use the spotlight continually, though it risked betraying their approach.

As the skiff entered a deeper bay, the waves kicked higher, misting salt spray. From the bow Fry shouted, 'Dad, you see that?'

Skinner had already spotted it – the flicker of fire on a nearby shore. He cut the engine and dimmed the spotlight.

'Is it them?' Fry asked anxiously.

'Son, I don't know.'

The breeze and the tide were at odds, foiling his drift and nudging the boat onto the flats. Skinner tilted the engine and picked up the long graphite pole. Fry watched him scale a wobbly platform above the outboard motor and said, 'You're kidding me.'

It took Skinner a few moments to steady himself. 'The water's only twelve inches deep. You got a better idea?'

He planted the double-pronged foot of the pole in the mud and, with slow tentative strokes, began pushing the skiff across the bank toward the island where the campfire burned. Backcountry guides made it look easy, but Skinner felt awkward and tense, rocking on the thin wafer of molded plastic. One slip and he'd tumble into the water or, worse, fall backward and crack his skull on the propeller.

Fry said, 'You're the one who needs a football helmet.'

Skinner gently poked him with the dry end of the pole. 'Keep your eyes peeled, ace. We don't need a welcome party.'

'Where's the gun anyway?'

'Just relax,' said Skinner.

Fry felt like hurling, he was so anxious. He kept flashing back to the moment when Louis Piejack's pickup had nearly run him down at the trailer park, and he wondered what he could have done to stop the guy from pursuing his mother. Fry had hated Mr. Piejack for groping her at the fish market, but he'd pegged him as just some twisted old turd – not a mad stalker.

The boy drummed his fingers on the gunwale and thought: Relax? No way.

'I hear somethin',' his father said from the back of the skiff.

Fry stopped tapping and listened. 'Sounds like . . . like a funeral or somethin'. People cryin'.'

'Where's it coming from? Can you make out anything?'

'Just shadows.' Fry balled his fists to keep from shaking.

By now his dad had pushed the skiff close enough for them to see the orange flames dancing and to smell the woody smoke. At first the shapes around the fire had looked like small pines, bowing and shaking in the breeze. Now Fry wasn't so certain. The moaning chorus swelled and faded, making him shudder. His father poled faster.

'We'll go ashore here,' Skinner announced, angling toward the beach. Four long strokes and the hull scraped up on the sand.

Fry hopped out and was beset with dizziness. 'It's gettin' cold,' he murmured to himself.

His father jumped down and with both hands hauled the skiff farther up on land, so that the rising tide wouldn't carry it away. Then he tossed Fry a sweatshirt, which the boy absentmindedly attempted to put on without removing his bulbous helmet.

'Dad, I'm stuck,' he said sheepishly.

Once extricated, he jogged after his father as they hurried away from the shoreline, into the trees. He felt like he was five years old again.

Skinner said, 'If I tell you to run for it, you damn well run.'

'Yeah, but where?'

'The other way, son. Opposite of me.'

'But—'

'Don't be lookin' back, either — I'll come find you later.'

'I can't go fast with this stupid thing on my head.'

'Pretend you're Mercury Morris.'

'Who?'

'Pitiful.' Skinner pretended to kick him in the pants. 'Come on, let's do it.'

Watchfully they moved through the scraggle and scrub, keeping parallel to the beach. The eerie keening sounds grew louder as they neared the campfire. Skinner dropped to a crouch and motioned for his son to do the same. They crossed a sandy clearing in a faint circle of moonlight and took cover in a stand of Australian pines.

Fry counted five hooded shapes twirling and dipping around a crudely dug fire pit. They wore white robes and weren't actually crying; it was a strident, wailing chant, with no discernible melody. A tall wooden cross had been planted on a dune overlooking the campsite.

'It's the Klan!' Fry whispered.

'They're a long way from home,' said Skinner.

Fry saw him reach beneath his sweatshirt and adjust a gun-shaped bulge in his waistband. It was possible he clicked off the safety.

'What're you gonna do, Dad?'

'Be my usual charming self.'

Nervously Fry followed him out of the pines. Skinner walked with casual purpose as he approached the moaners, who one by one stopped dancing and fell silent.

'Howdy,' Skinner said.

'Who are you, brother?' It was the tallest one; a man's voice.

'State wildlife commission. I'm lookin' for a man named Louis Piejack – he's wanted for poachin' shellfish.'

'Don't know the sinner,' said the tallest moaner. The others closed ranks behind him.

'How 'bout losin' those hoods?' Skinner asked genially.

The hoods turned out to be part of their white robes, each of which bore a breast emblem that read FOUR SEASONS – MAUI.

Definitely not the KKK, thought Fry with relief.

'We've nothing to hide,' the tallest moaner declared. He and the others obligingly revealed their faces. There were two men and three women, all shiny-cheeked and well fed. Neither Fry nor his father recognized them from Everglades City.

'I'm Brother Manuel,' the tall one volunteered, 'of the First Resurrectionist Maritime Assembly for God. We believe that Jesus our Savior has returned and is sailing the seven seas' – he paused to acknowledge the lapping surf – 'preparing to come ashore in all His glory and inspire the worldly to repent. We will welcome Him with prayer and rejoicing.'

Skinner nodded impatiently. 'Where you from, Manny?'

'Zolfo Springs, sir, and we're up to no mischief. We're here upon this blessed shore to baptize our newest sister, Miss Shirelle.'

She identified herself with a perky wave.

'You folks been drinkin'?' Skinner inquired.

Brother Manuel bridled. 'Wine only, sir. I can show you the passage in the Scriptures.'

'I'm certain you can. See anything strange out here tonight? We believe Mr. Louis Piejack is in the vicinity.'

One of the female moaners asked, 'How might we know this man?'

'One of his hands is taped,' Skinner said, 'like a mummy's.'

'Ah!'

'Plus he stinks like dead mudfish,' Fry added, quoting his mother.

One of the male celebrants revealed that they'd heard gunshots earlier in the evening. 'From over there,' he said, pointing across the waves.

'How many shots?' Skinner asked. He avoided eye contact with Fry, whom he knew would be alarmed. He purposely had not told his son about the shotgun that he'd seen in Piejack's johnboat on the river.

'Two rounds,' the man said.

'Sure it was gunfire? Sometimes campers bring fireworks.'

'Brother Darius is a deer hunter,' Brother Manuel explained. 'God's bounty, you understand.'

Sister Shirelle, the stoutest of the moaners, asked, 'May we invite you to stay for the baptism? Join us in the divine waters where our Savior sails.'

'Some other time,' Skinner said tightly.

Another woman called out, 'Sir, may I inquire about the boy?'

'That's my son.'

'I couldn't help but take note of the headpiece. Is he afflicted in some way?'

'Yeah, he's afflicted with one motherfucker of a migraine. He crashed his skateboard into a truck.'

Brother Manuel clasped his hands. 'Then let us pray for the youngster's healing. Come, brothers and sisters!'

The moaners re-hooded and commenced a new chant, as dissonant as the others. Sister Shirelle, dauntingly braless, led the group in improvisational writhing.

Fry jerked his father's sleeve and whispered, 'You think they really heard a gun?'

'*Vamos ahora*,' Skinner said.

They'd gone about fifty yards down the beach when Brother Manuel broke from the dance ring and barreled after them, yelling, 'Friends, wait! Whoa there!'

Away from the firelight, Fry could no longer see his father's expression. Not that he needed to.

'A-hole,' he heard him mutter.

'Should we run?' the boy asked hopefully. He was aware of Skinner's low opinion of preachers and zealots. One time his dad had turned a fire hose on a roving quartet of Jehovah's Witnesses who'd accosted him at the crab docks.

'See, this is the problem with religion, son. They

can't keep it among themselves, they gotta cram it down everyone else's throat.' He'd hurried his pace, but the long-legged moaner was gaining on them. 'It's been a long time since I looked at the Bible, but I don't recall Jesus makin' a damn nuisance of Himself.'

'He's almost here, Dad.'

'Yeah, I know.' Perry Skinner stopped and whirled around.

Huffing and sweaty, the tall moaner advanced with the grinning, witless confidence of the self-righteous. From his purloined hotel robe he produced a folded pamphlet, which he held out to Skinner as if it were a deed to a gold mine.

'No offense, sir, but by your coarse language I could tell it's been awhile since you brought your soul to church. Here, please take the Word.'

Fry held his breath. Slowly his father drew the .45 and placed the barrel upon the florid tip of Brother Manuel's nose.

'Manny,' Skinner said, 'I got my own word: *Semiautomatic.*'

The leaflet fluttered from the moaner's fingers. 'Easy, dog,' he said.

'*This* is my church,' Skinner went on, 'this island out here and all the others — so many islands that nobody's counted 'em all. And the sky and the Gulf and the rivers that roll out of the 'glades, all of it's *my* church. And you know what? God Almighty or whatever His name might be, I believe He'd approve.'

Fry said, 'Come on. Let's go find Mom.'

The boy was more worried than before. Learning of the gunshots plainly had set his father on edge, too.

'Manny, I'm gonna ask you a personal question and I expect an honest, upright Christian answer,' Skinner said. 'You're fornicatin' with Sister Shirelle, aren't you? You already baptized that young lady in your own special way, am I right? Told her to close her eyes and get down on her knees and wait for sweet salvation.'

Half-lit by the moon, Brother Manuel blinked once in slow motion, like an anemic tortoise.

'Thought so,' Skinner said. 'Look – me and my son are gonna leave now, and you're gonna go back to your people and boogie for Christ and forget you ever laid your sorry heathen eyes on me. Got it?' Skinner lowered the .45.

'Amen,' said the moaner and ran away, his white robe flapping like a shredded sail.

Eighteen

Boyd Shreave dreamed he was working at Relentless, phoning suckers at dinnertime. He was trying to sell residential lots on a sodded landfill in a future housing development called Lesion Hills. To the east was a pig farm and to the west was a dioxin factory; upwind, a crematorium. All unsavory details were perversely included in the telephone script, and elucidated with appalling candor to prospective customers.

It was a nightmare. Everyone whom Shreave called would insult him savagely then hang up. When he turned to commiserate with Eugenie Fonda, he was aghast to find her cubicle occupied by his wife, who menaced him crudely with a Taser. And the dream got worse: Shreave neglected to observe that the last number on his call sheet belonged to one D. Landry, a disaster compounded by his failure to recognize his own mother's voice until he was midway through the sales pitch, when he heard a string of witheringly familiar debasements that culminated with the phrase 'worthless pile of muskrat shit.'

Shreave awoke in a sweat. He remembered where he

was, though it gave him no comfort. His wristwatch showed 3:46 a.m. He called out Genie's name but didn't get a response. With larval contortions he shed his sleeping bag.

The stars were gold and the temperature was falling and the campfire was dead. In such a setting it seemed reasonable for a man to seek a snuggle with his girl-friend. Through the shadows Shreave crawled toward the tent that held Eugenie, only to find it empty.

'She hit the bricks,' Honey Santana said, startling him.

'Not funny.'

Honey's head popped out of the other tent. 'She ran off with an Indian. I peeked.'

'You can do better than that,' said Shreave.

'Some big Indian with a gun. I know what I saw.'

'Just tell me where she is.'

Honey said, 'This is hopeless,' and closed the flap.

Shreave shouted for Genie again and again. He grabbed his flashlight and went stomping into the trees, a decision quickly reconsidered and reversed. Angrily he stood outside Honey's tent and com-manded her to reveal what had really happened.

'I told you already,' she said.

Shreave foolishly reached inside, snatched the end of the sleeping bag and attempted to shake her out. Honey's second kick landed flush on his chin, causing him to buckle. Through a starburst of pain he fumbled to realign his lower jaw with the rest of his face.

She said, 'I'm nominating you for the Dickhead Hall of Fame. Seriously.'

Once again, assertiveness had brought pain and indignity to Shreave. It seemed doubtful that he'd ever transform himself into the sort of physical beast that aroused women such as Eugenie Fonda. His only consolation was that she hadn't been there to witness him getting kicked in the kisser.

'This is all on you,' he whined at Honey, 'for scamming us into this trip. It's your fault she got kidnapped.'

'Kidnapped? That Indian was ripping off our supplies when your girlfriend begged to sneak away with him. She practically offered to ball him on the spot.'

'Liar!'

'She moves fast, Boyd.' Honey emerged from her tent and started to build a new fire. 'I pretended to snore so he'd think I was sleeping.'

'Why the hell didn't you do something?'

'Gosh, I don't know. Because he was holding a rifle?' She set a match to the tinder and watched it flare. 'Anyway, we're alone now, so let's have a talk.'

'What about?'

'You,' Honey said.

The subject appealed immensely to Shreave.

'Tell me an enthralling life story,' she said, 'so I can understand you better.'

'Not a problem.' Shreave misread her interest in the predictable way. His jaw was throbbing but if she wanted to talk, he'd talk. Whatever floated her boat.

Honey said, 'First, you should get up off your knees – no, never mind. That'll work.'

Turning away, she opened the remaining duffel and removed some items out of Shreave's sight. She asked him to shut his eyes and, idiotically, he complied. His dismay over Eugenie's defection was rapidly evaporating at the prospect of intimacy with another handsome woman, even if she happened to be wacko.

The campfire was blazing again. The heat felt good on Shreave's face. He heard Honey stepping across the broken oyster shells and then moving about the bushes. He hoped that she'd snuck off to get undressed.

Moments later she was standing behind him, whispering: 'Give me your hands, Boyd.'

He was delighted to oblige. She smelled wonderful, and he noticed he was getting hard – a marvelous development in the wake of the stun-gun accident. Not even the sound of duct tape being ripped from a roll crimped Shreave's rising anticipation.

When he turned to peek, Honey thumped him smartly on the head. Thinking only of his erection and the daring ways it might be gratified, he obediently remained motionless while she taped his wrists and ankles behind him. Then something as light as a lei, though more coarsely textured, settled around his neck.

'Don't dare move,' Honey said.

Again she slipped away. Soon there was a slight noise behind him.

'What're you up to now?' Those were Shreave's final words before the rope drew snug around his throat.

His eyes popped open and Honey reappeared, divinely backlit by the fire glow. Shreave was disappointed to observe that she was fully clothed. She informed him that he was attached to a noose looped over a poinciana bough. If he attempted to pull free, she said, the slipknot at the base of his neck would come tight and possibly strangle him.

Shreave believed her, although he clung like an ape to his carnal ambitions. He'd watched a cable documentary about asphyxiating sexual practices, and he speculated that Honey was seeking to initiate him. Spurred by Eugenie's drop-of-a-hat betrayal, he'd decided to let himself be seduced no matter what the dangers might be.

Honey said, 'Sorry about this contraption, but you already assaulted me twice.'

Shreave grunted an objection but said nothing. He feared that even the smallest muscle twitch required for speech might cause the rope to cinch down a crucial millimeter or two.

'Go ahead and talk. It's really not that tight,' Honey said.

Kneeling ramrod-straight, he wheezed, 'I didn't "assault" you, I just tackled you.'

'You'd be in jail if you tried that on Biscayne Boulevard.'

'And that business with the sleeping bag, *I'm* the one who got hurt!'

'The veins in your neck are bulging.'

'Whatever. Can we hurry up and get on with this?'

'Certainly, Boyd.'

'Well . . . ? You gonna strip me or spank me, or what?'

Honey looked perplexed. 'It hadn't crossed my mind.'

'Oh, come on.'

She shrugged. Gloomily Shreave realized she was telling the truth.

'Goddammit,' he said. It was impossible to envision a brute like Van Bonneville being tricked and tied up by a deranged single mom.

Honey sat cross-legged by the fire and brushed her hair; short, emphatic strokes. 'What'd you do before you became a telephone solicitor?' she asked.

'Sales.'

'What did you sell?'

'My knees hurt.'

For padding, Honey folded a woolen blanket and scrunched it beneath him.

'So, what did you sell?' she asked again.

'The usual shit,' he muttered.

'Tell me all about it.'

'Genie's in on this, isn't she? You and her cooked up this sick little scene just for giggles.'

Honey laughed. 'You think very highly of yourself, Boyd. I'm sure Genie's got bigger fish to fry.'

He felt his ears get hot.

'Ever sell cars?' she asked.

'Sure. Buicks and Saabs.'

'What else?'

'TV sets,' he said. 'Pet supplies. Orthotics.'

'Oh my God, that's a riot!'

She has a great smile, Shreave thought bitterly, for a psycho. 'I'm glad one of us is having fun,' he said.

Honey scooted closer. She repositioned the rope above his Adam's apple and smoothed the collar of his ripening Tommy Bahama shirt.

'Don't worry, there's a point to all this,' she told him.

'I can't wait.'

What are the odds? he wondered. One sales call out of thousands – and some crazed bitch freaks out, tracks me down, lures me into a swamp and makes me her prisoner.

'You have kids?' Honey asked.

'Not me. Not for all the gold in Fort Knox.'

'Being a parent is no picnic, that's for sure. Good luck trying to raise a kid with a positive outlook. Face it, we live in a stinking shitwash of cruelty and greed and rotten manners. Look at you, Boyd. You're a classic specimen.'

'Not this again,' he sighed.

'Yes, this again! My one and only son is growing up in a culture where the values are so warped that a creep like yourself can masquerade as a respectable citizen.'

Shreave bridled and said, 'I never hurt anybody.'

'So, talk to me. Help me figure out what makes your engine run,' Honey said.

'First let's go look for Genie. What if she's in trouble?'

'We're *all* in trouble, Boyd. For heaven's sake, don't you read the papers—'

They were interrupted by a single gunshot, the brittle echo soaring away on the wind. A scream followed.

Honey jumped up. 'That's not poachers. It's the Indian, I bet.'

And away she ran, Shreave hollering after her: 'Don't leave me here! Don't you fucking leave me all alone!'

In his agitation he toppled sideways, the rope rubbing into the loose folds of his neck. It hurt, yet he seemed able to breathe without difficulty.

Until a voice at the edge of the shadows hissed, 'Don't be scared, asswipe. You ain't alone.'

Sammy Tigertail ordered his latest voluntary hostage to sit with Gillian and the white man who might or might not be a death spirit. The Indian kept for himself one jug of water and two power bars, and he strictly rationed to the others what remained in the stolen duffel bag. He hadn't meant to take all the kayakers' food, but there had been no time to sort the contents.

Alone he receded to the far end of the clearing and hunkered down with the Gibson. He was struggling to pick out the opening notes of 'Tunnel of Love' when his spectral nemesis, Wilson, lurched out of the woods. It was the first time that the deceased tourist had appeared while Sammy Tigertail was wide awake, and it caught the young Seminole off guard. He'd been hoping that he had seen the last of the carping corpse.

Wilson looked worse than ever. His sodden clothing was rotting to rags, and the scavengers had made a grisly patchwork of his flesh.

'*I asked you to move my body somewhere warm,*' he said reproachfully.

'Beat it,' said the Indian.

'*That goddamn river is colder than a witch's titty. And look here what the crabs and snappers did—*' Wilson displayed the most gruesome of his recent mutilations. '*It's lonely out there, man.*'

'I can't help you.' Sammy Tigertail had never felt so low. He was failing as a hermit, and failing as the great-great-great-grandson of a Seminole chief. His mission to isolate himself from the corrupt white world had backfired completely; he was now besieged by white people, dead and alive. He'd even kissed one.

'*Nice ax.*' Wilson nodded admiringly toward the guitar.

'Don't touch.'

'*Can you play "Folsom Prison Blues"?*'

'Never heard of it.' Sammy Tigertail thought a jolt of pain might expunge the nagging apparition, so he scratched his own forehead with the broken oyster shell that he'd been using for a pick.

The dead tourist did not disappear. '*That was really stupid. Now you're bleeding*,' he said. '*Actually, I'm jealous*.'

'Hey, don't blame me 'cause your heart gave out. Maybe you should've laid off the booze and french fries.' Sammy Tigertail felt a tickle of warmth roll down his nose.

Wilson said, '*What about Garth Brooks? You know his stuff, right? I'll sing one, so you can figure out the chords*.'

'I wish you wouldn't,' said the Indian.

Wilson waved him off and began crooning mercilessly about a girl in Louisiana. The lyrics made Sammy Tigertail remember the way he'd felt after his first night with Cindy, before learning of her problems with homemade methamphetamines, check kiting and serial infidelity. He expected he would be no less smitten by Gillian once he slept with her, and no less shattered when her true dysfunctional self emerged. Each new verse of the country song deepened the Indian's melancholy.

When the white man finished, he said, '*Well – can you play it?*'

Sammy Tigertail noticed that blood from his self-inflicted laceration was dripping onto the neck of the Gibson. He hurriedly wiped off the frets and braced the instrument upright between his knees. Then he reached for his rifle.

Wilson chuckled. '*Don't waste your bullets, bro.*'

With one arm the Seminole aimed the barrel at Wilson's algae-bearded face. 'Worth a try,' he grumbled, and squeezed the trigger.

Wilson didn't flinch, but on the other side of the

clearing one of the women hostages shrieked. Sammy Tigertail felt sick.

'*Now you done it*,' said the dead tourist, dissolving to fog.

For Dealey, dawn couldn't come soon enough. After the Seminole had shown up with Boyd Shreave's girl-friend, Gillian promptly had ratted out the private investigator.

Eugenie Fonda confronted him as if he were a common rest-room peeper: 'This is for real? Boyd's wife is paying you to spy on me and him?'

'And take dirty movies,' Gillian interjected helpfully.

'Pitiful.'

Dealey said, 'It's my job. No lectures, please.'

They were sitting in a semicircle sharing dried pineapple chunks and passing a jug of water. Sammy Tigertail sat off by himself, morosely picking at his guitar. There was a consensus that he ought to be left unbothered.

'That's some scummy job you've got,' Eugenie said to Dealey.

'The truth can be scummy merchandise, Miss Fonda. Which, by the way, is a totally bogus name. Your real one is Hill.'

Eugenie nipped her lower lip. 'I suppose I should be impressed.'

'Believe me,' Dealey said, 'I wish I hadn't touched this goddamn case – I've never run up against so many card-carryin' fruitballs in all my life.'

Gillian said, 'Tell her how much the guy's old lady was gonna pay for the money shot! Go on, Lester, she won't believe it.'

'My name's not Lester.'

'The *what* shot?' Eugenie asked.

'Mrs. Shreave happens to be a kink,' Dealey said. 'I got all the stills and video she'd ever need, but she wanted more.'

'Needed for what – a divorce? Oh please,' Eugenie said.

Dealey raised his hands. 'Why do you think wives hire me?'

Gillian couldn't restrain herself. 'Twenty-five thousand bucks! That's what she was gonna pay for a triple-X shot of you and your boyfriend. That's why Lester came all this way.'

'Twenty-five grand?' Eugenie had to laugh.

Dealey said, 'For what it's worth, nobody's seen the other tapes or pictures except me and my client.'

Which was untrue. However, Dealey felt no need to enlighten Eugenie about the on-line popularity of her stellar blow job at the delicatessen. After all, he'd scrupulously doctored the photograph to obscure her face.

He was surprised to hear her say, 'Show me what you got, Lester. I'm curious.'

Gillian piped up eagerly, 'Me too. Let's see.'

'Sorry. It's all in a lockbox back in Fort Worth.' The investigator thought: What is it with these women?

Gillian colorfully shared the tale of her sorority sister turning up on a *Girls Gone Wild* video, then she asked Dealey, 'What's the all-time freakiest thing you ever got on tape?'

'That's easy,' he said. 'Threesome in River Oaks – the two guys wore Road Runner masks and the woman was Wile E. Coyote.'

Gillian clapped. 'Tell me you didn't make copies of *that* one!'

Eugenie steered the conversation back to Lily Shreave's twenty-five-thousand-dollar offer. 'Now, what exactly did she want you to get?'

'The impossible,' Dealey said.

'Nothing's impossible.'

'She's got a thing for close-ups. Let's leave it at that.'

Eugenie smiled cheerlessly. 'If I'd known Boyd and I were on camera, I would've kicked it up a notch or two.'

'You did just fine,' Dealey said.

Gillian confessed that she'd seen only one porn film, at a fraternity-house party. '*The Fellatio Alger Story*. It was so boring I fell asleep.'

'Boring wouldn't be bad after the last two days I've had. Boring would be a treat,' the private investigator said.

Eugenie was pacing. 'How the hell do we get out of here?'

'Talk to *him*.' Gillian jerked a thumb across the clearing toward Sammy Tigertail, who appeared to have lapsed into a trance while playing his guitar.

Dealey helped himself to another chunk of pineapple. 'Well, I'm gettin' rescued tomorrow,' he said matter-of-factly. 'You're both welcome to hitch a ride – in fact, I'd strongly recommend it.'

'Done,' said Eugenie.

Gillian declined. 'I'm totally stayin'. He kissed me tonight.'

'The Indian?' Dealey smiled wearily, thinking: True love in the mangroves.

'He's an Indian? But his eyes are blue,' Eugenie said.

'A Seminole, most definitely,' Gillian reported. 'I'm

still waitin' to get the full story.' She turned to Dealey. 'So, Lester. Who's comin' to rescue you?'

The investigator said it wasn't important. 'I'm goin' home to Texas in one piece, that's all that matters.'

'Without the money shot,' Eugenie reminded him. 'Boyd's wife will be seriously bummed.'

'Ask me if I give a shit.' Dealey took a swig from the water bottle. 'Something real bad's going to happen on this island, and I don't want to be here when it does.'

'Me neither,' said Eugenie, a millisecond before the blue-eyed Seminole's rifle went off and Gillian screamed and Dealey dropped like a moose.

Nineteen

Honey Santana believed there might be hope for the world if she could save a man as empty as Boyd Shreave. She wanted to try one more time.

'The Indian shot somebody. I couldn't see who,' she told him when she returned.

'Get this goddamn noose off my neck.'

'It's just a slipknot, Boyd.'

The rope came undone as easily as a shoelace. Shreave rolled to his knees and whispered, 'You're a sicko.'

After peeling the tape from his ankles and wrists, Honey offered him some dry cereal. 'It's all we've got. The Indian took everything else.'

'There's somebody hidin' out there.' Shreave glanced anxiously behind him. 'I never saw the guy but he sounded real close. Said he's watchin' us the whole time.'

Honey made a torch by fastening Shreave's natty Indiana Jones hat to a driftwood limb, squirting it with lighter fluid and holding it in the embers. She walked the perimeter of the campsite and found no sign of another intruder. She didn't look inside the cistern.

'There's nobody in the bushes, Boyd.' She believed he'd cooked up the story to frighten her into fleeing the island with him.

'Who is he? Tell me!' Shreave demanded.

'Eat your Cheerios.'

Honey reflected upon what she'd done – tracking down this disagreeable stranger and suckering him with a phony Florida vacation. She didn't feel guilty and she didn't feel crazed; frustrated is what she was. After Fry was born, her low tolerance of cretins, liars and lowlifes had dwindled to zero. She came to regard all of them, from the leering bag boy at Winn-Dixie to the thieving third-term congressman, as potential threats to the happiness and well-being of her offspring. If a common bottom feeder such as Boyd Shreave could be reformed, Honey reasoned, the future would be incrementally brighter for all mankind, including Fry.

It wasn't an easy theory to sell, and Perry Skinner had never bought it. Neither had her son. Honey was aware that she sometimes appeared to them as naïve and obsessive, even borderline manic.

'You asked why I did this, Boyd, how come I went to all the trouble of tricking you down here,' Honey said. 'Well, apparently I'm trying to fix the entire human race, one flaming asshole at a time.'

Shreave sniggered. 'Good luck, sister.'

'You didn't even ask about your girlfriend. What's the matter with you?'

Shreave rubbed his arms nervously. 'The scream didn't sound like Genie. It sounded like a girl.'

'I couldn't get close enough to the Indian's camp to see who it was. Don't you love her, Boyd?'

'I'm not gettin' my brains blown out over some chick

273

who ran out on me.' He snatched a handful of cereal and crammed his cheeks. 'Let's go find those damn kayaks and get away from here.'

Honey saw that he was genuinely frightened. She said, 'They're hidden in some trees on the other end of the island. I spotted them on the way back from the Indian's.'

'Then what are we waitin' for?' Shreave leapt up and grabbed her arm.

Honey easily shook free. 'Dawn is what we're waiting for. There's something you need to see.' One last chance to awaken your shriveled soul, she thought.

He lunged toward her, then halted. Again he turned toward the woods, straining to listen. 'This was part of the setup, right? You got some goon in the trees, waitin' to kick out my teeth.'

Honey said, 'Nobody's there. Nobody's watching.' She had no fear of Shreave, who was as unimposing as any man she'd ever met.

His voice dropped to a growl. 'Listen, you psychotic twat. This is a goddamn suckhole and we're gettin' out *now*.'

'No, Boyd, it's an incredibly peaceful and inspiring place,' she said, 'and I'm not leaving until morning. You want to sail off on your own, be my guest.'

'Un-freaking-believable. You won't even show me where the kayaks are?'

Honey said no. Shreave called her another crude name and glared into the night. Then he sat down, fuming, by the campfire.

'Try to keep an open mind,' Honey told him.

'Just shut the hell up,' he said.

*   *   *

The rifle slug had ricocheted off a branch and passed through Dealey's right shoulder, exploding the rotator-cuff joint. As he rocked in and out of consciousness, he wondered if he was dying. It seemed possible, judging by the pain.

He found himself speculating about who might show up at his funeral, in the event his body was returned in a recognizable condition to Fort Worth. The visitor list would be short – two or three other private investigators with whom he occasionally hoisted a few beers; an aunt from Lubbock who was so senile that she was still mailing campaign donations to Barry Goldwater; his landlady and her yodeling poodle; a bisexual nephew who hung drywall in Austin; possibly one or two ex-wives, snorkeling for loose change.

Not appearing at the ceremony would be Dealey's next of kin, a younger brother who was a halibut fisherman in British Columbia and forbidden by the terms of his parole from leaving the province. Nor would any of Dealey's past girlfriends be at the funeral, all having married and long ago terminated correspondence.

Dealey was not sentimental, and the prospect of a sparsely attended memorial didn't bother him. A more nagging concern was the safe-deposit drawer he kept at the Bank of America branch on Ridglea Place. The private investigator regretted leaving no instructions in his will regarding the box, which meant the lock would be drilled and the contents inventoried for his modest estate. His avaricious ex-spouses would insist.

Inside the bank drawer, awaiting the eyes of some unwary probate functionary, was a small trove of trysts, betrayals and adulterous moments, including

Eugenie Fonda's virtuoso number at the delicatessen on Summit. Dealey's interest in such a collection wasn't salacious, but rather one of stout professional pride. The photographs and videotapes stood as triumphs of solo surveillance, the greatest hits from his life as a snoop. The paper files he diligently expurgated every three years, but the most sensational visuals were faithfully preserved. Having always felt underrated by his peers, Dealey found comfort and validation in this secret gallery, which he revisited no more than four or five times a month. Of course he'd never intended for such tawdry gems to reach the public domain, as the fallout would be both tumultuous and career-ending.

Hey, there's the wife of Zeke Gibbons, our new city councilman, checking into the downtown Hilton with her Bavarian riding coach . . .

And there's the husband of Mary Lisette Scowron, chair of the local Justice for DeLay committee, nestling on a Utah ski lift with a dancer for the Mavericks . . .

And, whoa, there's the middle daughter of the Rev. Jimmy Todd Barnwell, televangelist and on-call spiritual adviser to our governor, entertaining a vanload of longboarders on South Padre . . .

Fucking beautiful, thought Dealey. It's just as well I'll be six feet under when the shit hits.

He felt his suit jacket and shirt being cut away, and he shivered as the night air awakened his wound. Cracking one eye, he saw a handsome ash-blond woman kneeling over him. She appeared to be disrobing.

That cinches it, he thought. I must be dead already.

* * *

Eugenie Fonda capably administered first aid, irrigating the puckered entry hole with water heated over the campfire coals. Then she removed a sweater that she'd borrowed from Honey and used it to stanch the bleeding.

'One time a guy almost croaked on me in bed,' she was saying. 'Lucky I'd just passed a CPR class. I kept him goin' till the paramedics got there, and guess what? He still had his hard-on when they carried him out on the stretcher – that's all you need to know about men.'

Gillian said admiringly, 'Wow.'

Downcast, Sammy Tigertail hovered near Dealey's motionless form. 'It was an accident. It wasn't him I wanted to hit.'

Eugenie doubted that the injured man was going to die. 'But a doctor would be helpful,' she said, adding with a wink: 'Even a medicine man.'

Gillian tugged the Indian's shirttail. 'I told you he was real, Thlocko. I told you he wasn't a ghost.' She wiped the blood from the gash on Sammy Tigertail's forehead. 'What'd you do to yourself?' she whispered.

Dealey stirred and briefly fluttered an eyelid. The Seminole remained glum. He dumped out the stolen duffel bag in a futile search for a medical kit.

'Exactly who were you shooting at?' Eugenie asked.

'A dead tourist.'

'If you say so.'

'Thlocko is, like, haunted,' Gillian explained.

Eugenie snapped open Dealey's travel cases to inspect the camera equipment. The Seminole bent down and felt the investigator's wrist for a pulse. He said, 'At day-break you two take him back to the mainland. Somehow we'll squeeze his fat ass into the canoe.'

Gillian didn't want to go. 'Lester said he was gettin' rescued tomorrow. Why don't we just wait?'

Sammy Tigertail frowned. 'Who did he say was coming?'

'I dunno. Somebody he called on his cell,' she said.

'No! I don't want anybody else on this island.'

'What's the difference?' Gillian asked.

'The difference is, I don't want to go to jail.' Sammy Tigertail believed he would be arrested for shooting the white man in the business suit. He was also fairly sure that he'd killed the fishy-smelling white man with the bandaged hand; the one he'd clobbered with the rifle butt.

And last but not least: the Wilson situation.

The Indian said, 'We're not hangin' around waitin' for the Coast Guard or the Collier goddamn County sheriff, understand? You girls are takin' this poor bastard back to Everglades City soon as the sun comes up—'

'Just a minute,' Gillian cut in. 'Lester told me there's a motorboat somewhere on the island. That's how he got here.' She looked at Eugenie Fonda. 'You remember the way back, right? You don't need me.'

'No, sweetie, I'd need a miracle.'

Sammy Tigertail said, 'I'll find the damn boat and I'll draw up a chart, but you're *both* going. I'm through.'

He swung the rifle by the barrel, beating it furiously against a tree stump until it broke into pieces.

'Here. Don't forget this one.' Gillian reached for the sawed-off shotgun.

The Seminole shook his head. He stretched out on the ground and covered his face with his arms. Eugenie aimed Dealey's Nikon and snapped a frame.

Gillian drew her aside and said, 'He's really not a bad guy. Just majorly messed up.'

'I never meet the ones who aren't,' Eugenie said.

'But, see, I want to stay.'

'You slept with him yet?'

Gillian blushed. 'I'm workin' on that.'

'Well, he *is* good-lookin'—'

'Please don't try to snake him for yourself.'

Eugenie chuckled tiredly. 'Just so you know, I'd do whatever it takes to get off this island, and that includes hand jobs, blow jobs, butt jobs, even singin' opera stark naked. Nothin' personal, okay? But it's windy and cold and I'd love a bowl of French onion soup, so I'm definitely on my way to the Ritz, one way or another.'

'But Thlocko said he'd find the boat! He promised to make a map.' Gillian understood that Eugenie possessed advanced powers of persuasion over men. 'You don't have to screw him or anything. He's not like that.'

'Of course he isn't. You want some free advice?'

'Not really. Could you give us, like, some privacy?'

'First show me how to work the video.'

Gillian looked alarmed. 'I don't want me and him on tape!'

Eugenie patted her hand. 'Don't worry. I would never.'

Gillian instructed her about Dealey's minicam. 'I did a fake weather report – you can play it back with that button. I was thinking it might be cool to try TV.'

'You're cute enough for it,' Eugenie said.

'Check out the video and let me know. A "weather personality" is what they call the job. I'd have to take some, like, meteorology classes and probably switch majors, but that's okay.'

'So you'll go back to school?'

Gillian glanced at the Indian, who was lying mute and miserable next to Lester on the ground. She said, 'I guess. If this thing with Thlocko doesn't turn serious.'

Eugenie said, 'His kind of serious is too serious, trust me. You got a flashlight I can borrow?'

Gillian found one among the Indian's supplies and handed it to Eugenie, who went off toting Dealey's video case into the darkness. Gillian thought: That girl's not scared of anything.

'Where's she going?' Sammy Tigertail raised up on one elbow. 'Tell her to get back here.'

Gillian walked over and lay down on top of him, her lips lightly touching his neck and her breasts pressing against the warmth of his chest. She could feel his heart pounding, and it made her smile.

'This time you be the alligator,' she said.

The moaners had been right. Somebody was firing a gun.

'Dad?'

'Yeah, I heard it.' Skinner nudged the throttle and aimed the skiff into the waves.

Fry bounced like a sack of apples in the bow. The football helmet felt as if it weighed twenty pounds. Three hundred yards from the island his father raised the engine and started poling again. Fry was in charge of the spotlight.

'You sure this is where the shot came from?'

'Fifty-fifty. So damn windy it's hard to tell.'

'There's no beach like at the other place,' Fry observed.

'I'm gonna stuff the boat in the mangroves. Give me some light off the starboard.'

'You got it.' The beam cut a smoky purple groove through the dark. Fry was growing numb from riding in the cold, but numb wasn't bad. It kept him from breaking down when he thought about his mother.

'Does Mr. Piejack have a gun?' he asked.

Perry Skinner said nothing. He was huffing up on the platform, battling the wind and the current. Fry heard the tip of the pole crunching against a submerged oyster bar.

'Dad, does Louis Piejack keep a gun?'

'That was a rifle we heard.'

'Yeah, so?'

'Piejack's got a shotgun, a crappy little sawed-off. You can shut down that spotlight now, we're almost there.'

Fry hardly ever thought about the divorce; when it had happened, he wasn't surprised and certainly not traumatized. His mother and father were so different that he'd long been baffled by their marriage. He was now old enough to understand that Honey Santana and Perry Skinner cared in some eternal and deep-running way for each other, but from his earliest memories it seemed clear that they had no business living under the same roof. Just as Fry couldn't picture his own life without both of them in it, he couldn't picture the two of them together again. For his dad this trip was a mission of duty and not devotion, but Skinner would be shattered − Fry knew − if something happened to Honey.

'Dad, what's the name of this island?'

'Dismal Key.'

'That's sick.'

'I'm not jokin',' Skinner said.

'I know.'

They stepped out onto the flats and pulled the skiff toward the trees. The shoreline was longer than on the other island, and more densely foliated. Fry thought he smelled camp smoke but he couldn't see any fires.

After securing the boat, Skinner started threading through the mangroves. Fry stayed close and kept quiet, even when the barnacle-covered prop roots raked his legs. They followed the curve of a small bay, searching for an opening.

'Light,' Skinner whispered.

Fry aimed the beam.

'No. Over there.' His father pointed.

The spot fell on a red kayak and a yellow kayak, empty and tethered together.

'Those are Mom's!' At first, Fry was elated, then queasy with dread. What if they were too late?

Skinner weaved quickly through the trees. Once he broke onto dry land, he began to run. Fry struggled to keep pace but soon he fell, overcome by a shooting pain in his ribs and a hot wave of nausea. Before vomiting he adjusted his Dolphins helmet to avoid soiling the face guard. In a moment Skinner was there, steadying him by the shoulders.

'Go on. I'll catch up later,' Fry said. He was embarrassed to be puking in front of his father, who already felt guilty about taking him out of the hospital.

'Don't leave this spot – you understand?' Skinner gave the boy's arm a firm but affectionate squeeze.

Fry handed over the spotlight. 'But I want to help find Mom.'

'I'll be back in fifteen minutes. Do *not* move.'

'I heard you, Dad.'

He waited until he was alone before upchucking again. He hoped it wasn't fear that was making him sick. He hoped it was a flu bug, or even the knot on his head.

He sat back, resting against the rock-hard trunk of a gumbo limbo. His ankles stung from the barnacle scrapes, but at least his stomach was settling. Still, he meant to obey his father and remain right where he was. He had no intention of going anywhere . . .

Until he heard among the stirring leaves a soft voice. Fry cupped the ear holes of his helmet and listened – it was definitely a woman. She was speaking in a hurried, secretive tone.

The boy sprang up and ran toward the voice. He was moving at a steady jog, snapping branches and kicking deadwood, when he burst from a thicket and surprised her. He was crestfallen to see that it wasn't his mother.

'Well, if it ain't Dan Marino,' the woman said, 'scaring the holy crap outta me.'

Fry was out of breath and nauseated again. The woman steered him to an aluminum suitcase and made him sit on it. She had thick light-colored hair and wore a cotton pullover, and she was nearly as tall as his father. In one hand she held a cell phone and in the other a flashlight. Fry doubted she was the college girl who'd run off with the poacher; she looked too old to be in school.

'What's up with the helmet?' she asked.

'I got a concussion. I'm out here lookin' for my mom.'

'Yeah, and I'm lookin' for Johnny Depp.'

'I'm serious. She took some people on a kayak trip.'

The woman turned the flashlight on Fry's face. 'Oh my Lord. Are you Honey's boy?'

Fry pushed to his feet. 'Where is she? Is she all right?'

The woman was silent for a few moments. 'Damn,' she said finally.

'What's wrong? Tell me!'

'Oh, she's fine. It's just that I honestly wasn't planning to go back there ... but now here you are. How in the name of Mother Mary you found us in the middle of the night, I can't imagine.'

Fry said, 'Wait – you're one of the kayakers.' She was the woman he'd seen from a distance, outside his mother's trailer, while they were loading the car for the trip.

'Where's your husband?' he asked.

The woman made a pinched face. 'We are *not* married, thank you very much. He's my former travel companion and he's with your mom right now, griping like a brat and driving her crazy, no doubt. It's a long, pitiful story.'

'She said she knew you both from junior high. Said you were old friends.'

The woman was grandly amused. 'Where's your boat, by the way? Can I hitch a ride back to the real world?'

'But we heard a gunshot, my dad and I.'

'Yeah, some spaced-out Seminole accidentally plugged the guy who loaned me this cell phone, which unfortunately just ran out of juice in the middle of an extremely urgent call. My name's Genie, by the way.' The woman firmly shook his hand. 'It's okay, the guy who got shot didn't die or anything. Technically, he didn't even loan me the phone – I sorta borrowed it while he was passed out.'

Fry said, 'That's how I found you. I heard you talking to somebody.'

'The reservation desk at the Ritz-Carlton in Naples,' the woman explained. 'Tragically, the battery croaked before they could take my MasterCard number. You mentioned your father – where'd he waltz off to?'

Fry pointed. 'Out there somewhere.' He filled her in about Louis Piejack.

'Whoa, hold on – your old man's sneakin' around this godforsaken jungle in the middle of the night, risking his butt to rescue his ex-wife. Is that possibly true?' The woman named Genie seemed enchanted by the notion.

'Is there a gun in that suitcase?' Fry asked.

'Just a videocam,' she said, 'but don't worry, sport, you won't need to shoot anybody. The Indian's girl-friend told me he brained some pervo that sounds like your mom's stalker. She said the guy looked dead as a doornail.'

'Yesssss!' Fry pumped a fist.

Genie tossed the useless cell phone into the bushes. 'Let's go find your folks,' she said, 'and get the hell outta here.'

Twenty

In the summary of his report for the Smithsonian Institution, the Rev. Clay MacCauley thoughtfully editorialized about future relations between the Seminoles and the white settlers who by 1880 were flooding into Florida. The ethnologist foresaw that 'great and rapid change' was inevitable, and that the Seminole was 'about to enter a future unlike any past he has known.' MacCauley argued for justice and fairness in dealing with the tribe, so that the young braves would be friendlier toward whites than their jaded, battle-weary elders. It was the minister's hope that the Indians might in a climate of peaceful cooperation forget 'their tragic past,' but he warned that angering them could be a costly blunder.

Now that he can no longer retreat, MacCauley wrote, *now that he can no longer successfully contend, now that he is to be forced into close, unavoidable contact with men he has known only as enemies, what will he become?*

A gambling tycoon like my uncle Tommy, thought Sammy Tigertail, recalling the passage. Or a fucked-up half-breed like me.

He was pondering the irony of MacCauley's question while Gillian made love to him. It was the closest-possible contact one could have with a white person, and indeed it seemed unavoidable. Sammy Tigertail believed the pacifist preacher would have approved of what he and Gillian were doing – the conciliatory spirit of the act, if not some of the boisterously subjugating positions. It's better than smoking a damn peace pipe, he thought.

The Indian had succumbed to the college girl's advances because it wasn't a surrender, or the commencement of another foolish doomed affair; it was farewell. Gillian would be departing the island the next day, whether she wanted to or not. Never would Sammy Tigertail set eyes on her again. There was no other choice – not after his stray bullet had struck Lester. A wounded white man was apt to stir up more trouble than a dead one.

Reverend MacCauley was wrong about one thing, Sammy Tigertail thought. Retreat is always an option when there are ten thousand places to hide.

Gillian rocked briskly on top of him, her eyes half-closed and the golden lick of firelight on her skin.

'I wish you'd hold me the way you hold that damn guitar,' she was saying, 'like you'll never let go.'

'Quiet,' Sammy Tigertail whispered.

'Quiet's okay sometimes,' she said, slowing down. 'Sexy, even.'

'Exactly.'

'You know who's quite the talker? Ethan. In the sack, I mean.'

'Not now, please?'

She arched, playfully clenching a certain muscle. 'What's the matter, Thlocko, you jealous?'

Sammy Tigertail measured his response.

'Don't worry, you got him beat by a mile.' Gillian squeezed again. Then on she went: 'Ethan's gotta talk dirty or he can't keep it up. But at the same time he's, like, unbelievably shy. I'm serious, he won't even say the *F* word!'

Sammy Tigertail bucked his hips so forcefully that Gillian hiccuped. 'You go on with this story,' he told her, 'I'm gonna stuff Lester's socks in your mouth.'

'That old trick?' She giggled. 'I don't think so.'

He weighed the pros and cons of gagging her, then decided against it. Once she was gone, a life of sublime silence awaited him.

Gillian said, 'He was so shy – Ethan was – that whenever we did it, he spoke German. That's the only way he could make himself talk dirty! Problem is, *nothing* sounds dirty in German the way Ethan says it. But here he goes, poundin' away, yankin' on my hair, tellin' me do this, *Fräulein*, do that – only I haven't got a frigging clue what he's talkin' about. No lie, Thlocko, it's like he's reading from the owner's manual of his old man's Mercedes. Is that wild or what?'

The Indian said, 'I've got a question.'

'But this is only after he told me about setting free those dolphins – before then I wouldn't go to bed with him. What is it you just said?'

'I wanted to ask you something.'

'Like?'

'Could you check and see if we're still having sex?'

Gillian smiled. 'We are,' she said. 'In front of Lester, too. Does it still count if he's unconscious?'

Sammy Tigertail began pumping at such a pace that Gillian quit gabbing and hung on with both hands. Somehow they finished together, he with a low sigh and she with a sequence of piercing, feral yelps. Afterward he gently rolled her onto a blanket, where she curled up like a kitten.

He was standing away from the campfire, struggling to turn his khakis right-side out, when a gun barrel poked him in the small of the back. His first thought was that the wounded white man had made a miraculous recovery.

But it wasn't Lester.

'Be still,' the voice warned.

'Yes, sir.'

A pause, then: 'Sammy, is that you?' The gunman spun him around and exclaimed, 'I'll be damned!'

'Hello, Mr. Skinner.'

'What happened to your head, man?'

'I fell on an oyster shell,' Sammy Tigertail lied.

Gillian drowsily looked up, tugging the blanket over her breasts. 'Who's that?'

'A friend,' the Seminole said hopefully.

He and Perry Skinner had met when Sammy Tigertail was a teenager and new to the tribe. Skinner had rolled his truck after swerving to miss an otter pup on the Tamiami Trail. Sammy Tigertail and his uncle had been the first to drive up on the scene, and they'd dragged Skinner out of the wreck moments before it caught fire. Later Sammy Tigertail learned that Skinner was an important and prosperous man in Everglades City. It was he who'd loaned the young Indian the crab boat on which Wilson's body was ferried to Lostmans River.

Sammy Tigertail assumed that's why Skinner had tracked him down – the cops must have sorted out what had happened, then informed Skinner that his vessel had been illegally used to transport a dead tourist.

'I can guess why you're here,' the Seminole said.

Skinner stuck the handgun in his belt. 'Excellent. Where is she?'

Sammy Tigertail was puzzled. 'Who, Mr. Skinner?'

'Honey.' For Gillian's edification he added: 'My ex.'

Sammy Tigertail tried to conceal his relief that Skinner's surprise appearance was unconnected to the Wilson fiasco.

'She's out here somewhere, Sammy. You remember what she looks like, right?'

'It's big country, Mr. Skinner. I haven't seen her.'

The Indian had met Honey Santana only once, but that was enough. Every autumn since the truck accident, Skinner had given Sammy Tigertail twenty-five pounds of fresh stone-crab claws to take back to the reservation. The gift was always picked up on October 15, the first day of the trap season, when the largest crabs were caught. One year when the Seminole came to get the cooler, Honey Santana happened to be at the packing house. She was reaming out her then-husband about a cracked exhaust pipe on one of his boats, which she said was polluting the air on the river, gassing the herons and ospreys. Sammy Tigertail had never seen a woman so lovely and so possessed. She had rattled him, and he hadn't forgotten the episode. He had also not forgotten the sight of Perry Skinner calmly slipping on a set of Remington earmuffs to block out his wife's fulminations.

'What's she doing out here?' Gillian asked. 'Did she, like, run away?'

Skinner didn't answer. He said, 'We heard gunfire on this island.'

'That was him' – Gillian was pointing at the

Seminole – 'shooting *him*.' She turned and nodded toward the prone pudgy white man.

'I didn't mean to, Mr. Skinner,' Sammy Tigertail said. He noticed that the sky in the east was beginning to turn lavender. The sun would be coming up soon.

Skinner bent over and studied the man with the bloody shoulder, who was breathing loudly but steadily. Skinner said he didn't recognize him.

'We call him Lester. He's a private eye,' Gillian volunteered.

'Sammy, listen to me,' Skinner said. 'There's a sick fucker with a taped-up hand chasing after Honey. He's got a johnboat, and he's also carryin' a sawed-off. You seen him?'

Gillian started to blurt something but the Seminole silenced her with a glare.

'Sammy?' Skinner said evenly.

'No, I haven't seen anybody like that.' Sammy Tigertail hated lying to Mr. Skinner, but he didn't need another corpse in his life.

'Tell him the truth. You didn't do anything wrong,' said Gillian.

The Indian watched helplessly as she wrapped herself in the blanket and hurried to the other side of the campsite. She came back holding the sawed-off shotgun for Perry Skinner to see.

'Band-Aid Man was gonna shoot Lester, so Thlocko whacked him on the head,' she said.

'You kill him?' Skinner asked.

Sammy Tigertail shrugged. 'He looked pretty dead. Smelled dead, too.'

'That would be wonderful news.' Skinner came very close to smiling.

'I didn't mean to hit the man so hard.'

'We'll take care of it, Sammy. Don't worry.'

'Where was your wife headed?' the Seminole asked.

'Out here somewheres. And it's "ex-wife," Sammy. She was taking some friends on a kayak tour.'

'How many people?'

'A man and a woman from Texas,' Skinner said.

'The kayaks, were they red and yellow?'

'That's right. I found 'em tied in the mangroves not far from here.'

Sammy Tigertail was pleased to know that soon he'd have the island all to himself. 'I think I know where she's campin', Mr. Skinner. Sorry, but I stole their food and water.'

'The boats, too,' Gillian chimed in.

'Water was all I wanted but the munchies were stashed in the same bag,' the Seminole explained.

Perry Skinner said, 'You're gonna take me there right away.'

'Definitely.'

'First let me run back and get my boy. I left him in the woods.'

'We'll wait here,' Gillian promised.

After Skinner had gone, she said, 'You do *not* want to mess with that guy.'

Sammy Tigertail nodded. 'His old lady, either.'

Gillian leaned back and admired at the blushing sky. 'Hey, there's the sun!'

'Yup. Another day in paradise.'

'What should we do with the shotgun?'

'Toss it,' said the Seminole.

Waiting for sunrise, Boyd Shreave flailed at a lone mosquito floating about his head and shoulders. It felt too cold for mosquitoes, and Shreave feared he was being pursued by a dangerous rogue.

Earlier Honey had insisted upon reading aloud from a paperback text devoted to the insects, which were by far the deadliest creatures on earth. Shreave knew this was true because he'd seen a show about it on the Animal Planet channel. Millions of humans perished from hideous mosquito-borne maladies, including dengue fever, malaria, yellow fever, St. Louis encephalitis and the West Nile virus. Over the centuries the flying pests had brought painful death to popes and peasants alike, and ravaged robust armies.

However, of approximately 2,500 known species, the smallish mosquito common to the salt marshes of the western Everglades carries no pathogens lethal to man. The fact would have thrilled Boyd Shreave, had he been aware of it. Desperately he continued slapping at his tiny tormentor, which he could not see in the dim pre-dawn but whose sinister presence was betrayed by a faint taunting hum. Any cessation in the buzzing sound unnerved him, for it meant that the mosquito surreptitiously had alighted somewhere – probably upon a vulnerable tract of Shreave's flesh. Occasionally he found himself clawing at imagined bites to dislodge the toxic microbes.

As Shreave conducted his frantic duel with the hypodermic predator, Honey Santana grew weary of watching him swing clownishly at thin air or scratch madly at himself like a psoriatic baboon. Finally she rolled up her paperback and, with one deft swipe, flattened the mosquito on a button of Shreave's flowered shirt. He aimed a flashlight at the small death splotch, the sight of which comforted him until he remembered from the Animal Planet program that mosquito blood wasn't red. It was his own mortal nectar that had squirted from the mushed corpse; the sneaky prick had pricked him after all.

'I'm dead,' he groaned.

Honey sneezed. 'Don't be such a wuss,' she said.

Her allergies had been acting up all night. She sneezed again and said, 'How about a "bless you"? Were you raised by wolves, or what?'

Shreave flicked away the dead bug. 'Don't these things carry the bird flu, too?'

'No, Boyd, that would be a bird.'

'How about HIV?'

'How about a Xanax?' Honey said.

Shreave worriedly examined himself for telltale bumps. 'I could damn well die out here thanks to that little bastard.'

'Only the females bite,' Honey remarked.

Shreave looked up and made a sour face. 'Christ, somethin' stinks.'

Honey couldn't smell anything because her nose was runny. She wiped it somewhat undaintily on her shirt.

'Like fish,' Shreave complained. 'Smells like a ditchful of rotten fish.'

'It's low tide, that's all.' Honey sneezed again. She stood up and said, 'Let's go, Boyd.'

He eyed her uncertainly. 'Where to?'

She pointed upward, toward the top of the royal poinciana.

'What if I said no?' he asked.

'Let me guess: You're terrified of sparrows, too.'

'What if I just don't feel like it?'

'Then you can find your own damn way off this

island,' Honey said, and started up the gnarled, winding trunk.

Shreave followed reluctantly and with an ungainliness that was almost painful to observe. The man's a born straggler, Honey thought, another lucky exception to the rules of natural selection. A million years ago he would've been an easy snack for a saber-toothed tiger.

She heard his panting call: 'How far up?'

'All the way, Boyd. Otherwise there's no point.'

At the top of the old poinciana, forty feet off the ground, Honey selected a sturdy bough. She sat down facing east, dangling her long legs and rocking in the mild breeze. It made her feel like she was sailing.

By the time Shreave finished the climb, he was red-faced and wheezing. 'I bet I got a fever. I bet that fuckin' mosquito was loaded.'

Honey told him to be still, and to watch.

She was thinking of her son, as she always did at that time of day. Dawn was when she felt the safest, the surest, the most optimistic about sending into the world a boy of Fry's earnestness and full heart. Dawn was when her private terrors disappeared, if only briefly, and warm hope shined. The evening news made her wonder if God was dead; the morning sun made her believe He wasn't.

As the first shards of light appeared along the pinkish rim of the Everglades, Honey drew in her breath. To her the moment was infinitely soothing and redemptive; Boyd Shreave seemed oblivious.

'Long way down,' he mumbled, glancing anxiously below.

'Hush,' Honey told him.

Fry had been born precisely at sunrise, and

motherhood had crashed over her like a hurricane tide. Nothing afterward was the same, and no relationships went untested – with her husband, her family and the rest of humanity. Honey's life had jumped orbits, and shining alone at the new center of the universe was her son.

'I'm dyin' to hear your plan for getting us out of here,' Shreave drawled.

Light spilled into the cloudless sky like a blazing puddle.

Honey said, 'I'll go see the Indian and get my kayaks. Then you and I will head back to the mainland and say our good-byes.'

'Right. Genie's Indian.' Shreave laughed harshly. 'You're gonna straighten his ass out, are you?'

'Would you please shut up? Look what you're missing.'

The moment the sun cleared the horizon it started draining from red to amber. Simultaneously the wind died, and a crisp stillness settled upon the island.

The vista from atop the poinciana was timeless and serene – a long string of egrets crossing the distant 'glades; a squadron of white pelicans circling a nearby bay; a pair of ospreys hovering kite-like above a tidal creek. It was a perfect picture and a perfect silence.

And it was all wasted on Boyd Shreave.

'I gotta take a crap,' he said.

Honey rocked forward, clutching her head. The man was unreachable; a dry hole. For such a lunkhead there could be no awakening, no rebirth of wonderment. He was impervious to the spell of an Everglades dawn, the vastness and tranquillity of the waterscape. Nature held nothing for a person incapable of marvel; Shreave was forever destined to be underwhelmed.

It's hopeless, Honey told herself. The cocky telephone hustler would go home to Texas unchanged, as vapid and self-absorbed as ever. That a dolt so charmless could attract both a wife and a girlfriend was as dispiriting as it was inexplicable. Once again, Honey felt foolhardy and defeated, the queen of lost causes.

'Didn't you hear me?' Shreave snapped. 'I gotta climb down pronto and pinch a loaf.'

Honey straightened herself on the bough and breathed in the morning. The salty cool air had cleared her sinuses. 'All right, Boyd, let's go.'

'What is it you wanted to show me up here, anyway?'

'You missed it, I'm afraid.'

'Missed what?'

Honey heroically resisted the urge to knock him out of the tree.

'Come on,' she said, 'before you soil yourself.'

In his tenuous and trembling descent Shreave resembled nothing so much as an arthritic sloth. Twice Honey caught hold of him when he lost his grip, though it never occurred to him to say thanks.

Upon reaching solid ground, Shreave snatched his copy of *Storm Ghoul* from the Orvis bag and hurried into a stand of buttonwoods.

'Don't forget to clean up your mess!' Honey called after him. Shreave scoffed, dropped his pants and started to read:

All during the trial I acted strong and composed, but on the inside my heart was in shreds. The haunting truth was that I still cared for Van Bonneville, even though he was a monster. When the day came to take the witness stand, I vowed not to look at him. I kept reminding myself that what Van had done to his wife was unforgivable and wrong, even though he'd done it for me. He was a cold-blooded killer, and he deserved to be locked away.

For the first hour or so I was fine. The prosecutor asked his questions and I answered promptly and honestly, the way I'd been coached. But as time wore on, everything blurred together and my own voice began to sound flat and unfamiliar, like a stranger was reciting my testimony. Soon my gaze wandered to the defense table . . . and Van. His sexy tan had faded in jail, and they'd dressed him in a cheap blue suit that barely fit. He could have split the seams just by flexing his arms!

In his eyes I expected to see hate or at least disappointment, but I was wrong. Van was looking at me the same way he had that morning we met by the grapefruit tree in front of the Elks Lodge; the same way he looked at me that night in the cab of his truck as he unbuttoned my Lilly Pulitzer blouse. The harder I tried to vanquish these moments from my mind, the more vivid and arousing they became.

Then I made a foolish mistake. I looked at his hands, those incredibly strong and knowing hands. His fingernails had been scrubbed for the trial, but the scars were still visible – those mysterious pale marks on his knuckles. They would never wash away, nor would my memories of the wondrous ways his hands had touched me during our many nights together. When I looked up I saw Van smiling fondly, and I knew he was thinking the same thing. My eyes brimmed with tears, so quickly I turned to the judge and begged for a recess . . .

Boyd Shreave tore the page from Eugenie Fonda's memoir and, with a contemptuous flourish, wiped his ass with it.

Had he screwed up the courage to confront Genie, she would've willingly informed him that the best-selling account of her affair with the notorious wife killer had been ludicrously exaggerated to juice up the sales, and that Van Bonneville had turned in an unskilled and utterly forgettable performance the one and only time they'd had sex. Clueless as usual, Shreave believed – and suffered over – every salacious sentence in the book.

'Boyd!' It was Honey shouting.

'I'm not done!'

'Boyd, hurry!'

'Leave me alone, for Christ's sake.'

'Please! I need you!' Then she screamed.

Awkwardly he shuffled out of the trees and was instantly poleaxed by the stench of dead fish. Beneath the poinciana stood Honey with a rope cinched tightly around her neck, possibly the same rope she'd used on him. He was about to say something snarky when he noticed movement behind her.

It was a man. The end of the rope was tied around his chest and secured with a substantial knot. One hand was wrapped in dirty bandages and the other hand hefted a branch of gumbo-limbo.

'Can I help you, fuckwad?' the intruder asked.

It was the same voice that had hissed at Shreave from the shadows in the dead of night.

'Boyd, for God's sake,' Honey said. 'Do something.'

Shreave blinked.

The stranger peered. 'Darlin', who is this noodle dick?'

Humiliated, Shreave looked down at what was left of himself after a shriveling by cold fear. He was too petrified to pull up his pants.

'Boyd, he doesn't have a gun or even a knife. All he's got is a stupid stick!' Honey winced as the man twisted the rope.

She was right. There was no good reason for any young able-bodied man to stand by and let her be hauled off by some teetering, drool-flecked deviant. Obviously he was in sorry shape. His swollen face had a greenish tint, his shrunken eyes were bloodshot and he carried himself stiffly, as if riven with pain. To further advertise his sickliness, he was gnawing like a starved squirrel on a capped pill bottle.

'Boyd, please,' Honey implored. 'For once in your life.'

'Wh-what?' Shreave thinking: You're a tough broad. You can take this loser. 'What d-do you expect m-me to do?'

'Come on! You outweigh him by forty fucking pounds!'

That was undeniably true. All he had to do was sit on the guy, and Honey could free herself. Still, Shreave didn't move.

The foul-smelling stalker seemed richly entertained by the standoff – Honey shouting at Boyd, and Boyd standing there half-naked, cupping his privates.

'You're bettin' on the wrong rooster,' Louis Piejack said to Honey. 'Come on now, angel. Let's go make us some magic.'

With a stained and lopsided grin, he yanked roughly on the rope. Honey let out a small cry as she was led away from the campsite and, ever so slowly, up the slope of the oyster midden.

And Boyd Silvester Shreave – mouth open, eyes dull, respiration shallow – stood with his Tommy Bahama boat shorts bunched around his bug-bitten ankles, doing what he did best.

Absolutely nothing.

Twenty-one

Louis Piejack had deteriorated in all aspects during the long night in the cistern. Grime-borne infection had erupted beneath his cheek-to-shin stubble of cactus needles, promoting a startling dermatological resemblance to a puffer fish. Meanwhile his moldy surgical bandages had been fully colonized by fire ants, creating a live insect hive on the terminus of his left arm. Protruding from the putrid gauze were Piejack's skewed finger nubs, which had plumped and ripened into a parody of Greek olives. A medley of extreme pain stimuli – stinging, searing, throbbing, burning, grinding – was being transmitted in hot static bursts to Piejack's brain stem, yet he remained benumbed by the derangement of lust.

'Jackpot! Jackpot!' he chirped at Honey Santana as he exultantly led her across the island.

'Louis, you're hurting me.'

'Then be good.'

'The rope's cutting into my neck.'

'Don't worry, angel. I'll kiss it and make it better.'

'What is it you want?' Honey asked, as if she didn't know. The man looked quite ill, and she aimed to overpower him at the earliest opportunity.

'What do you *think* I want?' Piejack waggled the pill bottle in his lips like the stub of a cigar.

'There are easier ways to get laid, Louis. Call an escort service, for heaven's sake.'

He sneered. 'Ever seen them girls? Oinky oink oink!'

'Really,' Honey said. 'And when's the last time you were mistaken for Sean Connery?'

'Who?'

'You know. The old James Bond.'

Piejack grunted. 'So you're makin' a goddamn joke.'

'No, I'm making a point. Think about what you're doing, Louis. You rape me, they'll lock you up for twenty years.'

'Who says it's gonna be a rape?'

'*I* do.' Honey yanked on the rope, halting him in his tracks.

Piejack spun around. 'So, how come it's gotta be that way? Why?' His eyes were twitching. 'I know you want me – that's how come you stopped over my house. So why don'tcha just roll with it?'

Honey longed to say: Because you're a loathsome lump of shit, Louis, and I'd rather die than let you touch me . . .

But Piejack still toted the gumbo-limbo branch, so Honey's reponse was: 'Because I don't sleep with men who treat me like this, that's why.'

'Treat you how?'

'Like a dog, Louis. You're dragging me along like a hound dog on a leash. Is this supposed to put me in a romantic mood?'

Piejack clicked his teeth. 'You're just tryin' to con me into takin' off the rope. Here'— he spit the pharmacy bottle at her feet— 'Twist the cap off that sucker, would ya?'

Honey picked up the bottle, glanced at the label and opened it. 'How many?' she asked.

'Three would be nice. Four would be scrumptious.'

She tapped the Vicodins into her palm. 'Where you want 'em?'

Piejack opened his jaws and unfurled his tongue, which resembled a scabrous brown sea slug.

'Put that nasty thing away,' Honey told him. 'Open wide.'

Predictably, he slurped at her fingers as she dropped the pills into his mouth. She was too quick for him.

He swallowed the painkillers dry. 'How many do I got left?'

'Just one, Louis.'

'That's okay. My man at the drugstore owes me a refill.'

'So we're going home soon?' Honey asked.

'Yes, ma'am. The johnboat can't be far.'

'Can we bring my kayaks?'

Not wishing to abandon her expensive purchases, Honey had no qualms about asking Piejack for a tow. She figured it was the least he could do after abducting her.

'Don't see why not,' he said, resuming the march. 'But 'member, one good deed deserves an even better one. That means you gotta give up the velvet, angel.'

Honey's outlook on men was sinking to a point of abject revulsion. The day was new, yet already she'd been ridiculed by a soulless twit and kidnapped by a reeking pervert.

'You might even like it.' Louis Piejack winked over his shoulder. 'I never had no complaints in the bedroom department.'

Honey no longer could stand it. 'Know what? I need a potty break.'

Piejack stopped walking. 'Well, hurry it up,' he said.

'Right here – in front of you? I can't, Louis.'

'Okay, I won't peek. But I ain't undoin' the damn rope.'

As soon as he turned away, Honey pretended to unzip her pants. After lowering herself into a credible squat she began searching the ground for something sharp, heavy or both.

'I don't hear nuthin,' Piejack grumbled suspiciously.

Honey said, 'It's hard to do this while you're standing there listening. Just give me a minute.'

She found a gnarly chunk of coral the size of a mango; the weight was perfect. Clutching it in her right hand, she rose slowly and took aim at the back of Piejack's crusty head.

'You lied,' he was saying. 'You don't really gotta go.'

'Louis, would you please shut up so I can concentrate?'

'Concentrate on what? It ain't a chess match, angel, it's just pissin' in the woods.'

Honey Santana raised the piece of coral to strike him, but Piejack was already half-turned, swinging the gumbo-limbo like a boom. The blow landed flush on the left side of her face, and she heard a bone break. Then the sun exploded into a million flaming pink raindrops.

Like flamingos, Honey thought as she fell.

Flying home.

Fry had been confident he could locate the clearing where his father had told him to wait, but the lay of the island looked different in the morning light. After twenty minutes of circular meandering he admitted he was lost.

'Let's take a time-out,' said Eugenie Fonda, whose own navigational skills were better suited to the city.

Fry put down the metal camera case and leaned against a buttonwood. 'I don't feel so great.'

When he told Eugenie about the skateboard accident, she said, 'Your old man should've left you in the hospital.'

'We were worried about Mom.'

'I've seen her in action, bucko. She can take care of herself.'

'What's that shiny thing in your mouth?' Fry asked.

Eugenie smiled self-consciously. She'd never been asked about it by a boy his age. 'A pearl,' she said.

'Is it real?'

'Yessir.'

'Can I see?'

She extended her tongue in a prim and clinical way, so as not to give the kid any wild ideas. Fry adjusted the football helmet to get a better look.

'Sweet.' He leaned close. 'Did that hurt when they made the hole?'

'Like a mother,' she said.

'There's this girl in eighth grade, she's got a gold safety pin in her nose and a platinum screw through one eyebrow and an I-bolt in her right ear. They call her "Toolbox."'

Genie said, 'Kids can be awful.'

'I like your pearl.'

'Thank you, Fry, but I believe I've outgrown it.' She unfastened the stud, wiped it on the front of her pullover and dropped it in the palm of his hand.

'Ma'am, I really can't take this,' he protested. 'No way.'

Genie closed his fingers over the pearl and said, 'It's for when you meet that certain girl. But first you gotta make me a blood promise.'

'Like what?'

'Don't ever change. By that I mean don't grow up to be a jerkoff like ninety percent of the men I meet.'

'Mom always tells me the same thing. Except she says it's more like ninety-five.'

'Best advice you'll ever get: Stay a gentleman, and you'll never be alone. Don't lie, don't bullshit, don't fuck around – Christ, I can't believe I said "fuck around" to a fourteen-year-old boy! I'm sorry.'

Fry laughed. 'I'll be thirteen in June.'

Genie made a gun with her fingers and cocked it to her temple.

'Don't worry,' he told her. 'I hear worse stuff every day at school.'

'Now you're depressing me. Let's get movin'.'

Fry pocketed the pearl. Eugenie said it was her turn to be the bellhop, and reached for the Halliburton. They'd walked for only a few minutes when the boy began to lag. Eugenie went back and entwined her free arm in one of his.

'My dad's gonna be so pissed,' he said dejectedly.

'Tell him it was my fault you ran off. You were rushing to the aid of a damsel in distress – what's wrong, sweetie?'

'I dunno, all of a sudden it's like I'm in a cave.' Fry blinked and started to weave. 'I'm getting really cold again,' he said.

Genie dropped the metal case and grabbed for him, but he was already falling. His head struck first, the helmet making a hollow *tonk* as it bounced off the trunk of a strangler fig.

'Oh God, no,' Eugenie murmured.

Kneeling at his side, she lifted his head onto her lap. His eyes had rolled back, and his skin was damp and ashen. The pulse at his neck felt fluttery, and a burgundy trickle ran from his bitten lower lip to his chin. Genie rocked the boy, softly pleading with him to wake up and cursing the day she'd met Boyd Shreave.

Gillian said, 'Let's talk about what happened. The sex, I mean.'

'We already talked,' said Sammy Tigertail, 'the whole time it was happening.'

'But you never told me what you thought. Am I worth all the hassle or not?' She stepped into her flip-flops. 'My sister goes through, like, twenty boyfriends a year. I don't say a word.'

The Indian felt another impulse to kiss her, which was unnerving. He was supposed to be done with it; that was the plan. He picked a red bay twig out of her hair and said, 'It was real nice.'

Gillian slugged him in the arm. '*Nice?*'

'Wonderful,' he said. 'I meant wonderful.'

'Right. Vundebar, as Ethan used to say.' She was steamed. 'You're quite the fucking poet, Thlocko.'

Sammy Tigertail tried to put his arms around her but she spun away. He opened his carry bag to look for some warm clothes. Nearby, the white man with the gunshot wound was making an odd flutish sound through his nose.

Gillian fumbled with the strings of her bikini top. 'Know what my problem is? I want everything perfect, see, like at the end of a movie. I always want the damn dolphins to swim free. I always want to sing like Jewel when I'm playin' the six-string. And I always want guys to fall totally in love with me after one night.'

The Indian handed her a sweatshirt and fleece pants. 'It's getting colder,' he said.

'No staring at the ta-ta's allowed.'

'You'd be bored to death out here with me. Plus, you're allergic to mosquitoes – that's what you told me.'

Gillian said, 'I'm not high-maintenance, okay? My sister, she's high-maintenance. My mom, big-time. Compared to those two, I'm easy.' She plopped down beside him and rolled up the cuffs of the pants. 'Hey, I know I talk when I shouldn't. I'm workin' on it.'

Sammy Tigertail wasn't sure what steps to take if she refused to leave the island the next day. He wasn't even sure he still wanted her to go.

He kissed her lightly and said, 'Truth is, it was better than wonderful.'

'I thought so, too. Wanna do it again?'

'Mr. Skinner and his boy will be here soon.'

Gillian faked a pout. 'Mean old man,' she said.

'Anyway, your buddy Lester's gonna wake up any minute.'

She clucked and affected the proper accent of a British headmistress. 'Well, goodness, we most definitely don't wish to offend Lord Lester.'

As if on cue, the sleeping man snuffled and quaked.

Sammy Tigertail said, 'There's something I didn't tell you. I'm only half Seminole.'

Gillian smiled devilishly. 'Bet I know which half.'

'Seriously. My father was white.'

She pretended to look him over. 'Wild guess – did he have fantastic blue eyes?'

Sammy Tigertail found himself talking about his childhood in the suburbs of Broward County; about how he'd moved to the Big Cypress and started his life over.

'That,' Gillian said, 'is *insanely* cool.'

'Some days it was a bitch.'

'But you hung in!'

'So far,' he said.

She reached for his hand. 'Thlocko, I've got a little confession, too. I lied about not being high-maintenance.'

The Indian broke into laughter. He couldn't stop.

Then all of a sudden he was kissing her again.

Until she took a deep breath and said, 'You're probably right. I wouldn't last very long out here in the boonies.'

'Do you want to try?' He was stupefied to hear himself ask the question.

She said, 'God, I'm already jonesing for a Starbucks. Is that pathetic or what? And Krispy Kremes.'

'My dad's favorite,' said Sammy Tigertail. 'Every Sunday morning we'd eat a dozen, just the two of us.'

'Stop, you! I could inhale a whole box of those bad boys.'

He said, 'Look, Gillian – you want to stay and give it a shot, I don't mind.'

She lifted his hand to her lips. 'That's, like, the most romantic thing anybody's ever said to me – least in English. But I gotta think about it, 'kay?'

'Take your time.'

'Meanwhile, Big Chief Thlocko, let me show you what my people call a "quickie."'

Sammy Tigertail rose to a crouch. 'Ssshhh. Somebody's comin'.'

Perry Skinner wasn't inclined to panic – not after the many close calls he'd survived in his dope-running days. He had trained himself to keep calm because those who got rattled usually made poor and life-altering decisions.

Fry was gone but there was no reason to think something terrible had occurred, which would have been his mother's automatic assumption. The kid had his shit together; he wouldn't do anything stupid. He'd probably started feeling better and decided he could catch up to Skinner on his own.

After searching the woods around the clearing, Skinner jogged to Sammy Tigertail's camp, hoping to find Fry waiting for him. The Seminole and his girlfriend had heard Skinner's footsteps and hidden behind some bay trees.

When they saw who it was, they came out waving. Fry wasn't with them.

Sammy Tigertail said, 'I'll help you look, Mr. Skinner. The island's not that big.'

'Maybe he went and found his mom,' said Gillian.

The thought had occurred to Perry Skinner, too. It was something to hope for.

'I'll stay here with Lester, in case they show up. You guys go,' Gillian urged. 'And take some food – if you find 'em, they'll be hungry.'

Skinner and the Indian didn't get far before they heard the helicopter. It was working a search grid, back and forth. Sammy Tigertail said it must be the Everglades park rangers.

'We're not in the park,' Skinner said. 'We're on Dismal Key.' From the pitch of the turbines he could tell it was the Coast Guard.

The Seminole looked distraught as he ducked into the bushes. 'It's me they're after, Mr. Skinner.'

'Why? What'd you do?'

'A white man died on my airboat and I sunk the body.'

'Did you kill him, Sammy?'

'No, but they'll never believe me,' he said, shaking his head. 'Just like they won't believe I didn't mean to shoot Lester.'

Skinner had a feeling that the Indian might be right about the cops arresting him.

'I can't go to prison, Mr. Skinner. That's what they did to Tiger Tail and the other chiefs.'

'All right, Sammy.'

They hurried back to the campsite and found Gillian preparing to flag the chopper with an Allman Brothers *Eat a Peach* T-shirt that had once belonged to Sammy Tigertail's father. The Seminole snatched the cherished relic from the girl's hands and ordered her to stay low. Although they couldn't yet see the helicopter, it sounded close.

'But that's Lester's ride!' Gillian exclaimed. 'Remember? He phoned somebody to come get him.'

The engine noise roused Dealey, and he struggled to sit. 'Finally,' he said thickly. 'Somebody help me up.'

Sammy Tigertail told him to forget it. 'There's nowhere to land that thing on this island.'

Perry Skinner was impatient to search for Fry and Honey, but he knew what had to be done first: The man with the bullet wound needed a doctor. It would be bad for everybody if Lester got worse and died on Dismal Key.

'Grab his legs,' Skinner told the Indian. 'I'll get the other end.'

'Go easy,' said Gillian.

Skinner pointed to an expensive Halliburton valise. It was the same brand he'd used for hauling cash in the old days; durable and waterproof. 'That yours?' he asked Dealey.

'Yeah, but where's my other one?'

Gillian picked up the travel case. The Seminole took hold of Dealey's ankles while Skinner hoisted the private investigator from behind, clutching him Heimlich-style around his bare chest.

'Goddamn, that hurts!' Dealey blurted.

Skinner said, 'Suck it up. You're goin' home.'

They carried him to the notch along the creek where the kayaks were tethered, and with great effort they positioned him in the red one. Gillian propped the Halliburton between his knees.

Dealey was unable to paddle because of the shotgun hole in his shoulder. Skinner hastily devised an anchor from an old cinder block and attached the rope that had been used to secure Honey's kayaks. He instructed Dealey to push the hunk of concrete overboard in the middle of the creek; that would hold the lightweight craft in the current and make it easier to spot from the air.

Skinner spun the red kayak and aimed the bow toward the open water. Gillian waved and sang out, 'Bye, Lester,' but her words drowned in the roar of the approaching chopper. On a count of three, Skinner and Sammy Tigertail gave a firm shove and sent Dealey gliding out of the mangroves.

The tide took the kayak and tugged it toward the Gulf. Dealey clumsily kicked the cinder block over the side, the line came tight and the boat swung to a halt halfway across the creek. From the shore, Gillian clapped and whistled.

A large shadow appeared, skittering like a water bug over the waves. Perry Skinner looked up to see a flash of blaze orange, the official striping of the Coast Guard air-search fleet. He herded Gillian and the Seminole into the shelter of the tree line as the helicopter circled and dipped. They watched with consternation as Dealey endeavored to stand in the kayak, undoubtedly with a mind to signal for help. He was every bit as graceful as a walrus on a boogie board.

The juggle of Dealey's ample heft caused the boat to list ominously, and the nose began to tunnel in the current.

'Look at that fool,' Sammy Tigertail said.

Skinner was furious. 'Sit your fat ass down!' he yelled at the man called Lester, who paid no heed.

Gillian gasped. 'Holy shit, he's sinking!'

The Indian pulled off his shoes. 'I'll go,' he said.

Skinner said no. 'They might lock you up, Sammy. Let me do it.'

Thinking: *I don't have time for this nonsense.*

The kayak capsized with hardly a ripple. Dealey didn't fall so much as he rolled. Invigorated by terror and a torrent of cold water, he thrashed until his good arm caught hold of the upturned hull, which had remained anchored in the channel.

'Poor old Lester,' Gillian said, and began stripping off the clothes that Sammy Tigertail had given her.

The Seminole watched, dumbstruck.

'Don't worry,' she told him when she was down to her mesh panties. 'I was on the crew team, 'member? Plus I did the whole *Baywatch* thing one summer in

Destin. It was, like, eight-fifty an hour and you had to buy your own sunblock.'

She stuffed the clothes in Sammy Tigertail's arms and kissed him wildly on the mouth and said, 'Bye, Thlocko. You're the fucking best.'

'Don't do this!'

'Write a song about me later,' she said, 'when you're a rock star.'

Then she was gone, splashing out of the mangroves and into the swift creek.

The Indian started to chase her but Perry Skinner caught him by the belt. Skinner pointed up at the helicopter, which already had begun lowering a rescue basket over the flipped kayak. A full-suited Coast Guard diver was poised on one of the aircraft's skids.

'You think those guys're gonna let that pretty girl drown?' Skinner said. 'Lester's the one who ought to be worried. He'll be lucky if they save him a towel.'

Sammy Tigertail watched Gillian scissor through the rotor-blown chop and latch onto the wallowing white man. 'She's a good swimmer, for sure,' the Seminole said. 'And pretty, like you say.'

'Save it for a valentine, Sammy. Right now I need you to help me find my son and my wife.'

'You mean your ex.'

'That's what I said.'

'Sure, Mr. Skinner.' Sammy Tigertail stooped to put on his shoes.

When Fry awoke, he was weak but no longer dizzy. His lower lip stung where he'd chomped it when he fell.

Eugenie Fonda was elated that the boy hadn't croaked in her arms. She pecked him on the forehead and said, 'You got a concussion, bucko. We're stayin' right here until your old man tracks us down.'

Fry didn't argue. He had no strength for another hike. The sun on his legs felt good; so did lying on Eugenie's lap. Were it not for the football helmet, he would have been basking in the warmth of her outstanding breasts. He tried not to dwell on that.

'Hey, check out the chameleons,' he said.

There were two of them, as bright as emeralds, sharing a bough in the strangler fig. One of the lizards inflated its wine-red dewlap and began pumping its featherweight body, as if it was doing push-ups.

'That's the male,' Fry explained. 'He's showin' off.'

'Go figure,' said Eugenie.

She opened the Halliburton and removed the video camera. After rewinding the tape, she touched the play button. The young Seminole's girlfriend appeared on the display screen, auditioning with the shotgun as a prop.

Good morning, this is Gillian St. Croix bringing you the weather! A winter storm rumbled through the Rockies last night, dumping snow from Montana to New Mexico. The ski resorts in Vail are reporting three feet of fresh powder, and it's even deeper in Aspen and Telluride. Meanwhile, waaaaaaay down in sunny southern Florida, daytime temps are expected to reach the low seventies by noon. It's ideal conditions for being held hostage by a stud-hunk Native American on a deserted tropical isle. We're talkin' about a serious blue-eyed Bone Machine—

Eugenie Fonda hastily shut off the tape.

'Who was *that*?' Fry asked.

'Just a girl gone wild.' Eugenie rewound the cassette and activated the record button.

'Where are those lizards?' She pointed the camera toward the fig tree.

'Little higher.' Fry twisted around to show her.

'They're cute little buggers, aren't they?'

'Yes, ma'am.' The boy's neck ached, so he turned back the other way.

'And real fond of each other.' Genie toggled the zoom.

'Do you have any kids?' Fry asked.

She thought: One of the few mistakes I haven't made. 'I never grew up enough to be a mom. That's a serious gig,' she said.

'Nah, you could do it.'

'I was wondering – do lizards make noise?'

'Geckos, yeah. Not chameleons,' he said.

'Too bad.' Genie fiddled with the focus control.

'What kind of job do you have?' the boy asked.

She chuckled dryly. 'I sell an incredible amount of crap to people over the phone. But once upon a time I had a book published.'

'Sweet.'

'The phony true-life story of a doomed romance,' she said, 'but don't be too impressed. I didn't write a damn word of it.'

'What's the book called?'

Genie said, 'Never mind. It's not in your school library, I promise. Aren't chameleons the ones with the big buggy eyes and the superlong tongues? Like that guy in Kiss.'

'Those are old-world chameleons. The species here in the Everglades is called the American anole.'

Eugenie was enjoying herself; the kid was an encyclopedia. She said, 'Maybe I can sell this tape to the *National Geographic*. You could help me with the script.'

Fry cocked his head and listened. 'You might want to wrap it up,' he said.

'In a minute.'

He sat up. 'Hear that? It's a chopper!'

'How can you tell from so far off?'

The boy raised one arm to block out the sun. 'They're headin' our way.'

Eugenie switched off the camera. Honey's kid was right – it sounded like a helicopter, not a plane. She remembered the man called Lester bragging of secret arrangements to leave the island; possibly she'd underestimated him. Although Gillian's young Seminole had promised to provide a boat and a map for returning to the mainland, air travel was much more appealing to Genie.

'I need to ask you somethin' important,' she said to Fry. 'Say I caught a ride outta here – would you be all right until your old man shows up?'

With a whoosh the helicopter passed over the treetops.

'Coast Guard. They're circling.' Fry craned for a better view. 'You get going. I'll be okay,' he said.

Genie helped the boy to his feet. 'Or how about you and me leave together? They'll send somebody back to find your folks, for sure.'

'No, ma'am, you go.'

Hurriedly she packed the video gear. 'Promise you'll wait right here for your dad? Don't be a typical dumb-ass male and get yourself lost in the woods.'

'Promise.'

'Hey, I know you're quite the jock. I saw all those track trophies at your mom's place.'

Fry said, 'I'm not goin' anywhere. I feel like crap.'

Genie shielded her eyes and pivoted on one heel,

following the hum of the chopper. 'How they gonna land with all these damn trees?'

'They're not. You've gotta get in the creek or they won't see you.' Fry pointed. 'Try that way – the kayaks are stashed in the mangroves. Dad and I found 'em last night.'

She squeezed the boy and thumped the side of his helmet. 'If you were ten years older, bucko, you'd be in serious trouble.'

Fry squirmed and said, 'Better hurry.'

Eugenie Fonda snatched up the camera case and took off. She laughed when she heard him call out: 'Wait! Are you sure you don't want your pearl?'

Priceless, she thought. One in a million.

Shortly before sunrise, the U.S. Coast Guard station in Fort Myers Beach had received a call from Fort Worth, Texas. A woman who gave her name as Lily Shreave reported that a cousin named Dealey had contacted her by cellular phone to say he was stranded without provisions on an unknown island near the town of Everglades City. The woman said her cousin was a well-known nature photographer working on a documentary about orphaned pelicans. She said he suffered from a rare condition known as aphenphosmphobia, of which the petty officer taking the report had never heard and didn't even attempt to spell. Ms. Shreave went on to say that her cousin was in dire need of his anti-aphenphosmphobia medication, which he'd forgotten on the front seat of a rental car parked at his motel.

When the petty officer inquired how Mr. Dealey had come to be marooned, his cousin said he'd blacked out

319

in a small boat while photographing a rookery. She said the battery in her cousin's phone had gone dead during his call, so she had no other information to help pinpoint the location. She provided a thorough description of the missing man – fifty-seven years old, brown eyes, balding, five ten, 215 pounds. Ms. Shreave also said he was wearing a slate-gray Brooks Brothers suit. When the Coast Guard officer remarked that such attire seemed strange for a field trip to the Ten Thousand Islands, Ms. Shreave explained that her cousin, like many artistic types, was an eccentric.

At 0700 hours, an HH60 Jayhawk helicopter carrying a search-and-rescue crew lifted off and headed south along the coast, passing directly over Naples, Marco Island and then Cape Romano Shoals. The chopper angled slightly toward the mainland and dropped altitude before looping around the fishing village of Chokoloskee. The pilot then banked westward to place the rising sun behind the spotters who would be searching the green tapestry of mangroves and hammocks for Mr. Dealey. It was a limpid morning, and visibility was superb.

Lily Shreave was rolling up her yoga mat when a Coast Guard ensign called with good news. Her 'cousin' had been pulled alive from a creek near an uninhabited island called Dismal Key, a few nautical miles outside the boundary of Everglades National Park. Also rescued were two women, who gave their names as Gillian St. Croix and Jean Leigh Hill and stated their respective occupations as a TV weather personality and a freelance videographer.

Ms. Shreave said she had no idea who they were.

Twenty-two

As soon as Boyd Shreave heard the helicopter, he began scrambling up the old poinciana. Without Honey's assistance he couldn't reach the top, but he got high enough to consider it a lifetime achievement.

As a boy, Shreave had avoided tree play, impaired as he was by flabby musculature and a loathing for exertion. Now, wedged snugly into a crook of three branches, he felt like he belonged in an episode of *Survivor*, his favorite TV reality show. Every season a crop of youthful competitors was deposited on some remote tropical location and put through a delightfully pointless series of physical challenges resulting in the elimination of the weak and unreliable. While the program usually featured one or two contestants who were as desultory and unathletic as Shreave himself, he never rooted for them. It was the sunburned babes in their frayed cutoffs and ill-fitting halters whom he avidly tuned in to watch.

From the tree, Shreave flagged his arms and hollered for help. The crew of the hovering helicopter never glanced his way, and Shreave realized that he needed to go higher. However, he was intimidated by the prospect of scaling to a more visible position above the canopy – the breezy conditions, the slipperiness of the branches and his own lack of agility argued for caution.

From a pocket of his windbreaker he extracted what he falsely believed to be a portable marine radio, which along with two granola bars he'd pilfered from Honey's belongings after she was snatched by the club-handed lunatic. Shreave started pressing buttons on the compact gadget and barking, 'Mayday! Mayday!'

There was no response from the Coast Guard pilot or any other human, and for good reason. Except for its LED screen, the instrument in Shreave's possession was electronically dissimilar to a radio in all significant respects. Most crucial was the absence of either an audio receiver or a transmitter.

'SOS! SOS!' he persisted. 'Help!'

The device was in fact a mobile GPS unit, as technologically impenetrable to Shreave as the Taser gun he'd found beneath Honey's bed. Commonly carried by boaters, campers and hunters, a GPS enables users to precisely track and then retrace their movements anywhere on the planet. Satellites record intermediate points in longitude and latitude in the instrument's memory, which displays the information in a mapping format so elementary that even a drooling moron can read it.

Not Boyd Shreave. The singular result of his frantic button pushing was to engage the satellite signal and successfully identify his location as approximately 81°33' west of the prime meridian and 25°53' north of the equator. However, the flashing numerals were a meaningless jumble to Shreave.

'Mayday! SOS! Nine one one!' he screamed at the

mute GPS as he watched the orange-and-white helicopter repositioning above the creek. From his bushy perch, Shreave couldn't see what the Coast Guard spotters saw, so he was unable to appreciate their gallantry and resourcefulness. A routine search mission for an ailing middle-aged photographer had been complicated by the unexpected appearance of not one but two extremely attractive female evacuees.

The first woman had dived nearly naked into the chilly water to assist the wayward photographer as he clung to a small overturned vessel. Minutes later the second woman had emerged in a yellow kayak from the mangroves, waving what appeared to be a festively colored undergarment at the chopper. Swiftly the crew members took action to expand the retrieval operation, proceeding with an unbreakable focus and esprit de corps that reduced to zero the chances of them noticing a lone pale figure halfway up a distant tree and obscured by heavy foliage.

Bitterness engulfed Boyd Shreave as three times an empty basket unspooled from a cable in the belly of the aircraft, and three times the basket ascended holding a blanketed human form. Shreave was too far away to see who was being rescued; he knew only that it wasn't he. When the helicopter buzzed away, he thought: Screwed again.

A silken quiet fell briefly over the island, but soon the seabirds began to pipe and the trees began to stir. From his lonely roost, Shreave watched a zebra-striped butterfly alight on a nearby poinciana leaf. With a sour cackle he hurled the GPS at it.

He missed by three feet, and the butterfly flitted away.

*　*　*

In the four years following her divorce, Honey Santana had gone out with five men. Only three of them got a second date, and only two of them got to see her bedroom.

The first was Dale Rozelle, who had advertised himself as a professional bowler from Boca Grande. He was thin and handsome and eleven years younger than Perry Skinner. During sex he slapped his own ass and grunted like a constipated hog, which distracted Honey and on at least two occasions awakened Fry down the hall. Honey might have overlooked the barnyard sound effects had Dale Rozelle distinguished himself in other ways, but he had not. An Internet troll by Fry revealed that Dale Rozelle was lying not only about his bowling career but also about his lifetime membership in the Sierra Club, a fictitious credential that he'd correctly surmised would boost his standing with Honey. Disgusted by her own gullibility, she had (against Fry's counsel) stormed into the bowling alley on Mixed-League Night and confronted the duplicitous shithead in the ninth frame of his last game. The one-sided encounter had ended with Honey dropping a sixteen-pound Brunswick on Dale Rozelle's left instep. Eventually he agreed not to prosecute, but only after Perry Skinner had promised to pay the medical bills.

The other man with whom Honey had slept was Fry's orthodontist, Dr. Tyler Teehorn, whose wife had sold their Volvo sedan and run off to Montserrat with her husband's star hygienist. It had happened on the same day that Tyler Teehorn was fitting Fry for a retainer, and the man was a mess. That night Honey had dropped her son at Skinner's house, driven back to Naples and dragged Tyler Teehorn out to Ruby

Tuesday's for a drink. Never had she seen anyone so bereft, and in a moment of rum-soaked pity she'd invited him to go home with her. The sex, while slightly better than Honey had anticipated, was quite obviously the most spectacular in Dr. Tyler Teehorn's sheltered experience. No sooner had he pulled on his socks than he proclaimed his eternal love for Honey. Not wishing to be the second woman – or possibly the third, considering how hard it was to find a top-flight hygienist – to break Tyler Teehorn's heart in a twelve-hour span, Honey had murmured an endearment that she'd hoped was adequately tender yet vague. For the next four weeks the man had clung to her like a mollusk. In contrast to Dale Rozelle, Dr. Teehorn's integrity and devotion were unassailable. Unfortunately, he was a suffocating bore. Ignorant of politics, world affairs and even sports, his personality sparked only when he steered the conversation to the topic of teeth. Honey had finally dumped him during a candlelit dinner when he'd offered to fix her overbite for free.

'Wake up!' she heard Louis Piejack say, yet she didn't move. She intended to fake unconsciousness as long as possible. In addition to fracturing her jaw, the gumbo-limbo bludgeon had knocked all the songs out of her head. Inexplicably, the void had filled with that dispiritingly detailed recap of her post-divorce sex life. It made her long for a dual blast of Ethel Merman and the Foo Fighters.

'Giddup right now!' Piejack snapped.

The toe of a shoe poked Honey in the ribs, and a fog of fish stink confirmed that Piejack was looming over her. She hoped that her face was so pulped that he would lose interest in raping her.

'C'mon, goddammit, I didn't hit you that hard,' he said.

She noticed a new sound – not a tune, but rather a single distant note, rising in volume. Soon it grew to a sustained chord, complete with percussion. Honey was relieved that Piejack could hear it, too.

'What the hell?' he cried with alarm.

Honey recognized the noise and smiled. She peeked up just in time to see an orange-and-white shape streak overhead. Impulsively she tried to shout, but only a bubble of blood came out; the left side of her face was numb, and her tongue felt like she'd been licking broken glass.

'You be still!' Louis Piejack was ducking and bobbing as he watched for the return of the Coast Guard helicopter. His level of alertness was impressive, considering the gorilla dosage of Vicodin that he'd consumed.

'Don't get no ideas,' he warned her.

Honey was brimming with ideas. Unfortunately, she was also tied to a tree. It had happened while she was knocked out, when the dexterously challenged Piejack had had time to work.

'Long as we stay still, they won't never see us,' he said confidently. He hunkered beside her and, with his misassembled hand, stroked her thigh. When he lasciviously wiggled a blackened pinkie, she swatted it away.

Piejack chuckled. 'You'll feel better soon, angel. When we're snug at home.'

Honey knew that he was too weak to carry her; otherwise they'd already be on his boat, speeding back to the mainland. Slowly she sat up, testing the rope that he'd secured to her wrists and then looped around her neck. The fit was tight enough to limit her options – and to make her slightly sorry for having pretended to tie up Boyd Shreave.

'Damn, I'm thirsty,' Piejack said.

Honey was parched, too. Her throat felt like she'd been gargling sawdust.

She heard the chopper hovering nearby yet she couldn't see it through the trees. *Maybe it's me they're looking for*, she thought, although she couldn't imagine why. Fry wasn't expecting her home until the following day, so he had no reason to call out the Coast Guard.

Unless . . .

Honey stiffened.

. . . unless it was her exhusband who'd summoned a search helicopter, which he wouldn't do unless there was an emergency back in town.

Like something awful had happened to Fry.

Honey Santana lunged to her feet, nearly garroting herself. Piejack brought her down with one sharp yank.

'What's your problem, woman?' he said.

Frantically she scanned the sky. A vision became fixed in her mind of Fry motionless on a stretcher in a speeding ambulance. The boy's head was bandaged and his father was sitting beside him, stroking his hair. The image was so vivid that Honey thought she could hear the ambulance siren above the high drone of the helicopter.

Then the chopper flew away and the vision faded. Honey was overtaken by a desire to murder Louis Piejack on the spot, and she would have tried had she not been bound by the neck.

He stood up shakily and said, 'Let's get a move on, 'fore that whirlybird comes back.'

Honey watched with a bent fascination as Piejack struggled to untie the rope from the tree, no easy task for a man with a set of jumbled fingers. After several frustrating attempts he decided to attack the knot with his teeth, freeing both hands to hoist the gumbo branch as a sobering reminder for Honey to behave.

Once the rope was loose, he managed to rehitch the free end around his chest. Wordlessly he headed into the woods, leading Honey like a pack mule. They walked for half an hour, following a dense and unfamiliar shoreline until they broke into a large clearing. At one end was an untidy campsite with a small fire pit that was piled with ashes. Piejack tethered Honey to another tree while he rifled the gear belonging to the campers, who were nowhere to be seen. He found an uncapped jug of water, which he guzzled without so much as a glance toward Honey, who was too proud to ask for a drink.

Louis Piejack tossed the empty water bottle and resumed foraging. He kicked something hard that was wrapped in a blanket, and it made a noise like a cat caught in bedsprings. Piejack kicked open the bundle and revealed a dazzling electric guitar, which he gathered into his foully stained lap.

Honey felt vindicated. Boyd Shreave had scoffed at her when she said she'd heard guitar music.

'Can you play one a these?' Piejack asked.

'Sure.' She was trying not to move her jaws.

'I'm a piano man myself.' Piejack began tweaking the strings with his infected nubs. 'This baby's worth some cash, ya think?'

'Go easy, Louis.' Honey was disgusted to see him smearing his rancid bandages across the beautiful finish on the Gibson.

'Will you do a song for me?'

'I guess so. If you untie this rope,' Honey said. She couldn't play a lick, but it was worth a shot.

Piejack hunched over to work one-handedly on the loops of the knot. As the moist stubble of his whiskers rubbed against her skin, Honey suppressed the urge to chomp a gaping hole in his neck.

Once her wrists were freed, he gave her the guitar. It was a magnificent thing to hold. With a sleeve she cleaned Piejack's grease marks off the polished wood.

He said, 'Now do me a love song, angel.'

'All right, Louis.'

Strumming lightly, she began to sing:

> Got a noose rope around my throat and a fractured face,
> From a man who swears he loves me true.
> He might break my bones, but he'll never break my heart
> 'Cause that only belongs to you . . .

Piejack wrested the instrument from Honey. 'I don't care for that fuckin' number.'

'But there's twelve more verses,' she said innocently. 'It's called "The Trapped on an Island with a Revolting Pervert Blues." You never heard it before? Fiona Apple does a killer cover.'

Piejack flung the Gibson into the fire pit and said, 'You ain't one bit funny.'

Honey touched the side of her face. She had a bruise the size of a pomegranate where he'd clobbered her with the branch.

'Louis, may I have a Vicodin?'

'I only got the one left – and it's for me.'

'Always the gentleman,' she said.

'We get home, you can have all you want. So quit yer bitchin'.'

'Where's this boat of yours, anyway?'

'Ain't far now,' he said, although he didn't sound certain. 'Gimme your hands,' he rasped, and fumbled at her neck for the loose end of the rope.

Honey spotted a bluish glint on the other side of the campsite – a pipe-like object on the ground beneath a bay tree. Piejack caught her staring past him, and he wheeled to see what had grabbed her attention.

'Jackpot!' he chortled.

'What is it?'

'Jackpot! Jackpot!' Piejack wobbled excitedly across the clearing and scooped up his sawed-off shotgun. Waving it high for Honey to see, he cried, 'I thought I'd lost 'er for good, but look here!'

'Wooooo-hooo,' said Honey. She felt like weeping.

Perry Skinner and Sammy Tigertail had split up to search for Fry. Given his limited wilderness instincts and chronic bad luck, the Indian didn't expect to find the boy. Yet there he was, in a splash of sunshine, sitting on a Dolphins helmet near a stand of green buttonwoods.

Fry appeared startled by the arrival of the stranger, though he tried to look brave. Sammy Tigertail introduced himself and said, 'Your father's lookin' all over creation for you.' He offered some water, but the kid declined.

'Where is he? My dad.'

The Indian checked his watch. 'We're supposed to

meet up in twenty minutes on the other side of the island.'

Fry said, 'I'm not going anywhere. I don't know you from the man in the moon.'

'Your father does. I saved his life once – me and my uncle.'

The boy eyed him. 'When he rolled his truck?'

Sammy Tigertail said, 'Yep. That night on the Trail.'

'You're one of the Big Cypress Seminoles?'

'Well, I ain't exactly from the south of France.'

Fry didn't crack a smile. 'You could be a Miccosukee is what I meant.'

'I could be, but I'm not.'

'How come you're wearin' blue contacts?'

'This the real color of my eyes.' It was a sensitive subject for Sammy Tigertail; conspicuous evidence of his mixed ancestry. He wasn't ashamed so much as uncomfortable. Skinner's kid was quick, and fearless with the questions.

He said, 'That fleece you've got on is a Patagonia.'

'My deerskin loincloth is at the dry cleaner,' the Seminole cracked. 'Don't you read the papers, boy? We're like the new Arabs. We got casinos and night-clubs and hotels. Our chief is now called the chairman, and he just sold his Gulfstream to Vince Vaughn. That's how far we've come.'

The boy looked stung. 'I didn't mean anything bad.'

'I know you didn't.'

'My mom had me write a paper about Osceola, what they did to him,' Fry said. 'What *we* did to him.'

The Indian felt sort of lousy about jerking the kid's chain. 'Come on. It wasn't you that killed him.'

'On the Internet I read how your tribe never surrendered, not ever. That's cool,' said Fry.

'Depends what you mean by "surrendered." They booked Justin Timberlake at the Seminole Hard Rock for New Year's.' Sammy Tigertail was ready to change the subject. 'I heard about your skateboard crash. How's the headache?'

'I'll live.'

'Mr. Skinner said for me to make sure you keep that football helmet on 'til we find your mother. That way, he won't get yelled at.'

'But it's too heavy.'

'Do what your dad says. We should go now.'

Fry put on the Dolphins helmet and followed Sammy Tigertail, who again asked if he needed water.

'Nope. I'm good,' Fry said.

The Indian had to laugh. 'You remind me of me,' he said, 'back when I was a white boy.'

'Was your dad like mine?'

'He cared just as much. He would've made *me* wear that damn thing, too.'

Sammy Tigertail wondered what his life would be like if his father were still alive. I'd probably be off at college now, he thought, studying business or accounting, and dating a trippy coed like Gillian.

Fry said, 'Hey, can you slow down a little?'

The Indian turned in time to see the boy teeter. He caught him under the armpits and slung him over a shoulder.

'Actually I feel like shit,' the kid murmured.

'Deep breaths,' Sammy Tigertail advised, traipsing onward through the scrub and hammock.

Perry Skinner had been waiting for the Seminole in the mangroves near the skiff. He took Fry and hugged him.

'Not too tight,' the boy squeaked, 'or I'll start hurlin'.'

Skinner lay him on the casting deck of his boat and looked him over. 'It's my fault,' he said, 'draggin' you out here with a goddamn concussion.'

'I'll be okay. Where's Mom?'

'Sammy and I are fixin' to go get her right now. Stay here in the shade.'

'But I wanna come, too—'

'No!'

The kid sighed unhappily. Skinner slipped a seat cushion under his head and told him not to worry. 'We won't be long. Sammy knows right where she's at.'

The Seminole nodded. He figured it would be easy to find the place again in the daylight.

'And it's just her and the guy,' Skinner said. 'Sammy said the girlfriend ran off.'

'I know, Dad.' Fry described his encounter with Eugenie Fonda. 'She was nice. She stayed with me last night after I got sick. The Coast Guard chopper picked her up this morning.'

Skinner turned to Sammy Tigertail. 'Well, that simplifies things. You ready?'

The Indian set off in the lead. He improvised a path through the cactus plants to the ravine that Gillian had named Beer Can Gulch, because of the hundreds of empty tall boys. Perry Skinner called it a 'recycler's wet dream.'

Sammy Tigertail pointed to the Calusa shell mound. 'She's camped on the other side.'

Skinner ran up the slope, the Seminole two steps behind. At the top, Sammy Tigertail pointed out a clearing, fifty yards away. They saw a couple of pup tents, but no sign of Honey Santana or the remaining Texan.

Skinner was halfway down the hill before realizing he was alone; the Seminole hadn't moved.

'What's wrong?' Skinner called out.

Sammy Tigertail motioned for him to return, and Skinner jogged back. There was no easy way to tell him, so the Indian said it directly: 'He's not dead, Mr. Skinner.'

'Who's not dead?'

'That guy I hit with the rifle butt. The one with the tape on his hand that you said was after your wife. I told you I killed him but I guess I didn't.'

Skinner grabbed Sammy Tigertail's arm. 'How do you know?'

'Because this is the spot where I hammered him. He fell into that cactus patch and now he's gone.'

'Show me.'

The Indian walked him to the place, careful to avoid the spiny plants. Skinner noted numerous crushed leaves and several loose threads of cloth.

'Maybe somebody moved the body,' he said quietly.

'No, sir, I don't believe so.' Sammy Tigertail pointed to a furrow where something large had slid down the shell mound into the pile of Busch cans.

'Like a gator drag,' the Indian said. Nesting alligators grooved similar trails while hauling themselves back and forth to the water. This one had been made by a human.

Skinner quickly scouted Beer Can Gulch. He discovered a line of unmistakable tracks leading up another slope; recurring impressions of kneecaps and elbows.

'The bastard's crawling,' he said.

Sammy Tigertail had mixed feelings. He was relieved that he hadn't killed the white man and set loose another bothersome death spirit. At the same time, he was sorry that the guy was still around to cause trouble.

'What's his name again, Mr. Skinner?'

'Piejack.'

'As bad hurt as he is, he won't get far.'

'He doesn't need to. It's a small island, like you said.' Perry Skinner pulled the .45 from his waist and clicked off the safety. He said, 'Sammy, I forgot to thank you for finding my son.'

'He's a good kid,' the Seminole said.

'It would destroy him if something happened to his mom.'

'Or to you, Mr. Skinner.'

Gun in hand, Fry's father disappeared over the crest of the Calusa mound. Sammy Tigertail sprinted after him, kicking up a dust of ancient shells and warrior bones.

Twenty-three

As the helicopter sped north along the coast, Eugenie Fonda frowned out the window. One minute she'd been watching snowy egrets scatter like confetti across a carpet of mangroves; then abruptly the view had changed to a dreary checkerboard of parking lots, condo towers and suburbs. Eugenie had anticipated a rush of relief at the first sight of civilization, but instead she felt depressed.

Gillian was chatting up one of the Coast Guard spotters, while another crewman tended to the private investigator. Eugenie couldn't hear a thing over the turbines, which was fine. Her thoughts turned to the boy in the football helmet, Honey's son. Eugenie tried to imagine what it was like living in the back-water of Everglades City, where there were no Jamba Juices or Olive Gardens or Blockbusters; where the only entertainment was a swamp bigger than Dallas.

Fry seems like a fairly normal kid, she thought. A happy kid, too. She was sure that his old man would find him soon, and run him to a doctor.

Eugenie also wondered about the tall blue-eyed Seminole. She was glad that she hadn't tried seducing him to get a lift off the island, because that would have hurt Gillian, of whom she'd grown fond. It also averted the humiliating possibility that the Indian might have refused to have sex with her. Eugenie was unaccustomed to such rejection because she was unaccustomed to dealing with men of character.

Exhibit A being Boyd Shreave.

On the regret meter, Eugenie Fonda had passed the 'What was I thinking?' stage and was cruising toward 'Boyd who?' Their fling had been an idle blunder of her own devising, and she bore him no malice. In fact, she would've been bummed if he were mauled by a panther, poisoned by a coral snake or otherwise savaged in the boondocks.

But Eugenie doubted that a fate so colorful would befall her dull Boyd. She saw him begging a ride back to the mainland with Honey and her ex, then hastening to Fort Worth on a doomed mission to head off a divorce. It was easy to envision his thunderstruck reaction as Lily Shreave presented the graphic pictorial and video evidence of his infidelity. A more endearing schmuck might win a reprieve, but Boyd didn't stand a chance. Eugenie had no reason to hope that being single and destitute would improve his personality, or his prospects. Boyd was what he was, and she'd already moved on.

Minutes after the helicopter landed in Fort Myers, an ambulance whisked Lester off to a hospital. A female paramedic examined Eugenie and Gillian while a Coast Guard petty officer took their statements. Gillian told him that she was a weather personality for WSUK, a non-existent television station in Tallahassee. Eugenie, using her real name of Jean Leigh Hill, was inspired to identify herself as

Gillian's videographer. The two of them had gotten lost, she explained, on a kayak expedition in the Ten Thousand Islands. Juicing up the yarn, Gillian said they'd befriended Lester, who while skinny-dipping was shot by a poacher who'd mistaken him for a manatee. The ski-masked assailant, she added, escaped in a silver-blue speedboat called *Wet Dream*.

The young Coast Guard officer showed no sign of doubting the yarn. He mentioned that *Wet Dream* was the most common boat name in Florida, followed by *Reel Love* and *Vitamin Sea*. He also reported that Lester was actually Theodore Dealey, and that he was suffering from a rare and unpronounceable medical disorder. The petty officer commended Gillian for diving into Dismal Key Pass to assist Mr. Dealey, who would have otherwise drowned. The petty officer then asked the women if they'd seen anyone besides the trigger-happy poacher on the island, and both of them – wishing to protect the fugitive Seminole – answered no.

The petty officer said they were free to leave, and offered to call a cab. Eugenie picked up the Halliburton that held Dealey's video gear; Gillian grabbed the one with the Nikon.

Outside it was getting warm, so they waited in the parking lot and soaked up the sun. Gillian yawned and said, 'So, whatcha gonna do now – go home to Texas?'

'I haven't decided. You?'

'Back to FSU, I guess. Try not to flunk out this term.'

'Bet you're gonna miss Taco,' Eugenie said.

Gillian laughed. 'It's *Thlocko*. And yeah, I miss him already,' she said. 'But, hey, at least we got to do it. Only once – but he was amazingly awesome.'

'Well, good for you.' It was the natural order of

things, and Eugenie didn't feel the least bit jealous.

'I could totally eat a horse,' Gillian said, stretching.

'Me, too.'

'Can I borrow a few bucks?'

'All I've got is a credit card,' said Eugenie, 'but you're welcome to join me. There's some stuff I need to tell you, anyway.'

'Cool. Where do you wanna go?'

'Looks like a good day for the beach.'

'I'm there,' Gillian said.

'And maybe a spa treatment?'

'Oh, momma.'

'And for lunch,' Eugenie said, 'a bowl of French onion soup.'

'You're my hero,' said Gillian.

'That's what I want to talk to you about.'

Tree-bound, Boyd Shreave was revisiting the high points of his telemarketing career:

Troy Marchtower, age seventy-three, who had dumped the last of his 401(k) into sixteen acres of abandoned soybean fields near Gulfport, Mississippi, with the expectation (based on Shreave's spiel) that the tract would be developed into upscale waterfront town houses. Hurricane Katrina obliterated Gulfport soon afterward, and Marchtower's property lay beneath seven feet of toxic mud, a bleak turn of events that Shreave couldn't have foreseen (and in any case fell under the contractually absolving 'act of God' clause).

Mr. and Mrs. Clement Derr, whom Shreave had signed up for supplementary health insurance that cost a whopping $137.20 per week. Unfortunately for the Derrs, the policy reimbursed only for treatment of cholera, Ebola virus, chikungunya fever, trypanosomiasis, and six other tropical diseases not likely to afflict a couple in their mid-eighties living in Skowhegan, Maine.

Mrs. Rosa Antoinette Shannon, who was so upset to hear that Hillary Clinton was secretly plotting to confiscate all privately owned firearms that she'd patriotically recited for Boyd Shreave her husband's Platinum American Express number, pledging $25,000 to a Republican PAC called Americans for Unlimited Self-Defense, which had hired Relentless to do its fund-raising. Rosa's donation was hastily returned after it was learned that her spouse was none other than Marco 'Twinkie' Shannon, the most prolific supplier of Mexican heroin on the eastern seaboard. His unappetizing past came to light in personal correspondence from the East Jersey State Prison, where he was serving twenty to life for kneecapping two associates on the driving range at Pine Valley. In a handwritten letter leaked to the *Washington Post*, Mr. Shannon – citing a previous commitment – regretfully declined an invitation to visit the White House with other GOP donors for a photograph with the First Lady and her Scottish terrier.

All three deals had been buttoned up by Boyd Shreave's supervisor but, being the one who'd chummed up the suckers, Shreave awarded himself full credit and glory. If Relentless wouldn't take him back, surely a competitor phone bank would.

His immediate challenge, however, was to escape the island. As the morning ticked away, Shreave felt less like a 'Survivor' and more like Gilligan. He was reluctant to attempt descending from the royal poinciana, partly because he didn't trust his balance and partly because he felt safer in the branches than he did on the ground. In addition to a nerve-racking assortment of wildlife, at least two dangerous outlaws were running loose – the vile-smelling derelict who'd kidnapped Honey Santana, and the elusive Indian with whom Eugenie Fonda supposedly had skipped off. Boyd Shreave had no desire to interact with either of them.

Nearly as daunting was the cactus dilemma: Directly below Shreave's roost was a thriving spray of prickly pear. An ill-chosen step, a gust of wind – and he'd be impaled like a cricket on barbed wire. He blanched at the sight of the long, pale needles on the beckoning green pads, and thought: *Not again*. Shreave flashed back to that doomed orthotics sales call in Arlington, the old crow practically tripping him with her oxygen tank and then cackling when he fell crotch-first into her potted dwarf saguaro. The pincushion tracks on his pubic triangle might have paled, but the excruciating memory had not.

Shreave hugged the poinciana and resolved not to look down until he was better prepared. Fastening his eyes on the sun-kissed treetops proved calming, and gradually he began inching his butt backward along the bough. Eventually he'd have to stand and traverse branch to branch, but why hurry? The slower he moved, the less noise he made – and until the next helicopter appeared, his plan was to remain silent and unseen.

It hadn't occurred to Boyd Shreave that absolutely nobody would be searching for him; that his absence would leave no void in the lives of those who knew him. He would have been stupefied to learn that the

Coast Guard crew that he'd fruitlessly signaled had been sent by his own wife to rescue the private investigator who was gathering ammunition for their divorce.

After barely fifteen minutes of worm-like exertions, Shreave needed a rest. Clinging with one hand to a sturdy sprig, he fished a granola bar out of his shorts and tore off the wrapper with his teeth. Cramming the dry shingle into his mouth, he began to crunch so loudly that he failed to hear the two men enter the campsite below.

'Yo!' one of them yelled.

Shreave jerked and let out a terrified gasp, spraying crumbs. Anxiously he lowered his eyes and appraised the strangers, one of whom was carrying a weapon flatter and sleeker than Honey's Taser. Shreave assumed that it was a real handgun and felt compelled to make a case for his own harmlessness, yet he was unable to speak. With his gullet spackled by damp oats and mushed peanuts, he was left to pant like a pleuritic mandrill.

'Get your ass down here,' said the man with the gun. He was middle-aged, with broad shoulders and a real outdoor tan.

His companion was taller and much younger, with brown skin, high cheekbones and light eyes. Shreave suspected that he might be Eugenie's Indian. The man held up the foil wrapping from the snack bar and said, 'You drop this?'

Shreave was so dry that he couldn't make himself swallow. Theatrically he pointed at his bulged cheeks and began huffing, to demonstrate that his speech was temporarily impeded.

The man with the handgun asked, 'Are you one of

the kayakers? Did you take the tour with Honey Santana?'

Shreave saw nothing but risk in admitting the connection, so he shook his head and shrugged in fake puzzlement. He was confident that he could mime a lie as convincingly as he could vocalize one, and as usual he was mistaken.

The Indian said, 'The guy's bullshitting, Mr. Skinner.'

The other man nodded impatiently. 'I don't have time for this bumblefuck.' He trained the handgun on the imaginary center point of Shreave's shiny forehead. 'Last chance, junior. The truth shall set your sorry ass free.'

Shreave's response was a rude quiniela of fear-based reflexes. First he soiled himself and then he volcanically expelled the remains of the honey-nut granola bar. The intruders alertly stepped back from the poinciana, avoiding the volley.

'Nasty,' the Indian said.

The gunman re-aimed. 'Get outta that tree,' he commanded again.

Shreave wiped his face with the back of his hand. It was time for a desperate change of strategy: the truth.

'A man took her!' he shouted down hoarsely. 'Took Honey!'

'What'd he look like?' the gunman demanded.

'Sick,' Shreave replied. 'All fucked-up – his hand, his face . . .'

'Where'd they go?' the Indian asked.

Shreave pointed feverishly. 'That way! He had her on a leash.'

'A leash?' The older man slowly lowered the gun.

'Yeah! Can you guys help me down?'

'What for?' The Indian crumpled the foil from Shreave's snack bar and shoved it into his pocket. He spat in the cactus patch and said, 'Damn litterbug. I hope you rot up there.'

Then he followed the gunman out of the camp.

For diversion, Honey composed in her head another letter to the newspapers. Inspired by her predicament, the topic was sexual harassment.

> *To the Editor:*
>
> *Recently I had an altercation with an employer, Mr. Louis Piejack, who groped me in the workplace. I fought back to defend myself, and then immediately quit my job.*
>
> *In retrospect I should have reported what happened to the authorities and contacted a lawyer, to deter Mr. Piejack from future misbehavior. Unfortunately, he has persisted with his unwanted advances and is presently holding me captive at gunpoint on a deserted island in the western Everglades.*
>
> *The lesson to be learned from my experience is that women must aggressively discourage mental and physical intimidation at the job site – not just with a crab mallet, but with the force of law.*
>
> *Most sincerely,*
> *Honey Santana*

She thought it was a darn good letter; succinct and low-key, the way the newspapers preferred them. If she'd had a pencil and paper, she would have written it down.

'You ready, angel?' Piejack asked woozily. The pain pills were working their magic.

'Ready for what, Louis?'

'A ride in my boat.'

He was sprawled beside her, befouling an otherwise-splendid morning. He hadn't stirred in so long that the fire ants had quietly returned to their dank hideaway inside his surgical swathing. Piejack had found another bottle of water in a duffel bag but, after laboring to open it, had lost interest. Listlessly he'd watched Honey drink the whole thing. She was grateful to be free of the ropes but mindful of the sawed-off shotgun, which Piejack had wedged erect between his legs.

'Look here, I don't need no hands!' He moved his hips to make the barrel sway.

'Adorable,' Honey said.

'You think *this* is a monster, wait'll you see ol' John Henry.'

'That's what you named your cock?' Honey laughed. 'Sorry, Louis, but that's lame.'

He lifted his head. 'You got somethin' better? I'll call him whatever you want.'

Honey said, 'Okay. How about Charlemagne?'

Piejack snorted. 'Sounds like a girl.'

'He was a king, Louis.'

'King a what?'

Now that Piejack was half-stoned, Honey had decided to make a grab for the stubby shotgun.

She said, 'He was king of the Franks.'

'Then why don't I just call my dick Frank? It's easier to say.'

'Because Charlemagne sounds better,' Honey said. 'Hotter.'

Piejack smiled. 'You like that, huh?'

He pumped his pelvis twice, bobbing the gun. The weapon was small enough that Honey believed she could handle it.

'He was the master of Western Europe, Louis. Emperor of the Romans,' she said. 'How about another pill?'

With his good hand, Piejack picked up the rope. His eyelids drooped and his head began to loll. 'Charlie Main,' he murmured. 'That ain't so hard.'

'You want the last Vicodin or not?'

'Sure. Bottle's in my pants,' he said. 'But first I need you to take care a somethin' else down there. See, I got this special itch I can't scratch 'cause my fingers are messed up.'

Honey said, 'Don't even ask.'

'It's Charlie Main's boys.'

'Yeah, I figured.'

'Aw, come on. They got a rash that won't quit,' he said.

Honey scooted close and nearly gagged on his smell. 'Be a good boy and take your medicine. Here, let me help with the bottle.'

She leaned over as if reaching toward his pockets, then locked both hands around the sawed-off. She yanked, but the barrel wouldn't budge – Piejack had clamped his thighs on the grip. Honey was shocked by his strength, and the quickness of his reflexes.

He cursed and rolled to his right, dragging her body across his torso. The shotgun's muzzle stuck hard in the ground, causing both of them to lose hold. As Honey tumbled she heard a muted concussion, and then a cry.

Her ears were ringing when she sat up. Piejack's face

was spattered with sand and leaf fragments blown back from the point-blank blast. He moaned dolefully and pinched his knees together, the heavy recoil having replaced his private itch with a stupendous bruising.

Honey couldn't believe that the man was still conscious. Wobbling to his feet, Piejack retrieved the wisping gun, which looked as if it had been used to dig a grave.

'Don't you fuckin' move!' he rasped at Honey.

She didn't. Her jaw was pounding again, and a sharp pain in her belly made her wince – one of Piejack's slimy cactus needles, poking through her shirt. Honey wondered if any infection could be worse than his company.

Desolately, she asked, 'What now, Louis?'

He hunched forward. 'Louder!'

'I said, what now?'

In frustration he screeched, 'You think this is funny? Huh, bitch?'

Honey realized that his ear holes were plugged with dirt. As a test, she said, 'Louis, you're nothing but a rancid bucket of scum.'

He squinted quizzically yet gave no indication of registering the insult.

Swell, Honey thought. Now I get to play charades with a sex fiend. She tugged at her earlobes and shook her head.

'You can't hear nuthin neither?' Piejack asked loudly.

Honey made a rowing motion and shouted, 'Where's your boat, Louis? Let's go find the boat!'

'The boat?'

'Bravo!' she said, clapping.

Piejack smiled crookedly.

'Mom! Dad!' A voice from the woods.

Honey went white – it sounded like Fry, but that was impossible. Fry was far away, safe at home with his father, and neither of them would've known where to find her. Honey told herself that she was imagining what she heard; cracking under the stress.

'Hey, Mom?'

The voice was closer now – too close. Honey didn't answer. With all her heart she wanted to shout back, but she knew better. If it was really Fry, he'd come running. No matter what she told him to do, he'd come running to save her.

And he couldn't possibly save her, not all by himself. He was twelve and a half years old, for heaven's sake.

'Mom, Dad, it's me!'

Honey already knew.

Run away, kiddo, she thought. *Please, God, make him go the other way.*

There was still hope, because Piejack couldn't hear him.

'Where are you?' the boy hollered.

He was dangerously close now. Tragically close.

Honey couldn't stop herself.

'Fry, go away!' she blurted. 'Go get help!'

Piejack was momentarily preoccupied, pawing at a string of fire ants that had greedily attached themselves to his neck.

'Fry, do what I say!' Honey cried out. 'Go away—'

But there he was, sprinting out of the trees as fast as he could, which was fast indeed . . . and wearing, of all things, a football helmet.

Honey held out her arms and blinked away hot

348

tears. Fry practically knocked her down with a flying hug.

'You okay?' he asked breathlessly. 'God, what happened to your face?'

'I'm fine. Just fine.'

The boy stared at Louis Piejack and the stubby shotgun.

'He's nearly deaf,' Honey said.

Piejack was glaring at both of them. 'Git lost, kid!'

Fry whispered to his mother: 'I heard the gun go off and I freaked. Have you seen Dad?'

'What are you talking about?'

'Dad's tryin' to find you. We came out here together.'

Honey thought: *I'm gonna brain that man.*

'I tole you to beat it!' Piejack bellowed at Fry.

'Chill out, Louis,' Honey said.

'It's just you and me, angel, that was the deal. You and me for all time.' Piejack coldly leveled the sawed-off at Fry. 'I ain't gonna be nobody's step-pappy. Now git movin', boy. Go home to your old man.'

Honey firmly turned her son. 'You heard him. Get outta here.'

'I'm not leaving. No way.'

'What'd you say?' Piejack tilted his head. 'I can't hear a goddamn word. You gotta speak up.'

Fry pulled free of his mother's grasp and stepped toward Louis Piejack until the barrel of the shotgun touched the face guard of his helmet.

'I said, I'M NOT GOING ANYWHERE!' the boy hollered.

Then he doubled over and puked on Piejack's shoes.

Twenty-four

For once, Honey Santana's head was absolutely clear. No tunes blared. No sirens whined. No trains whistled. A rare and welcome clarity prevailed.

A brutish criminal had clobbered her son, and there was only one appropriate response: Honey clamped both hands around Louis Piejack's oily neck.

It felt right; empowering, as Oprah might say.

Honey knew that if the man shot her, she would die strangling him. Saving Fry was all that mattered.

Honey forced Piejack against a pigeon plum tree, trapping the shotgun between their bodies. The barrel lodged lengthwise in her cleavage, the dirty muzzle sticking up at her chin. Fire ants began pouring out of Piejack's bandaged hand, which he flogged against his thigh until the surgical dressing fell off in a putrid husk.

To hinder his movements she pressed harder, though at first the lecherous fishmonger seemed to enjoy the rough frontal contact. He winked moistly and ran his spotted tongue around his lips.

When Honey squeezed harder, Piejack's smirk faded. His yellowed eyes began to bulge and seep.

Brownish spittle bubbled from the corners of his mouth, and his rank breath came in short, croupy emanations. As she dug her fingertips into his Adam's apple, Honey regretted having trimmed her nails the week before. She nonetheless felt capable of inflicting mortal damage, and, despite his narcotic intake, the sonofabitch was definitely uncomfortable. She could tell by his gurgling.

'Watch out!' It was Fry.

To Honey's immense relief, the boy hadn't been hurt. Piejack's gun butt had cracked the football helmet and knocked him flat, but Fry had sprung up quickly. Honey caught glimpses of him circling the scene, darting in to throw wild, ineffectual punches.

'I told you to get outta here!' When she opened her mouth to yell, her broken jawbone clacked like a castanet.

'No way!' Fry shouted back.

'Do – as – I – say!'

'Mom! Look!'

'Oh shit.'

From wrists to shoulders, her sleeves shimmered with fire ants. They were abandoning Piejack en masse, using Honey as a bridge. By the hundreds they streamed down her arms, but she was afraid to release her grip on Piejack to slap them away. He'd need only a moment, Honey knew, to regain control of the sawed-off.

As Fry flayed at the insects with a palmetto frond, Honey tried not to think about where the blood-red hordes might be heading. Piejack's misshapen face was darkening due to loss of oxygen, yet he continued to grapple ferociously with good hand and bad for possession of the shotgun. So heated was the scuffle that Honey failed to notice a column of ants disappear between the top buttons of her shirt. The stings seared, like a sprinkle of hot acid, and she wondered how much she could endure.

Not enough, it turned out. Within seconds she was breathless from the pain. She let go of Piejack, tore off her shirt and flung herself down. When she stopped rolling, he stood over her panting and clutching the sawed-off. His shoes still reeked of Fry's vomit.

Honey sat up and crossed her arms, to cover her bra. Her chest was burning along a sinuous track of tiny crimson bites.

'They's one in your curls,' Piejack croaked.

As shaky as he was, the man had managed to hook one of his reconnected digits, possibly a pinkie, over the shotgun's trigger. With the more nimble fingers of his good hand he was grubbing dirt from his ears.

Honey flicked the ant from her hair and thought: *Where the hell is my son?*

To find out if Piejack's hearing had returned, she asked in a level tone, 'What're you going to do now, Louis?'

'What the hell d'ya think? I'm gonna shoot yer fine ass,' he said, 'but first I'm gonna fuck it.'

He coughed up something, scowled at the taste and spat. Honey peered out between his knees, looking in vain for Fry.

Piejack said, 'Your kid's run off. But I'll catch him later, don'tcha worry.'

His eyeballs rolled and he gulped slowly, like a toad. It was plain that Honey had injured him.

'Lose them pants,' he told her.

'Not a chance, Louis.'

'You know damn well I'll shoot.'

'And that's the only way it would ever happen between us – if I was dead,' Honey said.

'Now, that ain't too bright.' Piejack touched the sawed-off to her forehead. 'But if that's how you want it . . .'

Honey expected her whole life to flash past, like people said it would, yet only a single event from her thirty-nine years replayed in fast-forward: Fry's arrival.

She'd gone into labor on a Monday afternoon, six weeks early. Radioed Perry out on the crab boat. He raced home, carried her to the truck and sped ninety-five miles an hour across the state to Jackson Hospital in Miami. A sweet old Cuban doctor asked if she wanted an epidural, and Honey answered no because she figured the baby would be small and it wouldn't hurt so much coming out. But it hurt plenty, and lasted way longer than she'd expected: fifteen hours and forty-one minutes. Perry stayed by her side. When there was pain he'd squeeze Honey's hand, and when there wasn't, he'd read to her from a book of fishing stories by Zane Grey. Honey had no interest in fishing, but it was the first time she'd heard her husband read aloud and for some reason she found it calming.

Then the cramps got fierce. Doctor told her to push. Nurses told her to push. Perry told her to push. Honey remembered biting her lip, thinking: *Thank God the little guy didn't go full term. He'd split me open like a melon!* And all of a sudden there he was, wriggling on the sheets like a purple tadpole: Fry Martí Skinner, four pounds and fourteen ounces.

From the first breath he seemed uncommonly self-assured. Never cried once in the delivery room, not even when Perry snipped the cord. The nurses were freaking because the child wouldn't make a peep, but Honey wasn't worried. Boy was smart. Knew he was safe and loved.

Mom and Dad were the ones who'd wept when the nurses bundled Fry off to the preemie ward and wired him up like a mouse in a laboratory tank. Fluid in the lungs, the doctor said, avoiding the term *pneumonia* so as not to further derail Honey, who was already frantic. She refused to leave the hospital, Skinner bringing her meals and books and fresh clothes. Fifteen days later Fry was home and his mother was whole, though not unchanged.

It was natural now, with time running out, that the final thought in her head would be of her son.

Who now emerged helmetless from behind the pigeon plum tree. He was carrying a bleached and broken two-by-four.

Honey willed herself to be silent and locked her gaze upon Louis Piejack's shotgun. Best that he kept pointing it at her, not elsewhere.

Slowly Fry crept forward.

What colossal balls, marveled Honey, and steeled herself for the end.

Louis Piejack had never been enthralled by the great outdoors. The unsentimental commerce of seafood had drawn him to the Ten Thousand Islands. It was simple: If you were a fish peddler, you went where there were fish. Piejack couldn't fathom why tourists and tree huggers gushed about the Everglades. He had no use for the vicious bugs and the infernal heat; his free hours were spent at home with the windows latched and the AC blasting and a case of Heinies cooling in the refrigerator.

It was into that cozy chamber of comfort that Piejack had dreamed of moving Honey Santana, but he now wondered if it was worth all the grief. Pretty as she was, her attitude remained piss-poor.

She was tough and outspoken and damn near fearless – qualities which in a female did not appeal to Piejack. Plus she had a rotten temper; for squeezing her boob she'd walloped his nuts, and for clocking her bratty son she'd nearly strangled him.

Piejack preferred not to shoot her, but he was running out of fight. As the dreamy effect of the painkillers ebbed, so did his optimism for a blissful union. From the day he'd set his sights on Honey, physical affliction had been his only companion. Anesthetized by lust, he'd doggedly pursued the quest, convinced that he could melt Honey's frigid resistance. So far he'd failed spectacularly. Even in his addled state, Piejack comprehended that this was a woman who wouldn't settle easily into the role of obedient homemaker-slash-sex slave. He'd have to battle for every lousy feel, and she was strong enough to make him pay with blood. Piejack knew a Key West shrimper who'd gotten himself into the same sort of fix, with an Internet bride from the Philippines. Three nights into the honeymoon, the girl had pinned his scrotum to the mattress with a cocktail fork, then set fire to the motel room. Piejack shuddered at the thought.

He allowed the muzzle of the shotgun to kiss Honey's forehead. 'I don't really wanna shoot ya, angel, and I gotta feelin' you really don't wanna die. So just do what Louis says and everything's gonna be fine.'

Expressionless, she gazed up the barrel.

'Now, git yourself naked and let's start this romance off proper,' Piejack said. 'Then we'll take the boat home and be happy ever after, just you, me and Charlie Main. As for your boy, well, he's better off with his daddy. You can visit him maybe on Saturdays, if I don't need you at the market. That's the fuckin' deal, angel, take it or leave it.'

Honey said, 'I need time to think, Louis.'

'How long, goddammit?'

'About three seconds.'

'Okay,' Piejack said. 'One . . . two . . .'

On the count of three, something sharp and heavy struck him from behind and knocked the air from his lungs. Piejack pitched sideways, thinking: *This ain't love.*

The first white person to betray Sammy Tigertail had been his stepmother, who'd dumped him at the reservation the morning after his father was buried. The second white person to betray him had been Cindy, his ex-girlfriend, who'd started screwing anyone with a functioning cock after the Seminole demolished her backyard meth lab and confiscated a butane-powered menorah that she'd swiped from a local Hanukkah display.

Sammy Tigertail would concede that his Native American heritage wasn't a factor in either instance of treachery – his stepmother was simply a self-centered shrew who didn't want to be saddled with a teenager, while poor Cindy was a buzzed-out tramp who would have cheated on Prince William for a thimbleful of crank. As it turned out, both women had done Sammy

Tigertail a favor. One had liberated him from his pallid existence as Chad McQueen, and the other had sprung him from a destructive and potentially gene-thinning romance.

Like many modern Seminoles, he had never been personally abused, subjugated, swindled or displaced by a white settler. The 'injurious accompaniments' to which the Rev. Clay MacCauley had alluded in his nineteenth-century journal were old, bitter history; there had been no significant perfidy or bloodshed for generations. By the 1970s Florida was being stampeded from coast to coast, and the fortunes of the Seminoles had begun to change in a most unexpected way. It all started with a couple of bingo halls, and the knowledge that bored white people were fools for gambling. Soon they were swarming to the reservations by the busloads, and the bingo venues expanded to make room for card games and electronic poker.

Even as its numbers dwindled, the tribe's prominence was inversely escalating to a dimension that boggled the elders. Wealth brought what three bloody wars had failed to win from the whites: deference. Once written off as a ragged band of heathens, the Seminole Nation grew into a formidable corporate power with its own brigade of lawyers and lobbyists. The Indians found themselves embraced by the lily-white business establishment, and avidly courted by politicians of all persuasions.

Some tribal members called it justice while others, such as Sammy Tigertail, called it a sellout. His uncle Tommy, who had helped mastermind the Seminole casino strategy, respected and even sympathized with the misgivings of his half-blooded nephew.

'My heart was in the same place,' he'd once told Sammy, 'but then one day I asked myself, Who is there left to fight? Andrew Jackson's dead, boy. His face is on the twenty-dollar bill, and we've got suitcases full at the casinos. Every night we stack 'em in a Brink's truck and haul 'em to the bank. It's better than spitting on the old bastard's grave. Think of it, boy. All their famous soldiers are gone – Jackson, Jesup, Clinch – yet here we are.'

Yeah, thought Sammy Tigertail, here I am. Risking my dumb ass to help a white man rescue his wacko ex-wife.

The shot had sounded odd; like a firecracker in a toilet.

Skinner was running hard, the Indian close on his heels. Still it took several minutes to cross the island, choked as it was with vines and undergrowth. Eventually the two men burst into a broad clearing and Sammy Tigertail saw, on the other side, his own campsite. Some sort of unholy fight was under way – yelling, grunting, writhing amid the dirt and shells.

No one appeared to have been wounded, despite the ominous echo of gunfire earlier. The Seminole briefly considered dashing to his canoe, for the frenzied scene in front of him promised a messy climax that was certain to further complicate his life. There are at least 9,999 other islands, he thought, where a man might find peace and isolation.

And Sammy Tigertail might have bolted if it weren't for the improbable sight of Skinner's adolescent son whaling at a figure whom the Indian recognized as the malodorous mutant he'd clocked with his rifle butt, the one Gillian called Band-Aid Man and Skinner called Piejack. The man had rebounded impressively from the head bashing, for he was able to fend off the boy while at the same time wrestle a youthful and athletically built woman. From her salty dockside vocabulary, Sammy Tigertail pegged her as the kid's missing mother, Skinner's former wife. She and Band-Aid Man were struggling for control of a metallic object that looked like a modified shotgun of the crude, chopped-down style favored by redneck felons and myopic urban gangsters. The Seminole heard the weapon make two dull clicks, as if a shell had jammed in the chamber.

Ahead he saw Skinner go down at full speed, tumbling and grabbing at his left knee. What happened next took only a few seconds, but it unfolded before Sammy Tigertail with a halting and grim inevitability. Skinner's ex-wife pushed away from Piejack and scrambled to Skinner's side. Their son made two steps in the same direction before Piejack grabbed his ankle and jerked him violently backward, causing him to drop the piece of lumber he'd been wielding.

The man then leered and displayed for the boy's horrified parents the shiny black .45, which had been jarred from Skinner's grasp when he fell. 'Lookie who's here!' Piejack cackled at Skinner. 'This is perfect! Now I aim to pay you back for what your Latino gorillas did to my hand.'

As the fiend placed the weapon to Fry's temple, Sammy Tigertail regretted losing his composure and busting his rifle into pieces, as now he had no means by which to end the mayhem. Without moving a step, he took inventory. Skinner was still down and in terrible pain. Honey Santana embraced him, whispering and sniffling softly. Her lower jaw was badly bruised and hanging slack. A few yards away, Piejack kept one arm hooked around their son's neck, the kid looking sick and dizzy again. Balanced tenuously in Piejack's bare and gangrenous left hand was Skinner's semiautomatic, the trigger covered by a discolored kernel of a finger. The discarded sawed-off was on the ground.

'Get lost, asswipe.' It was Piejack, finally taking notice of the Seminole. 'This ain't yer bidness.'

The creep might be right, Sammy Tigertail thought, but here I am.

'Be on your way,' Piejack said, ''less you wanna hole in your belly.'

The Indian could almost hear his uncle saying: What's happening there has nothing to do with you. It's more crazy shit among white people, that's all.

'Can I get my guitar?' Sammy Tigertail asked. He had spotted the Gibson, his fondest connection to the white world, in the cinders of the dead campfire.

Piejack said, 'That thing's yours? Ha!'

Sammy Tigertail recalled a quote he'd memorized as a teenager. It was from Gen. Thomas Jesup, appraising the long Indian war in Florida:

We have, at no former period of our history, had to contend with so formidable an enemy. No Seminole proves false to his country, nor has a single instance ever occurred of a first rate warrior having surrendered.

Sammy Tigertail's uncle had said it was mostly true. He'd also said there were some in the tribe who'd dropped their weapons and run like jackrabbits; others who'd taken bribes from the U.S. generals in exchange for scratching their names on worthless treaties.

Many Seminoles were first-rate warriors, Sammy's uncle had said, but a few were not.

'What're you waitin' on? Take the fuckin' guitar and

vamoose,' Piejack said, ' 'fore I shoot your red ass off.'

That's ugly, Sammy Tigertail thought. Ugly and unnecessary.

Crossing the clearing, he could sense the boy watching him. Skinner's ex-wife, too. The Seminole fixed his eyes on the blond Gibson, shining among the ashes.

'Mister, wait,' the kid said.

Sammy Tigertail didn't look up. He lifted the guitar and wiped it with a bandanna. With chagrin he noted a nasty ding in the finish.

'Don't you dare leave us here,' said the boy's mother. 'Please.'

The Indian offered no response. He'd made up his mind.

'For God's sake, Sammy.' It was Mr. Skinner, rising.

The Seminole thought of his great-great-great-grandfather, Chief Thlocklo Tustenuggee, tricked with promises of peace and then imprisoned. Manifest destiny, otherwise known as screwing native peoples out of their homelands, had been a holy crusade among white men of that era. Immune to guilt or shame, they dealt suffering and death to mothers, infants, even the elders. One American president after another, breaking treaties and spitting lies – the boundlessness of their deceptions was altogether stunning.

Sammy Tigertail in his young life had never betrayed a soul. He owned a working conscience that could have sprung from either of his bloodlines. His mother was a moral, hardworking woman; his father had been a decent and truthful man.

'You some kinda retard, or what? I said to get the hell outta here,' Band-Aid Man barked.

'Just a minute.'

'I said *now*!'

The Indian looked up and saw Piejack waggling the .45.

'Bad idea,' Sammy Tigertail said, and began moving toward him.

The man told him to back off, or else. The Seminole continued to advance with long, even strides.

Wide-eyed, Piejack struggled to level the gun.

'Louis, don't be an imbecile!' Honey pleaded.

When he got six feet away, Sammy Tigertail turned. He stepped up to Perry Skinner and held out the guitar. All he said was: 'I believe Mr. Knopfler would understand.'

'Who?' Piejack croaked. 'Unnerstand what?'

Skinner took the instrument by the neck and, limping forward, poised it like an ax.

'Duck,' the Indian advised the former Mrs. Skinner, and then he dived to cover her son.

The gun in Louis Piejack's paw spit an ice-blue spark, but the blond Gibson came down hard, splintering his filthy skull.

Twenty-five

Eugenie Fonda sat on the balcony of her sixth-floor room, fanning her freshly painted toes and watching the sun melt like sorbet into the Gulf of Mexico. Her third Bacardi was sweating cool droplets that snaked down her bare tummy.

The sliding door opened, and Gillian St. Croix stepped out wearing camo flip-flops and a baby-blue tank dress that Eugenie had bought for her at a shop in the lobby. She announced that her mosquito bites had practically vanished, thanks to a magical mint unguent recommended by a Moroccan lady at the spa.

'Check out the sunset,' Eugenie said.

'Yeah, it's awesome.' Gillian arranged herself cross-legged on the other patio chair. 'Wanna hear what he said? Ethan, when I called him?'

Eugenie sipped her drink. 'I can guess what he said, sweetie. "All is forgiven. Come back home."'

'Yeah, but you know what I said? "Find another girl-friend, loser." He's such a loser, not tellin' me about those dolphins. Makin' me think they swam off like Free Willie when all they did was hang around and beg for treats like trained poodles.'

Eugenie had heard the story before but she listened politely. Looking south, she wondered if Boyd Shreave had gotten off the island yet. She hoped that he wouldn't come searching for her, that he wasn't dim enough to believe he was still in the mix.

Gillian went on, 'Ethan doesn't really care about me. It's just the sex.'

'Well, he's a boy.'

'Why are they all like that?'

'Oh, they're not.' Eugenie was thinking in particular of Honey Santana's ex, who'd obviously never stopped loving her. There was no such man in Eugenie's past; even Van Bonneville had quit writing from prison.

'Rate the massage,' Eugenie said.

'Awesome. Eleven on a scale of ten.' Gillian paused and frowned. 'Know what? I gotta find a new word. I'm so over *awesome.*'

'It's been beaten to death,' Eugenie concurred.

'Hey, how about *super*? I had a *super* massage.'

Eugenie shook her head. '*Super* is over, too. Especially if you're gonna be a big-time TV weather woman.'

'God, who knows what I'm gonna be.' Gillian laughed. 'Did you have the Japanese guy or the deeptissue redneck? I had the redneck.'

'Me too. Showed me pictures of his darling twin boys.'

'Did he?'

'Yeah,' Eugenie said, 'then he took out a vibrator the size of a hoagie and asked me if I was into toys.'

Gillian hooted. 'See! They're all the same!'

Eugenie drained her glass. The sun was gone, the horizon aglow. There were scads of little kids running up from the beach, shouting and giggling and kicking up sand.

'Patience,' she said to Gillian. 'That's the secret. Once you start rushin' into these things, making lousy choices, it's awful hard to dig yourself out. By that I mean it's hard to change.'

Gillian said, 'You haven't done so bad. Look where we are, Genie – the beach, the ocean, rum drinks! The rest of the country's freezin' their butts off.'

Eugenie thought: Treading water is where I am. Maxing out my credit card.

'What happens is, you start to give off a certain vibe,' she said. 'Why do you think that masseur came on to me and not you? Because he knew, sweetie, that I'm not above fucking the help when I get bored. They've got radar for it, men do, the boredom vibe. You be careful about that, okay?'

Gillian went and got a beer from the minibar. She took a slug and said, 'Wait for the good ones – that's what you mean by patience?'

'They're out there. I know for a fact,' Eugenie said.

'Like Thlocko?'

'Find one from earth, Gillian. His *baggage* had baggage.'

'But he's different. I like him.'

Eugenie said, 'Me too.'

'Totally not boring.'

'That's true.'

'Thanks for not sleeping with him. I mean it.'

'Anytime,' said Eugenie.

Gillian tipped the last half of her beer into a clay planter. 'I better head back to Tallahassee tomorrow – I've gotta buy my books for the new term. What about you?'

'I'm on a non-stop to DFW. Gonna quit my shitty job and start over.'

'Yeah? And do what?'

'Quilts. I hear they're coming back. Or maybe scented candles,' Eugenie said with a straight face. 'Something where I can work at home and never have to meet any jerks.'

Gillian watched a flock of gray pelicans crashing bait in the waves. 'What a crazed trip – I mean *crazed*. Maybe we should, like, celebrate.'

Eugenie Fonda agreed. 'I'm thinking lobster,' she said, 'and a Chilean chardonnay.'

'Magnificent,' said Gillian with a wink. 'How's that for a word?'

Ninety-one miles away, Boyd Shreave finally got to change his pants.

He'd waited in the poinciana tree until dusk, listening for the two men who had accosted him at gunpoint. Then he had commenced a nervous descent that transpired in stages, the first being baby steps and the second being a spontaneous heels-over-head plummet. By some miracle, he'd landed short of the cactus patch. And although he'd torn off his windbreaker and bloodied his palms on a ridge of loose oyster shells, Shreave was overjoyed not to have crippled himself.

He removed his soiled boat shorts and searched hurriedly through the Orvis bag for a dry pair of Tommy Bahamas. He settled for apple-green Speedos, which he'd packed in the fanciful expectation of appearing well matched with his bethonged mistress on the beach.

In the pup tent that he and Eugenie Fonda once shared, Shreave found an open bottle of water, which he chugged. From Honey Santana's tent he appropriated bug spray and a small halogen headlamp; from his own gear he took his NASCAR toothbrush and the paperback of *Storm Ghoul*, for toilet paper.

Choosing an escape route was easy – Shreave aimed himself in the opposite direction of that taken by the men searching for Honey. While cowering in the tree he'd heard two small concussions that might have been gunshots, several minutes apart, indicating that something dangerous was happening on the other side of the island. Shreave headed briskly the other way, flaying a rough path through the vines and bushes and spiderwebs.

There was still a rim of amber along the skyline when he lurched through a slender opening in the mangroves. Heedlessly he waded into the water, the soles of his expensive deck shoes grating across a jagged shoal. He hoped to position himself to signal the first passing vessel, but of course no boats would be coming; mainly dope smugglers and poachers traveled at night through the Ten Thousand Islands, and they were not renowned for their Samaritanism.

The flats were turbid and cold, and Shreave in his glorified jockstrap began to shiver. As darkness closed in, he employed Honey's headlamp to scan the intricate tree line for the menacing reflection of panther eyes. Instead what he spotted was a shiny tangerine-colored canoe, canted among the spidery roots.

Excitedly Shreave dragged the craft to open water and, on his fourth attempt, bellied himself over the side. With his lacerated hands he snatched up the paddle and felt an exultant rush – at last he would be free of the place!

He navigated Dismal Key Pass with equal measures of zeal and ineptitude. Despite the slack tide he expended more energy correcting his frequent course oscillations than he did advancing the canoe. The exercise served to warm him, however, and present the illusion of pace. Never had Shreave attempted anything so daring as a getaway, and he regretted that neither Genie nor Lily was there to witness it. He chose to believe that they would have been dazzled.

After an hour he paused to rest, the canoe drifting noiselessly. With a stirring anxiety he contemplated the depth of the night; nothing but shadows and starlight and a pale sickle of moon. Far from being soothed by the silence, Shreave was fretful. It was as if he'd been sucked through a time tunnel into a bleak primeval emptiness with no horizons. He couldn't remember feeling so alone or out of place, and he yearned for evidence of human intrusion – a car's horn, a boom box, the high rumble of a jetliner.

Not being the spiritual sort, Boyd Shreave saw no divine hand in the unbroken wilderness that lay before him; no grand design in the jungled labyrinth of creeks and islets. Such unspoiled vistas inspired in Shreave not a nanosecond of introspection; when it came to raw nature, he remained staunchly incurious and devoid of awe. He would much rather have been back in Fort Worth, watching *American Idol*, swilling beer and gorging himself on microwave burritos.

Grimly he picked up the paddle and went back to work. He hadn't a clue where he was or what direction he was heading, although he suspected that the vast gray body of water to his right was the Gulf of Mexico – no place for a puny canoe. After an hour of ponderous stroking he was in profound discomfort.

Unfamiliar with toil, his arms burned, his lower back ached and his abs were cramping. He'd already decided to quit for the night when he heard what sounded like an engine, and the soft slapping of waves against a hull.

Shreave shoved the paddle between his knees and fumbled to activate the small lamp strapped to his forehead. He swiveled his neck owlishly, playing the narrow white beam back and forth across the water until he located the source of the noise: a small flat-bottomed craft motoring parallel to the canoe, about seventy-five yards away. A tall man stood in the stern of the boat, facing away, one hand on the tiller of the engine.

'Hey!' Shreave called out. 'Over here!'

The man appeared not to have heard him.

'Help!' Shreave steadied the headlamp, trying to center the light on the passing boat. 'Hey, you! Come get me!' he yelled.

The man continued to look the other way. Shreave was nettled; even if the guy was unable to hear him over the motor, he surely saw the flickering from the headlamp.

'What the hell's the matter with you!' Shreave hollered angrily. 'I'm lost out here! I need help!'

The flat-bottomed craft was moving so sluggishly that Shreave wondered if it had mechanical problems. He saw no smoke when he shined the light at the engine, although he noticed two ropes leading tautly from the transom to a lumpish object dragging in the backwash. Shreave couldn't see what the stranger was towing, and he didn't care. The guy obviously knew his way around the islands, and Shreave desperately needed a ride out.

'Hey! Over here!' Shreave shouted again. 'Are you fucking blind?'

The stranger stiffened, turned and scowled into the light. Shreave sucked in his breath.

It was Genie's Indian. The one who'd called him a 'damn litterbug' and left him to rot in the poinciana tree.

The man's response was firm and unambiguous. He took his hand off the tiller and held it up, flush in the headlamp's beam, extending the middle digit for Shreave's mournful contemplation.

Shreave dimmed the light, slumped low in the canoe and waited for the sound of the motorboat to fade away. Then he picked up the paddle, cursed under his breath and went back to work.

Sister Shirelle was bent over at the waist, bracing her arms against a storm-toppled pine, when she saw the light.

'Look there!'

Brother Manuel was deeply absorbed – gripping her by the hips, thrusting from behind while breathlessly invoking a deity. His robe was undone and his chest beaded with perspiration. The other moaners were well out of earshot, dancing and spinning around the fire pit on the beach.

'Brother Manuel, there's a man on the water!'

And indeed there was a man, pale and spectral, wading across the shallows and pulling a fruity-colored canoe. A harsh pinhead of light shone from the stranger's brow.

'Help me!' he called out.

Brother Manuel withdrew from Sister Shirelle and hastily tucked his unholy wand.

'Is it Him?' Sister Shirelle rose upright, tugging at her undergarments. 'Is it our Savior, home at last from His divine voyage?'

'Hush, child,' whispered Brother Manuel. 'Compose thyself.'

The man sloshed ashore and, after removing a canvas satchel, flipped the canoe to drain the water. He was garbed in a flower-print shirt and an alarming green pouch of a swimsuit, to which Sister Shirelle's gaze was wantonly drawn.

'Are you ailing?' Brother Manuel inquired.

'Freezin' my *cojones* off,' the man said. 'I'd kill for one of those bathrobes.'

'What's your name, brother?'

'Boyd.'

'And how long have you been at sea, Brother Boyd?'

'Too damn long,' the man replied through chattering teeth.

'We've been waiting for you!' Sister Shirelle exclaimed.

'You have?'

'Tell him, Brother Manuel!'

The self-anointed pastor of the First Resurrectionist Maritime Assembly for God was skeptical. His sermonizing to the contrary, he'd never seriously expected to run across Christ the Almighty during a camping trip in the Everglades. However, not wishing to dampen Sister Shirelle's spiritual fervor – which often overflowed rather lustily – Brother Manuel kept his doubts to himself.

'We've been faithfully awaiting a visitation,' he acknowledged to the stranger, 'or any holy sign from the Father.'

'Know what? I just wanna go home. You folks got a boat?'

'The hands! Behold the man's hands!' Sister Shirelle began to hop, her formidable and unbound breasts jouncing in tandem.

With impatience Brother Boyd directed the head-lamp toward his own pudgy palms, which were raw and oozing as a result of his tumble from the tree. He failed to behold the stigmata resemblance.

'I had a fall,' he explained.

Brother Manuel nodded. 'As have we all. Come.'

They led the stranger down the shore to the camp-fire, where the other moaners ceased their dancing and fell quietly into a half circle. The women were eyeing Brother Boyd's bathing attire in a manner that made him uncomfortable.

'Can I borrow one of those robes?' he asked. 'How about a beach towel?'

Brother Manuel steepled his long pink fingers and began: 'Sister Shirelle and I were praying together in the woods, communing most strenuously, when we saw a mysterious light – like a star descending from the heavens – and then, lo, this weary mariner appeared on the water. Show them your hands, Brother Boyd.'

The moaners gasped at the sight. 'It is He!' exulted one of the women.

'No, wait!' one of the others interjected. 'He could be that poacher – the lawless heathen we were warned about by the visitor with the boy. He was said to have a damaged hand, remember?'

Brother Boyd looked stricken. 'I'm not a poacher. I'm in telemarketing!'

Sister Shirelle hastened to his defense. 'But there are

wounds on *both* His hands, not just one. And He has arrived alone by sea, exactly as foretold by Brother Manuel, bearing a cargo of forgiveness and salvation for all worldly souls. His long, lonely crossing is over.'

Another female moaner raised an arm. 'What's up with the Speedos?'

Sensing that doubt was coiling like a serpent amid his flock, Brother Manuel sidled close to Brother Boyd and whispered, 'I'll take it from here, dog.'

'Hey, are those rib eyes on the fire?'

'Sisters, brothers, listen and be joyful!' Brother Manuel commanded. 'Tonight He appears to us just as He departed this world more than two thousand years ago – nearly naked, wounded and pure of soul. Instead of thorns He is crowned with light, the symbol of hope and rebirth!'

Here Brother Manuel spread his arms to righteously welcome Brother Boyd, who appeared to the other moaners as somewhat lacking in serenity.

'What are you goony birds talkin' about?' he demanded.

Sister Shirelle gently spun him by the shoulders, the beam of his headlamp falling upon the stark wooden cross that was planted on the dune.

Brother Boyd stared and said, 'You're shitting me.'

Sister Shirelle put her plump lips to his ear. 'See? We've been expecting you.'

'Rejoice! It is Him!' a bearded moaner crowed.

'No, *He*!' corrected the woman who had earlier commented upon Brother Boyd's swimwear.

Sister Shirelle pressed the case: 'Can there be any doubt that He is our Savior? Is today not the Epiphany?'

The moaners murmured excitedly, and then one

spoke up: 'But wait, sister – the Epiphany was, like, last Thursday.'

'Close enough!' boomed Brother Manuel.

Whereupon a spontaneous frolic broke out, the moaners twirling and gyrating euphorically around the fire. Bottles of cabernet were passed around, and before long Brother Boyd worked up the nerve to ask Sister Shirelle if they intended to nail him to their homemade cross. She laughed volcanically and tweaked his chin and said he was an extremely cute Messiah.

'I'm in sales,' he whispered confidentially.

'And a carpenter, too, don't forget.'

'C'mon, sis, tell me – where's your boat?'

'As if you needed one,' she said with a wink.

His headlamp illuminated the blue stenciling on the front of her white robe. 'Four Seasons, huh? Not bad,' Brother Boyd remarked. 'That's *my* kinda religion.'

'Are those goose pimples on your arms?'

'Duh, yeah. It's cold as a well digger's ass out here.'

'Well, we definitely can't have our Savior catching pneumonia. Here—' With an operatic flourish, Sister Shirelle shed the plush hotel garment and presented it to him.

'God bless you,' said Brother Boyd, liking very much the way it sounded. 'God bless all of you.'

Honey Santana said, 'Don't die on me, you big bonehead.'

'Slow it down.' Perry was laid out and breathing hard in the bottom of the skiff. She'd given him Louis Piejack's last Vicodin but he was still in monstrous pain.

He said, 'You're gonna hit an oyster bar, and this ain't my boat.'

'Is Fry asleep?'

'Can't you hear him? He snores worse than you.'

'Not nice.'

'Slower, Honey. I promise I'm not gonna die.'

She eased off the throttle. 'Me and my two sick boys,' she said. 'You with your hip shot away, and him with a concussion. Knuckleheads!'

'See the channel markers?' Perry asked.

'Sure do.'

'Remember, stay left of the red ones and right of the greens.'

'I heard you the first time, Captain Ahab. You're still bleeding, aren't you?'

'I got a pint or two left. Is your jaw broke?'

'It looks worse than it feels.'

'I doubt that. Was it Piejack?'

Honey nodded. 'My own dumb fault. I tried to be Wonder Woman.'

'Tell me what the hell you were doin' out here – and no more bullshit about an "ecotour." '

So she told him everything, beginning with Boyd Shreave's sales call from Texas. He didn't interrupt her once.

After finishing, she said, 'Perry, this is all my fault and I'm sorry.'

'It ain't exactly normal. You know that.'

'I'll go back to the doctor. I'll try the pills again.'

'Won't work, Honey. This is how you are. It's how you'll always be.'

'Please don't talk like that.' But she knew he was right. 'Can I ask you something – was that the first time you ever killed somebody?'

'It's been a week or two, at least.'

'I'm serious, Perry! I never saw a man die before – have you?'

'Not like that,' Skinner said. 'Not killed by a damn guitar.'

'But Fry didn't see it, right? The Indian was on top of him.'

'I'm pretty sure he didn't see a thing.'

Honey said, 'You've got no idea how sorry I am—'

'Just watch where you're goin'.'

The pass opened into a broad expanse of water, and she spotted a twinkle of lights – Everglades City. It had to be.

Perry lifted his head. 'Good work, babe. We're almost home.'

Chokoloskee Bay. She remembered the first time she'd been there at night. Perry had brought her out in a crab boat to see the sunset. They drank some champagne, made love – the water glassy at dusk and the sky like grenadine. He'd asked if she was sure about staying with him. Said he'd understand completely if she changed her mind and went home to Miami.

This was two days before they got married.

It's the middle of nowhere, not everybody can handle it, Perry had said. Especially the skeeters.

Honey had told him she'd never seen anyplace so peaceful, which remained a true statement nearly twenty-two years later. When she'd told him that she wanted to visit all ten thousand islands, he'd promised to show her every one. Build a fire and make out on the beach. What woman could have said no?

Fry stirred in his father's arms. Honey was chilled to think that she'd almost gotten both of them killed.

'Perry, I'm gonna dock at the Rod and Gun, okay?' She was in a hurry because of all the blood.

'Hey, Perry?'

The channel was well marked, so she goosed the engine and planed off the skiff.

'Perry, you awake?'

She sped up the mouth of the Barron River, eased back the throttle and – as if she'd done it a thousand times – kissed the bow against the pilings of the old Rod and Gun Club.

'Perry!'

Nothing.

Fry sat up, rubbing his neck. He said, 'I got the worst headache in the history of the human race.'

'Can you run?'

'What for, Mom?'

'Just answer me. Are you good to run?'

'Sure. I guess.'

'Then go get help.' Honey boosted him to the dock.

Fry looked down at his father lying in the boat. 'Dad? Hey, man, wake up!'

'Just go,' his mother told him. 'Fast as you can.'

One day not long after Fry was born, Perry Skinner had brought home a CD by the Eagles, a group that he claimed was more country than rock. He'd told Honey there was a song on the record that reminded him of her, and she'd picked it out immediately: 'Learn to Be Still.'

At first her feelings were hurt because it was the story of a restless woman who heard voices; a woman who wouldn't slow down long enough to let happiness find her. But the more Honey had listened to the lyrics, the better she'd understood that Perry wasn't being mean; he was trying to let her know that he was afraid of what was happening.

But if I hit the brakes now, she remembered thinking, *I'll skid for ten years.*

The funny thing was, Honey secretly liked the song. It made her feel that she wasn't the only one struggling with that particular demon. One afternoon, Perry had come home early from the docks and caught her playing the CD, but she'd insisted it was only because she had the hots for Don Henley.

Although Honey couldn't carry a tune – Fry forbade her from singing in the car; said she sounded like a wildcat riding a jackhammer – she knelt down, gathered Perry Skinner close and sang to him. As always she switched the words to first person.

'*Just another day in paradise . . .*'

Listening to his choppy breaths.

Squeezing one of his wrists, counting the heartbeats.

'*As I stumble to my bed . . .*'

Feeling the sticky warmth of his blood on her bare leg.

Thinking that he'd promised her he wouldn't die, and he'd always kept his word, for better or worse.

'*Give anything to silence . . .*'

She shifted him slightly in her arms so that she could watch his face in the lights from the dock.

'*These voices ringin' in my head . . .*'

'Have mercy,' Perry said weakly.

Honey giggled with relief. 'Ha! You want me to stop?'

'No offense.'

''Member those letters I wrote you in prison? Did you read 'em all?'

'Except for the ones that started 'Dear Shithead.' Where's Fry?'

Honey said, 'It's so perfect out here. Look at the sky.'

'Better than church.'

'Oh, so much better.'

Perry coughed. 'Damn. I'm all run-down.'

'How come you filed first? Don't you dare go to sleep on me! Let's discuss this stupid divorce.'

He said, 'The stars are burnin' out one by one. I'm tired, babe.'

Honey shook him. 'Nuh-ughh, buster. We're not done yet.'

She heard a siren. She prayed it was real.

'Oh no you don't,' she said. 'Wake up, Skinner.'

'I'm not afraid.'

'You are too.'

He said, 'Hush now. Doesn't it hurt to talk?'

'Wake up or I'll start singin' again. Honest to God.'

He smiled but didn't open his eyes.

'You hear that?' she asked. 'That's the ambulance.'

'I don't hear a damn thing.'

'Yes you do!' she said. *Please tell me you do.*

Twenty-six

On the thirteenth day of January, overcast and crisp, Lily Shreave sat before the bedroom television and replayed for the fourth time a VHS cassette that had arrived that morning by courier.

The tape was only six minutes long, and after it ended she made a phone call.

'You lied to me,' she told the man on the other end.

'Not completely. I said I got penetration, which is true.'

'But it's not Boyd!' Lily snapped.

'Obviously. Nothing was happening between him and the girlfriend, so I had to wing it.'

'Oh please, Mr. Dealey.'

'This was the best I could do.'

'Lizards? Two lizards humping?'

'I was on an island, Mrs. Shreave. Lost in the god-damn Everglades.'

'And you'd still be stranded there if it weren't for me,' Lily said. She clicked the remote to rewind the tape. 'I hope you're not expecting twenty-five thousand dollars for *this* spectacle.'

Dealey chuckled. 'No, ma'am. But remember I took a bullet for the cause.'

Lily hit the play button. 'I do like the music,' she remarked.

'Ravel's *Bolero*. It's pretty standard.' He'd dubbed it himself, to erase the conversation between Eugenie Fonda and the boy in the football helmet.

Lily went on: 'I'm not fond of creepy critters, but these slinky little rascals are cute, I've gotta admit. And definitely hot for each other.'

'I'm told they're chameleons,' Dealey said. 'Green is their happy color.'

Lily was impressed by the male's lithe piggybacking. It couldn't have been easy maneuvering around his mate's tail to achieve the glandular docking.

'You still there?' Dealey asked.

'I'll give you ten grand, but that's it.'

'Sounds fair.'

'To help with your out-of-pocket medical.'

'Much appreciated,' said the private investigator. He could hear *Bolero* rising in the background, along with Mrs. Shreave's breathing.

She said, 'FYI, I'm filing the divorce papers next week.'

'Should be a breeze.' Dealey figured that she'd finally closed the deal on her pizza joints.

'Just out of curiosity, where exactly is my husband?' she asked.

'I have no earthly idea.'

'Then I'll assume he ran off with his six-foot bimbo.'

Dealey didn't say a word.

Lily wasn't finished. 'By the way, the Coast Guard said they rescued two women from the same island.'

'Campers,' he said. 'They were lost, too.'

'Serves 'em right. It sounds like a perfectly awful place.'

'Good-bye, Mrs. Shreave.'

Dealey hung up smiling. When Eugenie Fonda asked him what was so funny, he told her about the ten grand.

She whistled and said, 'What'd I tell ya? The woman's seriously gettin' off on those reptiles.'

'Nice job with the camera. Helluva job, actually.' Dealey's shoulder, bolted together with three titanium pins, was throbbing. He hunted through the desk for some Advils.

'You got any normal clients?' Eugenie asked.

'A few. You'll see.'

'So, what's the dress code around here?'

'Surprise me,' Dealey said.

Eugenie had strolled into his office two days earlier offering a deal: She would return the two Halliburton cases containing the costly surveillance equipment if he promised to deliver the chameleon sex tape to Boyd Shreave's wife. During that conversation it had occurred to Dealey that Eugenie, with her vast and intimate knowledge of human frailty, could be a valuable addition to his staff.

'Does this mean you're taking the job?' he asked.

'Just don't try to get in my pants. You've got no chance whatsoever.'

'Understood,' Dealey said.

'And if you set me up with any of your loser buddies, I'll personally break your other arm. Think compound fracture.'

'Right.' He was almost certain that she could, and would, do it.

'One other thing – those tapes and pictures you took of me and Boyd. Did you make copies?'

Dealey frowned and shifted in the chair.

'Burn 'em,' Eugenie said.

He thought ruefully of his masterpiece, the delicatessen blow job. 'They're in a safe box at the bank. Nobody but me has a key.'

'I said burn 'em.' Eugenie leaned forward, tapping her fingernails on the desk. 'Did I or did I not just make you ten thousand ridiculous dollars?'

The investigator slouched in resignation. 'But I thought you wanted to see 'em – the videos and prints.'

Eugenie said no, she'd changed her mind. 'It's ancient history.'

'You looked pretty damn fine, for what it's worth.'

'Don't make me tell you what it's worth, Mr. Dealey.'

He uncapped a pen to write down her Social. 'When can you start?'

'Hang on. I'm not done,' she said. 'Did you make those calls for our friend?'

She was talking about Gillian, the spacey college kid with whom Dealey had been forced to share a sleeping bag. It was not an entirely unpleasant memory.

He said, 'Nobody at the Indian reservation would tell me a damn thing. They acted like they'd never heard of Mr. Tigertooth.'

'Tigertail.'

'Whatever. Guy could be anywheres by now.'

'Gillian's determined to find him.'

'I don't get the attraction.'

'If you've gotta ask,' Eugenie said, 'then you definitely need my help around here.'

Dealey's inquiries to Collier County had not been altogether fruitless. From a newspaper reporter he'd learned that Louis Piejack, the freak who had kidnapped him, was missing in the Ten Thousand

Islands. Having no wish to be subpoenaed to that dreadful part of the planet, Dealey had elected not to enlighten the authorities about Piejack's many crimes.

'What about Boyd?' Eugenie Fonda asked.

Dealey flexed his hands and shrugged. 'No John Does at the local morgue. He probably got off the island and hauled ass. Were you expecting him to call?'

'Oh, I'd be very surprised,' Eugenie said. She had changed her phone number the day after arriving back in Fort Worth. It was the first call she'd made after quitting her job at Relentless.

'Now let's talk salary,' she said to Dealey.

'Fire away.'

With the exception of Sister Shirelle, the moaners had become disillusioned with the one who called himself Boyd. For a savior he seemed whiny and graceless.

One afternoon, Brother Manuel took him aside and said, 'You blew it, dog.'

Boyd Shreave bridled. 'Bite your heathen tongue!'

'They took a vote. Gimme the damn robe.'

'No way.' Shreave locked his arms across the sash.

'You had a sweet gig here,' said Brother Manuel. 'Why couldn't you just smile and look wise and keep your trap shut?'

'But I read somewhere that Jesus was like a rock idol.'

'*Charismatic* is the word, but that ain't you, man. You're just another loudmouthed schmuck.'

'Okay, fine. I'll tone it down.'

'Too late,' the chief moaner said curtly.

The moment reminded Shreave of his many past

failures in sales. Over the phone he could be a master of persuasion; in person he seemed doomed to rankle. This he blamed not on multiple character defects but rather on miscalculating his target demographic. From now on he would upwardly skew his efforts toward a more cosmopolitan market, with needs yet unrevealed.

Brother Manuel went on: 'Fact is, you're way too obnoxious to be the Son of God. I can't cover for you anymore.'

'Was it unanimous?'

'Everybody except Shirelle, and she'd go down on Judas Iscariot if he was a hottie. Now hand over the robe.'

'I don't think so,' Shreave said.

Brother Manuel calmly punched him in the gut and he doubled over. The glorious Four Seasons vestment was peeled off his shoulders like a snakeskin.

'We're headin' back to the mainland tomorrow,' said Brother Manuel. 'The girls are gonna leave you two loaves of sourdough and a jug of Tang. If you're ever passin' through Zolfo Springs, stop by the AAMCO and I'll cut you a break on a pan gasket.'

Shreave was wheezing. 'This is a joke, right?'

'No, friend, this is adieu.'

'You can't leave me out here! Even on *Survivor* the losers get to go home.'

Brother Manuel said, 'We'll call the Park Service on our way out of town.'

'But you don't even know the name of this friggin' island! How're they supposed to find me?'

'Worse comes to worst, you've always got the canoe.'

'But I'll die out here! I've got a heavy-duty disease and I need my medicine,' Shreave said. 'Aphenphosmphobia!'

Brother Manuel snorted. 'That's not a disease, it's a disorder. And if you were truly afflicted, *brother*, you wouldn't have asked Sister Shirelle to rub your feet last night.'

Boyd Shreave wilted.

'My cousin's an aphenphosmphobic,' Brother Manuel added in a frosty tone. 'That's how I know.'

There was nothing left for Shreave to do but beg. 'Christ, please take me with you.'

'If He were here, perhaps He would. However, it's my boat and it's my call.' Brother Manuel slung the white robe over one arm and turned away.

'Gimme another chance!' Shreave called out, but the preacher kept walking.

That night Shreave built a feeble fire on the dune, using a book of matches that Sister Shirelle had tucked in his Speedos shortly before the moaners cast off. For tinder he sacrificed his ragged copy of *Storm Ghoul*, rendering to ashes the only keepsake of his fizzled affair with Eugenie Fonda.

Slumped against the wooden cross, Shreave stared out across the Gulf of Mexico and assayed his prospects, which were not as gloomy as he'd initially believed. The running lights of several large vessels were visible offshore, so he knew it was only a matter of time before somebody spotted him. At that point a major life decision would be required. Shreave ruled out a return to Texas, having no desire to face Lily's wrath and his mother's scalding denigrations. It never occurred to him that neither woman was interested in his whereabouts or his intentions.

Florida might be worth a shot, Shreave mused. Boca Raton supposedly had more telephone boiler rooms than Calcutta.

He gnawed on a hunk of sourdough but nearly gagged on the lukewarm Tang. The waves whispered him to sleep, and he awoke at daybreak sucking on his NASCAR toothbrush. Glancing up, he was alarmed to see – preening on the crossbeam of the bogus cross – a large white-capped bird that he recognized from countless documentaries on the Discovery Channel as an American bald eagle.

'Boo!' Shreave yelled hoarsely. 'Beat it!'

The eagle was old and hunched, yet its amber gaze was penetrating. The flexed talons were larger than Shreave's hands, and he didn't doubt for a second that the predator was capable of removing his face with one swipe.

'Go away!' he brayed twice, whereupon the great bird hitched its chalky tail feathers, uncorked a prodigious bowel movement and flew away.

With a woeful moan, Shreave rolled himself down the dune, over the cold fire pit and into the water. There he threshed in hysterics, trying to slosh off the pungent stickum of feathers, bones, fur, mullet scales, cartilage and less identifiable ingredients of the jumbo eagle dropping.

It was in this frothing state of aggrievement that he was found by a passing park ranger, drawn to the scene by Shreave's howls. After being hauled aboard the patrol boat, he was transported in his befouled Speedos to the public landing at Everglades City. There he was hosed off vigorously and examined by a paramedic wearing full biohazard gear.

Later, sporting ghastly tartan shorts and a double-knit golf shirt donated by the local Red Cross, Boyd Shreave wandered alone to the Rod and Gun Club, where he slapped his wife's MasterCard on the old mahogany bar. The bartender was the same one who'd provided directions on the night that he and Genie had arrived, but the man didn't recognize him. Shreave's bearing had been considerably diminished on Dismal Key by a deleterious combination of sun poisoning, wind chafing and general character abasement.

After five Coronas, Shreave felt not nearly so adrift and out of sorts. A couple in their sixties, plainly from the Midwest, settled a few bar stools away and began rhapsodizing about their vacation to southwest Florida.

'It was twelve degrees at O'Hare this morning!' the wife chortled.

'Three below with the windchill,' said her husband.

'I don't want to go home, Ben. It's so incredible here.'

'McMullan called from the club – the lake on the seventeenth hole is froze solid. The kids are out there playing ice hockey with dog turds.'

'Ben, did you hear what I said? I really do *not* wish to go back.'

'You mean it?'

Boyd Shreave picked up his beer bottle and moved closer.

'We could get a place in Naples,' the wife was suggesting.

'Or right here on the river,' said the husband. 'Buy a boat and dock it behind the house.'

The bartender had heard the same conversation maybe a thousand times, but to a defrocked telemarketer from Texas it was revelatory; a thunderbolt of inspiration.

'It's paradise here,' Shreave heard himself say. 'Heaven on earth.'

The husband turned on his bar stool. 'Today I caught eight ladyfish, and a flounder as big as a hubcap. That's no lie!'

His wife said, 'But what about the mosquitoes? I hear it's torture in the summer.'

Shreave smiled. 'That's what the locals tell all the Yankees. You folks seriously in the market?'

'Aw, we're just dreamin' out loud,' the husband said.

'No, we're serious,' the woman spoke up. '*I'm* serious. Do you live here?'

Shreave didn't hesitate. 'Just up the road,' he said.

It had of course dawned on him that, being immune to the wonders of the place, he was ideally equipped to exploit it. Erik fucking Estrada, eat your heart out.

The husband introduced himself. Shreave shook his hand and said, 'I'm Boyd Eisenhower.'

'Like the president?'

'No relation, I'm afraid.'

The wife asked, 'Are you a broker?'

'I handle a few select waterfront properties, yes.'

Shreave was experimenting with a new, low-key style. The beers definitely helped. So far, the couple had not recoiled or grown even slightly leery in his presence; just the opposite. They were so eager to escape Chicago that they hadn't noticed he was half-trashed.

'And what would it cost,' the husband was saying, 'for, oh, a three-two on the river? Hypothetically, I mean.'

'Or a town house on Marco,' the woman added eagerly. 'Do you have a card, Mr. Eisenhower?'

'Not with me.' Boyd Shreave experienced a rush like no other. It was, he believed, his deliverance.

'Let me take your number,' he said, reaching for a cocktail napkin.

First thing in the morning, he would inquire about a real-estate license.

I am home, he thought. *At last.*

The eagle flew south and spent the night in the top of a dead black mangrove along the Lostmans River. Even from a distance Sammy Tigertail could see that the bird was ancient, and he wondered if it was the ghost spirit of Wiley, the demented white writer about whom his Uncle Tommy sometimes told stories.

At dawn Sammy Tigertail motored the johnboat to the base of the mangrove tree and called up at the eagle, which responded by yakking up a fish head. The Indian waved respectfully and headed upriver to check the spot where he'd submerged the corpse of Louis Piejack. It was the same deep hole in which eleven days earlier he had anchored Jeter Wilson, the luckless dead tourist. Recently, Wilson's rented car had been recovered from the murky Tamiami Trail canal, which was now being searched by snake-wary police divers. Sammy Tigertail wasn't in any hurry to come out of hiding.

No evidence of Wilson or Piejack had surfaced in Lostmans, so the Indian returned to his campsite near Toms Bight and carefully hid the johnboat. The day before, a chopper had passed overhead half a dozen times – it wasn't the Coast Guard or the Park Service, but nonetheless Sammy Tigertail was on edge. He knew somebody was looking for something, although he wouldn't have guessed that it was Gillian St. Croix looking for *him*, and that she was paying for the helicopter charters with a tuition refund from Florida State University. No longer was she a fighting Seminole.

Concealed by a clumsily woven canopy of palm fronds, Sammy Tigertail spent the daylight hours re-reading Rev. MacCauley's journal and constructing a new guitar. From the shattered Gibson he had salvaged the neck, the tuning pegs and five strings; the body he was laboriously shaping with his Buck knife from a thick plank of teak that he'd gotten from a derelict sailboat. Sammy Tigertail was by no means an artisan yet it was satisfying work, and a task of which the inventive Calusas would have approved.

A month's worth of gasoline and provisions had been delivered by Sammy Tigertail's half brother, Lee, whom Sammy had contacted with a cellular phone that he'd found in Piejack's johnboat. It was Lee who had delivered the news about Wilson's car, and he'd agreed it would be premature for Sammy to return to the reservation. During Lee's visit they had selected future drop sites and a timetable. Aware that his half brother's wilderness skills were not as advanced as those of a full-blooded Seminole, Lee had also provided a compass, a dive watch, a NOAA marine chart and a bag of flares.

At night Sammy Tigertail was occasionally pestered in his sleep by the spirit of Wilson, who would complain sourly about sharing eternity at the bottom of a river with Louis Piejack.

'I thought you'd like some company,' Sammy Tigertail said the first time the dead tourist appeared at the camp on Toms Bight.

'*The guy's a total scumbag! Not even the damn crabs want a piece of him,*' Wilson griped.

He'd brought along Piejack's ghost for dramatic impact, but the Indian was unswayed. The depraved fish peddler looked no worse in death than he had when he was alive; the river scavengers were avoiding him like a toxin. Wilson, meanwhile, was disappearing by the biteful.

Sammy Tigertail said, 'You told me you were lonely.'

'*Lonely, yeah – not desperate. The dude's a major perv,*' fumed the dead tourist. '*I can't believe you wasted a perfectly good guitar on this fuckwit!*'

His facial bones having been staved in by Perry Skinner's lethal blow, Louis Piejack was unable to respond effectively in his own defense. It wouldn't have mattered.

'I wasn't the one who killed him,' the Seminole said.

'*What happened to that guy you plugged?*' Wilson inquired. '*The porky one in the business suit. Hell, I'd rather hang out with* him.'

'He didn't die,' Sammy Tigertail replied.

'*Always some excuse.*'

'Go away now. I'm tired.'

'*Fuck you, and good night,*' said Wilson.

The dream visitations always ended the same way – the expired white men clomping away with their anchors dragging, two sullen figures deliquescing in a funky blue vapor. Afterward Sammy Tigertail would awaken and lie still, studying the stars. His uncle said that whenever a Seminole soul passed on, the Milky Way brightened to illuminate the path to the spirit world. On some crystal nights Sammy Tigertail worried that when his time came, the Maker of Breath would look unfavorably upon his white childhood as Chad McQueen.

He regarded the arrival of the hoary bald eagle as a powerful sign, and it remained near his camp as the days passed. Sometimes the old bird would drop a feather, which the Indian would retrieve and attach to a homemade turban of the style worn by his ancestors in the Wind Clan. Each morning he'd sneak from beneath the ragged palm canopy and scout the tree line to make sure that the great predator was still watching over him. During this period Sammy Tigertail's sleep was undisturbed, for Wilson and Piejack did not show themselves.

On the same day that Sammy Tigertail finished rebuilding the Gibson, he began composing a tune for his mother. Musically its roots were closer to Neil Young than to the traditional Green Corn chorus, but nonetheless he was pleased by his first effort. Later he took the johnboat on the river and started casting for snook. He hooked a good one that jumped several times, attracting a nine-foot alligator. The animal exhibited no fear of the Indian, who tried to spook it by shouting and smacking the water with a frog gig. Even after the fish was boated, the gator lingered, its black fluted profile suspended in the current behind the transom. The sight reminded Sammy Tigertail of his ignominious stint in the wrestling pit at the reservation; he vowed never to harm another of the great beasts unless it was for survival.

Back at camp he cleaned and fried the snook. Then he doused the fire, stripped off his clothes and swam into the bight to watch a pod of dolphins herding mullet. He was a hundred yards from shore when the mystery helicopter returned, cruising low from the north. Exposed and unable to hide, Sammy Tigertail went vertical in the water, moving his legs only enough to keep his chin above the muddy chop. He hoped that from the air his dark head would look like a bobbing coconut.

The chopper banked and then hovered near the dolphins, which began vaulting and turning flips, the mullet spraying like silver fireworks. The aircraft was near enough that Sammy Tigertail could make out the features of the pilot and, on the passenger side, a young woman watching the frenzy through binoculars. The Seminole blinked away the salt sting so that he could better focus on the woman, her hair showing chestnut in the afternoon sunlight. When she lowered the binoculars she looked very much like Gillian.

Sammy Tigertail remained motionless, treading water and resisting an urge to wave. He was not dismayed by the idea that a rambunctious college girl in mesh panties might be searching for him, but at the same time he was grateful to the dolphins for distracting her. He could imagine Gillian's half of the conversation on her cell phone, gloating to poor geeky Ethan about where she was and what she was seeing.

When the wild dolphin show was over, the helicopter moved on. Sammy Tigertail swam back to the beach and walked the shoreline for nearly an hour. There was no sign of the eagle, and the Seminole returned sadly to his camp, thinking the bird had been driven away by the noisy chopper. He sat down with the guitar in his makeshift hideout and resumed work on his song, which he suspected would have benefited from Gillian's frisky creative input.

Shortly before dusk, something substantial struck the thatching above Sammy Tigertail's sleeping bag. He grabbed Perry Skinner's .45 and scooted from beneath the canopy, where he encountered the freshly stripped skeleton of a redfish. Slowly the Seminole raised his eyes.

Overhead, on the tallest branch of a lightning-charred mangrove, the old eagle was chewing on a ropy pink noodle of entrails. The Seminole grinned and called out in fractured Muskogee to the bird, which pretended to ignore him.

Later Sammy Tigertail moved his bedding under the stars. Although the temperature was dropping, he didn't light a fire. The warrior spirit of his great-great-great-grandfather was traveling somewhere in the galaxy, and Sammy Tigertail wished him good night. Then the Indian closed his eyes and pondered what to do if Gillian came back tomorrow in the helicopter.

Maybe he would hide. Maybe he wouldn't.

Honey Santana noticed the pearl stud pinned to a lamp shade next to her son's computer.

'Where'd you get that?' she asked.

'From a woman,' Fry said.

'Miss Fonda had one of those. The telemarketer's girlfriend.'

'You sure talk an awful lot,' he said, 'for someone with their jaws wired shut.'

'Dinner's almost ready,' said his mother.

'So I guess you'll be skipping the corn on the cob.'

'You're enjoying this, aren't you?'

'Just a joke, Mom.' He gave her a hug.

She said, 'Go help your father up the steps.'

Perry Skinner had moved into Honey's painted trailer. They said it was no big deal because the arrangement was strictly temporary and didn't mean a thing. Fry only heard that about ten times a day, which is why he was certain they were getting back together. While it was fun having both of them around at the same time, Fry was apprehensive. He remembered how they used to fight, and he worried that it would start up again once their respective injuries healed and they went back to being their old hard-headed selves.

He went outside where his dad was trying to walk with a cane. Skinner had a new left hip joint; Louis Piejack had blown the old one to bits. At the hospital a sheriff's detective had gotten the same story from the boy and his parents: They'd gone out to Dismal Key for a picnic, and Skinner had accidentally shot himself while plinking beer cans. Fry's mother didn't think the detective believed them, but Fry's father said it didn't really matter. As vice mayor he enjoyed a solid relationship with the sheriff, who had never – even in the heat of a high-stakes poker game – questioned his credibility.

'When can I go skateboarding again?' Fry asked his dad.

'When the doc says so.'

'But my head feels fine.'

'Oh yeah? We can fix that.' Skinner playfully raised the cane like he was going to bop him.

'Glad *somebody's* feelin' better,' Fry said.

'Cut your mom some slack, champ. You'd be in a shitty mood, too, if you had to suck all your meals through a straw.'

'Know what she made herself for lunch? An oyster smoothie!'

'Dear God,' said Skinner.

For dinner Honey had broiled two fresh cobia fillets that she'd purchased at Louis Piejack's market, which was prospering in his absence. Piejack's long-suffering wife, Becky, had taken advantage of his unexplained sabbatical and fled to São Paulo with Armando, her orchid adviser, after cleaning out the joint money-market account. Nobody in town blamed her.

Fry and his father devoured the cobia while his mother sipped crab bisque.

'Skinner, did you happen to see your son's stylish pearl stud?' she asked. 'A lady friend gave it to him.'

Fry's father looked over at him and winked. 'What else she give you?'

'Nice,' Honey grumbled through surgically clamped teeth. 'Setting a fine example as always.'

'Aw, c'mon. He knows I'm kiddin'.'

Fry watched his father reach over and touch his mother's arm, and he saw her eyes soften. It was a good moment, but the boy had mixed emotions. He'd been trying very hard not to let his hopes rise. He was afraid of awaking one morning to the sound of an argument, and then the slamming of a door.

He put down his fork. 'Can I say somethin'? Even if it's probably none of my business?'

Skinner told him to go ahead.

Fry said, 'Okay, I'm not sure this is a swift move – you two in the same house again.'

Honey sat back, surprised at his bluntness. 'Honestly, Fry,' she murmured.

'I mean, everything's cool now,' he went on, 'but there was a reason you guys split up. What if . . . you know?'

His father said, 'We told you it's just for a few weeks, until I get the hip rehabbed.'

His mother added, 'It was a practical decision, that's all. Mutually convenient.'

'Nice try.' Fry knew they were hooking up late at

night, him with a gimp and she with a busted jaw. No self-control whatsoever.

'Just what're you getting at?' Honey asked.

Fry said, 'The walls are like cardboard, Mom. I've been crankin' up my iPod full blast.'

His mother reddened and his father's eyebrows arched.

'I can't believe you're talking to us this way,' Honey complained, 'like we're two kids who don't know what we're doing.'

No comment, thought Fry.

Skinner said, 'You seriously want me to move back to my place?'

'Dad, I just want you to slow down and remember what happened before.'

Which was: Skinner had burned out trying to deal with Honey's manic projects, and Honey had burned out trying to explain herself.

'People change,' his mother asserted.

His father said, 'Not true. But they do learn new tricks.'

Fry felt crummy about bringing up the past, but somebody had to break the ice. 'Hey, I always knew you guys still had the hots for each other. That's not the part I'm worried about.'

'Oh, I *know* what you're worried about,' said Honey.

'Never mind, okay? It's none of my business.'

'It's totally your business,' she said. 'All right, let's say your father and I got back together—'

'What happened to "ex-father"?' Skinner chided.

'You hush up and listen,' she told him, then turned back to Fry. 'Say we get back together or whatever. It wouldn't be the same as before – I've got a much better grip these days. Both hands firmly on the wheel.'

'Oh, come on, Mom. The Texans?'

'Nobody's sayin' she's normal,' Skinner cut in, 'not even *her*. But there's too many so-called normal people with no soul and no balls.'

'Thank you,' said Honey, 'I think.'

Fry smiled because he'd spent lots of time trying to figure out his mother, and that was one of his theories: Her affliction was one of the heart, not the brain. She felt things too deeply and acted on those feelings, and for that there was no known cure. It would explain why all those medicines never worked.

'I believe I've heard you use the word *crazy*,' Honey reminded Skinner, 'more than once.'

'Yeah, well, there's good crazy and bad crazy.'

At Honey's place the topic of Louis Piejack had arisen only once, when she'd asked Fry if he understood that by killing Piejack his father had almost surely saved Fry's life. The boy had never doubted it, although he would have preferred to forget the desolate crunch of wood on bone. Later the Seminole had departed with Piejack's body, the remnants of the shattered guitar and a blood-stained map provided by Perry Skinner.

Fry did not need to be told that he hadn't seen a thing. It was a secret they would keep as a family, and he wondered if it was enough to hold them together.

His father said, 'Everybody screws up, son. I made a big-time mistake that put me in prison, but your mom still stuck around. If she hadn't, you wouldn't be here right now, givin' us grief.'

His mother said, 'Eat your sweet potatoes, kiddo.'

Fry nodded. 'Okay, fine. If the shit hits the fan, we'll just call Dr. Phil.'

Skinner laughed. 'Smartass,' he said.

Honey said they were both impossible, two peas in a pod. 'And I don't care what you say, people can change if they want to.'

The phone started ringing.

'Dammit,' Honey muttered. 'Always in the middle of dinner. God knows what they're selling tonight.'

Irritably she pushed away from the table.

Fry and his father looked at each other.

'What?' Honey crossed her arms.

'Nothing. Here's your chance is all,' Fry said.

His mother rose, glowering at the phone. 'They've got absolutely zero manners. Zero respect.'

'Just let it ring,' said Fry's father.

'But they're so incredibly rude to call at this hour.'

Fry said, 'Sit down, Mom. You can do it.'

Eight, nine, ten times the phone rang.

'I forgot – the answer machine's off,' she said.

'Perfect.' Perry Skinner slugged down his beer. 'Let it ring, babe.'

'Sure. *Nooooo* problem,' Honey said, but she didn't sit down.

Thirteen, fourteen, fifteen rings.

She looked achingly at Fry, as if to say, *I'm trying*.

He gave her a thumbs-up.

'Finish your soup, Mom. Before it gets cold.'

The phone stopped ringing.

Honey sat down with her boys.

THE END